SMALL TOWN
HORROR

RONALD MALFI

SMALL TOWN HORROR

TITAN BOOKS

Small Town Horror
Hardback edition ISBN: 9781803365657
E-book edition ISBN: 9781803367583

Published by Titan Books
A division of Titan Publishing Group Ltd
144 Southwark Street, London SE1 0UP
www.titanbooks.com

First edition: June 2024
10 9 8 7 6 5 4 3 2 1

A CIP catalogue record for this title is available
from the British Library.

Printed and bound by CPI Group (UK) Ltd, Croydon, CR0 4YY

Thinking of Peter Straub…

... and of Rebecca: burn bright

"And his dark secret love
Does thy life destroy."

—William Blake

"The past is never dead.
It's not even past."

—William Faulkner

"Every love story is a ghost story."

—David Foster Wallace

PROLOGUE

M aybe this is a ghost story.

If it is, then I am both the haunter and the haunted. Do I still hear the echo of that night, repeated forever, until it bursts across the firmament of space? Do I still sense all of those dark mementos nestled tight and unmovable in the blackened corners of my memory, stirring from time to time just to let me know they are never going away?

It was a sudden jolt, a disruption in the fabric of the universe, an unexpected divergence in the timeline of things. An *accident*. That one fateful incident has resonated in me with all the clamor of a star imploding, and no matter what I do—no matter what I've done— it never stops resounding. That steady war drum *boom . . . boom . . . boom*. I can't move out from under it; I can't escape it, no matter what I do to balance the good with the bad. No matter how many wrongs I try to right.

Listen: I'll never stop looking at the palms of my hands, never stop studying the pallor of my flesh in mirrors as I pass by. I'll never quit listening for the sloshing, liquid rattle in my lungs, or sniffing the air for the acrid stink of burning black powder whenever my eyes begin to sting and the tears spill down my heat-reddened face.

Tell me one of your stories?

No.
Not this one.
Never this one.
We were doomed from the beginning.

PART ONE

KINGSPORT . . .
. . . AND THE WRAITH

ONE

Three months into Rebecca's pregnancy, I began to worry that something terrible was going to happen to the baby. It didn't hit me all at once, but rather it gradually insinuated itself inside of me: a seed taking hold in loose soil, casting its pale, sinuous roots to great distances. It started as a solitary notion, lighting upon me soft as a feather: *what if something happens?* It was a thought I was able to brush aside at first, but in the days and weeks that followed, it became a steady, worrisome drumbeat in my head: *what if something terrible happens to the baby?* Things like that happened all the time, didn't they? Accidents, miscarriages, complications: a host of shadowed malignancies that caused in me inexorable concern.

As Rebecca's pregnancy progressed, I found myself waking in the middle of the night from some disremembered nightmare, certain that there *was* no baby, that the pregnancy was actually the dream. I'd place a hand to my wife's abdomen while she slept, the warmth of her body radiating through the thin fabric of her nightshirt, desperate to seek out confirmation that everything was as it should be. At work, I would sometimes be overcome with the certainty that Rebecca, wherever she was, had miscarried, and I would fumble my phone to my ear just to hear her voice. I told myself these were normal fears, that I was nervous about becoming a father, but that didn't help quell my anxiety. My mind filled with innumerable baseless terrors—of stillbirths and nuchal cords and all manner of physiological defects. A dispossessed *thing*, large-eyed and staring, milky-blind, congealing in a forever soup inside my wife's body. I envisioned a womb full of life one moment, vacant the next . . . as if a fetus was something as tenuous as a wish or a dream, and just as liable to disappear in the same fashion.

It was an irrational fear—there was nothing in Rebecca's or my genetic makeup to suggest there'd be a problem, and by all accounts, the fetus was strong and healthy—yet by the end of that first trimester, I couldn't shake the certainty that some dark wraith had arrived unbidden into our lives. That this thing had moved into our home, had latched onto us—or, more specifically, onto the *baby*—and would not go away.

I handled this the way I'd learned to handle most things in my life—I put on a false face and practiced the art of human mimicry. To keep my mind off my mounting unease about the baby, I plunged headfirst into work. This was nothing new to me—since my graduation from law school, I had always put my nose down and gotten it done—but I let work consume me, let it take all the time it wanted, and relished the evenings when I had to work late at the firm or bring reams of legal documents home to pore over deep into the night. The result of this extra time and energy got me high praise at Morrison and Hughes, the Manhattan law firm where I'd been working for the past five years. Desperate for distraction, I had sweated my way for months through a particularly daunting legal entanglement dealing with one of Bryce Morrison's wealthiest (and shadiest) clients, Remmy Stein. The issue ultimately went before a judge, where my dedication to this client's cause paid off; he and I left the courtroom that afternoon, sweat pooling in my armpits, an ear-to-ear grin on Stein's ruby-red face. For my efforts, I received an engraved crystal award, thick as a phonebook, and a shiny new office on the fifth floor, where a wall of windows gazed dizzyingly through a maze of skyscrapers and office buildings downtown. Before I was fully moved in, I rested my sweaty forehead against the cool glass of one window and peered down. Below was a trash-strewn alleyway, cluttered with dumpsters and a blazing bit of brick-wall graffito that, quite ominously, proclaimed:

THE PAST IS NEVER DEAD

This, admittedly, did not help ease my state of mind.

Rebecca didn't notice this change in me at first. She was still working, editing manuscripts from a pool of clients she had cultivated after leaving the publishing house where she'd worked previously, and was in overall high spirits. She looked perpetually radiant, with her curled copper hair swept behind her ears, and her green cat's eyes alight. The freckles across the delicate saddle of her nose had become as pronounced as flecks of mica. It was like the baby was emitting some spectral light from inside her.

One morning I came out of the bedroom to find her sitting at the kitchen table eating raspberries from a small bowl, one of her client's manuscripts on the table in front of her. She was in her robe, one bare leg tucked under her thigh, her hair shining in a slant of midday sun. I had spent too many hours at the office the night before, had gotten only a few scant moments of restless sleep, and so I staggered over to the coffee pot, took a mug down from the cupboard, and poured a full cup.

I sensed something in my wife. Her thoughts, moving about in that brilliant head of hers. I turned and looked at her—stared at her for several moments, in fact, unobserved. Losing myself for a time in that pale white tract of scalp where her coppery hair lay parted. The constellation of earrings along the perimeter of one ear caught the sunlight and momentarily blinded me.

"How's the novel?"

"Oh," she said, curling one corner of the manuscript page between her thumb and forefinger. "The author is obsessed with head hopping."

"What's that?"

"He's telling the bulk of the novel in first person, then he jumps at random into some other character's head in third person. It's jarring."

"Maybe there's a reason for it in the end," I said. I kept looking at my wife, sensing some disquiet moving around inside her, just beneath the surface.

"Hey," she said, looking up at me. "Can we talk for a second?"

"Of course."

I sat at the table. The manuscript in front of her looked as thick as a cake box. There were red pen marks on the top page where she'd been editing.

"Will you level with me?" she said.

"About what?"

"About what it is that's been haunting you for most of this pregnancy."

I set the coffee mug on the table. My wedding ring accidentally knocked against the handle, eliciting an eerie, discordant chime that seemed to hang in the air for much longer than it should have.

"It's nothing, Bec. It's just stress, worry, about to be a new father. All of that."

She shook her head, so slowly that it was hardly perceptible. Her eyes, those perfect green jewels, glittered. "No." Her voice was small but firm. "No, that's not it. It's something you're keeping from me. I can tell. You're not sleeping. You're more restless than the baby. You *kick*. Also, you've been so . . . preoccupied."

"Honey," I said, and reached out to her.

She drew away, just as slowly as she'd been shaking her head a moment ago, yet still managing to evade my hand. "It's something more than just stress and worry, Andrew." She took a breath, and in that instant I could tell she had been concerned about this for much longer than I realized. "Do you not want to have this baby with me?"

Her words struck me like a mallet.

"Hey," I said. "Listen to me. I want nothing more in the world than to have this baby with you. Am I scared? Yeah, okay, I'm scared. But I will get through it."

"We," she said. "*We* will get through it."

"Yes," I said. "We."

"And that's it? That's all this is?" She was watching me with some lingering measure of skepticism, her jade eyes having narrowed the slightest bit.

"That's all this is, I promise."

And then we stayed there like that for several heartbeats. Those luminous green eyes, sucking me in like twin tractor beams . . .

"Okay," she said eventually, turning back to her manuscript, and just like that the spell was broken.

Five months into the pregnancy, I was on the subway heading home from work when I glanced up and saw an advertisement that depicted a fireworks display over New York Harbor. I stared at it, became transfixed by it, just as the lights in the subway car began to flicker. I grew unsettled and twisted around in my seat. My shirt collar suddenly felt too tight, and I could feel a bead of sweat roll down the left side of my ribs. In the grimy window glass beneath the advertisement, my reflection stared back at me. I took in the drawn lines of my face, the haunted, weary expression that made me appear much older than my thirty-five years. When the lights went dark again, my face became a smudged black nothingness right there on the glass. The roar and hiss of the train sounded like those fireworks come to life. I shifted around uncomfortably in my seat again, and that black reflection in the window moved in a way I felt did not match my own movements. It was like looking at someone staring up at me beneath the surface of dark water—not a reflection at all, but an entirely separate entity. I watched as a spark of light flickered in the right eye socket of that black smudge of a face, or maybe it was something beyond the window in the subway tunnel that had flickered—either way, I felt my mouth go dry and my palms grow clammy. I was unreasonably grateful when the lights came back on, the doors shuddered open, and I could get off at the next stop.

Seven months into the pregnancy, lying beside me in bed, Rebecca said, "Do you still not want to know?"

"Know what?"

"The sex."

Something tightened in my belly. I had been lying there with my eyes closed, attempting to force sleep upon me, but I was wide awake now, staring at the lights of the city through the slatted blinds of the windows across our bedroom.

"No," I said, after a time. "I still don't want to know. I can wait a couple more months." I rolled my head toward her. She was already facing me, a pair of luminous eyes in the dark. "Unless *you* want to find out?"

"I don't need to find out." Her voice was a soft whisper, her breath warm and gentle on my face. "I already know."

"This is mother's intuition? Something you feel?"

"It's something that beats in me like a pulse," she said. "A little patter of Morse code, beep boop beep, right there in my temples, whispering to me in dots and dashes."

"So what is it?" I asked her.

"You said you didn't want to know."

"Well, I want to know if *you* know."

"Are you sure?"

"Yes."

"It's a boy, Andrew."

I didn't know what to say to that. So I leaned in and kissed her. She kissed me back. A moment later, we were making slow, lazy love while someone's car alarm fractured the night. When it was all over, she got up and went to the bathroom. I heard the shower clunk on, the old pipes shudder. That sliver of horizontal light beneath the bathroom door changed something in the bedroom—shadows seemed to rearrange themselves, items throughout the room furtively changing form.

Across the room, a figure stood just beyond the open closet door.

I sat up in bed, my flesh hotly prickling. I could see the outline of this person with perfect clarity, a black shape superimposed against the blacker background of my open closet. Most clearly, I could make out the tips of this person's shoes, illuminated by the light spilling from beneath the bathroom door.

As I stared at the figure, I sensed its slow retreat as it receded, measure by measure, into the closet, its distinct, black silhouette growing more amorphous. As though it knew it had been spotted and was trying to quietly back away.

I climbed out of bed, went to the closet, and turned on the light.

There was no one there, of course. Just a file of dark suits, some boxes on a shelf, and a platoon of neckties hanging from a single wire hanger. I looked down and saw that those shoes I'd glimpsed were actually my own.

"Packing for a trip?" Rebecca said, coming out of the bathroom with a towel wrapped around her head, another around her torso.

"I thought I heard a noise," I said, kicking my shoes deeper into the closet and closing the door.

"It's probably the Constantines upstairs. They're renovating."

"At midnight?"

"Well, I sure as hell don't want to think it's rats." She tossed both towels over a chair and climbed into bed. "Come," she told me.

I crawled in beside her, the clean, warm smell of her body and the dampness of her hair splayed partially across my own pillow feeling like some perfect little snapshot of domesticity. I nestled my head in the crook of her neck. Her damp hair was cool against my burning face.

After a time, Rebecca's gentle snoring pulled me down with her.

Eight months into the pregnancy, and my single-minded focus on work afforded me another win for the firm. To celebrate my success, Morrison threw a small bash at The Winchester, a private supper club in the Village, resplendent with plush club chairs, crystalline chandeliers, and a piano bar. I did my best to avoid conversation that evening, negotiating between the bar for beers and the back alley of the club to smoke cigarettes. On one pass, as I sidled up to the bar and ordered another Heineken, I sensed a shadow looming behind me. I worried it might be Morrison, but it was Laurie O'Dell.

"Counselor. How does it feel to be the man of the hour?"

"Oh, I don't know about that," I said.

"Don't play coy." Her smirk was darkly suspect. Laurie O'Dell was attractive, slightly older than me, and direct as an arrow. "Morrison can't stop talking about you. It's like you're his long-lost son come back from the war. What's gotten into you these past few months? You're on fire."

I looked across the club and saw Bryce Morrison surrounded by a cadre of dark-suited sycophants. They could have been vampires paying homage to their leader. As if sensing my gaze on him, Morrison glanced over at me, caught my eye, and raised his martini glass in my honor.

"It's really kind of sick, don't you think?" Laurie said, cradling a short glass of amber liquor in both hands as she leaned against the bar. "I mean, he knows you didn't actually go to a real law school, right?"

"Harvard isn't the only law school in the country, Laur."

"Rumor has it Stein sent you a gold Rolex with 'scot-free' engraved on the back."

This was only partially true: the Rolex sent by Remmy Stein had my name engraved on the back. It was currently tucked away in a desk drawer in my office, still snug in its velvet box.

"Don't believe everything you hear, Laurie. Besides, everyone eventually pays in the end. You know that."

"Now you sound like a choir boy."

I laughed. "Far from it."

She finished her drink and set her empty rocks glass on the bar. "Where's your bride tonight? Doesn't she want to bask in your glory?"

"She's tired. Baby's been restless."

"Should be soon now?"

"One more month." I nodded toward Laurie's empty glass. "Refill?"

"If you're buying."

I ordered another Heineken for myself and a Macallan for Laurie, which made her chuckle.

"What?" I said.

"Be careful, counselor," she said, and actually reached out and straightened my necktie. "Your blue collar is showing."

It was then that I felt a gentle buzzing from the inside pocket of my suit jacket. I pulled out my cell phone, glanced at the unfamiliar number on the screen, and was about to decline the call when something gave me pause. Maybe it was the 410 area code that stopped me, or maybe it was that Morrison was headed in our direction, a toothy grin stretching the boundaries of his face; whatever the reason, I excused myself and hustled across the club toward the exit that led to the back alley, where I'd spent half the night smoking.

"Hello?" I said, answering the phone.

"Andrew? Is this Andrew Larimer?"

The voice was male, and it held the grogginess of someone freshly roused from a deep sleep.

"Who's this?" I said.

"Andrew, this is Dale. Dale Walls. You know..." He cleared his throat, then added, "From back home."

I pulled the phone away from my face, saw the Maryland area code for the second time, and became instantly aware of a cold, clammy sweat peeling down the center of my back. "Dale," I said, the name coming out in a breathy whisper. "It's been a long time."

"Been a lifetime," Dale said. "Look, man, I'm sorry to call so late. I've been drinking. And then I . . . I saw . . . something, I think..." He trailed off for a moment, with only his labored breathing on the line. Then: "It's not a good idea. But listen, Andrew, I need your help."

I closed my eyes. Said, "What's wrong, Dale?"

"No. Not on the phone. I need you *here*."

"Here?"

"Home," Dale said. I heard a glass or a bottle clink in the background. "Kingsport."

"What kind of trouble are you in, Dale?"

There was a beat of silence on the other end of the phone. I opened my eyes and saw my shadow stretched along the wet pavement of the alley in front of me, the lights of the city at my back—a distorted, alien shadow, long-limbed and monstrous.

"We got a lot of history between us, Andy." He was breathing too heavily into the phone again, his words punctuated by expulsions of static. "I need you to come here, back to Kingsport, no questions asked. Just come home, and I'll tell you everything. I'll text you my address. Come tomorrow, Andy. As soon as you can."

"Dale—"

"You don't have a choice," he said, and disconnected the call.

TWO

Around the same time I received the phone call from Dale Walls, a man named Matthew Meacham opened his eyes to a tomblike darkness. His body quaked, his mind raced, and his skin burned. He raked overlong fingernails down the tender flesh of his arms, praying for his eyes to adjust to the lightlessness. They never adjusted. After a time, he sat up in that dark space, feeling the elements of the world pressing against every inch of his body to inform him of where he was and what was about to happen.

What was about to happen?

"No," he muttered, his lips unsticking with an audible smack. His tongue felt like a wool sock in his mouth. "Please, no..."

Nothing at first—except the distant *plink plunk* of a steady drop of water coming from somewhere. He picked himself up off the hardwood floor and stood upon a pair of creaky legs. What felt like large flies thumped against his face in the still and humid air. This man was thirty-five years old, but the things he had done to his body since his teenage years had come home to roost. His heart raced as he peered through that chamber of darkness for a sign of . . .

What?

"Robert?" he said, his voice a brittle snap in that bleak, sarcophagal place. "Is that you? Let me see you. Let me see you. Let me see—"

The smell of sulfur crept into his nose, causing him to recoil.

Meach summoned what fading flicker of courage he had left in him and staggered through a dark gallery of hallways and corridors, Theseus without his ball of thread, lost but blindly pursuing some internal patter, some broach of contact from another place, beckoning, tantalizing . . . a figure he believed existed even if it did not. In a spark of clarity, he recalled where he was—his old friend Andrew Larimer's childhood home; *my* childhood home—yet that realization did not help anchor him back down to reality.

He kept thinking, *Robert? Robert?*

That sulfuric smell only grew stronger. Another smell behind that one—more earthy, brackish. Something of the land, and of the water that covers it.

And then he heard a voice, whispering in an almost singsong fashion: *"One . . . two . . . three . . . four . . . five . . ."*

"Yes," he said, the word, hardly a sound, an expulsion of air that wheezed from him as he staggered out into the warm, thick summer night in pursuit of that voice, his pores expelling gooey bulbs of perspiration. He dug his fingernails into his arms again, *scritch-scritch-scritch,* then focused his bleary eyes across a moon-wan night toward a stand of trees. Something shimmered in the dark. The boughs of the trees were wet and droopy from a recent summer rain, and if he listened carefully enough, he could hear the raindrops plinking from leaf to leaf, plunking in puddles cupped by black soil. Was that the sound he'd heard upon waking? *Plink-plunk, plink-plunk.*

A shape moved beyond the trees, causing him to freeze, his heart galloping in his chest. There was a crackle like static electricity in the air, and he became distantly aware of some transference taking place. Or taking *hold.*

(please no please please no)

The voice again, maybe in his head, or maybe calling out to him from just within the confines of those nearby trees: *"One . . . two . . . three . . . four . . . five . . ."*

"What do you want from me?" he shouted hoarsely into the woods. "Why won't you leave me alone?"

The voice repeated: *"One . . . two . . . three . . . four . . . five . . ."*

"What—"

"Dig," said the voice. And when he didn't immediately oblige, the voice said again, more sternly, *"Dig, Matthew."*

Meach felt his entire body shudder. He was hearing the *plink-plunk* again, and knew now without question that it was the sound of water dripping off a living corpse.

Something at his feet: he bent instinctively and drove his fingers into the moist soil, wiggling them around, feeling what was beneath the surface. Searching, searching. Nothing there. Nothing there. Searching some more. Thinking, *This is it. This is the end. I've gone over the edge, like I always knew I would.* Thinking of a boy who had once gone over—

(the edge)

But Meach did not go over the edge. This was not the end; more specifically, one might argue that this was the *beginning* of something, albeit something that owed its beginning to another time, another place. Whatever the case, tears dribbled down the waxen, pockmarked sides of Matthew Meacham's face as he knelt there digging in the muddy soil.

"One . . . two . . . three . . . four . . . five . . ."

A deep, shuddery breath, like the distant flutter of birds' wings. Fingers working greedily in the dirt.

"One . . . two . . . three . . . four . . . five . . ."

His fingers came into contact with a warm, moist cable buried beneath the earth. The feel of it caused him to pull away . . . but then something drew him back to it, and he gripped it tightly in both hands. It seemed to pulse against his palms as if with its own heartbeat. He tugged it out of the soil, uprooting it, and it came in segments, *thuk-thuk-thuk,* its wet, fibrous shaft thick as a powerline in his hands. It was an umbilical cord, or so his mind told him it was. He tugged at it with more authority, teeth gritted, but it would not uproot itself further. He took several steps forward and repositioned his hands along that slimy bit of rope, prying it out of the earth, *thuk-thuk-thuk,* the sharp little fibers bristling from the cord slicing through the soft meat of his palms, and Matthew Meacham, thirty-five years old, half a lifetime in and out of rehab and bars alike, his blood boiling with hepatitis, kept pulling, kept following the cord, kept pursuing his destiny.

It led him through a dense wood, where summertime trees, weighty with rainwater, bowed in supplication. He crossed beneath their boughs, forehead slapped by wet leaves, lacerated by pitchfork branches, blessed by the world around him, until he staggered out onto a muddy dirt road that overlooked the wide, black expanse of the Chesapeake Bay. He was suddenly standing on a platform at the edge of the world.

He paused for a moment, that taut umbilicus gripped tightly in both his bleeding hands, blood trickling blackly down his wrists. His lungs ached and his skin itched. His right eye was burning again, just as he claimed it had in the weeks after the incident back when the five of us had been teenagers. Beyond the road was a bluff that overlooked the tremendous expanse of the bay, ink-black and moonlight-shiny. It was a clear summer night, and even with Meach's bleary, burning vision, he could easily discern the pulsating glow of the lighthouse out there, surrounded by all that darkness. The umbilicus was strung like a booby-trap beneath the road, leading toward the edge of the cliff; Matthew Meacham tugged at it again, and it broke incrementally free of the earth in little staccato reports, *pop pop pop,* right through the muddy surface. It tunneled straight through to the opposite side of the road, toward the edge of the cliff that looked out across the inky black waters of the bay. Still stubborn in its buriedness.

Matthew Meacham staggered toward the edge of the cliff. A dizzying euphoria overtook him, and he momentarily closed his eyes and swayed on his unsteady feet. His lungs, burning a moment ago, now felt heavy and full of some thick, viscous liquid.

Robert, is that you?

What do you want?

What is there to find?

And the voice responded: *"One . . . two . . . three . . . four . . . five . . ."*

The umbilicus grew taut once more, and he looked down to find it snagged between two large rocks at the edge of the cliff. He yanked on the cord, but it wouldn't budge; his hands were slippery with blood now, and with whatever noxious fluid was seeping out of the cord itself.

No, not a cord.

A lifeline, he thought, for no discernible reason. *A life—*

The cord pulled *back,* and the next thing Matthew Meacham knew, he was tumbling over the side of the cliff, his heels carving trenches through the earth, then flipping forward, and he was airborne, head over ass, plummeting down, down, down . . .

In a flash, just before he struck the earth below, he thought he saw the figure of a teenage boy standing in the shallow water, watching him fall.

THREE

I've got a book, *The 365 Greatest Things Anybody Ever Said,* which my father gave to me upon my admittance to law school. The concept is like one of those word-of-the-day calendars, only it's a book, and they're famous quotes instead of words. In it is a quote from William Faulkner, from his novel *Requiem for a Nun,* I believe. I'm pretty sure you've heard it: "The past is never dead. It's not even past."

That was what it was like returning home.

Kingsport, an animal, carries upon its hide the fleas of humanity: chafe-knuckled watermen, sun-browned faces, the squinting, rheumy eyes of career alcoholics. Live to eighty, and you've gone blind from a lifetime staring at the reflection of the sun off the bay. Garrulous, whiskied female laughter cackles through the open doors of the dock bars in mid-afternoon. Seagull shit plasters the hot tracts of asphalt that cut beelines through cornfields and sand dunes alike, as it does the gas station parking lots, the cars and trucks, the palmists' hand-painted wooden signs, the neon lights of the Stop and Go out along U.S. Route 50. There's always some guy with his shirt off on a bike, calf muscles like machine parts, baseball hat backwards, Ray-Bans on, pedaling with a basket on the front (sometimes there's a transistor radio jouncing around in that basket, sometimes a large, bored-looking cat). The boats down at Kingsport Marina are sad refugees, barnacle-clad and hopeless, with hulls like rusted torpedo shells. They've got faded names stenciled across their sterns—*Rudder Disregard* and *Cirrhosis of the River* and *In Decent Seas*—and there are fishing nets draped over the sides of these vessels, and crab pots stacked like Egyptian monoliths on their moss-slickened decks. You can see the line of houses along the coast, with their storm windows at the ready, satellite dishes on their sun-bleached roofs. You can see, too, the tracks cut into the marshland by the rugged, unforgiving tires of all-terrain vehicles, and the litter of empty beer cans their riders leave behind in their wake. The bars stay open all hours of the night out here, filling cups for as long as there are patrons planted in seats to knock them back, county regulations be damned. They smoke, they fight, they sleep with each other's spouses. They spew racial epithets like it's some call to arms. Men here still call women "sweetheart" and "doll" and "babe," and the women take this without an ounce of resentment, or even the most remote inkling that something is out of balance; it's as if, at some pivotal juncture in their collective upbringing, their mothers had taken them out to the barn and explained, quite simply, that this is just the way it is, and now they carry that knowledge as some unknowable burden across their bowed and strained shoulders like sacks of wheat. The smell of the bay is year-round out here—a briny and vaguely fetid stench that becomes completely overpowering during the hottest, driest times of the summer. The beaches are littered with eviscerated clam shells, and mayflies congregate in knots in the air. Oyster beds are in such abundance, they crest above the surface of the water in bulging, irregular black pylons and gleaming, otherworldly outcroppings, so many it's like a breaching of a pod of humpback whales. Sometimes, you'll find a dead seagull snared in the reeds, its body garroted by fishing line, its red bill hinged at a ninety-degree scream, one blind, milky eye bulging from its black-hooded face.

As far as Rebecca was aware, Baltimore was my destination, where I'd meet with one of Bryce Morrison's legally challenged, unscrupulous clients. I told her nothing of the phone call from Dale the night before, nor of the text message I'd received from him this morning with his home address. I'd lied to her as I packed my bag in our bedroom, apologizing for having to leave her last minute on a Saturday and because I wasn't sure how long I'd be gone. She cursed Morrison under her breath for working me too hard, then made me a sandwich to eat on the train. And while I *did* take the Amtrak to Charm City, with its confusion of fire-scarred warehouses, Everest-like salt mounds, and winding, concrete ramparts like something out of a post-apocalyptic nightmare, I didn't stop there. Instead, I rented a car and took I-95 to U.S. 50, which shuttled me across the Bay Bridge. Far below, the Chesapeake lay sculpted in broken glass and streamers of molten metal, while a procession of cargo ships sat motionless on the horizon.

I'd spent the first eighteen years of my life in Kingsport—a small, insignificant creature bobbing along the whitecaps of this small, insignificant fishing and crabbing village, tucked behind fields of corn and wheat, bracketed by steel grain silos and CITGO gas stations, and flanked by the black-rock cliffs and brown, reedy beaches that comprised Maryland's Eastern Shore. It was a waterman's town, and nearly everyone who lived there made their living off the bay—crabbing, fishing, oystering, sailing. The crabbing and fishing boats would go out before dawn and return around suppertime, catch or no catch, and on quiet nights as a child, with my bedroom window open to let in whatever breeze there was to come on through, I could hear their mournful clanging down at the Kingsport Marina far across town. On clear nights, if you traveled the old Ribbon Road straight out to the cliffs of Gracie Point, you could see the lighthouse in the distance blazing like the finger of God in the middle of the bay; on foggy nights, it was still visible, only now as a smudgy cigarette burn poking dreamily through the misty veil.

When my father died six years ago, I became the sole owner of my childhood home. A rambling ranch-style farmhouse that had been in my family for generations, the only house on acres and acres of land, mostly hidden from the road by a confusion of overgrown, jungle-like trees, and a low chain-link fence woven with poison ivy. My father had been an attorney—a small-town lawyer who might have been destined for bigger things but was too preoccupied with raising a son on his own to pursue them—and he was a good man. He did his work from the house in an office in the back. He kept a wooden shingle dangling from the porch that said, simply, E. LARIMER, ATTORNEY-AT-LAW. While his profession obligated him to sit behind a desk, my father was also not afraid to get his hands dirty, so when he wasn't poring over clients' legal documents and offering advice on the occasional dissolution of a marriage, Ernest Larimer kept the old ranch house up as best he could. He'd do all the repair work himself—any necessary carpentry, but also plumbing and electrical work—and I have vivid memories from my youth of his broad shoulders sweating through the fabric of his threadbare work shirt, his eyes the color of steel pins narrowing in concentration, the beads of sweat trickling down his reddened, furrowed brow.

The last time I'd set eyes on the house—on this town—had been the week I'd come home to bury my father at St. Gregory's. It was a distant memory six years gone, but the emotion, I found, was suddenly very close to the surface as I turned the steering wheel of my rental car and pulled up the old gravel driveway. It was the same house, of course, but there was something hazy and remote about it now, noncommittal almost, like an image from some vaguely remembered dream—or like the Gracie Point Lighthouse on those cold, foggy nights.

Uncertain what I wanted to do with the place after my father's death, I opted to hold onto it for a while. Since I was already living in New York at the time, this required me to hire a caretaker to mow the lawn, trim the hedges, and just generally make sure the place didn't crumble to a pile of ash in my absence while I was still considering what I should do with it. Having kicked that can six years down the road now, and I was still forking over quarterly paychecks to Gil Wallace, the local caretaker.

As I pulled up to the house, I saw a rust-red pickup truck parked at an angle at the top of the driveway. Gil Wallace himself was leaning against the driver's door, smoking a brown cigarette and mopping the sweat from his creased and sunburned forehead with what looked like a dirty oil rag. I'd phoned him ahead of time to inquire about the condition of the place, since I'd planned to spend the night here, and he'd assured me all was tip-top, Mr. Larimer, sir. I hadn't asked him to meet me here, yet here he was, sweat boiling off his flesh while he sucked the life out of that cigarette.

What the hell am I even doing here? That I'd come running back to this place in the wake of Dale's cryptic phone call only confirmed how deep some roots grow.

Gil squinted at me, shielding his eyes from the setting sun, as I shut down the rental car's engine and climbed out into a swampy summer heat. Despite having spent the majority of his fifty-odd years doing manual labor in this town, Gil Wallace was an errant hangnail of a man, his loose skin like football leather. His shoulders came to points and his legs were noticeably bowed. He wore a belt that could have wrapped around him twice.

"Nice trip down, Mr. Larimer?"

I crossed over to his truck and shook his hand. "You didn't have to meet me here, Gil. I've got a key. How long have you been waiting?"

"Well, now, wasn't much waiting as I was getting some things ready for you, Mr. Larimer. Last minute notice and all, but I wanted everything to be good to go, sir."

"I thought you said the place was tip-top," I reminded him. "And please, call me Andrew."

"Oh, she is, she is . . . the place, I mean . . . only, well..." He twisted up his face into some semblance of a frown or a scowl—I couldn't be sure which—and then I watched as his cigarette rolled from one corner of his mouth to the other, like some magic trick.

"Well what?" I said.

"Well, I hate to tell you, but I think you had a squatter."

"A what?"

He pointed in the general vicinity of the house. "A squatter, Mr. Larimer. Someone broke in through the back door—I only just realized it today, when I was giving the place a final once-over for you—and they was living in there, I think, for a time. Found some fast-food wrappers, beer cans, stuff like that. Even some clothes and an old sleeping bag and backpack, which I took straightaway out to the trash." He raked a set of fingers through his short, silvery hair, and I watched as dry flakes of scalp trampolined into the air. "Of course, it could just be neighborhood kids, breaking in here to have a good time. You know how kids are."

"Great," I said, looking up at the old place.

"Anyway, I replaced the lock on the back, where it had been jimmied, and like I said, I cleaned everything out. Water's working, electric's on."

Sudden movement in the periphery of my vision caught my attention. I looked up in time to see a pair of massive black wings swoop down from the roof of the house and coast over to a low tree branch in the front yard. The thing settled there, the branch bowing under its weight. It was a turkey vulture, one of God's ugliest creations. I glanced up at the roof and saw two more perched up there like sentinels.

"I hate those things," I said, more to myself than to Gil Wallace.

"Well, they're ugly as sin, but they won't hassle you. They're carrion birds."

"Why are they hanging around here?"

"Maybe something has died," Gil suggested. Then he shrugged his shoulders and added, "Or it could just be the smell."

"What smell?"

He looked suddenly sheepish as he blotted the sweat from his brow again. "There's a godawful smell in the house, Mr. Larimer, just to warn you. Did all I could about that, some air fresheners, sprays and whatnot, but I'm afraid it's a stubborn stink. Smells like death, so maybe that's what brought the birds. And of course, the stink brings the flies, too. Did what I could about that, as well, Mr. Larimer, but I'm afraid it ain't been enough."

"Flies?"

"Afraid so, Mr. Larimer. Big black ones. Droves of 'em."

Gil followed me up the porch and was already digging a ball of keys out of his khakis when I said, "It's okay, I've got it." I took a key fob that said DAD'S HOUSE from my pocket. Before unlocking the door, I observed my father's shingle, still hanging there by a pair of rusty chains—E. LARIMER, ATTORNEY-AT-LAW.

I stepped inside a tomb, where the air sat stagnant and foul-smelling and humid as a sweatbox. Flies swarmed the air all right, the tiniest of them clustering around my nose and eyes. Strips of flypaper hung from the ceiling, so many brown, curling bits of tacky paper that they looked almost festive. I fanned flies from the air as I came through the door, and saw them swarming along the walls of the hallway.

"You weren't kidding," I commented.

Despite the infestation, I could see the place was mostly clean—old Gil had been busy all afternoon, eager to impress—and when I went to the sink and turned on the faucet, the old caretaker made a sigh of relief as crystal-clear water chugged unimpeded out of the tap.

"See?" he said, blotting dead gnats from his sweaty forehead with his dirty rag. "Tip-top."

"You're right about that smell, though. What *is* that?"

"I think," Gil said, "that if you keep the windows open for a bit, it might air the place out."

I nodded, although I knew this wasn't the smell of mustiness. The house smelled *putrid*, as if something dead was rotting away in here.

"You want me to bring your bags in from the car, Mr. Larimer?"

"That's all right, Gil. I'll take care of it."

"How long you staying for, you don't mind me asking?"

"I'm not really sure." I pinched a curled section of wallpaper between my thumb and forefinger, and gave it a decisive tug. It was so brittle, it made a sound like tearing burlap as it came away from the wall, and expelled a clot of dust particles into the air. "If this smell doesn't get any better, I might just get a room out by the highway. These flies aren't helping matters, either."

"Chicken necks," Gil said.

I looked at him. "What's that?"

"You ever hoist a crab trap from the water that's got chicken necks in it? Been under for a few days? That's what this smells like."

"Chicken necks," I muttered.

"Crazy thing is, I was out here just last month, Mr. Larimer, and everything was tip—"

"Was tip-top, right," I finished for him.

"Room by the highway might not be such a terrible thing, is what

I'm thinking, Mr. Larimer. Meanwhile, I could get an exterminator in here. Someone to come see about the smell."

I told him that wouldn't be necessary, thanked him for his help, then handed him some extra cash. He blotted his brow with that rag one last time, then tromped out of the house. I listened as his rattletrap pickup shuddered down the driveway toward the road.

What am I doing here?

I had never properly cleaned the house out after my father's death, so most of his belongings were still here—the kitchen table, the sofa and loveseat in the den, the bedrooms perfectly made up. His personal effects still resided here in the house, and it would be easy to believe he was still alive and well, with his pipe on a stand in the living room, a rack of magazines in the vestibule, an old percolator on the stove, polished and shiny as an old Chevy fender. I meandered through the place, taking it all in, like a spectator despite the fact that I'd spent the first eighteen years of my life living inside these walls. The floral-patterned wallpaper, the arched doorways, the multitude of claustrophobic little rooms with their hodgepodge assortments of furniture—this place felt like a shoe I'd outgrown. My mother had lit out for the Great Beyond when I was just a toddler, so it had just been my father and me for all those years, without so much as a modicum of female jurisprudence to brighten our lives. We were just two men, bound by blood, negotiating the creaky corridors and passageways of this cramped and musty dwelling. This house never felt more like that to me than it did now—a thing whose sole purpose was to *contain*.

I peered into the parlor with its scuffed hardwood floors; a closet off the laundry room with a collapsible ironing board protruding from it like an obscene gesture; the kitchen with its antique appliances; my father's office, with its shelves of ancient hornbooks, a desk with a dusty ink blotter, a silver letter opener, and a mug that said SHOW ME YOUR BRIEFS. There were photos of me as a child in this room, fishing rod in hand, or a baseball bat slung over one shoulder.

I went down the hall to my childhood bedroom last. I'd packed most of my things once I left for college, and then packed up the rest when I'd returned six years ago to bury my father, so all that remained in this room now was a single twin bed, a too-small desk, a dusty wall mirror, and a braided throw rug in the middle of the floor. There was a nightstand, too, with an old lamp on it. I stared at it for several seconds—or, more precisely, stared at the nightstand's single drawer. *It can't still be in there,* I thought, then on the heels of that: *Where else would it have gone?*

I pulled open the drawer. Inside was a tattered paperback copy of William Blake's *Songs of Innocence and of Experience.* The sight of it caused my throat to constrict. I took the book out, and thumbed open the cover. Printed on the title page in a faded, feminine script were two words:

burn bright

I slipped the book back in the drawer and closed it.

On my way out of the room to retrieve my luggage from the car, the toe of my right foot struck something, sending it rolling across the hardwood floor. I glimpsed it disappear beneath the bed.

Getting down on my hands and knees, I peered under the bed and at a vast sea of dust balls until I spied the thing—a narrow, cylindrical tube with some writing on it. I reached for it, drew it out, then knelt there staring at it as it lay like some talisman across the palm of my hand.

It was a Roman candle, hollowed and spent, with a fringe of burned paper on one end. The waxy black wrapper felt almost greasy in my hands, and despite the burned edges, I could still read the words in jarring red font—MAD DOG TNT.

Reality grew fuzzy around the border. Even as I stared at it, I wondered if it truly existed, or if it was some hallucination from my past, conjured up by my overtaxed and stricken mind.

I brought it to my nose, gave it a sniff. The stink of black powder was so caustic that it burned my sinuses and caused my eyes to water. The Fourth of July was soon approaching, so it was perfectly logical to think that some local kids had broken in here—squatted, as Gil Wallace had said—and had shot off some preliminary fireworks on the property. Wanton boys with cigarette lighters and too much time on their hands were a staple of Kingsport. Why the spent cartridge was in the *house,* however, I couldn't fathom, but it was all perfectly logical. Or so I convinced myself.

I placed it on the nightstand beside the bed. Kept staring at it even though I had suitably rationalized its existence to myself a moment ago. The waning daylight coming through the single window above the bed cast a spotlight on it, or so it seemed.

I decided to go around and open all the windows in the place. I doubted it would do much good against the stench, but it was worth a shot. If I came back here tonight after meeting with Dale and it still smelled this awful, I'd pack up and find a motel out by the highway.

Outside, the light was growing dim, and I was exhausted from the trip down, so I knew I needed to head out to Dale's before it got too late. I checked into some fresh clothes—an Oxford shirt, pleated slacks, considered a necktie then thought better of it—then brushed my teeth and combed my hair in the hallway bathroom. My father's toothbrush still sat in a plastic cup atop the sink, the medicine cabinet still chocked with his various ointments and pills and plastic hair combs.

I closed the medicine cabinet, then stood there looking at my reflection. Stared at it. Felt something uncomfortable rolling around inside me. A dark wraith come home to roost.

The last thing I did before leaving the house was to pull my wedding band off my finger and leave it on the bathroom sink.

i

There is a gas station on the outskirts of my hometown of Kingsport, Maryland, that is just your average, run-of-the-mill gas station and convenience store, except for the fact that it has a large green frog floating in a jar of formaldehyde on a little pedestal next to the coffee station. The frog looks frozen in some perpetual surprise, its buggy eyes forever staring, its abbreviated forepaws thrust out in a simulacrum of shock. Even its webbed toes, splayed like a newborn's, suggest that this creature was just as surprised by its arrival on this planet as those who found it.

There is a plaque on the jar, a little plastic sign fixed to it by Tacky Tape, that reads:

"RAIN OF FROGS"
SUMMER 2003

For those curiosity-seekers, there is a man who doesn't necessarily work at that gas station, but rather lingers like an odor, shuffling up and down the aisles, the cuffs of his pants frayed, his brown feet in sandals, one eye milky from glaucoma. For a dollar, he'll talk to anyone who comes in asking about that frog. He'll talk about the strange happenings in the summer of 2003 in the Eastern Shore town

45

of Kingsport, Maryland—the witchcraft that befell the populace, the strange storms, the horrific nerve-shattering majesty of it all— and his half-blind eyes will go wide with the retelling, as if he's just hearing this business himself for the first time in his life, stupefied by the grandeur of it all.

When he's done, he'll make sure you peek in at that frog, just take a good long gander at the old gal, and as you're doing that, this man will creep up beside you, those sandals shushing mutely on the linoleum tiles of the convenience store's floor, and whisper into your ear: *"It came right outta da sky, saw it wit m' own eyes, I did. Wit m' own eyes."*

And the smell of him will drive you right back out to your car.

FOUR

The address Dale had texted me took me straight through town and out to a new housing development on a cliff overlooking the Chesapeake, where all the homes looked brand new and vacant. A large white construction sign stood at the entrance of the development, the company name—Four Walls Construction—emblazoned in three-foot-tall letters. Dale's house stood at the end of a freshly paved cul-de-sac, a handsome white Colonial with polished stone columns on the porch. A brand-new Lincoln Navigator, battleship-gray, sat in the stamped-concrete driveway beside a more economical Prius. Beyond the house was nothing but a swath of deepening sky hanging over the vast gray slate of the Chesapeake Bay.

I parked on the street and climbed out just as a procession of lampposts winked on up and down the block. It seemed almost orchestrated. The street itself was eerily silent, and I could see that Dale's was the only house with vehicles in the driveway and lights on in the windows.

I went to the front door and was about to put the heavy brass knocker to work when the door swung open and a woman nearly slammed into me. I jumped back, and she made a squeaky little cry of surprise.

"My God, you scared the life out of me," she said, and actually placed a hand to her chest. I saw a small boy, maybe eight or nine, standing beside her, gazing up at me from beneath a fringe of licorice-black curls.

"I'm sorry, I was about to knock. I didn't mean to—"

"It's Andrew, right? Andrew Larimer?"

"Yes, I—"

"Suzanne," she said, and afforded me a curt smile. She was maybe forty, but the evident stress lines carved into her face seemed to age her to some indeterminable number. "Dale's sister."

"Of course," I said. "I remember. I'm sorry, I'm a little fuzzy from the trip down."

"Dale said you would be showing up tonight. It's good of you to come. This whole thing…" She glanced down at the boy beside her. "And this is Barrett, Dale's son."

"Hey," I said to the kid.

He just stared at me.

"And we," Suzanne said, "are heading out for some pizza." She grabbed Barrett's hand and navigated him around me and down the steps. She left the door open, and said, "Go on inside. He's waiting for you."

I stepped inside just as Suzanne got Barrett into the Prius and drove off.

The place was sparse and immaculate. Some Native American art hung on the walls and the dining-room table, which was a queer yellow-green hue, looked like it was comprised of some environmentally friendly substance, like bamboo. It was an open floor plan, so I could see straight through to the opposite end of the house from the entranceway: red leather sofas and armchairs, a massive television taking up one whole wall, plate-glass windows that looked out upon a sloping lawn and, beyond that, the steel-gray basin of the Chesapeake Bay. I could see a rope swing hanging from a tree, swaying gently in the breeze coming off the water.

"Hello? Dale?" My voice echoed off the mostly barren walls and the high, vaulted ceiling. I glanced down the length of the room, past the aboriginal art, and realized there were no family photos on any of the walls, no mementos or keepsakes conspiring to make this house a home. In fact, the house hardly felt lived in. I wondered if maybe it was a show home for the development and not Dale's actual home.

To my left was a kitchen. It was roomy, with stainless steel appliances and what looked like white marble countertops veined with smoky gray swirls. The table in the center of the room was a solid white square, disconcertingly modern, with a flower arrangement at its center. The chairs, also white, looked like they were made of iron bands soldered together. The floor was a spotless black-and-white checkerboard.

"Andrew."

I turned around to find Dale standing behind me. The last time I had seen this man had been six years ago, at my father's funeral. He had been the only one of my childhood friends to come. In the intervening years, he had put on weight, and his hair, although perfectly parted to one side, had grown a little unruly around the ears. He wore a white button-down dress shirt and charcoal slacks, like he'd just come from the office, but as I studied his face, I could see dark purple pouches beneath his eyes and the shadow of beard stubble darkening his jowls. There was something *dispossessing* about him, like he'd recently evicted his own soul, and he stood here now, a hollow husk of a man.

"Look at you," he said, his voice grave.

"Dale. What's all this—"

"You came."

He took a single step toward me, then wrapped me up in his big arms. Despite the dress clothes, he smelled sour, like he hadn't showered in days. I felt the beard bristle on the side of his face scrape against my cheek. He gave me one powerful clap on the back, and then I was thankful when he let me go.

"You know what you said to me the last time I saw you, Andy?"

"What's that?"

"You said you were never gonna set foot in this town again. That it made you feel sad and dirty and you were never coming back for as long as you lived. That if a man could pull off one grand escape in his lifetime, it was better not to tempt fate and risk having to do it again."

"That doesn't sound like me."

Dale laughed, hard enough so that I could see the fillings in his back teeth. "Life is nothing but a bunch of curveballs, isn't that right? It's good to see you."

I decided not to remind him that the only reason I was back here was because of his drunken, late-night phone call that, if I were being honest, had possessed the slightest suggestion of a threat. *You don't have a choice . . .*

"Listen," he said. "You don't know how much this means to me, you coming out here like this."

"What's this all about?" I asked him.

His smile lingered, but I watched as a fogginess clouded his eyes. He did a curious thing then: he glanced down at the palm of his right hand, the way someone might if they were taking a test and had the answers written there. When he looked back up and faced me, there was something sad—hopeless, even—in his eyes. He nodded toward the hallway. "Come on back to my office. We'll have a drink."

Dale's home office was only slightly less sparse than the rest of the house. There was a handsome wooden desk, a perfect file of books on a bookshelf, and a pair of club chairs beside a window that overlooked the bay. There were several framed photos of houses in various stages of construction on the walls, and some architectural blueprints in large frames leaning in a stack against the side of the desk. I glanced at each photo on the nearest wall and recognized the street, the cul-de-sac, the house I was currently standing in.

"You own all these properties?"

"Well, the company owns all the property, all the houses. But I guess I'm the company."

"No partners?"

"Not anymore. I bought 'em out a few years ago."

"Good for you. You must be doing well."

He made a sound way back in his throat that suggested I might have been a bit off the mark.

I was looking at one photo in particular which showed a slightly less paunchy version of Dale leaning on a golden shovel. Beside him stood a plain but attractive woman with sandy curls and a schoolgirl's smile, a knitted sweater over a simple floral dress. Young Barrett, looking no more than three years old in the photo, stood between them, a thumb plugged into his mouth.

"This house looks brand new," I said. "Did you just move in?"

"We were renting a place out by the highway while this house was being built. A lot of my cash was tied up at the time. We've only been in this house for a few months now. I think the paint's still wet."

"I'm happy for you, Dale."

"So was I, for the first few years." He went behind his desk, opened a drawer, and took out a bottle of bourbon and two rocks glasses. "I was unstoppable, Andrew. I made a killing on a residential development down in Ocean City, a second one out on Chincoteague Island, and that one-two punch really set me up. That's when I bought out my investors, paid off my loans. I felt like a rocket taking flight. But it's always a gamble. I'm taking a bath on these homes out here. Half of them aren't even finished and we had to put the brakes on the whole thing until I can free up some more cash. God knows why I thought I could make a few bucks coming back here to Kingsport. Big mistake. I guess I just got nostalgic, or just stupid."

"What's the problem? The houses look nice, and you're right on the bluff overlooking the bay. Water-view homes in this area must go for big money."

"That's not the problem."

"Then what's the problem?" I asked, while at the same time, thinking, *Is he going to hit me up for money? Is that what this is all about?* I suddenly felt like a dupe.

"Don't you know?" he said matter-of-factly, pouring bourbon into both glasses. "I'm cursed, Andrew."

I gave him what felt like a dour smile. I didn't quite know what he was getting at and I sure as hell didn't understand what any of this had to do with me. If he'd lured me here to ask for a loan, he was going to be sorely disappointed.

"You married?" he asked me.

"No," I lied, and then immediately wondered if he could make out the slight indentation in the flesh of my ring finger, where my wedding band had been. Self-conscious, I slipped my hands into my pockets. "I'm not."

"Sit down," he said, and slid a glass toward me across the desk. He crossed over and sat in one of the club chairs, the darkening vista of the back lawn and the Chesapeake Bay beyond, and I sat in the other one, facing him. "I asked you to come here, Andrew, because I'm in a little trouble."

"What kind of trouble?"

"It's my wife. Cynthia. She's gone."

"Gone where?"

He executed the slightest shrug of his shoulders. "I guess that's the big question," he said.

I just stared at him, watching his eyes as they hung on me. It felt like some great weight was suspended in the balance between us. I guess, in a way, that was true, although it had nothing to do with Dale's wife.

"Is that her in the photo?" I asked, pointing to the one with Dale leaning on the golden shovel. I'd never met Dale's wife.

"That's her." He leaned forward, closing the distance between us, his rocks glass dangling between his knees. His pant legs were a pinch too short and I could see he wore dark blue dress socks with tiny red boat anchors on them. "I spent close to a decade building my business, working hard, trying to be smart, and finally making some money. It was good for us, for our marriage. And things were fine between us at first, me and Cyn. But then, a little less than a year ago . . . something happened."

"What?"

"She *changed*. Started drinking too much, running around with guys from town. She quit being a mother to our son, and she quit being a wife to me. I'm talking the flip of a switch, man. Unbelievable. It's like, she cultivated this *hatred* for me, Andy, that kept building and building. I don't know why; we had everything we'd ever wanted, everything we'd worked for. But for some inexplicable reason, it just got to where she couldn't stand the sight of me anymore."

"I'm sorry to hear that."

He lowered his voice a pinch, as if someone might overhear, and said, "You ever have a woman laugh in your face? Just some spiteful, hate-filled laugh? The kind of laugh where you can just look at that person and see nothing but the fires of hell in their eyes?"

"No," I said, and it was the truth.

He looked past me and up at the photo on the wall behind my head. Something in his eyes grew distant. "It's like the woman in that photo ceased existing, replaced by some . . . well, I don't know. Someone else."

"Were you sleeping around on her?"

"No. No. Nothing like that." He looked down at his drink, and for the first time, I could see the barricade come down. The stress that had been pressing down on him, the desperation that was his current predicament—all of it, right there on the surface even if just for a moment. "It's not me who's caused this thing. I haven't done a single thing to her. I'm telling you, Andrew, it's like she became possessed or something. I don't know how else to say it."

"Did you guys talk about divorce?"

"Oh, yeah. Sure. She said she spoke to a lawyer. She wanted two-thirds of my business, two-thirds of all my assets. And full custody of our son."

"Full custody of the son she's just abandoned?"

"It's just to hurt me, Andrew. She's not interested in being a mother. She's drunk half the time she picks him up from school. I get phone calls from all the local bars whenever Cynthia's leaving all tanked up. She's more interested in running around doing God knows what with some local water jockey than raising a kid and being a wife. I'm telling you, the past year of my life has been an absolute living hell, man. I don't know what happened to her. It's like . . . like some poison has come into this whole . . ."

His voice trailed off, and he glanced away from me.

"How did you leave it with her?" I asked. "About the divorce?"

"I told her she'd never get full custody of my son. That she's out of her fucking mind."

"Where do you think she is now?"

"Banging one of her boyfriends and trying to drive me nuts. Making me look like some fucking pariah in my own hometown. This isn't the first time she's split, you know."

"How long's it been this time?"

"Nine days."

"Nine days and no word from her? Nothing?"

"No word. Nothing."

"Have you spoken to any of her friends?"

"What friends? Boyfriends? We haven't socialized together for nearly a year. I don't know her friends."

"What about her family?"

"She's got no family."

"I guess you've notified the police," I said.

"I've reported her missing. Yeah. I spoke to Eric repeatedly."

"Eric?"

"Eric Kelly," he said, then he must have seen the drawn look I felt crawl over my face at the sound of that name. "Oh. I guess you don't know." He glanced back down at his drink. "Eric Kelly's deputy sheriff."

"He's a cop? Here in Kingsport? I don't believe it."

"His old man was a cop," Dale said, as if this was some path toward explanation.

"Eric hated his old man," I said.

Dale shrugged. "People change."

Do they? I wondered. I asked Dale what our old friend Eric Kelly had to say about his current situation.

"What's to say? He knows my wife. He knows what she's like, what it's been like for me this past year."

"What do you think her endgame is here?"

"She's gonna file papers and make a move for my son."

"But why disappear? It won't help her get custody of the kid."

"You don't know my wife. She's become this devious . . . *thing* . . . over the past year, man. She thinks three steps ahead of everyone. Sometimes, when I look at her, it's like looking at a puppet that's being manipulated by some evil fucking puppeteer."

I tried to reconcile that statement with the image of the woman in the photo at my back—those simple curls, her simple smile. Tried to imagine her laughing spitefully in this man's face and found I couldn't do it.

"So what's she thinking now?" I asked him.

"She's setting me up. Wherever she is, she's gonna come back, say she took off because she feared for her life. Like I'm some kind of animal to live with. This whole thing, it's to make me look bad. It's a power play so she gets what she wants in the divorce."

"And that's why I'm here, Dale? I'm not a divorce lawyer. You could have called someone local."

He shook his head, then knocked back the rest of his drink. I watched him hoist himself up from his chair, refill his glass from the bottle on his desk, then knock that one back, too.

"Eric says I might be in some kind of trouble here," he said, leaning against his desk. "Like, something happened to her, and they're looking at the husband, right? Everything was procedure at first, normal stuff, a statement to the police, but now I don't know. Now *Eric* don't know. I asked him if I should get a lawyer, and he's the one who suggested I call you."

"Eric did?"

He nodded, then poured himself a third drink.

I let this sink in, unsure what to make of it. The last time I'd seen Eric Kelly, we'd both been eighteen years old, just before I had gone off to college. A lifetime ago.

"You're telling me you're a suspect in your wife's disappearance," I said. It wasn't a question; I could tell just by looking at his face what the answer was.

His wet eyes jittered away from me.

"Dale, did you do something to your wife?"

Something went solid inside him: I could see his body tense, his muscles constrict. He looked back at me, and his eyes held fast on mine. I could see that they were glassy and pink. We'd once been close friends, Dale and I, but it was difficult to see that teenage boy behind this man's wan, panicked, sweaty face now.

"How could you even ask me that, Andrew?"

"It's what the cops will ask, if they haven't already."

"They haven't," Dale said. "They won't. But I need reassurance, Andy. I need your help. I looked you up online. I know you've still got a license to practice in Maryland. You could be my lawyer."

"You looked me up online." This whole thing suddenly felt too much like a setup for my comfort. "Is this what you meant when you said I had to come out here and I didn't have a choice?"

He ran a hand through his hair. "I didn't mean it like that."

"Because it sounded like a threat," I told him.

He shook his head. "I had too much to drink last night and I was worried and desperate. I kept putting off calling you, but then I thought, *shit, I need this guy's help. Your* help, Andrew."

"So then answer my question," I said. "Did you do something to your wife, Dale?"

He looked me square in the eyes and said, "No."

I studied his face until he turned away and looked out the window.

"All right," I said, and leaned back in the chair. "When was the last time you saw her?"

"Listen," he said, and I watched as his eyes slid back over to the bottle on his desk. He didn't pour another drink, but I could tell he wanted to. "This is gonna sound shitty. You just gotta believe what I'm telling you is the truth, okay?"

This made me bristle inwardly. I didn't like hearing it, didn't like considering what this actually meant. When someone implores you to believe them, they're often about to tell a lie.

"What is it, Dale?"

"She was out drinking one night at The Rat. I was asleep in bed, middle of the night, when I get a call from Tig. She says she—"

"Tig?" I said, cutting him off. "Antigone?"

"Yeah, man. She runs The Wharf Rat now, ever since her parents retired and split for Florida. You didn't know?"

In my head, I pictured a soulful, dark-skinned beauty, in crop tops and frayed jean shorts, shells in her hair like a mermaid. Antigone Mayronne. Tig.

"No," I said, some weakness evident in my voice. "I didn't know. I didn't realize she was still in town. I always thought…" But I didn't finish the sentiment.

"She called me, asked me if Cynthia got home okay, because she was drunk off her fucking gourd when she stumbled out of there. I told her, yeah, she got home just fine, thanks for calling, Tig. But that's not true, Andrew."

"What do you mean, that's not true?"

"Cynthia never came home that night. I was embarrassed to say that to Tig, so I lied, and I told her everything was fine. But it wasn't. And that's the night Cynthia disappeared. And now the police are focusing on that."

"Where did you think she was that night when Tig called?"

"Some guy's house? How should I know? I mean, I'm close with Tig, but I didn't want my business out there, you know? You gotta understand why I said what I said—"

"I understand."

"She never came home that night, so the next morning I went out to The Rat. I found her car with all her shit in it, still in the parking lot."

"What do you mean, 'all her shit'?"

"Her purse, her cell phone. Everything."

"She left the car and all that stuff behind in the parking lot of a bar? What do you think she did, walk off somewhere?"

"How should I know? She was probably drunk and split with someone. Like I said, she's done this before. So, anyway, I drove the car home. But then after I reported her missing, the police came and took her car. They still have it."

"It's been impounded?"

"Yeah, I guess."

I looked down at my drink, untouched in my hands. "This is a big deal, Dale. You're being straight with me on this, right?"

"As an arrow," he said.

"What else have you said to the cops so far?"

"Everything I've said to you. That's it. It's just been Eric. I guess he's handling this . . . whatever the hell it is. He took a statement from me when I reported her missing. Then he came back and asked some follow-up questions. I know he spoke to Tig, too. But he's been laying low these past couple days. I think that's on purpose. Like, he doesn't want to be seen hanging around me right now."

"He shouldn't."

Dale nodded, and looked instantly miserable.

"Is there anything else you haven't told me? Anything I should know?"

Dale's body seemed to stiffen again, and I saw him glance toward the open doorway and out into the hall. He was absently rubbing at the heel of his right hand—the same hand he'd stared at back in the hall—like a nervous tic.

There's more to this story than he's telling me, I thought.

"Dale?" I repeated.

He blinked, like someone coming out of a trance, and then looked at me. Said, "Maybe you should talk to Eric."

Maybe I should go home, I thought, because the last thing I wanted was to be wrapped up in whatever bullshit this was. We already had enough baggage between us, Dale, Eric, the rest of us, and this town, and I didn't need to lug around any more. My arms had grown tired. Spiritually, my back ached.

"It wasn't a threat, you know," Dale said, and I looked up to meet his eyes. "Last night's phone call, I mean. I'm not gonna do anything stupid to fuck us all up, Andrew, is what I'm saying. I'm not using what happened to us back then as any kind of leverage. I wouldn't do that to you guys."

I said nothing.

Just stared at him.

"But you gotta help me, Andrew. You gotta help me."

Still, I said nothing.

Just stared.

FIVE

I returned to my childhood home that night to find a light on in one of the windows. Had I left it on or was my squatter back? Those neighborhood kids, leaving empty beer cans, fast food wrappers, and—

(a Roman candle)

—random clothes strewn about?

Lightning pulsed in the distance, followed by the gathering rumble of thunder as it bowled through the sky. I decided not to unnerve myself by sitting there in my car worrying about it, so I went inside and saw that nothing looked any different than it had when I'd been there earlier in the day. The kitchen light was on, which I'd probably done during my walkthrough with Gil Wallace. There was still that stink in the air, and while the flies had grown lethargic in the nighttime, I could still see them crawling about the walls and buzzing from the tacky strips of flypaper dangling from the ceiling. I sat down at the kitchen table, and dug my cell phone out of my pocket. It was growing late, but I hadn't touched base with Rebecca yet, and I knew she'd still be up. She hadn't been sleeping well in this last month of her pregnancy. Neither had I.

I dialed the number, waited as it rang. When it went to voicemail, I felt a cold disquiet overtake me. I set the phone on the kitchen table, then watched the flies scale the walls as another flash of distant lightning filled the windows. I felt the small hairs along my arms stand at attention.

I pictured my dad sitting across from me at this table, his reading glasses hanging from a cord around his neck. Clear-eyed and somber, sensing some dark secret inside of me, eating me up, reaching out to place a comforting hand on my shoulder . . .

My phone lit up on the table, vibrating in a semicircle. I scooped it up.

"Sorry, I was in the bathroom," Rebecca said.

"I wanted to call before it got too late. Everything okay?"

"Everything's fine. Where are you?"

"Uh, at the Sheraton downtown."

"Is it nice?"

"It's Baltimore," I muttered, and she hummed a little laugh. "But you know Morrison. He spares no expense."

"So what's the big emergency?"

I closed my eyes, rubbed my weary lids. My mind felt scrambled. I chased a stampede of thundering lies through the valley of my skull, finally landing on one: "Just one of Morrison's older clients who needs coddling. It's not a big deal. I'll know more tomorrow."

"This is what you get for being so good at your job."

"I guess so. I'll try to be more of an unproductive malcontent at work when I get back."

"That's the spirit. Everything else okay?"

"Everything's fine. I just don't like being away from you this close to the—"

Something moved at the far end of the hallway—a figure, a shape. Undeniable. I could see this person over the kitchen's half wall from where I sat, a man-like shape cloaked in shadow, staring right back at me through a wall of darkness.

Rebecca said, "You still there?"

"Yeah. Sorry." I got up from the chair and stepped out into the hall. The figure was still there, staring back at me from the far end of the hallway, seemingly unflustered by my appearance. When I spoke next, I felt something click at the back of my throat: "Listen, Bec, I'm . . . I'm gonna go over some paperwork and then get to bed. It's been a long day."

"Call me tomorrow?"

"Of course," I said, the phone suddenly hot against my ear. The person was there, all right—it wasn't some trick of the light or a slip in my psyche, like when I'd imagined someone standing in my closet back in New York. There was someone *right here with me.*

"I love y—"

I disconnected the call, then stood staring at the shape of a man at the opposite end of the hallway.

"Who's there?" I called out. "I see you. You're trespassing in my home."

To my horror, the man moved slowly toward me down the hall.

"Stop," I said. "Stop walking. Stay right there."

He *did* stop. For a moment, anyway. I could hear the rattle of his respiration that, to my ears, sounded very much like the flies currently buzzing around my head. And then I heard him say, "Wow." An undeniable sense of awe in his voice, which didn't serve to alleviate my concerns, but rather only heightened my apprehension. "Oh, wow," he said. "Is that really you, Andrew? Or am I dreaming again?"

For a second, I thought I'd misheard him.

"Now I get it," he said, and he advanced another step toward me, limping as he did so, until the light from the kitchen brought him into relief. "One, two, three, four," and then he pointed at me and said, *"five."*

I took in the stained and tattered clothing, the red gouges along the twisted flesh of his arms, the grime-black hands, and the pasty, haunted expression on his gaunt face. His eyes were burnt fuses, and there was a disconcerting cluster of sores at one corner of his mouth. His feathery blond hair hung down to his shoulders, like some surfer boy's, only dirty-looking and unkempt.

"Who the fuck are you?" I said, my voice shaking.

"Andrew," said the man, holding both hands out like some religious statue on a mount. "It's me, man. It's Meach."

Matthew Meacham and I were both five years old when we first met. I had been walking along the shoreline of Kingsport Beach after a particularly nasty summer storm, whacking at the cattails with a big stick and searching among the reeds for any interesting debris that had washed up. I saw a scarecrow-thin boy crouched in the sand up ahead, his hair shining platinum in the sun, his shoulders freckled and tanned. He was staring at something at his feet. When I approached, I saw it was a small bird tangled in fishing line, flapping its wings and making these shrill little squalling sounds as my shadow fell over it. I had seen seagulls with fishing line wrapped around their wings, their legs, even their beaks, but this bird was smaller than a gull, and I knew it wouldn't survive snared in that nylon web. Without saying a word to each other, we dropped to our knees in the sand and I gently pressed my fingers to the bird. It fluttered beneath my hands, terrified and wanting to escape. When it finally went still, I could feel its tiny heartbeat strumming against my fingertips. His tongue poking out of one corner of his mouth in concentration, Matthew Meacham slowly untangled the length of fishing line from the bird, delicate as a surgeon. And when he was done, I lifted my hand, and that tiny bird fired off into the clear blue sky. We both watched it for as long as our eyes could follow it.

Matthew Meacham—Meach, as we'd started calling him once we got older—was a different person now. There was no trace of that child I'd met on the beach that afternoon behind his red-rimmed, bloodshot eyes. And he seemed to know this. When he looked at me now, there was a twinge of apology in his gaze, an element that suggested he was sorry about what he'd done to the life of that young platinum-haired kid who'd once saved the life of a tiny bird out on Kingsport Beach.

"Meach," I said, and just shook my head in disbelief.

There was a box of fried chicken and a six-pack of National Bohemian in the fridge; Matthew Meacham dug them both out, carrying them to the kitchen table. He chugged a full can, then yanked a grayish drumstick from the box, which he offered to me, but I declined. I took one of the beers, though, and cupped its cool aluminum container in both my hands.

"So you're my squatter," I said, sitting opposite him at the table.

"I hope you're not pissed about it," Meach said as he simultaneously gnawed some grayish bits of chicken off the bone. Slimy flecks of meat clung to his lower lip, and I wondered how old that chicken was. "I knew this place had been empty for years. And it's not like I'm disturbing nothing. I don't even sleep in the beds, just on a sleeping bag in the living room . . . which, I guess, is gone now. All my stuff is gone."

"There's a sleeping bag and a backpack in one of the trashcans out back," I told him. I'd noticed the stuff there earlier when I tossed the empty Roman candle in the trash.

"It's just a roof over my head, you know?" he said, as if he hadn't heard me. He licked the bits of chicken off his lower lip.

"What happened to your house?"

"The bank came and took it after my grandmother died."

"I'm sorry."

He shrugged, noncommittal. "It was for the best, I guess. Her dying, I mean; not losing the house. She was making me nuts, and I know I wasn't some great guy to live with, either. It became like the fuckin' Bates Motel over there, to be honest."

"Do you still own the motel? You can't stay in one of the rooms?"

Meach gave me an empty stare. Meach's grandmother had owned a motel out on Rockfish Road, a cement saltbox with five rooms facing a crumbling strip of asphalt, with an overgrown jungle of trees separating the motel from the road. When he wasn't in school, Meach had worked there with his grandmother, an obese, despotic woman who smoked cigarillos and wore a silver cross around her neck big enough to anchor an ocean liner.

"Motel's been shut down for years now. County came and condemned it. Probably should have been knocked to the ground a decade ago." He seemed to shift uncomfortably in his seat, then added, "I was staying there for a while anyway, but things have happened there lately. I didn't want to stay there no more."

"What things?"

He rubbed the back of one hand across his forehead, and I could see more clearly the twisted lumps of flesh there, the ghostly vestiges of stitches and scars. "I don't . . . I mean, I'm not sure," he said. "I was pretty fucked up when things started to happen, is what I mean."

"Were you in some kind of accident?" I asked him, nodding at the ugly swirls of flesh along the backs of his hands and arms.

"Accident?"

"Your hands. Your arms."

He glanced down at his arms, as if just noticing the scar tissue there for the first time, and looked suddenly ashamed. "It's kind of an embarrassing story, really. I've had some problems with, you know, drugs and alcohol and whatever else in the past. I got pretty bad at one point. The guys, they all came to me, gave me one of them . . . whatchacallit? An intervention."

"The guys?" I said.

"The old gang. Dale, Eric, and Tig." And I swore he looked at me a bit funny, as though I were putting him through some sort of mental test. "Anyway, they said they were worried about me, didn't want me to drop dead of an overdose, wanted to see me get clean. All the things you say. It was a whole scene, and I guess I didn't want to let them down in the end. Dale ponied up some cash for a stint at some rehab facility in Baltimore, so I went."

"That was generous of him."

"Dale's a generous guy," Meach said. "He takes care of me sometimes. They all take care of me, you know. Eric's got me out of more jams than I can count, and Tig, she lets me work at The Rat, washing dishes and taking out the trash, whenever I need a few extra bucks. I try to, you know, repay them however I can. Tried to help Tig, get her out of this town for good, but . . . well, I don't know. Sometimes I don't think things through, and I just wind up making shit worse."

It sounded strange to hear that these people had remained close after all these years. Meanwhile, I had run away and done my best not to look back.

"Anyway, after a couple of days in that facility, I started to freak out. I needed to *get* out. Things were messing with my head, you know? Was like the walls were closing in on me. So I started a fire." He held up his arms so I could get a good look at the tracts of shiny, grafted skin. "Wasn't the smartest plan in the world, in hindsight."

"You couldn't have just walked out?"

His mouth slowly tightened into a knot. "I wasn't thinking too straight at the time, Andy."

"What about now?" I asked him. "Are you thinking straight now, Meach?"

"You mean, am I on something right now?" He gazed past me, at some indeterminable distance beyond my face. His eyes looked like they were two different sizes. One of his lower lids kept twitching. "I try to do the best I can, you know? Life ain't been so good to me. And lately, things have been…" He shook his head, as if to clear the cobwebs off his thoughts. "I mean, I've cut out all the hard stuff, swear to God, man. I'm just trying to drown out the noise, you know?"

"I understand." I had spent my first year in Manhattan working as a public defender. The bulk of my clients were drugs addicts, petty criminals, and the hopelessly indigent—people not much different than my childhood friend. They weren't inherently bad people, they'd just often been dealt a bad hand, and couldn't find their way out. Lost souls, really.

"Why do you think you've been brought back here, anyway?" he asked, and I noted the strange way he'd phrased the question.

"I came back to help Dale with something."

"It's about his wife, isn't it?" He posed it as a question, but I could tell he already knew the answer. "Everyone thinks she ran off, but that's not what happened."

"Oh, yeah? You know something about Dale's wife?"

Matthew Meacham might have spent the majority of his adult life as a strung-out junkie, but his eyes looked stone sober now. "You're gonna think I'm nuts," he said. "Sometimes *I* think I'm nuts."

"Try me."

"It's Robert," he said. "He's come back."

Something tightened in my belly—no, not exactly *tightened,* not like a muscle constricting or anything, but more like some serpent coiling thickly about itself in the hollow pit of my abdomen.

"No," I told him, and I physically drew back from the table, chair legs scraping along the floor. "I don't want to talk about that."

"Doesn't matter what you want, Andrew. Doesn't matter what *any of us* wants. It's time to make good for past sins, man. I always knew it would come back around to get us. I always knew we'd have to pay the fucking piper in the end."

"Meach, I don't want to talk about—"

"Hear me out," he said, and there was an edge to his voice now. "The five of us are *cursed,* man. For what we did to that kid all those years ago. Robert fucking Graves, the son of Ruth Graves, Kingsport's very own goddamn *witch.*"

I felt myself slowly shaking my head. "That's just an urban legend from when we were kids, Meach. She was just a sad old woman who lost her son. She's not a witch, she never was, and no one is cursed."

Meach placed his greasy hands flat on the table and leaned toward me. I could smell his unwashed flesh and his filthy clothes, a clot of stink hovering around him and wafting now in my direction. A fly lit onto his bottom lip and scuttled across the lower half of his face before taking flight again. It made Meach look like a corpse, and this unnerved me. I recalled what Gil Wallace had said about the turkey vultures earlier that day: *They're carrion birds. Maybe something has died.*

"You see, Andrew, I know why you're *really* back." His grease-slickened fingers drummed on the tabletop. "You've been *summoned.* All five of us, right back here in Kingsport, just like back then. One, two, three, four, five. The whole gang."

"Meach, I don't—"

"I've *seen* him, man. I've been seeing him for over a month now."

"Robert Graves is dead," I said, my voice barely above a whisper.

"Sure," Meach said. "But that doesn't mean he's not here."

The lights above the table flickered. It reminded me of that subway ride a few months ago, and how I'd questioned the legitimacy of my own reflection in that filthy window. We both looked up at the light, a choreography that might have been comical had Meach's words not rendered me so uncomfortable.

I leveled my gaze and saw Meach's moist, red eyes on me.

"I want to tell you a story, Andrew," he said, and then he did.

He couldn't say exactly when it started, because to some degree, it had always been there ever since that terrible night so long ago now. A haunting. A thing glimpsed in the periphery of his vision. A sensation that some sentient shadow was always just a few steps behind him, keeping tabs. In the weeks and months after that terrible thing had happened, he would wake with a scream snared in his throat, his right eye burning, and his lungs feeling as if they'd been pumped full of seawater. Meach, just a teenager back then, grew paranoid about birds and began collecting frogs in glass jars. Meach claimed the frogs weren't *real* frogs, and so he never fed them, and soon he had nothing but mason jars full of dead frogs lining the walls of his bedroom. It was anxiety teetering on madness, all of which stemmed from that night out on the old Ribbon Road, and what we had done to Robert Graves. Over the next several years, he had learned to blunt this anxiety with drugs and alcohol, and while those sedatives had ruined Meach's life in other ways, they had mostly kept the haunting at bay.

Until recently.

He began waking up in the middle of the night, feeling like something was caught in his throat. He'd roll out of bed, dropping to his hands and knees on the floor of the motel room where he had been living since the bank had reclaimed the house, gagging onto the fire-retardant carpet. One night, he coughed up a plume of dusty black feathers; they collected in a heap on the floor, glistening with spittle. He began to imagine invisible insects crawling around on his arms and along the nape of his neck, fearing that pale white grubs would come bursting from his flesh at any second. He would smell the smoke from ancient fireworks only to find himself in some sort of trance, setting *actual* fires down at the local dump or in the dry reeds and cattails along the shoreline down at Kingsport Beach. Was it the drugs causing these hallucinations, or something more sinister? Meach didn't know . . . until that sentient shadow in the periphery of his vision finally came up behind him and placed its cold, rotting hands on Meach's shoulders.

A dead boy named Robert Graves began to visit Meach in his dreams. But *were* they dreams? Meach couldn't be sure. Robert was drawing him out, tasking him with something that Meach could not quite comprehend. How long had this been going on? Days? Weeks? He couldn't be sure, and his recollection of such things was dulled by the drugs and the booze he continued to pump into his system in an effort to keep the dead boy in his grave.

One night, Meach awoke in the darkness of his room at the motel to find Robert standing at the foot of his bed. This was most certainly *not* a dream. He could smell the sulfur on the dead boy, could hear the water dripping from the dead boy's clothes and thumping mutely on the carpeted floor: *plink-plunk.* He had come through an opening in the wall of the motel, had been *birthed* from it, Meach understood; he could see a pulsating white light shining through the opening at Robert's back, could hear the crashing of the waves against the black rocks of Gracie Point. For a moment, Meach became disoriented, and believed that maybe he *was* down at Gracie Point, and that the light pulsing through the hole in the wall was, in fact, coming from the lighthouse.

Hello, Matthew, Robert had said. He stepped around the side of Meach's bed, the dead teenager's sodden sneakers squelching wetly on the carpet. When Robert leaned over the side of the bed and peered down, Meach felt droplets of water plink-plunk down upon his face. One drop fell between Meach's parted lips, and his mouth exploded with the briny taste of the bay. *Time to get up, Matthew,* Robert told him. *Time to get to work.*

Time to dig.

Meach fled the motel and spent the next few nights sleeping in an abandoned boathouse along Kingsport Beach. But he kept seeing Robert standing atop the water in the middle of the night, the dead teenager's empty eye socket blazing with a white light that lasered through the darkness. Ultimately, Meach broke into my old house, which he knew had stood empty for years. But when Robert began to appear to him right here in this house, trailing wet footprints across the hardwood floors, Meach knew it was hopeless to resist him.

Last night, around the time I'd gotten the phone call from Dale Walls, Matthew Meacham had woken up in this house and had gone on a trek, led by the dead boy. He told me about digging some strange cable out of the ground—what he called the *umbilicus,* or the *lifeline*—and following it straight out to the old Ribbon Road and right to the edge of Gracie Point, where he'd promptly tumbled over the side and was lucky he hadn't killed himself.

"Me falling off the side of that cliff was my own stupid fault," he said. "He wasn't trying to kill me. Robert, I mean. He still needs me. To follow that . . . that *lifeline,* or whatever it is." He paused here, studying my face. I could only imagine what mask of horror I wore at having heard his psychotic story. "I know how this sounds," he said, his voice a notch lower now. Apologetic, almost. "When I first started seeing him—*glimpsing* him, *smelling* him—I thought I was losing my mind. I even considered talking to a therapist about it, but then I—"

"No," I said, sharply. "You can't talk to anyone about that. You can't talk to anyone."

"I know, Andrew. I'm not a fool." His voice was eerily calm now. "But whether you believe me or not, you're not gonna be able to avoid this. None of us are. He's already worked his way in. He's already latched onto Tig. Dale and Eric, too, I'm sure, though they don't talk about it, at least not to me. I'll bet he's even gotten to you in some way, Andrew. Have you sensed him? Have you felt like something has been a little off in your life lately? Have you felt like your lungs are filling up with water and you keep breathing smoke? That there's someone . . . or something . . . watching you from just beyond your line of sight?"

I had no answer for him. I was suddenly thinking of Rebecca and the baby, and of the past few months of this pregnancy where I'd felt some dark presence had infiltrated our family. It was all just a manifestation of my concerns about being a father, coupled with the strains of old guilt. I knew that without question. Yet sitting across from Meach now, hearing his drug-fueled, lunatic story, and his proclamations about a curse on our heads for what we had done all those years ago, I couldn't shake the unease I felt.

"He showed me a reflection, too," Meach said. "A vision of Dale's wife."

"What do you know about Dale's wife?"

"Only what Robert showed me. A reflection of the past, I think. Something . . . something that happened."

"What, Meach?"

"I saw her standing in the night beneath a full moon, right in front of the old witch's house. There were things floating in the air around her, like bits of ash." He frowned, his eyes growing distant, as if this detail still confused him. "I think she'd been drawn there, led there, you know? Like she was sleepwalking or maybe only half awake. And I saw something dark go inside her. She just . . . she just breathed it in, like smoke . . ."

"Was this another dream?"

"Not a *dream*, man," he said, startling me as he pounded the table with a fist. "None of these things that have been happening are dreams.

I know that now." He placed his hands on the table, palms up, and I could see the fresh lacerations in the tender flesh there, crisscrossed like latticework. "Those cuts didn't come from a dream, Andrew. I sliced up my hands pulling that fucking *thing* out of the ground last night! Maybe that lifeline isn't there no more, but these cuts are real. And my limp, it's from falling over the side of that cliff and spraining my ankle. I woke up this morning on the beach. These things didn't happen in some goddamn dream or hallucination, Andrew."

"So how did you see this vision of Dale's wife? What does it mean?"

He seemed to consider this, his eyes ticking toward one darkened corner of the kitchen. Flies hummed around his head. "Maybe calling it a vision is wrong, too. It was like watching something on TV, only it was right there on the surface of the water. A reflection, just like I said."

"What water? Down at the beach?"

Meach's face tightened. He eased back in his chair, wiping his sticky hands along the thighs of his filthy jeans. A low susurration of thunder barreled through the night, and I watched as the lights flickered. Then Meach got up from the table, his chair legs scraping along the kitchen floor. The flies crawling along the domed ceiling light dispersed, vanishing into the darker depths of the house.

"You're not gonna like this," he said.

I followed him out of the kitchen and down the darkened hallway toward the rear of the house. I ran a hand along the wall to switch on the light, but no light came on: Gil Wallace may have had BGE turn the power on, but he'd forgotten to replace the bulbs. That rotten smell was stronger back here in this part of the house, powerful enough to wring water from my eyes. It hung in the humidity like a physical thing.

There was an old highboy that had been in my father's home office when I was a boy, but it was here now, against the wall of the hallway; in the gloom, I nearly ran into it before I saw it.

"Give me a hand with this, will you?" Meach said, moving around the side of the highboy and leaning into it with his shoulder. "I was able to drag it out here on my own, but my ankle is killing me right now from the fall."

"Why's it here?"

"I thought it might . . . stop him from coming up, but I was wrong," he said, and I didn't like the sound of that.

Together, we dragged the highboy a few feet farther down the hall, revealing in the wall behind it the narrow wooden rectangle of the cellar door.

The cellar. That claustrophobic little antechamber that had terrified me as a child, with its black, cobblestone walls, and its oily dirt floor. A root cellar, really, and something that I'd forgotten even existed as a part of this house until just now.

The cellar door was a bit narrower than a typical door, its wooden frame peeling and in need of a paint job. The doorknob wasn't brass like all the other doorknobs in the house, but a cut-glass diamond shape that was always icy cold to the touch, no matter the time of year.

"What's down there, Meach?"

"Go on," he said, and motioned toward the doorknob. "Go on down and see."

I gripped the knob—it was cold—and gave it a good turn. The cellar door squealed open on ancient hinges . . .

. . . and the stink rushed out at me.

Chicken necks, old Gil Wallace had said, and while I couldn't confirm or deny that, it certainly did smell like something was dead and rotting down there.

A terrible, terrible thought came to my mind then. I glanced at Meach, took in the haunted, lunatic eyes, the leaky sores clustered at one corner of his mouth, the ruined flesh of his arms that he kept scratching. The dirt that might have been dried blood in the creases of his knuckles and beneath his fingernails. The way his whole body suddenly seemed at unease, all shifty angles and twitchy musculature. As a child, he had saved a tiny bird's life; as a teenager, he had grown paranoid of them and kept dead frogs in mason jars.

"What have you done, Meach?"

"Don't be scared, Andy. Go on down and have a look."

"Meach..."

He backed away from me, until the darkness of the hallway swallowed him up.

I turned and stared down the black tunnel that descended into the cellar. My neck was prickly with sweat, my mouth dry. Every fiber of my body told me not to go down there, but I couldn't help myself: I set one foot, and then another, on the creaky wooden risers, slowly crawling down into that black pit. I paused only once, when I thought I heard a strange mechanical beeping, but when I stopped to listen, it was no longer there. I felt futilely along the wall for a light switch before remembering that there wasn't one: there was only a single exposed light bulb down there in the ceiling, accessible by a slender chain. I took another step, and the smell down there was so raw and thick, I covered my mouth and nose with one hand.

I took another step down and felt my foot splash through the surface of a tepid pool of water. I quickly retracted my foot, hearing the water slosh below. After a moment of consideration, I dug my cell phone from my pocket, clicked on the flashlight app, and directed that meager beam of light down the stairwell.

The basement was flooded with water, thick and black as squid ink, and it lapped lazily against the wooden stairwell and the dark cobblestone walls of the cellar as though someone were gently rocking the entire house. Patches of brownish scum floated lazily on the surface from one end of the cellar to the other. This stagnant water was the source of that awful stench.

There was a creak on the stairs behind me. I whirled around, and Meach shied away from the light on my phone.

"What the hell happened down here, Meach?"

Instead of answering my question, Meach posited one of his own: "You ever think that maybe we all died that night? Not just Robert, but all five of us? That we're ghosts, just shuffling along, without knowing any better? I mean, maybe I'm dead right now—maybe I died falling down that cliff last night—and you're standing here having conversation with a ghost."

I watched as a frond of black seaweed rose to the surface of the water. It waved lazily like something alive, and I found myself momentarily transfixed by it.

"I can't get away from him," Meach said, "so I've stopped trying. He's got something he wants me to do, and I guess it's my curse to do it. I'm not going to fight him anymore . . . it's pointless."

"What does he want you to do, Meach?"

A long silence, with only the distant rumble of thunder to keep me rooted to the here and now. And then Meach said, "I think he wants me to find something. I don't know what it is, but I think he wants me to find it."

I watched that snakelike strand of seaweed undulate atop the surface of the gently rippling water.

"Let's not come down here again," I said, pushing past him and heading back up the stairs.

◇

I offered Meach the master bedroom, and he was grateful enough to hug me. I offered him the shower, too, and he spent the next hour using up all the hot water. When he was done, he lumbered down the hallway in a cloud of steam, stomping wet footprints on the floor on his way to my father's old bedroom without another word to me. It was almost if he had forgotten I was there. I stood in the hallway, unmoving, smelling that rancid odor crawling up from the cellar. Thinking for a moment about the young boy Meach had been, and that day all those years ago when I'd met him at Kingsport Beach, kneeling before the bird snared in the fishing line. He used to talk with a slight lisp, his tongue poking between his teeth on any s-words. He used to keep pencil shavings in a plastic bag because he liked the smell of them. When he got older, he traded in that bag of pencil shavings for weed, which he'd sell in the parking lot after school.

Christ, Meach . . .

I felt momentarily unhinged at the strength of those memories.

That night, while a thunderstorm pummeled Kingsport, a cold dread overtook me as I lay in bed. What sleep I managed was fitful and furious with nightmares. Several times I awoke—or thought I awoke, because maybe I was still dreaming—to the certainty that someone had crept into my bedroom and was hovering over my bed, dripping water on my steaming forehead and into my burning eyes. I heard footsteps drifting up and down the hall, and thought, *Meach?* Because, yes, who else could it be? What else—

(the wraith)

—would it be? Footsteps advancing stealthily down the hall, into my room, around my bed, wandering through the valley of my half-sleep. The more I heard these footsteps, the more laborious it became to breathe, because my lungs were filling up with seawater, drowning me, and I was suddenly certain that I could smell the sharp, sulfuric reek of exploded fireworks, and I held my drowning breath, and my eyes twitched in the direction of the partially open bedroom door, that stark black sliver of space leading out into the hall, my lungs going *hssst-hssst*, a gargle, really, and I waited, waited, petrified as a small child, for whatever might ease that door open a bit more and come shambling into the room, a single, shining white orb of an eye, and smoke trailing from a ragged, empty socket, *hssst-hssst*, while at that very moment—

I awoke to a crash of thunder shaking the house. The storm sounded very loud—too loud—and I kept hearing a banging sound whenever the wind picked up. I climbed out of bed, went down the hall, and saw that the front door stood open. Lightning flashed beyond the porch and rainwater had wetted the floorboards of the front hall.

I shut the door, then went down the hall to peek in on Meach, which was when I noted his wet footprints still winding down the hall. The door to the master bedroom was open; I poked my head inside and turned on the light.

Meach was gone.

I stood there for a while, and I'll admit: a part of my mind wondered whether or not Meach had been here at all. What had he said as we stood on the stairs, looking down at the flooded cellar? *You ever think that maybe we all died that night? Not just Robert, but all five of us? That we're ghosts, just shuffling along, without knowing any better? I mean, maybe I'm dead right now—maybe I died falling down that cliff last night—and you're standing here having conversation with a ghost.*

Had I spent the night talking to a ghost?

Stop, said a voice in my head. Rebecca's voice. *Stop it.*

I headed back down the hall toward my bedroom, but paused midway down the corridor when I realized something curious about those wet footprints: they did not lead from the foyer, where I had found the door open and the front hall wet with rain, and they did not appear to come from the bathroom. In fact, they appeared to move in the opposite direction: from the cellar to the front door. As if something had risen up out of the water down there and crept out of the house.

ii

In 2003, around the second week of a sweltering July, a man named Brumley drove out to Kingsport to buy his son a truck. Brumley's son, a quiet, passive kid with little interest in sports or girls or anything else for that matter, rode with him. The boy had gotten his driver's license two months earlier, and Brumley thought that maybe if the kid had some wheels of his own, he might go out on a few dates. Or at the very least, maybe make some friends.

The vehicle that Brumley went to see was an old white pickup truck with a large bull's-eye crack in the center of the windshield. It wouldn't win any beauty contests (though neither would his son, Brumley understood), yet something in the eyes of Brumley's son came alive at the sight of the truck.

"What happened here?" Brumley asked, pointing to the cracked windshield.

The kid who was selling the truck—a teenager about the same age as Brumley's son—said, without affectation, "A rock hit it."

"It'll cost a pretty penny to have it repaired," Brumley said, hiking up his pants. Brumley worked in sales.

"I just need to get rid of it," said the teenager.

"How about I give you half the asking price?" Brumley said. It was something he had planned on saying before he ever even laid eyes on the truck, though now he at least felt justified. He kept looking around for the teenager's father, or some adult in the vicinity, but with the exception of a police car parked across the street, they were alone.

The teenager quickly agreed to the reduced price, and Brumley paid the boy two hundred dollars in cash for the truck.

He went home that day feeling like he'd gotten one hell of a deal.

SIX

Around the time I was staring down at a set of wet footprints in the hallway of my father's house, an old childhood friend of mine, Antigone Mayronne, was half asleep when she heard footsteps moving through her own house. They came pattering into the bedroom, deliberate but unhurried, and stopped at her side of the bed. Tig did not roll over, did not even open her eyes, but told the girl to climb into bed with her. All of it: habitual these past several weeks. Even as she spoke, the words were incorporated into a foggy dream where she was walking through a field of wildflowers, sunlight in her eyes, despite the sound of the storm raging outside.

Bonnie had been suffering from nightmares on and off for the past month or so, and Tig had begun to anticipate her climbing into bed with her at some point during the night. But on this night, when she did not sense her daughter crawl into bed beside her—when she did not feel the familiar bounce of the mattress and Bonnie's cold feet sliding against the backs of her legs—Tig rolled over and opened her eyes.

There was no one in the room.

"Bonnie?"

She sat up, feeling the haziness of sleep fall away, the dream of the field and the wildflowers replaced by the darkness of her surroundings and the slashing of rain against the house. She looked around the bedroom, her eyes acclimating to the dark. A flash of lightning pulsed behind the windows, printing rectangular panels of blue-white light across the foot of the bed. Otherwise, the darkness was impenetrable.

She heard it then—the muted *ring ring* of the bicycle bell, coming from Bonnie's bedroom. *Ah,* Tig thought. *There it is.* Why had she thought the girl had come into her room? Had she mistaken the sound of thunder for footsteps in her partial dream state?

Tig reached out and grabbed her own bicycle bell off the nightstand. She cranked the lever twice in reply, *ring ring,* a little call-and-answer routine that they had developed, and then set it back down. Listened. Listened. Listened. If Bonnie rang hers again, that meant come, hurry, I'm scared. Or sometimes Bonnie just discarded a second series of rings altogether, only to scurry into her mother's bedroom and climb into her bed. But tonight, there was only a wall of silence behind the storm that replied.

There, Tig thought, relaxing. The bicycle bells had been a suggestion of an old friend who had some insight into child development—not so much a therapist as a woman who had researched such things and written a handful of articles that were ultimately published in various lifestyle magazines. It was a crutch, something that Bonnie could do instead of climbing into bed with her every night, that might ease the poor girl's anxiety about sleeping alone. One ring calls out in the night, and Tig's ring would respond. Communion in the darkness. Why Bonnie had started having these night terrors in the first place, Tig was at a loss. She hadn't taken Bonnie to a doctor yet, but if things continued down this path . . .

Leaning over a mound of pillows, Tig squinted at the alarm clock on the nightstand and saw that it was a quarter after two in the morning. This desperate hour seemed to confirm her exhaustion, and so she dropped back down onto her pillows, the mattress springs groaning beneath her. The flesh on her arms tingled, the small hairs standing to attention, as if in anticipation of another lightning strike. She closed her eyes and tried to claw her way back toward sleep. It used to be that the din of a nighttime thunderstorm had borne a comforting, anesthetizing quality. But now, Tig found that the gears in her head were engaged. Despite her fatigue, her mind felt alert. Even with the storm outside, the stillness of the house was suddenly loud in her ears.

Something wasn't right.

Then—*ring ring!* Coming down the hall from Bonnie's room. A panic to the rings this time. A desperate urgency.

Tig got up and crept out into the darkened hallway. It was early summer, yet despite the A/C, the house felt overly hot. Her skin was clammy with perspiration. Bullied by the storm, the overgrown shrubbery in the front yard scraped along the aluminum siding of the house—a sound, Tig thought, that seemed to contain some hidden, coded message: *scritch-scratch-scritch, scritch-scratch-scritch* . . .

She went to Bonnie's room, saw the door standing open, and peered inside. Bonnie's bed was against one wall, her slight form buried beneath a mound of blankets and stuffed animals despite the heat. There were schoolyard chants about girls being made of sugar and spice and everything nice, but ever since Bonnie had turned six, Tig had begun to question such wisdom. There were LEGO blocks on the floor and the dresser drawers stood open, eager to trip Tig in the dark as she moved through the room. Adding to it was the briny reek of the fish tank on Bonnie's desk. Tig couldn't remember the last time the damn thing had been cleaned, and the smell of it unsettled Tig in that moment more than it should have.

"What is it, baby?" she said to the girl. "Another nightmare?"

Lightning strobed beyond the single bedroom window, illuminating the tiny glass eyes of a dozen or so stuffed animals perched on the shelf above Bonnie's bed. It was like watching bats stirring to consciousness in the depths of a cave.

"Bon?" she said, and took a step further into the room.

Bonnie had been a difficult baby, with terrible acid reflux and a disinclination toward breast feeding. Tig had worn herself ragged trying to keep up with the child—a child who apparently required no sleep, and who seemed in a state of perpetual discontentment. (And it wasn't like Reggie had ever been around to lend a hand back then, the son of a bitch; they'd never been married, so the unplanned addition of a daughter in their lives was all the motivation the son of a bitch had needed to hit the bricks. It was only in the past two years when Reggie suffered an attack of conscience and decided to start popping back up in his daughter's life, much to Bonnie's delight and Tig's dismay.) She had taken Bonnie into bed with her early on in those endless, gray, drawn-out days, which afforded Tig an opportunity to doze in the brief periods when Bonnie fell silent. But this also inadvertently cultivated an expectation in Bonnie that they would forever sleep as a duo in the event of some late-night discomfort. When Bonnie got older, it had been a struggle to get her to stay in her own room— Tig had bribed her by allowing her to pick the paint for her walls (a startling, almost nauseating Kermit the Frog green, but hey), and she had encouraged Bonnie to arrange her toys and furniture in any fashion she liked. To make this room *her* room, in other words. Still, Tig would awake most mornings to find her daughter tucked in bed beside her, the girl's thumb plugged into her mouth, sleeping soundly.

But that was something Bonnie had outgrown years ago. This new development—the nightmares, the crawling into Tig's bed in the middle of the night—was somehow different. It concerned Tig on some deeper emotional level.

Another flash of lightning, and something in the collective stare of those spider-like dolls' eyes unnerved her, even more than her daughter's refusal to respond to her. Tig flipped on the bedroom light to find the bed empty, except for a pale pink sheet pulled over a heap of stuffed animals. Bonnie's bicycle bell lay on the little pink nightstand beside her bed.

Something like panic inched its way up Tig's throat.

"Bonnie?" More sternly this time—some weight behind it.

The house shuddered.

Outside, the storm raged.

Tig moved down the hall, sensing something out of place, something in disarray: an element shunted slightly off-center. She glanced into the bathroom, switching on the light, but the room was empty.

There was water on the floor at the far end of the hallway, and a runner of dead, black leaves, greasy as tar paper, leading down to the kitchen. Tig's bare feet came down on them, and they were shockingly cold and wet despite the humidity in the house. She could hear the storm all the better from this end of the hallway—almost too clearly, for some reason, in fact. Crossing into the kitchen, where the roar of the storm was loudest, she found the side door standing open, and rain shelling the linoleum tiles of the kitchen floor. A loud *bang, bang,* that was thunder, and then a muted *crack* as the open door whacked against the wall in the wind. The kitchen floor itself was puddled in rainwater and a tapestry of dead, slimy leaves.

Tig went to the doorway and peered out into the yard. The house sat on five acres of land, the backyard skirting up against the bay, and on this night, staring out, she could see only the slight, timorous sway of the tall grass being bullied by the storm, and the tumult of the rain on the surface of the bay beyond. When she looked down, she could see small footprints in the mud just beyond the concrete steps.

"Bonnie!" she shouted into the night. "Bonnie! Bonnie!"

And then she was rushing down those steps, clutching at the oversized T-shirt she wore, her bare feet plashing through puddles of thick, brown muck. When she crossed into the wet stalks of that tall grass, they whipped against her bare thighs, and when lightning once again bisected the night sky, causing her to freeze midway across the yard, it was as if the devil himself had lit his lantern and shown the world all the darkness and degradation that existed beyond what the human eye could see.

"Bonnie!"

Thunder clashed.

In a secondary flash of lightning, Tig saw a slight figure standing out there in the water, chest-deep, staring up at the downpour—a small, helpless child in the throes of Armageddon.

She rushed to her, barreling through the frigid water, her bare feet sucked into the gray silt, staggering until she fell forward into the surf. She inhaled a lungful of brackish water, then immediately began to choke. She climbed back to her feet, her T-shirt clinging to her torso, her entire body trembling, and closed the distance between her and Bonnie, who remained standing in that chest-deep water gazing up at the storm . . .

"Bonnie, Bonnie, what are you *doing*, baby?" She wrapped the girl up in her arms, squeezed her tight. What was *this*, now? Sleepwalking? She could've *drowned* . . .

Bonnie's body was stiff and unresponsive at first . . . but then she seemed to snap from her daze, and slowly brought her arms up to circle around her mother's neck. Tig lifted her in her arms, feeling the pull of the silt at her feet—that desperate, hungry sucking—and she was about to turn and trudge back through the water toward the house when she saw someone standing several yards out in the distance, right there on top of the water.

A trick of the eye, though, right? A distortion created by her panic mixed with the pelting of the storm, wasn't it?

No—it was the thin frame and stooped shoulders of a teenage boy. She knew this without question, yet without seeing any details, since he was truly just a smudge of blackness superimposed against the never-ending backdrop of the storm-rattled bay. Even when lightning cracked the sky again, the boy remained a featureless black smudge.

Except for a spark of fire in one eye.

Robert, Tig thought, fear numbing her entire body. She squeezed her daughter more tightly against her.

The boy was staring at her from that impossible distance, that illogical place atop the surface of the water, *all of it* illogical, but staring at her with an iris of sparkling white flame nonetheless . . .

Tig turned and rushed back through the water, climbed back up onto the land, and carried her daughter the rest of the way to the house. There, she sat her daughter on the kitchen counter then shut and bolted the kitchen door. As if whoever—or whatever—that was out there on the water was already pursuing them across the yard.

"What were you doing out there?"

The kid was bleary-eyed and looked disoriented. She was shivering, too. A streak of mud darkened one side of her face.

"Come on," Tig said, gathering Bonnie up again. She carried her down the hall and into the bathroom, where she sat the girl on the edge of the tub and then cranked on the faucet.

"Was I dreaming, Mom?"

"I don't know, baby. I don't know what's going on."

Robert, she thought again. Her body was still numb. Her reflection in the bathroom mirror looked ghoulish, her own face streaked with mud, her eyes wide and jittery. Her hands wouldn't stop shaking.

Robert.

No. Not Robert. Robert Graves was dead. *Robert Graves was dead.* There was no one out there on the water. There was no one. There was—

And then a thought occurred to her, one that suggested she hadn't imagined this at all, and that something—

(some wraith?)

—was already in the house with them, and had been for some time now. And this realization scared the shit out of her.

Who rang that bicycle bell?

SEVEN

When we were thirteen years old, Eric Kelly and I were picked up by the local police for shoplifting at the Stop and Go out on Route 50. We'd loaded our pockets with packets of Trident gum, bags of candy, a few Slim Jims, and even wedged a couple of bottles of Dr Pepper into the rear waistband of our jeans, and for no reason other than we had been bored and had dared each other to do it. It was the summer of the Dare Club, as we called it, and Eric and I had both dared each other to steal as much from that convenience store as we were physically able.

The owner of the Stop and Go wanted to press charges. If he had been any other local business owner, we would have likely been cut loose after a good scare and a stern reprimand, but as it happened, the Stop and Go catered primarily to the string of tourists and beachgoers traveling east on Route 50 toward Ocean City, and was often the site of random thefts, vandalism, drunken fights in the parking lot, and at least one armed robbery that I was aware of. The owner—not a local—was tired of being victimized, and had wanted to set an example with Eric and me.

My father, being an attorney in good standing in the community, had a long discussion with the owner. To this day, I do not know what was said, but in the end, the storeowner agreed to have us repaint the outside of his store instead of pressing charges. Afterward, my father had a long talk with *me*, as we both sat at the dinner table gloomily twirling spaghetti around on our forks. "Why'd you take those things?" he ultimately asked me. "It was just junk. I don't understand. It was nothing you needed."

"I don't know."

"Did that friend of yours put you up to it?"

I had wanted to say yes, that it had all been Eric's idea, but that wasn't the truth, and I had always found it difficult to lie to my father. I told him no one put me up to it. It was just something I did and I didn't think about the consequences.

"The older you get, Andrew, the more impact your decisions will have on your life. You should learn that lesson now."

"Right. Okay. I know. I'm sorry."

He must have seen the tears welling up in my eyes in that moment—tears of shame and embarrassment—because he set his fork down on his plate, reached over, and gave my shoulder a gentle squeeze.

"If you've learned something from all this," he told me, "then it wasn't all bad."

Eric and I spent the next two months of Saturdays whitewashing the exterior of the Stop and Go until all was clean and pristine.

Eric's father took it a bit differently. He was the sheriff back then, so the fact that his only son had to be dragged down to the police station one afternoon for petty theft was an affront to everything Sheriff Dean Kelly believed in.

My father had never laid a hand on me my entire childhood, but I could not say the same for my friend Eric and his old man. Two days after we'd been caught shoplifting and hauled in to the police station, we both showed up early in the morning in old work clothes ready to paint the back wall of the Stop and Go. Eric's face was bruised, and each time he lifted his arm to run the paintbrush down the brick-alley wall, he visibly winced in pain. Moreover, I could discern a nondescript agony behind his eyes, too—a flicker of dim, low-reaching light that suggested there were worse horrors waiting for him at home than there were here, on this day, whitewashing the exterior alley walls of a gas station convenience store along the highway.

In the fall of 2003, a few months after the incident with Robert Graves, Eric's father got into his police car in the middle of the night and drove out to the Narrows Bridge. He parked along the shoulder of the bridge, the only vehicle on that desolate stretch of midnight roadway. He stripped out of his uniform, right down to his stark white briefs, then folded the uniform neatly on the passenger seat, his shiny gold sheriff's badge right on top. Despite the chill of that late fall, the interior windows of the police car were most likely fogged from his nervous breath, or so I imagine. After a time, Dean Kelly stepped out into the cool night. He'd left his gun belt in the foot well of the passenger seat, but wandered to the edge of the Narrows Bridge with his service weapon in one hand. Lord knows how long he stood there, staring down at the churning black waters below, contemplating things, before he put the barrel of the gun to his head and pulled the trigger.

I had gone to the funeral and stared across the gravesite at Eric. We'd both been sixteen that year, and the thing with Robert Graves was still a fresh wound on our collective consciences. I hadn't seen Eric much since the summer because of it, but in the aftermath of his father's suicide, I felt obligated to be there for him. Eric's face had been an impassive mask throughout the service. Emotionless. Shock, my father had suggested to me later. But I wondered what other emotions were fighting just below the surface of my friend's heart and mind. In that moment, he wasn't a sixteen-year-old beside the gravesite of his father, but a thirteen-year-old boy wincing every time he lifted his arm to paint a streak of white along the wall of the Stop and Go.

All these years later, and it was that same thirteen-year-old boy I pictured when I pulled my car into the gravel lot that ran alongside the docks of the marina, and saw a man standing beside a police car, dressed in a khaki uniform and a shining gold badge. Eric Kelly had been a good-looking kid back in the day. He'd played football at Kingsport High, dated the best-looking girls, and had this enviable aura about him that, even all these years later, as I crossed the parking lot in his direction, I imagined I could still sense. For all his good fortune in those arenas, though, he'd actually been a shy kid, prone to bouts of self-doubt, mostly due to his difficult relationship with his father, and he did not have many close friends outside our small circle. As kids, he had stayed at my house on more than one occasion when he was in deep with his old man, and I possessed a distant memory of him weeping silently in the night from a sleeping bag on my bedroom floor when he thought I was asleep. I wasn't bullshitting when I'd told Dale I was surprised to hear that Eric Kelly had become a cop just like his father. Back then, Dean Kelly had seemed like the one thing his son would most want to distance himself from.

"Andrew Larimer," he said as I approached. He was holding two paper cups of coffee, so I just stood there awkwardly, my own hands on my hips. He handed one of the coffees to me, then came in for a one-armed embrace, quick and efficient. He smelled like aftershave and leather.

"I can't believe you're a cop," I said.

"Want the truth? Sometimes I can't, either." His smile was genuine. "But you? Some big-time New York lawyer? I read about a case of yours online recently. You're a powerhouse."

"Don't believe everything you read."

"You look good."

"So do you."

"Let's walk," he said, and headed down toward the piers. I followed him, trying not to get the white powder from the granulated clam shells that comprised the parking lot on my shoes. He asked how long it had been since I'd been back in town, and I told him.

"I heard about your dad's funeral," he said. "I'm sorry I couldn't be there for you."

I waved off the sentiment.

"So fill me in," he said. "I know you're a lawyer with some big firm in New York City. But give me the rest of the story."

"Not much else to tell."

"Married? Kids?"

"No," I said. "How about you?"

"A wife and three kids, if you can believe it," he said. "If I'm not working, I'm at baseball practices and dance recitals."

"Is your wife someone from town?"

"A townie?" He laughed. "I burned my bridges with every local girl back in high school."

I smiled at that. He probably had.

"It's good you came out here," he said, and I sensed some unfathomable depth to that statement.

"To be honest, I didn't feel like I had a choice. I met with Dale last night at his house," I said, although I wondered how much he already knew, given that he and Dale appeared to have had some discussion about my having part in this already. "He thinks he needs a lawyer. How bad is this thing?"

"It's not great," Eric said. He paused along the bulwark and looked at me. "Cynthia, his wife, she's been missing for nine days. Well, ten days now. No one's heard a peep from her. She hasn't withdrawn any money from their accounts, and hasn't made any phone calls to anyone, far as I can tell. Last time anyone saw her, she was getting drunk at The Wharf Rat. I interviewed a bunch of people from that night, and everyone says she was there, flirting with some local jerk-off, but that she left without him. Alone."

"Who's the local?"

"Fella named Dan, young guy, lives in a trailer on Shore Road. I know him. He's a nobody. Paid him a visit, and he said she's just some chick he sees from time to time. He knows she's married, didn't care. He met her at the bar that night, they had a few drinks, but he said she left alone. Said she was acting a little strange, too. Freaked him out."

"Strange how?"

"Probably just very drunk," Eric said.

"Doesn't sound so strange for around here. And drunk women rarely freak guys out. Usually, it's the opposite."

"Yeah, well, this guy Dan, he said she spooked him. Said she'd been in a good mood all night, kissing up on him and everything, but then right before she left, she got all serious in the face, and she gripped his arm really hard. Hard enough to leave marks. He said she put her mouth right up to his ear and whispered something."

"What?"

"Well, according to Dan, she said, 'I'm smoke.' And then she laughed. Nearly burst his eardrum, he said."

"What does that mean?"

"Who knows? She was drunk. And then she just got up and left. Practically ran out of the place, is what people said."

I didn't like the sound of that. I said, "Do you know her at all?"

"Cynthia? Yeah, I guess you could say I became . . . familiar . . . with her."

"What's that mean?"

"For the past year, while Dale was having that development built up on the bluff, they were renting a house out by the highway. I met her a few times early on. She seemed nice enough at first. Type of girl you'd think someone like Dale would marry, because Dale likes to be the one in control, you know?"

As a teenager, Dale had been quiet and reserved, an observer rather than a performer, as my dad might have said. Our group had drawn out a more daring streak in him, but I couldn't say I ever found him to be someone who'd ever insisted on being in control. Then again, I didn't really know the guy anymore, so I just nodded and let Eric continue.

"I started getting calls from the local pubs. She was drunk, she was combative. I pulled her over a few times in the middle of the day, because she was swerving like a blind person down Main Street, but I just drove her home, or had Dale come and get her. I could see she was some kind of problem for him, and I felt bad for the guy. My wife and I went out with them for dinner one night, and it was the most . . . I don't know . . . surreal thing I'd ever seen. I don't think the woman said a single word throughout the whole meal. She just sort of stared off into space for much of the night. Then she ordered this whole chicken, and when it showed up, she meticulously picked all the meat from the bones, but didn't eat a bite of it. Just sort of . . . I don't know . . . arranged the bones in her dish. Dale was clearly mortified. I figured maybe she was on some heavy prescription or something. She made my wife very uncomfortable."

"Dale said some change had come over her in the past year or so."

"He told me that, too. Figured maybe he was making an excuse for her behavior." Eric didn't elaborate, but I could see the wheels turning behind his eyes. He was thinking of something—something he was reluctant to share.

"What else?" I prompted him.

"I mean, there was one night . . . I don't know, maybe like eight, nine months ago? Around the time all this crazy shit with her started, now that I think back. It was snowing, and you know how it is around here when it snows. We've got one plow, and if Eddie Merchant, the son of a bitch, is too drunk to operate it, which he generally is, we gotta wait for his son to get off shift at the fire station. So Merchant's kid was out plowing all the main roads out to the highway, and he was up on Graves Road, and it was kinda hard to see, almost a blizzard at that point, but he saw someone up ahead in the road, in the lights of the plow, just standing there. It was Cynthia, and she was wearing this flimsy nightdress and nothing else—I mean, it was so fucking cold out, Andrew, her skin was nearly blue by the time I drove out there. She was like a zombie or something, all doped up. But I didn't wanna take her in, you know? So I drove her out to where they were staying out by the highway—this was back before the house was built on the bluff—and I drop her off. Dale's there, he's a mess, all upset, and the whole thing was just so bizarre. You know I saw that woman's bare footprints in the unplowed part of that road, leading all the way back through town and back out to the highway? That's five, six miles in good weather, never mind barefoot in a fucking blizzard."

"What was she doing out there?"

"Beats the hell out of me. She didn't even tell Dale she was leaving, she just walked out of the house in her bare feet in the middle of a snowstorm. Like I said, when I started talking to her, she was like someone half in a dream. Drugs, I figured, or maybe some kind of mental breakdown. I don't know."

"Where exactly on Graves Road did you find her?"

Eric's face hardened. "She was standing in the road outside Ruth Graves's house."

"Doing what?"

"Doing nothing. Just staring up at the house. At least that's what she was doing when I showed up."

"Why would she go out there?"

"I have no clue, Andrew. Why would she make an art project out of chicken bones in a nice restaurant?"

"All right," I said. "So she's either got a drinking problem, a drug problem, or suffering some mental breakdown—"

"Or all three," Eric interjected.

"Right, okay," I said. "Maybe Dale can tell us if she's been seeing a psychiatrist or anything."

Eric shook his head. "She hasn't. I've already asked."

"Whatever the case, she's got a track record of strange behavior, and now she's just run off somewhere. Abandoned her husband and her kid."

"It's a bit more complicated than that," he said. "Dale's story is a little shaky."

"Shaky how?"

Eric looked out over the bay, wincing in the face of the sun. "What exactly did he tell you, Andrew?"

I relayed a rough sketch of the conversation I had with Dale the night before. Eric appeared to take it all in, and didn't speak until I had finished.

"For one thing," he said, "he lied to Tig about his wife coming home that night. That doesn't look good."

"He said he was embarrassed to tell her the truth," I said. "Makes sense to me."

"He also waited four days before he reported her missing."

I paused in my stride, and Eric turned to look at me. Dale had said nothing about this to me last night at his house, and it caught me off guard hearing it now. Still, I attempted to lawyer a response: "Dale told me this wasn't the first time she took off. Maybe he didn't get worried about her until a few days passed."

"But he went back the next day, saw she'd left her car behind. Saw her purse and cell phone inside. The *keys* were inside. So he drove the car home. Said nothing to the police—nothing to anyone—for days."

"He told me the police impounded the vehicle. Any evidence of foul play?"

"Nothing."

"Okay, good," I said. "That's something."

"Listen, Andrew, let's be straight with each other."

"All right."

"You've got a guy whose wife has been running around on him, embarrassing him all over town. Their marriage has basically fallen apart, and she starts threatening him with divorce, wants to take the kid. Then you've got Dale's business, which is in financial trouble, and there's a sizable insurance policy on his wife. I don't have to tell you how this looks."

"How it looks and how it is aren't the same thing."

Eric exhaled a long, weary breath. He said, "The district attorney wants him to take a polygraph."

"No," I said. "No way. He's not taking a poly."

"I agree," he said. "But it looks better for Dale if his lawyer says that."

"Eric, man, I really don't want to be involved in this. I gotta get back to New York."

"Listen," Eric said. "Dale's been a wreck. He's been drinking too much, and the son of a bitch, he's frayed, man. He's at the end of his rope. Not to mention he's been talking a little too much about things he should be keeping quiet. I warned him about keeping his cool, that he's got a kid to think about. That we've *all* got our lives to think about."

"What are you saying?"

"I'm saying Dale's a freaking mess. I've been keeping him grounded best I can, but the D.A. is hot on this, and now I'm trying to keep my distance so it don't look like we're so fucking chummy. But too much pressure and Dale's gonna snap like a twig."

"Did he tell you he did something to his wife?"

"I'm not talking about his fucking wife, Andrew. I'm talking about shit from the past—*our* past. What we did. Dale's become a liability."

A cold knot twisted in my gut.

"He wouldn't say anything about that," I said. "Why would he? How does that help him?"

"Because he's not thinking straight. The idiot thinks he's got some hex on his head. He thinks we're all cursed and we're all going to hell or something. Bottom line is, who knows what he'll say when he's backed into a corner?"

I let this sink in while the twisting in my gut intensified. "I saw Meach last night," I said after a moment. "He's been living in my old house. He said the same thing to me—about some curse. He told me this insane story about Robert coming to him in some . . . I don't know, some vision or something . . ."

"Meach is nuts," Eric said, and he glanced back out toward the bay where a cargo ship chugged its way across the horizon. "He's fucking hopeless. I've heard his Robert bullshit already. Where is he now?"

"I don't know. He was gone when I got up this morning."

Eric shook his head. "He's been spooking Tig with all his ghost story bullshit and now he's gotten Dale all freaked out about it, too. Everybody's losing their fucking minds all of a sudden. They're like a bunch of scared children. But not us, though, Andrew. You and I gotta keep this ship from sinking."

"We can only do so much."

"We gotta do everything we can. It's only a matter of time before this thing with Dale gets elevated, and I'm not gonna be able to run top cover for him anymore. And I don't want this guy to break during some interrogation with someone from the D.A.'s office and start talking about past sins. You get me?"

"He wouldn't do that."

"You keep saying that, but you don't know. It's not a chance I'm willing to take."

"So what are you suggesting I do here, Eric?"

"I'm suggesting you start acting like his lawyer, and you keep him boxed in. Keep his mouth shut and make sure he doesn't step on his own dick. I've been laying low, distancing myself from him for the optics of it, but you and me, we can talk, Andrew. We can devise a game plan behind the scenes, make sure this thing doesn't spiral. It's the reason I told him to call you in the first place."

"You think he killed his wife?"

"I don't think so," he said. "But I don't trust what he'll say if the pressure's on."

"I assume you've pulled the records from his wife's cell phone already?" I asked him.

"Yeah, of course. But I already told you, we've got her phone. She left it behind in the car that night. No one's using it."

"Yeah, but those older records will show who she was talking to before she vanished. Can you get a look at the data? You can cross-reference the numbers, see if any are connected with some local divorce lawyer."

"You think her lawyer's gonna talk to you or me?"

"If they know that she's hiding out somewhere, making things hard for Dale by *Gone Girl*-ing him, we'll have to make it clear just how badly this will play out for her in court."

One corner of Eric Kelly's mouth tugged upward in a smile. For a moment, he was that handsome young teenage boy on the high school football team again. "See?" he said. "I knew you were good."

I said nothing.

"Meet me at The Wharf Rat tonight at nine," Eric said. "It won't be crowded. There was a grease fire there last week, burned up a section of the kitchen, so half of it's been shut down. Point is, the place won't be too busy. I'll photocopy the case file, bring it to you."

I shook my head. "You can't do that. It's an ongoing investigation. Just look at the phone records."

"Don't tell me what I can't do, Andrew." He stared at me, his eyes hard. "I've got a family and a good job. I'm trying to keep those things. I don't need Dale Walls opening his big fat mouth and screwing that up for me."

"It won't come to that," I said . . . but my voice, to my own ears, sounded distant and false. As if I were someone else trying to convince me of some uncertainty.

"Yeah, well, let's make sure it doesn't."

"How bad was the fire?"

"No one was hurt. Truth is, it probably would have been best for Tig had the whole place burned to the ground. That's the only thing keeping her anchored to this miserable town. With a nice insurance check, she could pick up and go down to Florida with her folks. Forget about this lousy place for good."

"Is that what she wants?"

"Hey, you got out, didn't you?" He held out a hand, and I shook it. "It's good seeing you again, Andy. For a while there, I thought you'd forgotten about us."

"I don't think that's possible," I said.

He nodded, and then sauntered off toward his police car. I watched him go, his head low, his stride deliberate. I remembered how he'd winced each time he lifted that paintbrush, and I felt something roll over inside me at the memory of it. He got into his police car, cranked over the engine, then drove in a wide circle out of the parking lot and onto the road.

I stood there for a moment longer, a useless cardboard cup of lukewarm coffee in my hand, and forced myself to digest everything

I'd just been told. I realized, after several moments, that I had been unconsciously rubbing my thumb along the fleshy groove of my ring finger, where my wedding band was supposed to be.

EIGHT

M atthew Meacham opened his eyes to a cloudless, azure sky, and thought for a moment that he might, in fact, be dead. His mind ran empty and his body felt no pain. But then he was shocked into screaming by the unexpected assault of the tide as it rose to soak his clothes, straight up his back and to his shoulders. He bolted upright, a smaller cry escaping his chapped lips, his body a sudden jangle of nerves.

No, he wasn't dead—but splayed out like a bum on the beach, among all the other detritus that had washed up in the tide after last night's storm. Styrofoam cups, empty beer cans, an old rusted beach chair, something that resembled a birdhouse smashed among the rocks. Behind him was the cliff that climbed back toward the old Ribbon Road, and straight ahead, if he were to shield the sun's glare from his eyes, he could make out the distant barbershop pole that was the Gracie Point Lighthouse atop the silvery, shimmering horizon. As he looked at it, he was overcome by the strange sensation that something—

(the lighthouse?)

—was looking back.

The wind picked up, coming in off the bay, and something tickled the right side of his face. He pawed at his cheek, and when his hand came away, he saw, with sudden horror, a dark black feather stuck to his palm.

Things were coming to a head.

His memory of what happened last night was hazy, as it always was the following day, but he could recall it with enough clarity—enough *certainty*—to know that things were getting dire. He had awoken in the master bedroom of the old Larimer house sometime in the middle of the night, disoriented. A nightmare had awoken him, or so he had thought, but when he sat up in bed, Meach could make out, through bleary eyes, the slender, motionless silhouette of Robert Graves standing in the open doorway of the bedroom.

Meach kicked the sweat-damp flap of the sheet off him, then obediently rolled out of bed and onto his feet. He stood there, swaying like a drunk, running his tongue along the dry upper ridge of his teeth while listening to the storm rage outside.

Robert Graves jerked his head toward the foyer, beckoning Meach out into the hall. Meach followed him, pausing only once to peer in at Andrew, asleep in the small bed in the adjacent bedroom, illuminated in a panel of white light coming through the solitary window.

"I don't want to do this anymore," Meach said, his voice a hoarse whisper. "Please, Robert. No more."

Robert said nothing; he merely turned and continued on down the hall.

The front door of the house glided open at their approach, and Meach pursued Robert out into the night, linked dimly to some caveman knowledge that this was the way of the world and he was powerless to fight it. Robert crept silently down the porch steps, and Meach went after him, setting his bare feet down upon the cool, muddy soil. He opened his mouth to call out to his late-night visitor, but all that escaped the narrow pipe of his throat was a snake's agitated hiss.

Robert pointed at the ground.

Unquestioningly, Meach dropped to his knees and began excavating in the cool, wet, loose earth.

Dig.

Dig.

Dig.

His numb fingers found it buried right there between his feet, just a mere two inches down beneath the surface of the earth: the lifeline. The umbilicus.

He recoiled from it. Something—some lucid part of Matthew Meacham that was still hopelessly clinging to reality—told him this was enough, that it was time to stop. He eased back on his buttocks in the mud, his filthy hands shaking, rainwater cascading down his heat-reddened face. He looked at Robert, who stared back with that solitary blazing eye, and who slowly began to shake his head, as if in disappointment. Meach could smell the smoke coming off him in acrid waves.

"*Dig,*" said the apparition—less a voice and more a static-laden hum at the center of Meach's brain.

Again, Meach just shook his head.

The ground in front of Meach bulged and rippled. Pockets opened up in the earth, swallowing up the pooling rainwater, just as *things* began to wriggle their way out—large, pale grubs, probing collectively, blindly, in Meach's direction. Over the years, he had corrupted his blood and his body with enough toxins to cause hallucinations wherein his skin crawled with invisible insects, and while he never actually saw any, he suddenly knew, with perfect certainty, that these things were *them.*

His arms tingled and he glanced down at them, turning his wrists over to expose the scar tissue, twisted train tracks of lumpy flesh connecting the smooth bands of grafted skin, slick as a slalom.

Like the earth had done, his *flesh* now rippled, his *flesh* now bulged. Whatever things were inside of him, they were pressing against that taut scar tissue, desperate and greedy to escape the confines of his poor, ruined body. The *itch* of it was driving him mad, and he raked a set of long, dirty fingernails down the length of one arm.

His skin flayed open in a bloodless parting. A tidal wave of smaller white grubs tumbled out, pouring into his lap and spilling to the wet ground all around him.

Meach screamed, swiping frantically at the purging wound in his arm, which only served to whisk more of the ruinous flesh away, allowing more and more of those horrible, hideous things to come spilling out of him—

But then they were gone.

Wheezing and shaking, Meach brought his arm close to his face to examine it. Just the scar tissue. Just the lumpy railroad tracks. No flayed flesh, no tidal wave of blind, pale, squirming grubs. The larger ones that had tunneled their way out of the ground all around him were gone now, too.

Dig.

Dig.

Dig.

Still shaken, he drove his hands back into the soil, felt the fleshy stalk of the lifeline once more, and yanked it from the earth. Black mud spackled him from head to torso. He climbed unsteadily to his bare feet, pulling more, more. The thing uprooted segment by segment, and he could see, beneath the glow of the white summer moon and the intermittent flashes of lightning, that it ran all the way across the yard, across the road, and into the woods on the other side. The thing in his hands vibrated in the air, its tiny hair-like spindles dripping with a cool, viscous fluid. Its shaft was as thick and imposing as a serpent coiled in the branches of a mangrove tree.

He followed it, hand over bloody hand, his bare feet carving trenches in the muddy soil. The umbilicus pulsed with a living current against his abraded palms, as though respiring, and although that sensation repulsed him, he dared not let go and deny Robert again.

The dead boy stood in the middle of the road, watching him. Though the rain did not seem to touch him, Robert Graves was still soaking wet, his flesh a chicken-bone gray beneath the nearly full moon—

(and how is the moon out during a thunderstorm?)

—that looked down upon him like a luminous skull. That hollow black pocket where Robert's right eye should have been glowed with a cold, unearthly light.

"I don't want to do this anymore."

It was what Meach said, or at least what he believed he said, although he couldn't be certain that those words actually escaped his quivering lips.

No more. Please, Robert. No more.

Then he was following the lifeline into the trees, the storm driving down on him through the sparse canopy, sodden, weighty branches groping and slapping and tugging at him: things alive. Robert walked in step beside him for a while, reeking of gunpowder and dripping with foul-smelling, brackish water. The hole in his face now emitted a light strong enough to carve a channel through the darkness, leading the way. It made Meach think of—

(Gracie Point Lighthouse)

—revolutionaries carrying lanterns through a dense fog.

The light remained with Meach until he exited the woods and came out onto the old Ribbon Road, although Robert was no longer with him. The light, Meach realized, was the moon again, fat and nearly full and grinning like a jack-o'-lantern just beyond the bluff and out over the black waters of the bay. Moreover, he could see the light of the lighthouse glittering through the rain. Meach crossed the old Ribbon Road, that respiring umbilicus still gripped firmly in both his quivering hands.

The lifeline led down the far side of the cliff. Meach tugged at it lightly, cautious this time not to have it tug back and cast him over the side, as it had done the night before. But that didn't happen this time: it held taut.

Meach crept to the edge of the cliff and peered down. There were the black rocks below, the sash of pale beach frothing with foam. The storm tossed waves against the shoreline as if in a fury.

Like a tent pole, the lifeline ran from the edge of the cliff at an acute angle, where it vanished in the frothing surf below.

There was someone down there.

A woman.

Preposterously sitting on a bar stool in the water.

Something nearly as potent as lust or hunger prompted Meach to scramble over the side of the cliff. He gripped the umbilicus in both hands again, and lowered himself down the face of the cliff, much as a mountain climber might. He never lost his grip, despite the wind that lashed against the face of the cliff at this hour of the night, the pellets of rain that threatened several times to shake him loose during his descent, because those thorny spindles had *embedded* themselves into the soft, ravaged meat of Meach's palms. They didn't release him until he had both bare feet planted firmly in the wet, frigid sand of the beach.

The woman was watching him from the water. Yes, she was seated on a barstool, and there was another stool now—an empty one— beside her. For some reason, the tumultuous waters did not knock those stools over. And for some reason, this whole situation was no longer as preposterous to Meach as it had seemed just a moment ago.

She was beckoning to him.

Meach crossed into the surf, the water rough but not entirely unpleasant. He waded in up to his hips, then climbed upon the empty barstool beside the woman.

The woman.

Cynthia Walls.

His friend Dale's wife.

"Hello, Matthew," she said. "It's nice to see you again. Would you like a drink?"

"Y-y-y-yes," he stammered. He wasn't cold, necessarily, but there was something vertiginous about this whole thing all of a sudden that messed with his nerves. Messed with his *perception*. When he was just a boy, his grandmother had taken him on a trip to see the Grand Canyon, and he had gone right up to the edge, no railing or anything, and just peered over the side and down at the dizzying fathomlessness of it all. That was how he felt now—like staring into an abyss.

"She's watching you, you know," Cynthia said.

"I know," Meach said. "It's the birds. The big ugly ones. She sees what they see."

"Not just the birds, Matthew. She sees *all*."

Far out on Gracie Point, the lighthouse's beacon stopped rotating and fixed on Meach like a spotlight. Meach brought up one arm to shield the glare from his eyes.

"Oh," he said simply. As if this was the most basic revelation in the world.

Cynthia's grin was cadaverous. She reached out and lowered Meach's arm, and her fingers were pegs of ice against his burning hot flesh.

"I don't . . . I don't understand how ..." he stammered, and was unable to complete the thought.

Cynthia handed him a rocks glass filled with murky gray bay water.

When he brought it closer to his face, he could see one of those horrible whitish grubs flexing spasmodically at the bottom of the glass.

"Do you remember, Matthew? Sitting there with me, right at the bar one night, telling me how pretty I am?"

He did—vaguely. He would see Cynthia occasionally in one of the local bars. She knew he was one of her husband's childhood friends, so sometimes she would buy him drinks. Sometimes some food, too. More recently, she'd even kissed the side of his face, squeezed his thigh. Muttered fuzzy things into his ears. He'd been embarrassed by the erection he'd gotten one time as her warm breath tickled the side of his face.

She brought her face to his now, but he recoiled when he saw that the things tickling him were long black feathers sprouting from the hairline around Cynthia's ears.

"Do you remember me asking you questions and telling you things, too, Matthew?"

He had been drunk, had been stoned. He'd been even worse than drunk and stoned on other occasions. What could he remember? What questions? What things had she told him?

"I want to tell you again now," she said. "I want to remind you of what was said between us so you can tell your friends."

He realized that the storm was not bothering them here—that they were in some sort of protective bubble, calm and unencumbered. The light from the lighthouse was still on him, but for some reason it no longer bothered his eyes; in fact, he could stare right into it with no trouble at all.

"Listen to me, Matthew."

He turned to look at Cynthia and saw that she was radiant, her skin practically glowing, her hair parted in matching curtains of perfect platinum curls. Those feathers he had seen—had felt graze the side of his face—were now gone.

But there was something dark in her eyes. Something sinister. And for a moment, she was no longer Cynthia Walls at all, but Ruth Graves, the Kingsport witch, her irises limned in gold. Meach once more felt like he was gazing dizzyingly down at the floor of the Grand Canyon, all those pastel slats in the canyon walls blurring and making him feel ill and a little bit lightheaded.

"I want to remind you," she said again, bringing her lips very close to his ear now, her breath warm against his prickly, itchy flesh. "I want to remind you of *my* secret..."

He felt those feathers again, and drew back. Afraid, he just shook his head. He didn't need her to remind him, because in that moment, he had already remembered. She had sat right next to him on a barstool and told him—

"No," Meach muttered.

"I'm going to tell you anyway," she said.

And then she did.

And Matthew Meacham—

—looked around to see that he was still seated in the cold sand on that beach. Last night's thunderstorm had retreated, leaving in its wake a dazzling blue day with a sun that Meach could still see through his eyelids when he closed his eyes. He glanced down at his hands, gingerly brushed the damp sand from his palms. The puncture wounds were fresh, but they had already begun to scab over. The feather that he'd plucked from his cheek was gone.

He remembered it all now.

He had heard what she had to tell him. She had *reminded* him.

And even Matthew Meacham, who'd be the first to admit he'd spent a lifetime dulling his senses, poisoning his blood, and indiscriminately slaughtering his brain cells, understood the implication of it all.

NINE

I didn't wait for nine o'clock.

The Wharf Rat sat along the cusp of an inlet, surrounded by water on two of its four sides. It was a large, gray, barnlike structure, with narrow, wire-meshed windows, decorative buoys on pilings out front, and a rank of metal trashcans facing the gravel parking lot. Along the inlet, boats rocked against the pilings, their hulls draped in fishing nets, their pilothouse windscreens crystallized with sea salt. The tavern's pink neon sign was already lit, and seeing it triggered a rush of memories so achingly rich, I felt a sheen of sweat break out across my brow.

I parked my rental car in front of the arrangement of decorative buoys and stepped out into a wall of thick, humid air, so tangible it was like walking into a volleyball net. Something in the weather had changed in the time it took me to drive from the marina where I'd met Eric Kelly, to The Rat—a thickening of the air, a density in the sky directly above me. Afternoon heat hammered down on me with all the authority of a Roman god.

The Wharf Rat had been the most prosperous local tavern in Kingsport when I was kid, although in a town our size, that wasn't saying much. Watermen returning to port would shuffle in droves off their boats to come here, reeking of fish guts, to squander whatever cash they had left in their wallets at the bar. Tig's parents had owned the place back then, the only black family in a sea of white, sunburned faces, and that meant The Wharf Rat was just about the only place in town where my friends and I were consistently refused service because we were underage, and Tig's parents didn't put up with that nonsense. I remembered the summers Tig had worked here, all through high school, and how we'd sometimes pick her up in the evenings after her shift, all of us packed into Dale's rumbling, foul-smelling pickup truck, Metallica blasting on the radio, and Tig would come streaming out of the place, stripping the apron from her hips, her sleek, dark legs pumping, her eyes alight, bolting like some furious fire was burning off her heels and scorching the earth in her wake.

Thinking of this, something made me run my thumb along the smooth band of flesh at the base of my ring finger. Earlier that morning, upon waking in my old bedroom and staggering through a cloud of black flies on my way to the bathroom, I noticed that my wedding ring was no longer on the corner of the sink where I had left it the night before. Panic had quickly set in. I peered into the basin, but there was a little mesh screen over the drain, clotted with scummy hair, so it couldn't have fallen down there. I searched around the bathroom floor, to see if I had accidentally knocked it off the sink without realizing it the night before. But it was nowhere to be found . . . and a part of me wondered if Meach had absconded with it in the night.

Still staring up at The Wharf Rat, I took a deep breath then went inside.

It was much as I remembered from my youth: the walls draped in fishing nets and the lacquered carapaces of blue crabs, the ceiling lights were like medieval lanterns, and there was an overall air of desperation radiating about the place. I could smell the residual smoke caused by the fire still hanging in the air, and a section of one wall was covered in plastic tarp. Some remediation work had been left unfinished behind that smudgy, partially opaque sheet, where I could make out a part of the wall that was opened up, exposing a ribcage of slender copper pipes. The wall itself was singed black, and the acoustical tiles in the ceiling above that area of the bar had turned brown and melted.

The place was quiet and practically empty. The only customers were two men in sleeveless flannels perched at the bar, drinking beer and playing Keno, and a young girl of about five or six sitting by herself at a table near a window, furiously scribbling on a piece of pink construction paper with a crayon. Three steps in from the front door, and I realized the place was hot as hell, too—an easy eighty-five degrees in here, which wasn't providing much reprieve from the summer heat. The fire must have taken out the HVAC unit, too.

As I stood there trying to catch my bearings, a woman came around the side of the bar clutching two fresh beer bottles in one hand. She wore a white tank top, frayed denim shorts, and had her hair pulled back to reveal a face jeweled with perspiration. I walked up to the bar as she cranked open the beers and set them down in front of the two men playing Keno.

"Hey," I said.

She looked over at me, offered a casual smile . . . and then recognition dawned on her. Emotion swam quickly across her face—something akin to fear, I thought, although maybe that was just in my head.

"Hey, Tig," I said again, more cautious this time.

"My God," she said. "Andrew fucking Larimer."

"Classy as always, Tig."

She kept looking at me, her dark eyes ticking back and forth as she took in mine. Maybe it hadn't been fear I'd glimpsed in her face after all—maybe it had been surprise, or even a twinge of guilt—but whatever it was, it still simmered there behind her eyes.

I suddenly felt like I shouldn't have come here.

"Wait," she said, as if sensing my desire to flee. She came out from behind the bar, closed the distance between us, and gave me a hug. I hugged her back, feeling the stiffness of her spine within my embrace. The last time I had hugged this woman had been on the morning of my sixteenth birthday, mere hours before all our fates would be sealed forever.

"It's been such a long time," she said into my ear, and then we were separated. Her dark eyes kept moving over mine, over me, much as mine did over hers and her. "I can't believe you're actually standing here. Dale said he was thinking about calling you, but I never thought you would actually . . ."

I gave her a sad smile. "You look good, Tig."

"You look old." And then she shook her head, a humorless half-smile on her face. "No, that's not what I meant. Just . . . you know . . . *older*, I mean. We were kids the last time we saw each other."

"Yeah."

"I'm, uh . . . well, I'm at a loss. I don't know what to say." She ran a hand across her hair. "I'd offer you something to eat, but we had a fire here last week and now the kitchen's been shut down. I swear, this place is falling apart all around me."

"I'm not hungry." It was true, even though the only things I'd eaten all day was a gas station hot dog, a Mountain Dew, and a handful of mint green Tic Tacs.

"Hey," she said. "I'm sorry. Looking at you is like . . . looking at a ghost. I guess I'm in shock, is all."

"It's all right. I understand."

"Yeah, well, it's a shitty hello to an old friend." She grabbed a bottle of some brownish liquor and two lowball glasses off the bar. "Have a drink with me."

"To steady our nerves?" I offered her a wan smile, trying my best to look harmless. "I'm not really a ghost, you know."

"Yeah? Well, maybe I am. Come on."

I followed her to the back of the bar, where she slid into a booth. I sat down opposite her while she poured the drinks.

"I hear you're some big shot attorney in New York now," she said, and pushed one of the lowball glasses across the table to me.

"I don't know about that," I said. "I keep busy, that's all. But look at you, running the family business."

She laughed. "Yeah, more like running it into the ground. It's the American dream, right? Single mother, debt up to her eyeballs, and now there's an arson investigation underway for the fire, if you can believe that, so I can't even collect the insurance money to fix this dump until all that gets squared away. I'm quite the catch, so marry me up now, Andrew, while you still can."

"Arson?" I said.

"Eric said not to worry. It was probably just an electrical thing. You open up these walls, you'll see rats gnawing at the wires and building nests in the fuse boxes. But enough about this dump. Ask me something nice."

"How many kids do you have?"

"Just one. A daughter. She's six. Her name's Bonnie." Something swam briefly behind her eyes again—some dark shape, or so I thought. It moved too quickly for me to really be sure, less defined than the fear or shock that I glimpsed when she'd first recognized me. She pointed over at the girl coloring at the table beside the window.

"Oh, wow," I said. "She's a beautiful kid."

"Nice way to spend a summer when you're six years old, huh? Either with babysitters or hanging around your mom's joint while she works twelve-hour shifts."

"Hey," I said. "You do what you have to do, right?"

"I guess. I make sure we take a vacation every year. Hershey Park last year, the beach in August. We'll see. Money's been tight. What about you? Married? Kids?"

In that moment, I was unconsciously rubbing my thumb along the indented flesh of my ring finger beneath the table again. "No kids, no wife," I said.

"A free agent. Smart."

"It's really good to see you, Tig."

She knocked back her drink in one swallow then gave herself another pour. "I'm sorry I didn't come out to the funeral when your dad died. Dale told me about it. I'd been going through some shit with Bonnie's dad, it was a tough time for me. I thought about calling you, sending a card, maybe. I don't know."

"Don't worry about it."

She stared down at her drink. Ran a finger along the rim of the glass. "I know why you're here," she said, her voice lower now. "How bad is it for him?"

"You're talking about Dale?"

"He got you out here in a hurry." She looked up at me.

"He just wanted some advice."

"From an old friend or from a lawyer?"

"A little of both, maybe." I brought the drink to my lips, took a sip. I felt the liquor carve a trench down my gullet and detonate like a mortar in my guts. I winced and Tig's face softened a bit. "I just saw Eric a little while ago. He filled me in on some of the details. I'm meeting him here later tonight, in fact."

"I had to give a statement," Tig said. "To the police. I mean, it was just Eric, but it still freaked me out." She lifted her glass and I saw that her hand shook. She set it back on the table without drinking. "I'm so worried about Dale. She was here that night, you know. Dale's

119

wife. I mean, she's in here a lot, and she's usually drunk, but there was something . . . I don't know . . . out of sorts with her that night."

"That's what Eric said, too. That she was acting funny."

"I thought maybe she was on something."

"How well do you know her?"

"Not well at all. Dale only came back here once he started building that development on the bluff. I don't think she likes me being friends with her husband. I mean, not just me—it's just that she strikes me as the kind of woman who doesn't like her husband having female friends. You know the type?"

I wanted to ask her if there was a reason why Cynthia wouldn't approve of a friendship between her and Dale—if there was an *intimate* reason that may have crossed beyond the boundary of friendship—but I stopped myself. It was a lawyerly question, not something someone asks a friend after a twenty-year absence from their life.

"I heard you called Dale that night to see if Cynthia got home," I said instead.

"Yeah. After I closed the place down. I mean, I debated about it because it was so late. But I was worried. I mean, she was acting so strange when she left here."

"Did she say anything strange to you?"

"No, but I saw how she acted. Manic one second, like a zombie the next. It was like she had two personalities fighting for dominance, you know? And she spooked the guy she was flirting with, said something that creeped him out, though I don't know what that was."

I'm smoke, I thought.

"And she left alone?"

"Yes."

"What exactly did Dale say to you when you called him?"

"He said she was home and in bed."

"Which turns out wasn't true," I added.

"That's what Eric told me. And Dale, too, after the fact. He said he was embarrassed that she never came home, and so he'd lied to me."

"You didn't see her car in the parking lot when you left that night?"

"I didn't notice. I think she was parked around the far side of the building, down by the docks. This was before the fire," and she jerked a thumb over her shoulder in the direction of the construction work, "so we were doing good business that night, and the parking lot was crowded."

"How did he sound when you called him?"

"What do you mean?"

"When Dale first answered the phone. How did he sound?"

"Well, I guess he'd been asleep," she said. "Like I said, it was late. I guess I woke him up when I called." She lowered her voice further and leaned closer toward me over the table. "I know what Eric's so concerned about, Andrew, but you know Dale. He didn't do anything wrong. He wouldn't do something like that."

"Yeah, I know," I said, but I was reminded of the feeling I'd had when speaking to Dale the night before—that he was deliberately leaving something out of his story. "We're just covering all the bases, that's all."

"Circling the wagons, you mean." Again—that darkness resurfaced for a moment behind her eyes. She held her gaze on me a moment longer than necessary, as if to transmit some message to me without words.

"What is it, Tig?"

Her lips thinned as her eyes skirted away from mine. She glanced out across the barroom, clearly contemplating whether or not she should tell me something.

"Hey," I said, and reached across the table. I rested my hand on top of hers, and she let me stay that way for a second or two, before pulling away.

"You'll think I'm acting crazy," she said.

"Not a chance, Tig. What is it?"

"Things have been happening," she said. "At first, I didn't think anything of it. Not really. It started with Meach coming around, talking about how we're all cursed. How he's been having these . . . I don't know . . . these nightly visits from Robert lately."

I bristled at the mention of his name in public.

"Nightmares or visions or hallucinations," Tig went on. "Whatever you want to call them. He thinks they're real, and that Robert's come back. He's been saying it to all of us, and of course Eric thinks he's crazy. I thought he might be hooked on something again—he's got a lot of demons to battle—but lately . . . I mean, I don't know, Andrew. I know you'll just say he's filling my head with things, but I just don't know anymore."

"I saw Meach last night," I told her. "He's been squatting in my old house."

"Oh," she said, looking back at me. She appeared relieved. "I haven't seen him in a few days. I was worried something might have happened to him."

"He was high. Talking a bunch of nonsense."

"That's just it, Andrew," she said, and now she reached out and placed her hand on mine. "What if it's not nonsense?"

"Talking about seeing ghosts? Come on, Tig. I don't believe—"

"No," she said, cutting me off. "Not ghosts. *Robert*."

I glanced toward the two men at the bar. They were too far away to hear anything being said, as was Tig's daughter, but I wanted to convey my discomfort in talking about Robert in public.

"You know, I see his mother around town from time to time," Tig said. "She's still living in that creepy old house on the edge of nowhere, and she still sets up that creepy fucking table at the craft show every October. You remember those . . . *things* . . . she would make? Every time I see one, I cringe."

I recalled the eerie dolls Ruth Graves used to make and sell at the local craft show every year—those faceless, child-sized ghouls, assembled from wire and straw, bird feathers, and the bleached bones of road kill. I had forgotten all about those creepy things until just now.

"Meach says she's cursed the five of us over what happened with her son, and now we're—"

"Meach's head is scrambled, Tig. You know better. Don't let him get to you."

She held me in her gaze, and for the first time, I could see how glassy her eyes had become.

"I want to tell you about something that happened last night," she said, "but you've got to promise not to tell me I'm crazy. Even if you think it, Andrew, you've got to promise not to tell me, okay? Can you do that?"

"Yes, I can," I said.

"All right," she said.

She took a deep breath and told me about her daughter's recent struggles with sleeping alone. She told me about the bicycle bell, and how she had awoken last night to the sound of it ringing; only when she got to Bonnie's room, the girl was gone. When she told me about finding the kitchen door standing open and the rain coming in, I couldn't help but think of how *I* had found the front door of my father's house open last night, Meach's wet footprints stamped onto the hardwood floor.

"She was sleepwalking," Tig went on. "I found her standing in the water behind the house, up to her chest, and she was in some sort of . . . trance, I guess."

I glanced at the girl coloring beneath the window at the far end of the bar. She looked perfectly fine to me now. "A kid sleepwalking is hardly evidence of a curse, Tig."

"There was someone out there on the water," Tig said, and her voice trembled. "Just . . . just *standing* there, right on the surface. It was *him*, Andrew. It was Robert."

I shook my head. "Antigone, please—"

"I know what I saw."

"A person standing on the surface of the bay? A ghost?"

"You weren't *there*, Andrew."

There was nothing I could say to that. I just sat watching her from across the table, the right side of her face slivered in the sunlight coming through the high windows.

"I got Bonnie cleaned up, tucked her into my bed. She went right back down, as if nothing had happened. But I was wired. I raced around the house, making sure all the windows and doors were locked. I turned on all the lights, too, but then the storm knocked out the power, and everything—*everything*—went dark. And then I just stood there, because . . . Jesus . . ."

"What, Tig?"

"It's crazy."

"Tell me."

"Because I could *smell* him. The smoke? The fireworks? It was in the house, and the hallway was filling up with smoke. So I freaked, I thought even if there wasn't someone in the house, all that *smoke*. I ran back to my bedroom, grabbed Bonnie, and rushed back out of the house. I thought the goddamn place was on fire. But then as I stood out there, I wondered . . ."

She trailed off again, and I gave her a few moments before telling her to go on.

"I wondered if that's exactly what he wanted me to do—to come back outside. Like the smoke was some sort of trap to get me out of the house."

"And this was part of a nightmare you had?"

She shook her head and gave me a humorless smirk. "No, Andrew. No, this wasn't a nightmare. This *happened*."

I eased back in my seat and said nothing.

"Listen, I know how it sounds," she said. She poured herself another drink, then tipped the remainder of the bottle into my own glass, even though I'd hardly drank any at all. Her hands shook. "I'm not crazy. And don't look at me that way."

I didn't realize I had any expression at all on my face. "I don't think you're crazy, Tig. Of course not. I just think you've got a lot on your plate, you're worried about Dale, and you've been talking to Meach too much. That's all. But if you're trying to convince me of some supernatural interference here..."

"I'm not trying to convince you of anything, Andrew. I don't even know what *I* believe. But it's left me feeling uncomfortable and I'm worried about my daughter."

"That's understandable, but you can't—"

"Do you wanna know something else?" she said, cutting me off again.

"What?" I said.

"Meach said you'd come. He said Robert *told* him you'd come back here to Kingsport. He said we would all be drawn back together to pay for our sins. I thought nothing of it, swear to God, even after last night, until I looked up and saw you standing in my bar."

"I'm here because of Dale," I reminded her. "Not some voodoo curse."

"Meach told me this weeks ago, before Dale's wife ever went missing."

I said nothing, just let this sink in.

She knocked back the rest of her drink. "This isn't stress. This isn't some residual guilt, which I'll admit, I've always carried around with me, ever since that night. But you're *here*, Andrew, and I saw what

I saw last night out on the water. I see what's been happening to Bonnie. And I don't know how to reconcile any of that."

"It's not by getting drunk," I said, and moved my glass away from her just as she reached for it.

"Baby, I haven't been drunk since I was a teenager. It's just about maintenance now."

One of the men at the bar called for the check, and Tig said she'd be right with him. The quality of the daylight outside the wire-meshed windows had dulled to a murky seawater color. Tig's daughter—Bonnie—was still meticulously drawing on a piece of construction paper, none the wiser that her mother was over here, worried sick about her, and fretting about some witch's curse.

"Listen," Tig said. "What time are you meeting Eric here tonight?"

"Nine."

"I'll shut the place down early, order some food, and see if I can scrounge up Dale and Meach. We'll have a half-assed reunion."

"I don't know, Tig. I think Eric's trying to keep some distance from Dale right now."

"Yeah, I know, but it's eating Dale up and it makes him look guilty, like Eric believes he actually did something to Cynthia. It's the wrong move." She reached out and squeezed my hand again. "Please. It'll make me feel good to see us all together again. It'll make me feel sane, at least. Maybe you're right, and I just need to dilute Meach's craziness with some more grounded people in my life."

"Hey," yelled the guy from the bar, waving a hand over his head.

"Nine o'clock," she said, and got up.

"All right," I said, watching Tig head back to the bar, although still unsure if it was such a good idea. In truth, all I really wanted to do in that moment was to get back to Rebecca in New York and forget about this place and the people who still lived here.

I sat there awhile longer, nursing my drink and watching Tig.

When she vanished into the kitchen, I got up from the table and stole quietly across the floor. It felt like a coward's escape, but I was okay with that. I paused briefly beside Bonnie's chair, the girl unaware of my presence even as my shadow fell across the table, and I peered down at her drawings. Most of them were of birds, except for the one she was currently drawing: With a bright red crayon on yellow construction paper, Bonnie had drawn a long rectangle with what looked like five smaller rectangles in a row inside of it. They looked like doors on a boxcar. In the center of the larger rectangle stood the rudimentary shape of a human figure—only this figure Bonnie had filled in with a stark black crayon.

The girl looked up at me with large brown eyes.

"Hello," I said. "I'm a friend of your mom's. My name's Andrew."

"I'm not supposed to tell my name to strangers. I'm Bonnie."

I grinned. "What's your drawing supposed to be?"

"I don't know," she said.

"Who's the guy?"

"He's not really a guy."

"Looks like one."

"He's smoke," she said.

"Is he supposed to be a real person?"

"I don't know. Do you like it?"

"I sure do. It's very creative."

"Okay," she said, and handed it to me. "Then it's for you."

I reached for it, but she pulled it back, as if suddenly remembering something. She picked up the red crayon again and, after a moment of contemplation, printed a number at the top of the page, floating there in space above the collection of rectangles:

13

"Thirteen? What does *that* mean?" I asked.

With a slight speech impediment that swapped the *th* for an *f,* Bonnie said, "It's not a firteen."

"Then what is it?"

Bonnie shrugged, then handed me the drawing again. I stared down at it, while Bonnie went to work on a new drawing. Something about that stark black figure trapped behind those five door-like rectangles unsettled me, leaving me abruptly cold. More than that: it was as if I had seen this drawing, or something very much like it, someplace before.

"Thank you, Bonnie," I said, then hurried out into the waning daylight like someone guilty of some atrocity.

I grabbed a bite to eat downtown while I poured over some legal briefs on my laptop, answered a few work emails, and then headed back to the house to shower and change my clothes before meeting Eric back at The Wharf Rat. The house was silent and dark when I arrived, and the smell of the place slapped me across the face the moment I stepped through the front door. Flies hung in the air and I held my breath as I passed through them. I went down the hall, opened the cellar door, and glanced down there. The water, it seemed, had risen throughout the day—not much, but enough to swallow another full step on the stairs. Moist, humid breath roiled out at me, and I quickly closed the door.

I taped Bonnie's drawing to the wall of my old childhood bedroom, and happened to lay my eyes on the smooth band of flesh at the base of my ring finger. A wave of guilt and discomfort washed over me. A touch of panic, too.

I searched the bathroom again for my wedding ring, but couldn't find it. Despite the little screen in the drain, I found a wrench in the kitchen drawer and took the pipe apart, but there was no wedding ring inside that chrome elbow.

What the hell?

I went down the hall to the master bedroom, where Meach had spent the night. The room was in the same state as it had been the night before, except that Meach had apparently dug his backpack out of the trash at some point: it lay slumped on the floor beside a wooden chest at the foot of the bed. I knelt down, unzipped all the pockets on the bag, and emptied out their contents.

It was mostly unwashed boxer shorts and T-shirts that tumbled out, the smell of them rivaling the stink coming up from the cellar, but also a small orange vial of pills, a pack of cigarettes, a bag of weed, a silver Zippo, and a tattered Tarzan paperback with a library sticker on the spine. Something else, too: the spent Roman candle tube. The one I'd found in the house yesterday and buried in the trash, or at least one just like it. The sight of it caused the flesh along the nape of my neck to prickle.

My ring, however, was not among Meach's possessions. I stuffed everything back into his backpack, zipped it up, when—

—something struck one of the bedroom windows.

It was as loud as a gunshot and my whole body froze.

I stood and looked across the room at the windowpane. I could see nothing at first, but as I drew closer to it, I saw a small crimson smudge of blood. I stared at it for an inordinate amount of time, as if waiting for my vision to clear and for the bloodstain to vanish. But that didn't happen.

No way, I thought, and I could feel my pulse begin to race. *No fucking way that just happened.*

I went out back and walked along the perimeter of the house until I arrived outside the bedroom window. Snared in the branches of an overgrown hedge directly beneath the window was a dead bird.

No. No fucking way. Impossible.

Its neck was broken, its head twisted nearly all the way around. It was about the size of a robin, only it had a bright yellow bib and black-and-white speckled wings—a meadowlark. A thing not native to the Eastern Shore of Maryland. The way its head was turned around, only one of its dull black eyes was visible.

TEN

I called Rebecca from the parking lot of The Wharf Rat.

"I had a terrible dream last night," she said. "It was awful. I'm almost afraid to go to sleep again."

"Do you want to talk about it?"

"It'll just upset me."

"It was that bad?"

"You know how my dreams can be sometimes."

"I wish I was there with you."

"When will you be?"

"I'm still not sure."

"I miss you."

"I miss you, too. But you get some sleep, okay? And if you have that dream again tonight—"

"Stop."

"—you call me up, no matter how late it is. Deal?"

"Just finish up out there and come home."

I promised her I would. Then I told her I loved her, and told her goodnight.

Just as I was getting out of the car, a pair of headlights glided up behind me. Eric, driving some clunky old sedan. He got out of the car, dressed in a T-shirt and jeans now, and he held what looked like a plain white cake box under one arm.

"Did you see Tig?" he asked.

"I saw her earlier. She looks great."

"She *is* great."

"A single mom? How'd that happen?"

"The kid's father is a real piece of work. She's better off." He handed me the cake box. "Burn this shit when you're done with it."

"Any luck with those phone records?"

"She wasn't calling any lawyers, as far as I can tell. I can go back a bit further, just to make sure, but I think she was bluffing about that to Dale."

"He's here tonight, you know." I nodded toward Dale's Navigator, which sat in one of the parking spaces out front. "Tig wanted to have some sort of reunion. I tried to talk her out of it, but—"

"But, yeah, she's Tig. It's fine. She called me, too. Celebrate good times and all that, right?"

"Are you gonna come in?"

He seemed to consider this for a moment. "I guess I can stay for one drink," he said, and then he looked at something over my shoulder. "There's Meach."

I turned and saw Meach sitting on one of the trashcans behind the bar, smoking a cigarette. When he saw both of us looking at him, he raised a hand in salutation, then dripped off the trashcan and sauntered over to us.

Admittedly, I felt a calming sensation overtake me at the sight of him. It wasn't that I truly thought I'd spent last night in the company of a ghost—I didn't believe in such nonsense—but his hasty departure in the night had left me concerned about him.

"Wow," Meach said, his eyes volleying back and forth between Eric and me. "So fucking weird seeing you two standing here together. It's like . . . I mean, it's crazy, man. This is real, right?"

"Where've you been all day, Meach?" I asked him.

He offered me a wan smile, then sucked his cigarette down to the filter. "Long story, I guess, Andy," he said. And then he fixed his gaze on Eric. "Can I talk to you for a minute? In private?" He glanced back at me. "You don't mind?"

"Not at all. I'll see you guys inside."

I went to my car, stowed the box Eric had given me in the trunk, then went into the restaurant.

Dale and Tig were at the bar having drinks. There was a table behind them set up with some balloons tied to a picture frame with a photo of us as kids. There was a tray of sandwiches, a bucket of potato salad with a ladle poking out of it, and something that could have been a green bean casserole, too.

"Here he is," Dale said, smiling at me from over his shoulder. He looked awful, to be honest, and I wondered not for the first time if it was such a good idea for all of us to be here together like this. "What's your poison, Andy? Tig's letting me play bartender."

"Whatever you're having," I said.

"Okay, but make it a double. You need to catch up."

He poured some bourbon into a glass, squirted it with a spritz of seltzer, and then handed it to me.

"Should we make a toast or something?" he said.

"We can wait, if you want," I said. "Eric and Meach are outside."

"Meach," Tig said, almost breathlessly. She got up from her stool and went to one of the open windows. Shouted, "Meach! Eric! Get your butts in here!"

I looked at Dale and saw the way he was looking at Tig. Not lust, not appreciation, but a kind of sadness that was nearly heartbreaking and strangely misplaced. Or maybe it was just the booze I saw in his eyes. When he turned and saw me looking at him, I quickly lifted my glass and said, "Well, hey, we can do another toast when they get here."

He clinked his glass against mine, then finished off half his drink in two noisy swallows. I took a sip of mine, then set the glass down on the bar. Hanging on the wall behind the bar were several crayon drawings, presumably done by Tig's daughter. They were mostly of birds, but I also recognized the barber-shop pole that was the Gracie Point Lighthouse, and something that looked like a catfish with crab claws instead of fins.

"Kid's a good artist," Dale said, seeing that I was studying the drawings. "Smart as hell, too. I like that one in particular because it looks like a giant eyeball." He pointed to the drawing of the lighthouse. "Like Sauron in the watchtower from *Lord of the Rings*."

He was right: the lighthouse's lantern room looked disconcertingly like an eye in Bonnie's drawing. Staring.

"You guys remember the time we took my dad's boat out to the lighthouse? What were we, fourteen?"

"It was the summer of the Dare Club," Tig said. She was still leaning on the windowsill, looking out onto the parking lot.

Dale slapped his knee. "That's right! The Dare Club! I forgot about that. Like when we dared Meach to climb out to the middle of that train trestle in Cordova and take a shit over the side. Ha!"

"Meach was always good for a dare," I said.

"Yeah," Dale said. "He was always nuts."

"Don't talk about him like that," Tig said, not looking at us.

"The five of us took the boat straight out to the lighthouse," Dale said, ignoring her, "and I remember it was getting ready to storm. The water was real choppy and the sky looked like hammered fucking tin. I had stolen a bottle of Jägermeister from my sister's closet and we were getting sick on that stuff—"

"I remember," Tig said, turning away from the window. She was grinning. "And that rocking boat didn't help. I'm pretty sure I even puked over the side."

I grinned. "You did."

"Hey, I was fourteen!"

"We docked alongside that rickety little pier," Dale went on, "which I think is gone now, right at the base of the lighthouse. We were daring each other to see who would go inside all the way to the top."

"Dare Club," Tig said from over my shoulder.

"The door was locked with a chain, wasn't it?" I said. That day was coming back to me now, piece by piece. I remembered the roiling gray sky and the whitecaps crashing across the surface of the bay. It was the one and only time I had ever been out to that lighthouse, and I remembered standing there upon its rocky base, staring up, and feeling lightheaded at the sheer size and majesty of it.

"It was," Dale said, "but we managed to pry it open a few inches."

"Meach went in," Tig recalled.

"Always good for a dare," I repeated, grinning.

"His skinny ass slipped right through the opening in that door," Dale said. "We told him go straight to the top and wave to us when you get there."

"We picked up rocks and were going to throw them at him," Tig said, and she was shaking her head now. "God, we were horrible children."

"No harm," Dale said.

"But he never made it," I reminded them. "Meach never made it to the top."

"Yeah," Dale said. "Something spooked him."

I remembered the four of us standing around the base of the lighthouse, slimy, moss-covered rocks in our hands at the ready, waiting for Meach's face to appear in one of the crusty panels of glass of the lantern room. But he never appeared, and we started catcalling him and throwing those rocks anyway. When a flock of seagulls got spooked and took to the sky, I turned and saw Meach moving quickly in our direction across a landscape of slippery black stones. His face was pale and his eyes were wide. Something inside that lighthouse had frightened him terribly.

"He said there was someone else in there with him," Tig said. "I remember that. He said he could hear someone in there, at the top of the spiral staircase, calling down to him. A man. Actually calling him by name. Meach said he ran to the door and tried to get out, but it wouldn't open, and he thought he could hear the guy coming down those iron steps after him. Meach thought we were pranking him, leaning against the door to give him a good scare—"

"But we weren't," I said.

"Right. We weren't. And he looked so frightened when he came out."

"He got spooked by an echo," Dale said. "He was always so wound up. Only thing scares the old Meach-Man now is sobriety."

"Hey," Tig said, and shot him a look.

"Not the only thing," I said.

The moist grin on Dale's face grew tight. I caught him glance down at his right hand before picking up his glass off the bar. "To you, Andrew. For coming out here when I needed you most. Even after all these years."

We drank again, then set our empty glasses on the bar. A moment later, I heard footsteps coming up the wooden ramp outside. Eric and Meach came in, and Tig was quick to approach them. She kissed Eric on the cheek, then gathered up one of Meach's hands. She asked him where he'd been and how he was doing, but Meach looked like he'd been sucker punched and was unable to formulate a coherent sentence. Tig tucked a strand of Meach's blond hair behind his ear and asked if he was okay, but Meach said nothing. His eyes were wide and they kept roving between Dale and me.

Yet it was Eric whose stoic demeanor caused alarm bells to go off inside me. He stood there like a wax dummy, even when Tig had administered that kiss to the side of his face. Unlike Meach, whose eyes kept bouncing all over the place, Eric was staring daggers at Dale.

"Hey, Eric," Dale said, a rheumy grin on his face. He seemed oblivious to the sudden tension in the room. "Been a while."

"Meach just told me something," Eric said. "About your wife."

Dale sat up straighter on his stool. He had been about to pour himself another glass of bourbon, but he froze, then slowly set the bottle down on the bar. "What are you talking about?"

Eric came over to where Dale sat at the bar.

I took a step back.

"You dumb son of a bitch," Eric said. He looked angry, but his voice was strangely calm. "You told her."

Dale just shook his head. That ridiculous grin was now frozen on his face; he seemed incapable of losing it. "I don't know what you're talking about..."

"You told Cynthia about what we did," Eric said. It was not a question. "You told her, Dale. You told her everything."

"Eric, man, I don't know what—"

"She said something about it to Meach. Before she disappeared. She told him she *knew,* that you'd *told* her. She tried to get Meach to talk about it, but apparently he's smart enough to keep his mouth shut. But she knows, doesn't she, Dale? She *knows.*"

"Knows what?" I said.

"What do you think, Andrew? He told her about what we did. About Robert." He was still staring at Dale. "Meach said your wife came up to him one night at a bar, said she knew our little secret. Said you'd *told* her what we'd done, and that she laughed about it. Said she'd make us all pay for it..."

Tig stepped between the two of them. "Keep your voice down, the windows are open—"

"Shut the fuck up, Tig!" Eric shouted at her.

"Let's just calm down," I said. I looked over at Meach, who stood against one wall, his messy, bloodshot eyes volleying between all of us now. "She said this to you?" I asked him. "Dale's wife said she knew about Robert? About what happened?"

"Yeah, man. She did. She did." The words squealed out of him. "She told me for real, only I'd forgotten. I was fucked up, man. I didn't realize what she was saying! But then last night . . . I mean, it all came back to me . . ."

I looked at Dale, and could see the truth of it on his face. I felt a sinking sensation in my gut. "Dale," I said, and suddenly I felt like *I'd* been sucker punched in the stomach.

"What exactly did you tell her, Dale?" Eric said. "Tell us *exactly* what she knows."

Dale shook his head. Tears welled in his eyes, and his cheeks were beet-red. Breathlessly, he said, "It was years ago. When we were first married. She was my wife. And the guilt of what we'd done, you know . . . I confided in her . . ."

"Jesus," I said.

He glared at me. "You're not married, Andrew. You don't know. She was my wife."

"You stupid son of a bitch," Eric said, shaking his head.

"She kept that secret for *years!*" Dale shouted, and it came out like a sob. "How was I supposed to know things would get . . . all fucking twisted?" He looked imploringly at Eric. "You know how it is. You're married. You tell your wife everything. You tell—"

"Not *this,*" Eric said. "Not *this,* you imbecile."

"Eric, please, listen to me . . ."

"So this is what it all comes down to now. A fucking blackmail scheme. She hates your guts and now she's gonna ruin the rest of us, too? I've got a goddamn *life* here, Dale."

"I know," Dale said. He extended a hand toward Eric, to either stop him from coming any closer or to touch him fraternally on the shoulder—I couldn't tell which.

"We made a pact," Eric said. "We promised we'd never tell. But you've broken that promise, Dale, and now you've put all our heads on the chopping block."

"Eric, man, please—"

"What about Tig? They'll take her kid away. We'll all go to prison, Dale."

"It was a mistake, all right?" Dale's face was turning redder by the second, his jowls shaking. That hand kept hovering in the air between him and Eric but never seemed to find its purpose.

Tig came up beside me. She looked impossibly calm. She said, "Well, it's done. She's known this for a long time and she's never said anything. Let's not get too worked up."

"Yeah, Eric," Dale said. "Let's not get too—"

Eric slapped Dale's hand out of the air and shoved him one-handed off the stool. Dale grabbed one corner of the table where the food was set up to arrest his fall, but all he managed to do was drag the table with him as he went down. The casserole dish smashed and the potato salad sprayed in clumps across the floor. The balloons came free of the frame and drifted toward the ceiling.

"Hey," I said, though my voice shook.

"I'll tell you what we do." Eric jabbed a finger in Dale's direction. "When your wife finally turns up, you give her whatever she asks for. I don't care if it's your fucking business, your house, your goddamn kid—you let Cynthia have it all. She ain't holding this over our heads because you opened your big fat mouth and fucked up."

Dale pulled himself to his feet, but knocked his barstool over in the process; it struck the floor with a report as loud as a gunshot. He was nodding pathetically, unable to meet Eric's eyes, and there was potato salad on the cuff of his pants. "All right, all right," he said. Then he looked at the rest of us, his eyes bleary, his skin an unnerving shade of crimson. "I'm sorry, guys. It was a mistake. I don't know what else to say."

"You've said enough." Eric turned to the rest of us, meeting our eyes one by one. When his gaze settled on Tig, he said, very quietly, "I'm sorry for yelling at you like that."

Then he turned and walked out of the bar.

Tig went over to Dale, hugged him, and he rested his head against her chest.

I looked at Meach, who was standing with his back against the fishing nets on the wall, his arms crossed over his chest, hugging himself. I could see that he'd scratched himself badly, his fingernails having left fresh lacerations along the grafted skin of his arms. His eyes landed on me, and they looked huge and drug-fueled. I went over to him.

"Why'd you bring all this up now? Why didn't you say something sooner?"

He raked a set of nail-blackened fingers down the side of his face. "I didn't *remember* sooner. She *showed* me. Last night."

"Who showed you?" I said. "Robert?"

"No, not Robert." His moist, nervous eyes shifted over toward Dale at the bar. In a whisper, Meach said, "I saw her last night. Dale's wife. She reminded me of what she knew..."

"You're fucking stoned, Meach."

His eyes jittered back over to me. "She knows our secret. And Robert, he knows *all* our secrets. He knows a secret about *you,* Andrew."

"Yeah? What secret is that?"

"He ... he didn't say ... but I can sense it ... I can smell it ... he whispers these things to me..."

"Stop, Meach. Just stop."

"You shouldn't have come back here." His voice was a rusty hinge. "You set things in motion, man. It's almost twenty years to the day. You think that's some kind of coincidence? You ever stop and think about that? The anniversary of Robert's death looming just over the horizon. We're all gonna pay now."

"Meach," I said, "I don't think—"

"You hearing me, Andrew? We're cursed, man. We're cursed."

ELEVEN

I drove Dale home that night, got him out of the car, and assisted him up the walkway to his house. The door was unlocked, and I shoved it open, then pushed him over the threshold. He staggered through the darkness, weaving around the sparsely furnished room until he finally collapsed on the sofa, his head pitched backward over the cushioned headrest. The back of his head lay silhouetted against the far windows, where the nighttime sky glowed with a preternatural radiance.

I ran my hand along the wall for the light switch, found it, flipped it on.

"No, no, goddamn it, turn it off," Dale groused from the sofa.

I switched the lights back off, dousing us once more in darkness. The only illumination came from the procession of streetlamps that curled around the perimeter of the cul-de-sac and shined through Dale's front windows.

"Tell me," Dale said from the sofa. His voice was low, gravelly. He had proceeded to get drunk at Tig's place after Eric left, and hadn't stopped until I dragged him out to the car. "Do you see fireworks going off in any of those houses?"

"What the hell are you talking about, Dale?"

"Never mind," he said. "It was a mistake. Eric was right. I never should have said anything. I never should have told her." He shook his head slowly. "I just never thought she would betray me like this. She was my wife. I trusted her. You don't understand what it's like to have that, Andy."

"I think you should go to your room and get some sleep."

"Don't worry, Andrew. We'll be okay. All of us, we'll be okay."

He turned, half his face silvered in the light of the streetlamps coming through the front windows, the other half a black chasm of shadow. His was a haunted expression, one that I had glimpsed in my own face whenever I passed by a mirror or caught myself in the reflection of a subway-car window these past several months: the wraith. Only that loathsome devil had transferred from me to Dale . . . or maybe it now resided in both of us, some virulent disease jumping from host to host. The sight of him turned me cold.

"We'll be okay, Andy," he said. "Don't worry. Cynthia won't tell."

"Dale," I said, and my voice shook.

He sat forward on the couch, and I couldn't tell if I was hearing the couch or Dale's back creak. He brought his hands up, rubbed them up and down his face. Then he stared at his right hand—more specifically, at the heel of his right hand—while that hand trembled before him. I couldn't tell what he was looking at.

"We'll all be just fine. She won't say a word, Andy. She won't say a word." The words shuddered out of him, and he was breathing in gasps.

"How the hell do you know?" I asked.

"Because she's dead," Dale said. "I killed her."

PART TWO

DEAD IN THE WATER ...
          ... AND A RAIN OF
FROGS

TWELVE

July 4, 2003

It promised to be a sweltering Fourth of July, with heat lightning streaking the sky out over the Chesapeake Bay, and the Gracie Point Lighthouse looking like something superimposed against a Hollywood green screen. It would turn out to be one of the hottest summer nights in a hundred years, according to those who keep track of such things; it would also turn out to be something else, something that would change the course of all our lives moving forward. But of course none of us could have predicted that until it was all too late.

I was sixteen years old the night it happened—newly minted, you might say, since my birthday fell on the Fourth. My dad and I had gone into Annapolis for a steak dinner to celebrate earlier that evening, and then I'd come home and gotten drunk and stoned with my friends. Two days beforehand, Dale and Eric had taken a road trip to West Virginia to buy some fireworks that were illegal in Maryland, and the plan was to celebrate both my birthday and the Fourth with a dazzling fireworks display that night.

Earlier that morning, before any of that had happened, I had walked the winding curvature of Sea Grass Lane until I arrived at a small, two-story bungalow nested among wispy cattails, yellow fronds, and lush arbor vitae, a house whose backyard sloped down toward the muddy banks of the Chesapeake. Hidden in a stand of trees across the street, I waited as a large blue sedan pulled out of the driveway and motored on down the road, leaving a miasma of bluish exhaust funk in its wake. Once that car was out of eyeshot, I went around to the back of the bungalow (so no neighbors would see me on the front porch), knocked twice on the pane of semicircular glass in the patio door, and waited. A moment later, and Tig was there, kissing me on the mouth, and dragging me into the house.

We had been doing this for about a month at this point. No sex—Tig kept shunning me in that department—but a lot of making out. It had started seemingly out of nowhere: one day we were in her basement playing videogames and sharing a plate of Totino's pizza rolls, the next we were pressing our lips together, hands roving about each other's bodies. We'd managed to keep it a secret from the rest of the group, but I was beginning to suspect that Dale, who'd had a crush on Tig since grade school, had grown suspicious.

That morning, Tig and I made out for a while on her bed. She let me slip a hand under her shirt, but when I tried to wedge my fingers beneath the waistband of her jean shorts, she casually snared me about the wrist and tossed my hand aside.

"My dad would kill me if he knew I was bringing a white boy in here."

"He'd kill *me*," I said.

"Well, yeah. That's true. Hey—can I ask you something? For real?"

"Of course."

"You haven't told the guys about what we're doing, have you?"

"No way. It's none of their business."

I was lying on top of her, staring down at her, and I could tell she was hunting for a different truth in my eyes.

"Because I'd feel like shit if they knew."

"Because of me?"

"Because it's not something I want going around."

"I swear to God, Tig. I haven't said a word." And it was the truth. Something softened in her face. "Okay," she said. "I believe you." Then she pushed me off her and rolled off the bed. "I've got something for you, you know. A birthday present."

"Really? What is it?"

There was an old cigar box on her desk, which she opened, and took out something that shined in the early afternoon light coming through her bedroom window. She came over to where I still reclined on her bed, my hands laced behind my head, and held it out to me.

"What is it?"

"For you," she said. "I made it. Took me weeks to collect them all."

It was a bunch of metal pull-tabs from aluminum cans, strung together on a length of fishing line. A necklace, shoddy as it was, and gleaming in the sunlight poking through Tig's bedroom window.

"You did this? Really?"

"I did."

"Is there some significance to each of these tabs?"

"Those are tabs from all the crappy beer that you drank all year."

"Bullshit," I said. "No way you've been collecting them all year."

"You'd think there'd be more, right?"

She went to the beveled mirror in one corner of her room, and began fixing her hair. "Wear it tonight," her reflection said to me, "when you guys come to pick me up."

"Okay." I slipped the necklace over my head.

"But don't say I gave it to you."

"I won't say a word."

"Promise?"

"I promise."

"You should go," she said. "I'll see you tonight, birthday boy."

—◇—

Later that evening, after the celebratory steak dinner with my father, I met up with Dale, Eric, and Meach, and we plowed through a case of Natty Boh while sitting in the bed of Dale's pickup truck listening to music. The truck was an old beater, something he bought for a few hundred bucks when he'd turned sixteen a handful of months ago. He was the only one of us with a driver's license, which didn't necessarily preclude any of us from occasionally slipping behind the wheel, but he was the only one in our group who owned his own ride. And that meant freedom. He had spent a lot of time working on it in his parents' driveway in the spring and early part of that summer, and while the truck never ran like something off a showroom floor, it got us around town.

"Check this shit out," Dale said, sliding open the window at the back of the cab. He reached in and pulled out the colorful packages of fireworks he and Eric had purchased two days earlier in West Virginia. Dale passed them around, and one fell in my lap. I read the label on the wrapper—ZINGER'S THINGERS!—and saw the decorative cardboard tubes behind the window of cellophane. Their wicks were long, black, and oily, like rodents' tails. The words MAD DOG TNT were printed on each label in electric red letters.

Meach had one of the boxes on his lap, too, and he had punched a hole in the cellophane with one finger and was pretending to poke his lighted cigarette through it.

"You'll blow us the fuck up, you idiot," Eric said, slapping Meach's hand away. He snatched the box from him, looked at the items inside with some mild interest, then nodded at Dale. "Show 'em what else we got."

There was a metal toolbox in the back of Dale's truck, some rusted thing that hummed with tetanus. Smirking, Dale undid the latch on the toolbox, and the lid squealed open in protest. With a magician's flourish, he produced a small plastic bag with two joints inside. They looked like finger bones.

"You should've got some cherry bombs," Meach said, while Dale dug one of the joints out of the bag. Meach was our resident pyro, and had gotten kicked out of school last year for setting a fire in the boys' lavatory. "Those things can do some damage, man. I once saw a kid almost lose his head a few years ago, when a bunch of us went to Dump Field to blow shit up. Stuck a cherry bomb in an old potbelly stove, and *blam!* The cast iron door flew off and nearly decapitated some poor dummy."

We chuckled. The beer was going down easy, Dale was lighting the joint with Meach's lighter, it was my birthday *and* the Fourth of July, and we were going to have a celebration tonight.

Dale passed me the joint, then noticed the necklace of pull-tabs I wore around my neck. "The hell's that?" he asked.

"A fashion statement, you hillbilly," I told him, and cracked another beer.

Once it got dark, Dale and Eric piled into the cab while Meach and I held on for dear life in the truck's bed as the four of us whipped around the unpaved side roads of Kingsport. We skirted by the docks, saw the watermen chugging in from the bay, tiny white lights in their pilothouse windows, small red and green indicators on their bows. We replenished our beer at the Port Tack, where the senile old proprietor never carded anyone, then rocketed too fast along the winding, rutted surface of Graves Road, leaving the lights of Kingsport behind us in the humid, gnat-thick summer night.

"I feel my luh-luh-luh-luh-lunch coming up," Meach cried as he and I bounced along in the back of the pickup, stoned and laughing.

And then we were driving by the old Graves house, Dale slowing down. The house was dark, except for a light on in one of the downstairs windows—a milky, urine-colored light that looked unnatural out there among all that darkness.

The whole house looked unnatural.

Ruth Graves was a witch, and her home did little to dispel this rumor. It was a square cement house encased in ivy with an iron weathervane on its peaked roof. Black, barren trees twisted up from the ground and raked their claws across the sky, and the crooked teeth of tombstones leaned this way and that in the overgrown side yard. All of this was collected behind a low picket fence, some of the staves missing.

If that wasn't enough, Ruth Graves's front yard was adorned with those nightmarish, child-sized effigies she made—things that couldn't quite be called scarecrows but couldn't quite be called dolls, either. Things comprised of metal wire and bundles of straw, whose heads and shoulders were wreathed in bird feathers, whose faces were an assemblage of bleached animal skulls and piebald strips of hide. They were all out there in the front yard on this night, black and formless except for the vague suggestions of their somewhat human forms. It looked like a snapshot from some zombie movie, where these ghouls had all just wriggled their way out of the earth and were preparing to overtake the town.

Dale brought the truck to a slow stop. There was music on in the cab, some raucous, bass-heavy nonsense that fuzzed out the speakers.

"Ruth Graves, the Kingsport Witch," Meach said, and despite the excellent buzz he had going, there was an undeniable reverence to his voice. "Even her kids are weird."

Ruth Graves's daughter was too young for us to have paid her any attention, but her son, Robert, was our age. He was a homeschooled recluse, and the only times I ever caught sight of him was when I'd ride my bike past him along this very road. Sometimes he would be walking with his hands in his pockets and his head down, sweating buckets because he always wore heavy cable-knit sweaters and long pants, even in the dead of summer. A couple of times I saw him pulling a wagon behind him, a shovel propped on one shoulder. There would be roadkill in the wagon—more fodder for his mother's strange voodoo projects—and on at least one of these occasions, as I rode by on my dirt bike, he looked up and caught my eye. I don't know what I had expected him to do—grin a set of fangs at me, or maybe mutter some hex beneath his breath—but he only returned my stare with one of his own. Meach used to say that Robert and his sister weren't real people at all, but made up of wire and straw and bones and feathers: two of Ruth Graves's effigies that the old witch, with all her magic, had spirited to life.

The passenger door of Dale's truck popped open, and Eric climbed out. He was gripping one of those long, decorative cylinders that said MAD DOG TNT on the side, and held a lighter in his other hand. He looked up at Meach and me, who were leaning on the roof of the truck's cab. "What do you think, boys?"

"Oh, damn!" Meach howled. "I fucking *dare* you!"

"Dare Club back in session," Eric said, and then he thumbed the spark wheel and a flame popped up from the tip of the lighter. He touched the flame to the wick. A spark took, *sssszzz,* and then he thrust the thing straight up over his head. It was a Roman candle, I realized, just as the first fireball erupted from it.

That sizzling shooting star climbed into the night and exploded directly above the Graves house in a tinselly shimmer of golden light.

We cheered.

Another fireball arced across the night sky, detonating in an umbrella of sparkling purple light. A third caromed toward the distant trees and burst in a display of green light that we could only partially see. All around us, the world rumbled with the echo of the explosions, and I could already taste the black powder coating the back of my throat.

"Lower!" Dale shouted at Eric's back, leaning out of the open passenger door. "Shoot the house! Shoot the house!"

"Shoot one of those ugly fucking dolls!" Meach countered.

Eric laughed, and launched the next fireball much lower than the other three: it cut in a near horizontal path along Ruth Graves's property, exploding just beyond the creepy cemetery at the side of the house.

As I looked back at the house, I noticed someone watching us from a lighted window.

I banged a hand on the roof of the cab, and shouted, "Go, go, go! They're watching us!"

Eric dropped the Roman candle and hopped back in the truck, but before his door was closed, the fifth and final fireball shot in a spark through the picket fence and struck something halfway across the yard. It exploded in a flash of silver, like metal shards, and the air was suddenly thick with smoke. An instant later, a pillar of fire erupted in the front yard. It was one of the witch's voodoo dolls, all right, and the dried straw that made up most of its torso burst into flames. It looked like a person being burned alive.

Dale gunned the engine, the pickup bucked, and Meach and I nearly spilled out over the tailgate. A second later, we were speeding around the bend in the road, the truck's headlights too feeble to give enough line of sight. I shouted for Meach to hold on, and we were both laughing, and then out of nowhere there was a loud bang. It sounded like a blowout, and a second later, something whizzed right past the top of my head. The truck wobbled, its rear tires fishtailing across the bone-dry soil of the road. When the truck finally shuddered to a stop, we were engulfed in a cloud of dust.

"The hell was that?" Meach said. He was on his knees in the back of the truck, looking as if he wanted to stand, but maybe too fearful Dale might kick it into gear again.

"Flat tire?" I suggested.

"Come on."

Meach and I jumped out of the back and immediately began checking the tires. But they were all fine. I looked up and saw Dale and Eric climbing dazedly out of the cab. They moved with the palsied hesitation of someone in a state of confusion. "Tires are okay," I called to them, but neither turned in my direction. Together, they went around to the front of the truck, and stood before the glow of the truck's headlights in the middle of the road, staring at the windshield, matching expressions of shock on their faces.

I went around to the front of the truck, blocking out the glare of the headlights with one hand. It took my eyes a moment to adjust, but then I saw it: a massive bull's-eye crack in the center of the windshield. I took a step closer and saw an asterisk of blood stamped on the glass, too.

"What did that?" I heard myself say. My throat was suddenly dry and my voice sounded very far away.

"Guys!" Meach shouted from somewhere in the darkness. "Come see this!"

The three of us exchanged a look, then walked around toward the rear of the truck. Meach stood several yards down the road, his body devil-red in the glow of the truck's taillights. He was staring at something in the road.

As we drew closer, Meach said, "Don't get too close. It's still alive."

And just as he said it, I saw something flail on the ground, stirring up a cloud of red-tinged dust.

"Turkey vulture," Meach said.

"Fucking thing flew right into the windshield," Dale said.

"Maybe it's drunk," Meach suggested, and then he started to giggle.

I looked back in the direction we had come, where the road curved beyond the trees. The Graves house was not visible from this vantage, but I found myself suddenly occupied with the fact that someone had been looking out at us through one of those windows, and that we had been seen.

"Goddamn thing came straight at us," Dale said. He spoke quietly, almost reverently, and his voice trembled. "Cracked the fucking windshield."

"What do we do with it?" I asked. The way it was lying there mangled in the road told me it wouldn't survive, yet one of its wings kept cranking open and swatting futilely at the ground.

"Leave it the fuck alone," Eric said. "Let it die."

It seemed cruel to leave it there to suffer, but I certainly wasn't going to do anything about it. I looked back up in the direction of the Graves house, hidden beyond the wooded bend in the road, and saw nothing but a night spangled with fireflies. Yet I couldn't help but think—

Meach slapped me on the back. "Come on, birthday boy! We've got some celebrating to do." He bolted back toward the truck and launched himself over the tailgate and into the bed.

I looked at Dale and Eric, and although the three of us were still a little spooked—it was clear on their faces, as I was sure it was clear on mine—we all slowly regained some collective composure. Dale even started to chuckle, and then laugh outright.

I cast one final glance down at that broken, dying bird.

And then we ran back to the truck.

We picked Tig up at The Wharf Rat, she swinging her apron over her head as she came barreling through the doors, her body looking dark and sweat-sparkling in the moonlight. We were *all* sweat-sparkling from the heat, and although the local meteorologist had promised rain, it was holding off, allowing us all to boil under the pressure cooker that was the Fourth of July on Maryland's Eastern Shore.

Meach and I each grabbed one of Tig's hands and hoisted her into the back of the truck. Dale spun the steering wheel and gravel spat out from beneath the truck's tires as we growled out of the parking lot.

"That dummy!" Tig shouted, looking over her shoulder at the dwindling pink neon of The Wharf Rat. "What if my parents see!"

"It's my birthday," I said, grinning at her, my hair whipping about my face. "They'd understand."

We took the old Ribbon Road straight out to Gracie Point. Dale pulled the truck up onto a barren patch of shoulder then shut down the engine. In the distance, we could hear the fireworks coming all the way from Annapolis, or maybe someplace closer, off someone's barge anchored out in the bay.

I was pretty drunk and a little stoned by this point. We all were, except maybe for Tig, who was still rushing to catch up. The three of us spilled out of the back of the truck while Eric and Dale climbed out of the cab, those boxes of fireworks propped casually under Eric's arm. He turned and looked at me, and for whatever reason, I suddenly thought of that time the two of us had to whitewash the convenience store, and how Eric had winced every time he brought his arm up over his head.

He reached out and squeezed me on the shoulder.

"Happy birthday, you big douchebag," he said.

"Hey," I said, but then I said nothing more. My brain was too fuzzy, my mind moving too lethargically to keep pace with the sequences that were unfolding before me. Admittedly, I was still a little shaken up about that bird slamming itself into the windshield of Dale's truck.

Meach whipped around me, snatching both boxes of fireworks from beneath Eric's arm. He crooned as he ran in a wild circle in the middle of the road, and the rest of us laughed. He tore into the boxes, flinging bits of cardboard and cellophane into the air. He was insistent on lighting them himself, begging Eric for his lighter back. Eric dangled the lighter in front of him, but kept snatching it away each time Meach—the drunkest one among us—groped for it.

"Come on, man!" Meach bellowed.

"You think I'm giving you this lighter?" Eric said, laughing at him. "This was my grandfather's from the war. It's got his initials engraved on it and everything."

"I'm not gonna eat it, I'm just gonna light the goddamn wick!"

We just kept laughing.

Finally, Eric pitied him enough to toss him the lighter, cautioning him not to blow his fingers off.

"Or his dick," Dale chimed in.

Tig laughed and said, "What dick?"

"I saw that happen to a kid, once, too," Meach said.

"You saw a kid get his dick blown off?" Dale said.

"No, his fingers!" Meach was also our resident bullshit artist.

"Just be careful, Meach-Man!" Tig shouted at him.

Meach lit one of the fireworks at his feet. It shot up into the air, emitting a sound like a slide whistle, then erupted in a multicolored display out beyond the cliff, where it was reflected in the rolling black waters of the bay below.

We all cheered.

"You wore it," Tig said, coming up beside me and admiring the necklace around my neck.

"Told you I would."

I glanced at her, studied her profile as she stared up at the fireworks, their dazzling display of lights flashing in her eyes. Then

I looked past her to see Dale standing there, watching her, too. He must have sensed my stare upon him, because his eyes ticked in my direction, and there was something like embarrassment on his face. He smiled humorlessly with one corner of his mouth, then took a chug of his beer. Before he turned away, I caught him glance at the pull-tab necklace I wore, and for whatever reason, it made me feel like I'd been caught committing some treachery.

There was a lull in the activity as Meach tore into the second box of fireworks. The air smelled strongly of black powder and there was a serpent of thick charcoal smog creeping slowly across the old Ribbon Road. Whenever the beam from the Gracie Point Lighthouse swiveled back around, that swirling, gray miasma roiled and undulated like a thing alive.

I turned and saw a figure standing beyond that cloud of smoke, a few paces up the road. I almost didn't see him at first, to be honest. But then he moved through it, advancing at a slow but deliberate pace in our direction, and I realized, with a tremor of disquiet, that it was Robert Graves.

"Hey," Tig said, and nudged me with an elbow to my ribs. She had spotted him, too.

"Wait till I tell you the crazy shit that happened earlier," I whispered near her ear.

"Tell me now."

"Shhhh..."

The others took a moment longer to see him, but when they spotted Robert Graves coming through the smoke, their actions slowed until they ceased altogether, like animatronics winding down to a dead stop.

Robert stopped walking and just stood there, taking us all in. The smoke in the air was making my eyes water, but it seemed to have no effect on the local witch's son.

It was Eric who broke the silence: "Hey. Hey, man. Robert, right?"

"You guys were at my house earlier tonight," Robert said. His voice was flat and without affect, as if he could have been discussing the weather.

Eric said, "Us?"

"I recognized your truck."

"Lots of trucks in this town," Dale said. He had one elbow propped up on the hood of the truck, his belt buckle shining in the glow of the truck's headlamps.

"Not so many shooting illegal fireworks into my yard," Robert responded.

"I don't know what you're talking about," Dale said.

Tig leaned close to me, whispered in my ear, "What's going on?"

I said nothing, only shook my head.

"You guys started a fire in our yard," Robert said. He took another step forward, leaving a boy-shaped hollowness in the wall of smog at his back, as if it had been stamped with a cookie cutter. "I had to put it out. You scared my little sister."

Some alarm bell must have gone off in Meach's drink- and pot-addled mind: he raised both hands in surrender and backed away. His face looked pale, his hands shaking.

"I know who you are," Robert said. "I know who you *all* are." He looked at Eric and said, "You think the sheriff would be happy I tell him what his son's been doing tonight?"

"Relax," Eric said. "Come have a beer."

Robert lifted a finger, pointed it at each one of us, one by one. "One . . . two . . . three . . . four . . . five," he said. "I recognize you all."

"Come on, man," Eric said. "It was just a goof."

"I know what you people say about my family," Robert said. "I know what you think we are. Pretty fucking stupid to mess with us, if you believe in that sort of thing." And then something like a grin briefly swam across Robert Graves's face—so quick, I hardly had time to register it. He nodded at Dale's truck. "Nice windshield, by the way."

"Fuck you," Dale said.

"What is this?" Tig said, her voice rising. "What's this all about? What happened?"

"Don't come around my house again," Robert said.

And then I heard it—the *sssszzz* of a Roman candle being lit. I turned and saw Dale wielding one like a fencing sword, the tip of the candle drooling out black smoke. He leveled it just above his eye line, and the first fireball that came bursting from the tube sailed directly over Robert's head and exploded over the side of the cliff.

"Oh!" Tig shrieked, and when I looked at her, I saw the reflection of the fireworks across her face—a flash of greens and yellows. Flash flash flash.

"Hey," Meach said, but his voice was suffocated by the sound of the second fireball shooting from the candle—a piercing *flrrrr,* and then a purple explosion in the pitch-black sky above the bay. I thought I heard someone laugh, or at least utter something resembling a laugh. Dale had shot that second fireball even lower, and Robert Graves danced around like a frog on a hotplate to avoid it. The lights in the sky caused his shadow to flicker along the dirt road. Smoke roiled.

"What—" Tig said, gripping me high up on the forearm, painfully, her breath against the side of my face. "What is—"

A bright orange spangle of light erupted over the bay, streamers shimmering down toward the water, dissipating in the night air before they ever touched the surface. Dale took a few steps closer to Robert, that Roman candle sizzling and smoking, and launched another fireball in Robert's approximate direction. Robert hopped to the edge of the road, shielding his face with his arms, while Eric brayed laughter into the night. The fireball arced out over the cliff and exploded above Gracie Point in a display of bright red javelins of light.

"—the fuck out of here," I heard Dale say, as he finally lowered his arm.

At the edge of the cliff, Robert stood in a swirling miasma of smoke. He still had his arms up to protect himself, but slowly lowered them now. I could see the fear plainly on his face, in his eyes. The sweat leaking down his temples in sooty tracks. In the distance, the light from the lighthouse came back around, reflecting off the smoke and making it look alive.

There was a final *sssszzz* and a pop, and then a bright white fireball blasted from the tip of the Roman candle that Dale held down at his side. Dale was startled by it—he jumped back, confused—and then he quickly raised it at an angle up and away from himself just as the fifth and final fireball shot from the tip of the candle: it struck the center of the road in a heap of sparks, then ricocheted up into the air, a contrail of sizzling white lightning trailing behind it.

It struck Robert Graves in the face.

He didn't make a sound, but his hands came up to cover his face, and I could hear the soles of his sneakers sliding in the grit along the shoulder of the road as he staggered backward. Like some magic trick, a plume of smoke unspooled from between his fingers, hands still clutching at his face, and through that smoke I could see a series of fiery sparks and white zaps of light.

Then he *did* scream—the shrill, agonized cry of a banshee—as he stumbled backward, and—

"Hey!" I shouted, but it came out in a breathy whisper—

—and Robert Graves went over the edge of the cliff.

You would think there'd be a sound, a resounding gong, a plangent tolling of some distant bell, to commemorate the loss of a human life. But there was nothing. In fact, the silence that followed was so great, I imagined I could hear the whisper of that sentient cloud of black smoke shifting its way along the road—a feathery, rustling susurration that seemed to impart all the secrets of the universe.

And then the wind whisked the smoke from the road, carrying it out over the bay. We all stood there, our bodies trembling, our minds simultaneously alert yet also muddied and confused, unable to reconcile what had just happened. Tig was the first of us to move— she stepped away from me in a dazed, almost hypnotic trance. I even reached out for her before she had gone too far, groped for her loosely about the upper arm, my fingers grazing her elbow. She paused, glanced back at me . . . and I saw something oddly lucid and determined in her eyes. It scared me, to be honest. So I let her go, and she went across the road and stood at the edge of the cliff and stared down into that black abyss.

I looked at Dale, still standing in the middle of the road clutching the smoking black husk of the Roman candle, the front of his T-shirt damp with sweat. His face was pale, his cheeks nearly quivering. When he glanced over at me, I saw some measure of terror in his eyes. Then he looked down at the spent Roman candle in his hand, and his expression changed to one of mystification, as if he couldn't remember how he had come to be holding such a thing. He dropped it to the ground and stepped away from it. Then he glanced down at his right hand, where I could clearly see, in the glow of the truck's headlights, a powder burn across his palm. He began to rub at it furiously.

"That didn't just happen," Meach said. He was standing beside me, his hands pulling at his hair. When he met my eyes, a nervous sort of twitch was activated at one corner of his mouth. He began pacing like some jungle cat in a cage. "That didn't happen. That didn't happen. That didn't just happen, man."

Eric turned around in the middle of the street. When I met his eyes, I could see the fear in them, clearly as I could see the Gracie

Point Lighthouse shining through the dissipating smog. I watched as he glanced down at his own hands, as if there was some answer scrawled upon his palms for what had just occurred, some logic to it all, or maybe even a powder burn like the one on Dale's hand, but of course there was not.

"It was an accident," Dale said.

I went around him, heading toward the edge of the cliff to where Tig stood, peering over the side, but he gripped me, grabbing fistfuls of my shirt, and pinching the flesh beneath. I hardly felt it, although I distantly heard the string of the necklace snap, and a year's worth of pull-tabs rained down on my sneakers.

"It was an *accident*," he said again. His breath was sour in my face. "You saw it. A fucking accident."

I tore his hands off me then went over to where Tig was standing at the edge of the cliff, and looked down. I couldn't see anything at first, but when the lighthouse made its circuit, I caught the shape of Robert Graves's ruined body lying down there on the rocks, the surf washing over him, over and over again.

"He's alive!" Tig shouted. She was pointing at Robert's broken body. "He's moving!"

Eric went to her, gripped her about the arms. Pulled her back from the edge of the cliff. "He's not," he said. "He's dead, Tig. He's dead."

"No!" she cried. "He's moving! He's alive!" She swiveled her head in my direction. "Andrew, he's still alive! We have to help him! Please!"

I peered over the edge and saw Robert's body splayed down there on the rocks. The surf was coming in and there was foam collecting around his head and shoulders. One of his arms waved languidly in the surf, as if saying goodbye, but I knew it was just the movement of the tide. I couldn't tell if he was still alive down there or not—the distance was too great, the darkness too obstructive—but in that moment, I thought I saw his mouth come open, as if gasping for air.

"Jesus," I said, and drew back from the edge of the cliff.

"Andrew!" Tig shouted. "He's still alive down there!"

Before I could make a final determination, the light from the lighthouse continued along on its rotation, and everything down there went black again.

"We have to get out of here," Dale said, frantically scooping up our empty beer cans from the road and tossing them into the back of his pickup truck. "We have to go!"

"Come on," Eric said to Tig and me, a bit more measured. But the shock of it was wearing off and I could see a column of panic beginning to replace the fear I had witnessed in him a moment ago. I could feel that same panic beginning to rise in me, too.

"We have to call someone," Tig kept saying. She'd backed away from Eric and stood now silhouetted before the headlights of Dale's truck. She looked imploringly at Eric. "We have to call the police. We have to call your dad."

"Tig, are you crazy?"

"If he's still alive and he's hurt, Eric, then we need to—"

"He's not alive! No one could survive that fall. He's dead, and Dale's right—we need to get the hell out of here."

"Stop *yelling* at me!"

Eric's hand shot out and gripped Tig around the wrist. She cried out, in pain or surprise, and tried to pull herself free, but Eric was bigger and stronger, and he began dragging her across the road and back toward Dale's truck.

"Eric, stop, you're hurting me—"

"Cut it out," I said, and swatted his hand off her.

Eric whirled around and struck me across the face. It snapped my head back on my neck, and I staggered backward until I fell on my ass in the dirt. Momentarily, the world became gray and fuzzy around the edges. I blinked water from my eyes as I looked up at him. Eric's face was hard and flushed, and he seemed to be contemplating what else he should do to me in that moment. But in the end, he just turned and jogged back to the truck, where Dale was digging around in his pockets for his keys and where Meach was kicking the spent Roman candle tubes over the side of the cliff.

I rolled onto my side and Tig helped me up the rest of the way.

"Your nose is bleeding."

I rubbed an index finger beneath my nose and saw the comet trail of blood there.

"We have to do something," she pleaded with me. Her eyes were filling with tears and she looked utterly and completely terrified.

"Tig—"

"I saw him *move*, Andrew. What if he's still alive down there? We can't just leave him."

"You saw the *water* moving him. The tide. I saw it, too." And although I was thinking of it, I said nothing about how I'd seen his mouth fly open. Truth was, in that moment, I couldn't be sure *what* I had seen. "Eric's right—no one can survive that fall. He's gone. Let's go."

We ran back to the truck, and Meach pulled Tig up into the bed. I was about to jump in after her when I saw something wink at me from the dusty ground: Eric's Zippo lighter, the one with his grandfather's initials on it. I scooped it up, tossed it to Meach, then scrambled into the back of Dale's pickup truck. While I was still straddling the tailgate, Dale punched the truck into gear. The truck bucked, the rear tires spun, and then we were speeding around the bend of the old Ribbon Road, leaving all that we'd done behind us in the dark.

iii

There sits at the very bottom of the Chesapeake Bay a large, square ashtray made out of thick, sculpted glass. In a way it very much resembles the award I was given when I was promoted up to the fifth floor at my law firm. It sits there on the floor of the bay, grains of sand and vast particles of sea life washing over it, until it is completely buried not only by the gray silt that sits at the bottom of the Chesapeake Bay, but by the cold black waters of the bay itself. No one, as far as I can imagine, will ever find this large, square, glass ashtray. For all intents and purposes, one might even argue that it no longer exists at all.

THIRTEEN

I drove to Eric Kelly's house first thing the following morning. With last night's conversation with Dale still clanging around in my head, I was left unsettled and apprehensive, much as I'd felt back in New York as Rebecca's pregnancy had progressed. I'd hardly slept the night before, lying awake in the too-small bed in my old bedroom, listening to the fat, black flies thump mindlessly against the windowpanes, and smelling that dead-fish smell emanating from the flooded cellar.

Meach had split from The Wharf Rat after everything had gone down, and he hadn't returned to the house; yet even though I'd been alone last night, I would occasionally hear noises that suggested someone else was in the house with me. A thump here, a shuffle there. The creak of a floorboard that sounded too weighty to be the settling of an old house. Once, I even crawled out of bed and, groping blindly in the dark, staggered to the bedroom doorway. I called out for Meach, my voice echoing down the barren corridor, and got no answer. I went around the house, turning on what lights still worked, poking my head in all of the rooms. Tacky tendrils of flypaper stuck to my sweaty face as I roved about.

No Meach.

Maybe it was the confession Dale had leveraged on me hours earlier, or maybe it was the accumulation of all the ghost stories with which I'd been bombarded since my return to Kingsport—whatever the reason, I became convinced someone else was in the house with me. I even crept down into the cellar, stopping at the water line that had risen another few inches up the stairs, and peered down into that dank, gloomy catacomb. No one was down there, of course . . . but my heart had been racing the entire time, and despite the kiln-like heat in that house, I had gone instantly cold.

I turned and climbed back up the stairs, but paused when I heard what sounded like a high-pitched, mechanical pulsing. It was the same sound I thought I'd heard when Meach had told me to come down here the night before. I paused midway up the stairs and held my breath, hoping to discern the source of the noise. But the noise had stopped, and the smell was too potent to hang around much longer, so I had fled.

When I pulled up outside the brick-fronted split-foyer on Shore Road with the name KELLY on the lighthouse-shaped mailbox, I realized I had actually driven to Eric's old childhood home. I had no idea if he still lived here, only that I had no other location at which to find him. So I parked outside Eric Kelly's old house, sipped the coffee I'd purchased at the Stop and Go ten minutes earlier, and deliberated on whether or not I should knock on the front door.

As I sat there parked along the street, a police car came gliding up the block, and pulled right into the driveway of Eric's old home. I saw my old friend get out, dressed crisply in his uniform, and with his own cup of coffee in his hand. As he walked up the porch, the front door swung open, and two young boys in karate gis tumbled out. An almost-teenage girl followed them out. The girl had a backpack slung over her shoulder and was studying the screen of her cell phone; the boys looked like they could have been identical twins, and they sparred with each other on the front lawn, kicking and punching at the air, until Eric went over and snatched up one of them in a playful headlock. As they wrestled around on the lawn, a slim, attractive woman came out of the house, a handbag slung over one shoulder. Like her daughter, she was gazing at the listless white screen of her cell phone, but then looked up and smiled dimly at the rambunctiousness of the twin boys and their father scrapping around on the front lawn. Something about this scene struck a chord with me, and I suddenly ached to be back home in New York with Rebecca.

As Eric's wife and kids piled into a minivan, I got out of my rental car and sauntered over to his house. He looked up and saw me coming, and there was no denying the surprise on his face. He didn't look exactly happy to see me.

"You still live here?" I said.

"Where else would I go? When Mom died, I just took over. There's a bird that does that, I think—some bird that takes over another bird's nest." He nodded at the minivan pulling out of the driveway. "You just missed 'em."

"I saw," I said. "Beautiful family."

"Kids are a handful. Especially my daughter. She's at that age."

Eric's wife honked the horn and waved as she backed into the street. Like some Pavlovian reaction, I waved, and then felt silly for it. Eric and I watched them drive away.

"What are you doing here?"

I took a breath, and then told him about Dale's confession.

I was conscious of the way Eric's features gradually went slack as I spoke—how he seemed to become loose and boneless, yet at the same time, I could see the muscles tensing in his face. I watched as the color drained from his face, too, and his eyes grew hard and dark.

"That son of a bitch," he said, and then he lowered himself to sit on the porch steps. He gazed down the street, where his family's minivan was still visible chugging down the road. "What exactly did he do to her?"

I sat down beside him. "He didn't tell me that. He was too drunk, and he had stopped making sense. He just kept saying we shouldn't worry, and that no one will ever find her. And then he passed out."

"Yeah, right. Like I trust that idiot. Have you spoken to him this morning?"

"No. And I'm leaving today."

He looked at me, his stare laser-focused all of a sudden. "What?"

"I've got to get back to work, Eric. I can't sit around this town waiting for this shit to resolve. It may *never* resolve. I need to get back to New York." And I could tell he didn't like hearing that, so I said, "Go and see him today for yourself. He'll be a mess, but if you don't explode on him like you did last night, then I'm sure he'll talk. You can call me, let me know what he says. If there's something more I can do once you talk to him, you give me a call and I'll do what I can. But right now, man, I can't be here. No more."

"This fucking idiot has screwed us all," Eric said.

"You don't know that."

"He's going to get caught."

"You don't know that, either."

He made a face, like he was sucking on something sour.

"Listen," I said. "I never said anything to you. Do you understand? Far as I'm concerned, when I get up off this porch, Dale never said a single word to me last night, and I never said anything to you. And I'm going home, Eric."

"You think it's that easy?"

"I'm tired of being haunted by old ghosts."

Eric's face tightened. I could see a vein pulsing in his temple. "This isn't a ghost story, Andrew," he said. "This is reality."

I extended a hand. Held it there, waiting for him to shake it. He did, eventually. But there was no warmth in it. And when I got in my car and turned over the engine, I saw the way he was looking at me, sitting there on his front steps with his Styrofoam cup of coffee hanging between his knees, his uniform slightly disheveled from roughhousing with his kids on the front lawn. Something about the way he looked confirmed my decision to leave this place.

I went back to my father's house to pack up my stuff. As I did so, I wondered if I'd ever see this place again, or if I should just have Gil Wallace stake a FOR SALE sign on the lawn and finally put this part of my history to rest. Rebecca wasn't even aware that I still owned the place, and it would feel good to unburden myself of at least one old secret.

There were wet patches on the floor of the hallway. Several of them, in fact. I went over to one and saw that it held the shape of a footprint. They all did.

"Meach-Man? You here?"

No answer.

I followed them with my eyes down the hall, saw their pattern, a drunken weave, certainly Meach . . . yet something about them troubled me on some basic animal level.

The footprints began at the cellar door. As if something had crawled out of the water down there and slunk its way silently through the house at some point. I recalled seeing these prints the night before, only I had convinced myself they had been part of a dream.

Just leave, I heard a voice speak up in the back of my head. Rebecca's voice. *Just turn around, get in the car, and come home to me.*

I almost did.

Instead, I followed those wet footprints down the hall to the closed cellar door. That diamond-cut glass knob was cold when I wrapped my hand around it, despite the humidity in the house. I turned it, opened the door, and stood before the yawning black mouth of the cellar.

It was too dark down there to see how high the water had risen, so I dug my cell phone from my pocket, thumbed on the flashlight app, and directed that paltry white beam down the throat of the stairwell.

I counted four stairs clear of the water, the rest submerged. The water itself was a murky brown with bits of sediment floating in it. A burst pipe, for sure . . . although the smell of it now was more like the bay than anything else. I looked closer and saw that there was more seaweed waving languidly along the surface of the water. A brief flash of iridescence in all that murk, and I wondered, incredulously, if I'd just glimpsed a school of minnows winking by.

Something else winked at me from beneath the surface of the water.

I redirected the beam of light and saw my wedding ring twinkle on one of the submerged steps. I stared at it for a moment, unable to comprehend how it had gotten there. Had Meach swiped it from the sink, only to have dropped it down here? And if so, what the hell had he been doing down here in the first place?

I spoke his name then, my voice shaky and uncertain, the . . . *each* . . . *each* . . . *each* of it reverberating off those stone walls down below. I didn't know what to expect—to see him rise up in the center of that sunken room, breaking through the surface of that water?

Something *did* move, although not at the center of that sunken room: a movement of shadow in the dark antechamber, the room beyond the room, where the ceiling sloped downward and the black cobblestone walls drew in closer together. I could have convinced myself it was a trick of the eye until I saw the ripples moving along the surface of the water, lazily rolling in my direction. The seaweed parted and I gleaned something pale down there, so quick I was able to convince myself that it was only a trick of the light. Suddenly, I could hear it again—that strident, mechanical pulsing, a metronome of beeps. Not from down here, though, but from some remote plateau—behind the cobblestone walls, perhaps, like Poe's tell-tale heart.

I hurried down to the last dry step, grabbed the railing, and bent over. I plunged my hand into that stagnant, tepid water, and snatched my wedding ring off the stair. Just as I stood, I heard the stairs beneath me creak, followed by an audible snap. My foot plunged through the broken step to the one below it, soaking my leg to the shin. *Something is going to grab at me*, I thought, and despite the ridiculous nature of such a thought, it launched me up the stairwell and back out into the hall, where I slammed the cellar door shut a little too hard.

I opened my palm and stared down at my wedding ring.

Get in the car and come home to me.

It was still early in the day when I stepped out of that house and walked over to my rental car. Frogs were plentiful at this hour, peeping and chirping and wishing me a fond farewell. The birds, too.

I climbed into my rental car, started the engine, then looked up at the house.

Six or seven sizeable turkey vultures were perched along the roof, their wings splayed as if in preparation for an embrace, their heads slung low on their neck. I couldn't make out any details beyond that, but for some reason, I felt certain their black, beady eyes were staring right at me.

And if it felt like something dark and sinister followed me home from that bleak place, I did well to convince myself that it was all in my head.

FOURTEEN

A nd then I was back home, ensconced once more within the
protective shell of domestic bliss, waiting for the baby that was
mere weeks away from coming, nestling my face in the crook of my
wife's neck at the end of the night, smelling the shampoo in her hair,
smelling her skin, kissing the side of her face, tracing the faint red
freckles on her shoulders, the heart tattoo on her lower back, the
pert thrust of her rose-colored nipples, thinking, *This is where I'm
supposed to be,* thinking, *Nothing bad can happen when we're here like
this, together,* and then one night we even made love, me careful of her
condition, Rebecca less careful, more comfortable, more confident,
more *needing,* feeling it, rolling on top of me, straddling me, moving
her head in a certain way so that the curled copper ringlets of her hair
perfectly bracketed her face, such a face, those luminous cat's eyes
holding me in their tractor-beam stare, her hipbones grinding down
on me, hipbone against hipbone, her eyes never leaving mine, her
fingers digging into my shoulders, Rebecca coming down, Rebecca
coming, her face, that face, exhaling breath in *my* face, forgetting
which one of us is who, tasting her mouth, her tongue, the texture
of her teeth, those hipbones prodding my sweat-slick flesh, my
groin, the fullness of her, the swelling, the union of us, our green-
eyed fury, the dark and secret whispers as we climaxed together, one

particular murmur in my ear, not real, maybe real, but a memory of a memory, whispering, *Tell me one of your stories?* and I closed my eyes and disassociated for a while, just drifting along on a black current, and then it turned white, but in an expulsion of fireworks, *blam blam blam,* and then she was crying out, and those hipbones—those hot pockets, as I called them, sweet-smelling and warm, goose-pimpled as I worked my tongue around them in tiny swirls—working their magic, working their engine, working their communion with me, with me, with *me . . .*

I spent the next several days at the office, finding a comforting serenity in helping one of Bryce Morrison's clients untangle a particularly daunting legal matter. In the evenings, I would come home, sometimes with Chinese takeout or a pizza, and Rebecca and I would eat dinner together. She would talk about the current manuscript she was editing, and how the author was an odious piece of shit incapable of taking criticism, and then she would ask about my day at the office. And even though there was nothing exciting about my day at the office, it felt good to talk to her about it and not lie about anything.

"Your birthday is coming," she reminded me one evening. "Anything special you want to do?"

"Just spend time with you."

"I promise I'll keep the kid incarcerated a bit longer. No shared birthdays in this family."

"On the other hand," I said, "that just might be the coolest birthday present ever."

It was during the night that I found myself resorting to old fears about the baby. The wraith was back, creeping stealthily through our home, and the wraith was me. I found I couldn't fall asleep, my mind and body wired to intercept any misplaced, errant signals transmitted throughout our apartment, some beacon of communication, some noise, some smell, some flicker of an image glimpsed fleetingly in my periphery. One night, lying in bed beside Rebecca as she snored gently, I could abruptly smell that rotten, fishlike stink that had infiltrated my father's house back in Kingsport. Had I brought that smell home with me? Could Rebecca smell it on my flesh? Another night, I smelled smoke. I got up and wandered about the place, hunting down the source of that acrid burning stench: I checked the stove, the appliances, even stepped out into the hallway to see if something was amiss. The recessed lights in the hallway ceiling were out, dousing the corridor in shadow. I stared down to the far end of the hall, where a window faced back at me . . . yet on this night, I saw the silhouette of someone standing in front of it.

"Hey," I called. "Who's there?"

It could have been anyone.

It could have been no one.

His name, right there on the tip of my tongue—*Robert?* But I couldn't bring myself to say it, and I instantly felt foolish, letting Meach's crazy talk and Tig's stress-induced nightmares get the better of me. There was, however, someone there at the far end of the hall, and they appeared to be staring right back at me. I shouted at the person to come closer, to reveal himself, to be a man and confront me instead of standing there like someone looking to rob the place.

Mrs. Napier opened her door and scowled at me beneath a nest of hair curlers.

"There's someone standing at the other end of the hall." I conveyed this message in a hoarse whisper. I even pointed, and Mrs. Napier followed my finger down the length of the corridor. That silhouette was still there, blocking the view of the city beyond the window.

"What did you do to the lights?" the old woman asked me.

"I didn't do anything. They were off when I came out here."

"Why are you out here so late making such a racket?"

"Do you . . . Do you smell something burning?"

The unchanged expression on her face told me that she did not.

I muttered a clumsy apology, then glanced back toward the opposite end of the hallway just as the lights blinked on.

There was no one there.

I felt a twinge of unease at the base of my spine. I had spent two days in Kingsport telling old friends they were imagining things and jumping at shadows, and yet here I was, doing the very same thing.

I apologized again to Mrs. Napier, whose scowl remained. She pointed at me and said, "Your face. Your nose."

I pressed a set of fingers against the base of my nose, and they came away wet with blood.

Back in the apartment, the smell of smoke no longer lingered. This brought me little relief, since I felt like some part of me was slowly disassociating from the rest of my psyche. I went to the bathroom and saw that my reflection was sporting a bloody nose. I washed my face and hands, briefly examined the deep pockets beneath my eyes in the mirror, then crawled silently back into bed.

Laurie O'Dell noticed my preoccupation at work. She noticed how exhausted I was, too, from my lack of sleep. She joked about gunning for my job, but then genuinely offered her assistance, should I need any. I was appreciative, but the fact that she had so easily identified my aloofness only made me more self-conscious about my predicament.

It would be a lie to say that a part of my mind wasn't still back in Kingsport with Dale, Eric, Tig, and Meach. With each passing day, I expected to receive another phone call, or maybe see a news report about the body of an unidentified woman discovered in a block of cement at one of Dale Walls's construction sites. But those things did not happen. I brought the case file Eric had given me to work, and would occasionally thumb through it, searching for any element, any inconsistency, any loose thread, that might prove to be Dale's undoing. But the details were vague, and there was nothing in any of the reports or the paperwork that told me something I didn't already know. When I got too busy to study it at work, I took it home, and waited to read it after Rebecca had gone to bed. And when I heard a floorboard creak behind me, I quickly covered up the report and stuffed it back in my briefcase.

One night, I suffered a dream where Meach was standing at the foot of my bed, squeezing my ankle until I awoke. One of his eyes was missing, and there was thick, black smoke unspooling from the charred crater where it should have been.

"*One ... two ... three ... four,*" he said, and then he offered me a cadaverous grin. His teeth were gray tombstones.

The next Saturday, while Rebecca was out to lunch with some friends, I heard a sound like a fist slamming against the bedroom wall. I hurried into the bedroom, looked around, and even called out Rebecca's name in the event she'd come through the front door and let it slam. Was it the construction in the Constantines' apartment above us?

But no: I could suddenly see a greasy smudge on the window at the far side of the room. Dead center in the middle of the glass.

I went to it, opened the window. The sound of the city traffic rushed into the apartment. I leaned my head out over the windowsill and looked down upon the fire escape.

There was a meadowlark on the grate, lying on its back. Its neck was bent at an unnatural angle, its speckled wings splayed in a Jesus Christ pose. This close, I could see mites weaving in and out of the bright yellow feathers at its breast. I thought it was dead until one of its eyes snicked wetly in my direction. It unhinged its beak and released a shrill, vibrating cry that sounded like air rapidly escaping from a punctured tire.

I felt like someone was trying to shake me loose from my own body.

How can this—

From somewhere in the belly of the apartment, my cell phone began to ring.

I found it vibrating on the kitchen counter, Eric Kelly's number displayed on the screen. I stood there staring at it. Wanting to put Kingsport and everything it represented behind me for good. Wanting not to answer it. Rebecca and I were about to have a baby. I didn't need that old baggage weighing me down. I didn't want those old ghosts.

When the phone stopped ringing, I waited for it to chime with a voicemail, but it did not. I could forget about it, of course. I could pretend I hadn't heard it ringing. I could lie to myself and pretend that the call had never come. I could even delete the log that showed I had one missed call from Maryland.

Coward, I thought.

I picked up the phone and dialed Eric back.

There was no preamble when Eric picked up—he just cut to it.

"Cynthia's body has been recovered by police," he told me, and I felt a lead weight sink down into my bowels. "Meach found her."

"Meach? What do you mean, Meach found her?"

"It's as crazy as it sounds," he said. "And this changes everything. You have to come back."

I made a noise that could have been interpreted as staunch refusal.

"The D.A. is thinking about calling in the state police, Andrew. We've only had like two homicides here in the past decade, and they were the results of drunken brawls. The D.A. doesn't think we're equipped to handle something like this. Plus people know my connection with Dale. The D.A. needs this to be unbiased, and so I'm being marginalized. My hands are getting tied."

"Where was she found?" I asked.

"I don't want to do this on the phone."

I felt a sinking sensation in the pit of my stomach. I closed my eyes. "My God, she was in my father's cellar, wasn't she?"

There was a brief pause on the other end of the line. Then: "Andrew? What are you talking about?" Then before I could respond, he said, "Forget it. We'll talk in person. Grab the next train that you can and I'll pick you up in Baltimore and drive you back here."

"Eric, I can't just pick up and leave like that. I can't just jump on a—"

"I still don't think you understand the gravity of the situation, Andrew," Eric said. "I saw Dale this morning. We had to give him the news. He's about to break. And God knows what he'll say."

And that was all he said.

I exhaled a pent-up, shuddery breath. "All right," I told him. "I guess I'll see you tonight."

He hung up without another word.

I wandered back into the bedroom and went over to the open window. Peered back out at the meadowlark on the fire escape.

It was dead.

FIFTEEN

Aftermath, July 2003

I don't know how long we drove around that night until Dale pulled his pickup truck alongside the roadway that flanked the local dump. It was late and the fireworks from town had stopped hours ago. The night had cooled, too, but my entire body felt tacky with sweat. Dale shut down the truck but neither he nor Eric got out. Tig sat in one corner of the truck's bed, hugging her knees to her chest, her face buried.

"I can't sit here like this for another second," Meach said. He leapt over the side of the truck, his sneakers punching up a plume of dust from the road. His stuffed his hands in his pockets and walked over to the tall chain-link fence that surrounded the entire dump. I could hear gulls shrieking somewhere in the night.

Eric got out of the truck. He came around and peered over at me, then at Tig. To me, he said, "She okay?"

There was nothing I could say to that. *I* wasn't okay.

Eric looked over his shoulder. Shouted, "You doing all right, Meach?"

Meach gave a thumbs-up, but refused to look at him.

"Dale's wigging out a little," Eric said. "He burned his hand, but it doesn't look bad. He's also freaking out because there are so many cops on the road tonight. You know, because of the Fourth. I'm gonna give him a few minutes to get his shit together, and then we're gonna drive you guys home."

"What's gonna happen?" I heard myself say.

"Happen? What do you mean? We're gonna go home."

I looked over at Tig. She still had her face buried in her knees.

"Let's go now," I told him. "I don't want to wait. I want to go home now."

Eric gnawed on his lower lip. Sweat glistened on his forehead. After a moment, he said, "Okay," and shouted for Meach to get back in the truck. Meach slunk back and climbed into the truck's bed. I could see he'd been crying out there by the fence, his face blotchy and red, his eyes pink and glassy.

My heart was jackhammering in my chest.

Eric got back into the cab of the truck. The truck's engine kicked over, and then we pulled back out onto the road.

We dropped Tig off first. She didn't want us driving down her street, so we let her out at the nearest intersection, and watched her fade into the darkness. Once we lost sight of her, Dale cut a sharp left turn, and we coasted at a lethargic pace through the center of town. In our overtaxed state, we all forgot that Main Street was still closed because of the Fourth of July parade, so when we rolled up to the sawhorses at the intersection of Main and Sea Grass, I felt a lump form in my throat. *The police already know.* I looked over at Meach, who was already leaning over the side of the truck and staring at the roadblock, a measure of trepidation in his messy eyes.

But then I remembered, and said, "It's just the parade. Just the parade."

Meach looked at me—studied me, it seemed—and then nodded.

To this day, I'm not sure if he actually understood what I was telling him.

Dale backed the truck up and took us on the detour that ran us along the outskirts of town. Five minutes later, we came upon the Meacham Motel from the back way. The motel's sign was mostly dark, except for the glowing pink letters of the EL in MOTEL depicted in reverse high above the black swell of trees. Meach was out of the truck and hoofing it up the walk before Dale even brought the truck to a complete stop.

They took me home next, stopping at the bottom of our driveway to let me out. I climbed out of the back, thought about saying something to Eric and Dale, but decided against it in the end. I felt that if I opened my mouth to speak, I might be sick. My heartbeat hadn't slowed since we'd left the dump, and I wondered if there'd ever been anyone in the history of the world to die of a heart attack at age sixteen.

It was late and the house was quiet when I entered. My father was an early riser, which meant he was generally in bed before nine. I turned on no lights as I crept through the house, pausing to peer at the glowing emerald numbers on the microwave—11:58 p.m. Still my birthday. Still the Fourth.

I was as quiet as possible as I made my way down the hall to the bathroom. I was desperate for a shower, but I didn't want to arouse suspicion—to rouse my father—at this late hour, so I tugged off my shirt and settled for washing my face and body at the bathroom sink. Midway through the process, the pounding in my chest reached a crescendo. I curled up on the floor and waited for the heart attack to come, tears spilling down the burning flesh of my face, my hands trembling on the cold linoleum tile of the bathroom floor. I kept hearing Meach saying, over and over again, *That didn't happen. That didn't happen. That didn't just happen,* and I squeezed my eyes shut and prayed that his mantra would make things right.

SMALL TOWN HORROR

I didn't know how long I sat there on the bathroom floor, waiting for my heart to implode, but I was startled at some point by a pounding on the door. My dad's voice, muffled from the other side: "You okay in there?"

I cleared my throat, forced some composure, and said, "Yeah, Dad. I'm fine."

"You sick?"

"No."

"You and your friends do any drinking tonight?"

"No, Dad."

I prayed for him to go away. I prayed for him not to tell me to open the door so he could lay eyes on me. I prayed, I prayed, I prayed . . .

Silence.

I swallowed what felt like a lump of dirt, and said, very quietly, "Dad? You still there?"

More silence.

I got up and shut the sink off. I turned off the bathroom light before opening the door, in case my father was still out there waiting for me. But he was not out in the hall. I stepped out of the bathroom and tread along the old floorboards on my way to my bedroom, my heart still punching against my ribcage.

In my bedroom, I stripped down to my underwear then climbed beneath the sheet on my bed. I remained there, lying on my back, staring at the ceiling. Every once in a while, I would hear the distant explosion of fireworks from someplace, and the sounds of them drew fresh tears from my eyes.

Kill me, I told my heart. *Blow up. Explode. Kill me.*

Robert Graves's body was found on the morning of July fifth, down along the black, lichen-covered rocks below the cliffs of Gracie Point.

I heard about it from Eric, who showed up at my house at some time in the afternoon on that day, looking green and stricken and coated in a film of sweat from having walked all this way. Eric's father, the sheriff, had gotten called out in the wee hours of the morning after one of his deputies discovered the body along the shore. Eric had overheard the phone call, and deduced that Ruth Graves had reported her son missing sometime in the night, although he hadn't been able to glean much more than that.

My own father had gone out fishing early that morning with friends, and he was still out by the time Eric arrived on our front porch. I hurried him into the house, and Eric immediately asked to use the bathroom. He moved quickly down the hall, slammed the door, and I heard the water running for a very long time. I wondered if he was in there, curled up in a ball on the bathroom floor afraid his heart might explode, just as I had been the night before. I just stood there, growing nervous. I kept listening for the sounds of police sirens racing up my street, but they never came.

When Eric came out of the bathroom, I was relieved to see how calm he looked. He'd washed his face and hands, and had run his hands through his damp hair, slicking it back. "Had a Slurpee on the way over and I had to piss like a racehorse."

We sat together at the kitchen table, two glasses of iced tea between us, although I wasn't able to drink any of it. At one point, Eric said, "I got an uncle lives in a small town in West Virginia. Some kids set a fire in the woods out there a few years ago, completely by accident, but it killed a woman and her baby. Those kids went away to juvie for a whole year."

I just sat there, watching the droplets of condensation trickle down the side of the iced tea glass.

"Robert said he recognized Dale's truck," Eric went on. "Do you remember him saying that?"

I nodded. I remembered him saying it. I remembered him pointing at each one of us, too, marking us, and counting aloud: *one . . . two . . . three . . . four . . . five . . .*

"Do you think his mother or sister saw the truck, too? Like maybe they came to the windows when the fireworks were going off and saw us? Or when that thing caught on fire and started burning?"

"I don't know," I said, my voice small. I had my hands buried in my lap under the table; they wouldn't stop shaking and I didn't want Eric to see.

"I guess even if they saw the truck, that doesn't mean we were out at Gracie Point that night. The cops would have to prove that." He was rationalizing the situation to himself. "Which means that if they come around asking any questions, we all just have to deny that we were there. That's all. That's all we have to do."

"They'd ask Dale," I said.

"Huh?"

"It was his truck. The cops would ask Dale about it."

Eric appeared to consider this while slowly nodding his head. He sipped some of the iced tea that I had poured for him. "We picked up all those beer cans, didn't we?" he asked, then answered his own question: "Yeah, we did. We did." As if he was trying to convince himself.

I didn't know if we'd picked up all the empty beer cans or not, but I knew there were about a hundred aluminum pull-tabs scattered about the old Ribbon Road from when my necklace broke. I didn't know if that was something the police could pull fingerprints from—it probably was, I thought—and I was too afraid to ask Eric his opinion. Talking about this further, I feared, would only result in fueling our mutual anxiety.

"What do you think we should do?" I asked him.

"What do you mean?"

I cleared my throat and said, "Like, I mean, should we say something to somebody?"

Eric's eyebrows pinched together. "Say something about what?"

"I mean..." I didn't finish the sentence.

"We can't say a word," Eric said. "Far as we know, only Robert saw our truck and knew we were at the house and up on Gracie Point. And he's dead, Andrew."

"Jesus, Eric."

"Well, it's true. Don't be a baby about it." He sipped some more iced tea. "Look, if I hear anything more about this from my dad, I'll let you know. But don't say anything to anyone, Andrew. Not even your own dad. Do you understand?"

Numb, I nodded.

"Okay, good."

He finished his iced tea, then got up from the table, and let himself out of the house. I remained at the table, staring at his empty glass, and at my untouched one.

My father came home later that afternoon, cheerful because he'd scored the biggest rockfish. He was cleaning it in the kitchen sink when he asked me to come out of my room and take a gander at it.

"Yeah," I said. "Nice fish."

"Did you hear about the boy who died last night?"

I felt that tightening in my chest again. *Kill me, kill me, kill me.*

"No," I said.

"Kid about your age fell over the cliff along the old Ribbon Road last night. Ruth Graves's son."

I went to the fridge and pretended to search for something, just so I didn't have to look my father in the eye.

"Damn shame. I hope you and your friends are careful when you're out there by the cliffs."

"Yeah," I said, my face burning despite the cool air coming from the open refrigerator. "We're always careful."

"Let's throw this bad boy on the grille tonight, what do you say?"

"Sure," I said, then hurried off to my room.

A little while later, he knocked on my bedroom door. I did my best to hide my face behind a book before he poked his head in.

"Not much of an appetite tonight?"

"Guess I'm coming down with something."

"Maybe you should turn in early."

"Yeah. I think I will."

It wasn't my heart but my lungs that forced me out of bed that night. I felt like I was drowning, that my lungs were filling with water. I couldn't lie there any longer, so I climbed out of bed and got dressed. Checked the clock on my nightstand: 2:18 a.m. The house was as quiet as a mausoleum.

Something else on my nightstand—an old can of Sprite. I stared at the pull-tab on it for what felt like an eternity, while I felt something begin to curdle in my stomach.

And I thought, *Will the police see all those pull-tabs on the ground? Will they collect them as evidence and find my fingerprints on them? Find Tig's fingerprints on them? Will they come knocking on our door tomorrow to put me in handcuffs?*

I felt like I was going to be ill.

I went to the bathroom, where I hung over the toilet, waiting to vomit. Nothing happened. Back out in the hall, I could hear my

RONALD MALFI

father snoring like a locomotive. I crept down the hall, slipped my
sneakers on, and passed soundlessly through the front door and out
into the night.

Outside, the air smelled of smoke. I went around to the shed and
got my bike, then wheeled it down the driveway until I hit the street.
I had never ridden my bike all the way out to the old Ribbon Road,
but I had anxiety on my side now, and it would be enough fuel for
this trip. I pedaled to the outskirts of town and didn't pass a single
vehicle along the way. I thought maybe that was a blessing.

The old Ribbon Road was called that because it wound around the
coast of Kingsport in a series of undulating, circuitous passageways,
a scenic roadway that had become obsolete back in the sixties when
Main Street ultimately burrowed its way through the center of town.
I had never ridden my bike up the graduated slope of the old Ribbon
Road, but I did on this night, my breath coming in great whooping
gasps, my lungs aching, my legs straining.

I anticipated yellow police tape strung up around the trees, maybe
some sawhorses along the shoulder of the road where Robert had
gone over. Some evidence that something official had happened here.
But the road was empty—a desolate, unobtrusive tract of land that
looked as commonplace as the local dump, the marina, the empty
parking lots down by the supermarket plaza. I arrived in anticipation
of . . . something . . . only to find emptiness.

I wasn't sure if I was relieved or unnerved by it.

I dropped my bike in the reeds along the shoulder of the road
and wandered out to the edge of the cliff. There was a strong wind
coming off the bay, and it blew the hair off my sweaty forehead. That
heaviness was back in my lungs—I felt like I was drowning on land—
and I grew woozy peering over the edge of that cliff. I looked up and
at the distant point of light that was the Gracie Point Lighthouse in
an effort to anchor myself.

190

Something strange happened: I watched the light make its full rotation until it came back around to shine on me. But then it froze, spotlighting me right there on the cusp of the cliff, like someone attempting to escape a prison yard in the dead of night.

The light in the lantern room turned blood-red.

My heart slammed against the wall of my chest. I backed away from the edge of the cliff, suddenly certain that Robert Graves would scale that bluff and rise up over the edge, snatch a hold of my ankle, and drag me over the side.

Pull-tabs, I thought, and hurried back toward the road. If the police hadn't already collected them as evidence, they should be scattered about the ground somewhere . . . somewhere . . .

I couldn't breathe. I couldn't focus. I dropped to my knees in the dirt and swiped a hand through the soil, searching for the pull-tabs that had fallen here. *Where? Where?*

But I was looking in the wrong place. The necklace had broken closer to where the truck had been parked, in the middle of the road. I climbed to my feet and staggered in that direction. Saw something wink at me in the moonlight. *Yes. Yes.* Dropped to my knees. *Yes.*

They were there: scattered about the rutted dirt road, radiating with the pale—

(red)

—white light of the lighthouse, glowing like bioluminescence, all of those aluminum pull-tabs right there before me, *right there*—

I swept a mound of them into one hand, clods of dirt crumbling between my fingers. I hadn't brought anything to stow them in—I hadn't thought this through at all—so I just wedged them in the pockets of my cargo shorts, dirt and all. I ran my hands back through the dirt, feeling for any that might remain partially buried, any that I, in my panic, might have missed, but there were no more.

I ran to my bike, pulled it out of the reeds, and hopped on. The road was a steep decline on my return, and I picked up speed without effort, the summer's nighttime air whipping through my hair and pulling streamers of tears from the corners of my eyes.

By the time I got home, I was vibrating like a tuning fork. I was filthy from digging around in the road; all I wanted to do was wash up, strip out of these dirt-caked and sweat-stained clothes, and crawl into bed. I rolled my bike back into the shed, then went around to the side of the house and lifted the lid from the trashcan. I dug one hand in my pocket and pulled out a fistful of dirt. I sifted through it . . . but there were no pull-tabs. Just clumps of black soil. I emptied my other pocket and arrived at the same conclusion: no aluminum pull-tabs, just dirt.

They must have fallen out of my pockets on the way back, I tried to convince myself. Yet a deeper part of me wondered if I'd picked them up at all. Had it all been some panic-stricken hallucination? Because surely—

—surely the lantern house hadn't turned *red*.

I pulled the pockets of my cargo shorts inside out and shook the remaining dirt onto the lawn. On the porch, I was careful not to make too much noise opening the door. I moved so slowly down the front hall that my calf muscles began to ache from the strain of it. I decided to skip the bathroom and went directly to my room. I peeled my shirt off and shucked my grimy shorts to the floor. Despite the humidity, I was shivering.

I climbed into bed and prayed to wake up and find that all of this had only been a terrible dream.

The next morning, a storm rolled in off the bay. It arrived as an armada of undulating black storm clouds advancing down the throat of the Chesapeake toward Kingsport. Lightning was visible in those clouds, flashing and pulsing like brain activity, and dispatching great rolling peals of thunder out over the city streets for what felt like hours. The air hummed with electricity, and the sky darkened and remained that way for two days. When the rains finally came, the tides rose, and all the inlets and marinas flooded. People lost their boats—they were stripped from their moorings and ferried out to sea, many of them never to be seen again, although a few would be discovered days later, smashed to bits along the sharp gray rocks at the base of the Gracie Point Lighthouse.

It was during this storm that a number of Kingsport's residents reported frogs falling from the sky. I did not witness this firsthand, although it was hard to deny the aftereffects: two days after the storm had come, it drifted back out into the bay and, presumably, out to the Atlantic Ocean, leaving the land sodden and wet and drowning beneath several inches of rainwater. Frogs were everywhere—they sat in tidy little heaps on our porch, croaking a chorus of doom, and clung to the trees in the yard. They sat on the hood of my father's car and swam in puddles in the gravel driveway. People claimed that frogs had smashed through the roofs of their garden sheds, had dented the hoods of their cars and cracked the transoms of their boats. Some had been spotted snared in birdfeeders hanging four feet off the ground. One of the cashiers at the supermarket would later claim that a fat green frog came straight down her chimney and plopped wetly into her fireplace, where it proceeded to leap about the living room until she whacked it with a broom out the back door and into the yard. Their eyes could be seen poking up from the water that now covered the land, hundreds of shiny little eyes, *thousands* of eyes, and when they felt the need to migrate from one place to another—for whatever dim reason animals have for abruptly changing location—they were seen hopping in an amphibious cavalcade, and it was as if the entire earth had come alive.

One ... two ... three ... four ... five ...

The old palm reader on Back Bay Road dragged a table to the edge of her property, where she sold dehydrated frogs for five bucks a pop. She had them laid out on that table like neckties, their bodies brown and twisted like beef jerky, their eyes sunken deep into the optical cavities in their skulls. She sat in a lawn chair sipping a tall glass of pink lemonade and waved like an animatronic to people who went by, her diaphanous, bejeweled headscarf rustling whenever a breeze dared to creep in over the dunes and funnel down the sand-dusted roadway.

It wasn't just the frogs. Once the storm receded, it left in its wake a frothing, crimson shoreline surrounding the entirety of Kingsport. A red tide, some of the old-timers called it, suggesting that the recent storm, in all its rage and mystery, had stirred up some sort of toxins from the sea floor, or perhaps some microscopic algae or some such nonsense. To me, the water looked like blood, and it dyed the sand along the shores a deep, arterial red. Dead fish washed up on the beaches in droves, mostly small perch and sunfish, but also rockfish, eels, and even a few snakeheads among them. People talked about fish of a more cryptic variety, too—a catfish with crab claws where its fins should be, and a water moccasin with a fully functioning head at both ends of its body. After only a day of baking in the sun, the smell of them became unbearable. People stayed away from the beaches and the marinas for days, not just because of the stink, but because of the flies that had amassed on the carcasses and blotted out the sun in thick, dizzying clouds. These dead fish brought the turkey vultures, too, and they could be seen hunkered in black, dusty heaps down in the dunes, picking and tearing at the carcasses—turkey vultures so black they looked like the absence of light, or like the shadows of other birds that had fled so fast they'd left their shadows behind on the sand. It looked like Armageddon down there.

Fishermen came back from a day on the water telling stories about the strange fish they'd hauled out of the bay—rockfish with extra sets of eyes peering out of their flanks; eels with two heads; a stingray whose underbelly appeared to suggest that of a human face, as if someone were *inside* that stingray, pressing their face against its white, fleshy belly. I heard one man who'd come to our house to seek my father's advice on a legal matter talk about catching a mermaid, only this was like no mermaid from any of the Disney cartoons or fairytales, he said—this one had a face like a skull and hair like seaweed, and as he hauled it out of the water on his fishing line, it took a swipe at him with a hand whose fingers were capped in black, serrated claws. Terrified, the man cut the line and let the thing drop back into the water, but not before it sprayed him with some viscous pink slime that immediately calcified along his arms and shirt the moment it struck him. My father had listened to this tale with his usual bout of skepticism—he wasn't prone to the superstitious, my father—but I found myself believing this man. All the more, when he lifted his T-shirt and showed me the trio of jagged cuts that had just begun to scab over along the left side of his flank. And then he brayed laughter, and patted me on the shoulder, indicating that this had all been some elaborate joke meant to spook me.

The most horrifying story I heard—the one that haunted me for nights afterward; the one I believed to be one hundred percent true—was from a veteran drunk and longtime childhood friend of my father's, a waterman named Finn Barber. He'd been drunk when he showed up swaying on our porch one afternoon, less than a week after Robert's death, his eyes bloodshot, his upper teeth—dentures, they looked like—gnawing at his peeling lower lip. My father ushered him into the house, poured him a cup of lukewarm Folger's, and then they sat for a while talking in low voices at the kitchen table. Well, it was mostly Finn Barber who did all the talking; my father was a listener by nature, and apparently so was I, because I crouched down in my bedroom doorway where I could listen to Barber's tale:

Earlier that morning, in the sharp, cool moments before dawn, as the watermen made their way to the docks, boarded their vessels, their traps and lines baited, and puttered out into the dark, empty bowl that was the Chesapeake Bay, just as the sun was beginning to cut a blood-red artery across the horizon, and with the Gracie Point Lighthouse still puncturing the darkness with its stately rotating beam, Finn Barber carved a white froth atop the water with his twenty-five-foot Parker outboard. He commenced working, first baiting a trotline and then beginning the arduous process of hoisting crab pots onto the boat's deck by himself. This was generally considered a two-man job, but Finn had grown accustomed to loneliness and hard work, and anyway, he didn't want to split the day's catch with anyone else. The blues scuttled over one another, their carapaces clicking like castanets—*chickety, chickety, chickety*. When he turned the pot on its side, shaking it above a plastic five-gallon bucket, some of the blues clung to the meshwork of the pot, while others hung from what remained of the yawning, milk-eyed catfish head wired down into the food well. Once the pot was emptied and those armored sea spiders were clicking their pincers and spewing bubbles from their mandibular plates inside that five-gallon bucket, Finn hoisted the pot back over the side of the boat and into the water, which was when he spied what looked like the corpse of a woman knocking resolutely against the hull of his boat. The corpse was floating face-up mere inches from the surface of the murky brown water, skin as pale as parchment, a fan of dark hair gliding over the sunken, sallow features. The body was dressed in some sort of white shroud, which Finn said reminded him of pictures of angels he'd seen in the bible when he was a boy. Being the curious, industrious fellow he was, Finn snatched up his grappling hook and plunged it into the water. He figured he'd hoist the corpse onto the boat, radio the police, and take the thing straight to shore. (His tone intimated that he'd hoped there might be a reward or something for his efforts, although he never came right out and said this to my father.) But just as he'd hooked the corpse under one arm, her eyes flipped open, and Finn shrieked. He dropped the grappling hook into the water, though his shock prevented him from moving away from the edge of the boat, or from even looking away from the horrid thing. And as Finn stared at it, the corpse bared its teeth, and *grimaced* at him, before sinking deeper below the murky surface of the water, until all that was left was a series of small bubbles and then nothing at all.

"It was the witch," I heard Finn Barber tell my father. He sounded very close to sobbing. "Ruth Graves. It was her corpse, swear on my mother, Ernie, only it was *alive*."

"Ruth Graves isn't dead," my father clarified for this man. "It was her son who died. You're getting confused, Finn."

Finn Barber pounded a fist on the kitchen table. "Don't tell me what I saw out there on the water, Ernie! You weren't there. It was *her*. The Kingsport witch."

My father talked to him for a while longer, then drove him home. When he returned, it was well into the evening, and I was in the kitchen cooking up some grilled cheese sandwiches for dinner on the stove. My father carried in a stack of legal documents and sat at the kitchen table. I asked him if he wanted a beer, but he said no.

I had just flipped the sandwiches over in the pan when I heard a knock at the front door. "I'll get it," said my father, slowly ratcheting himself up from the table. I listened to his footfalls plod down the hall, heard the front door squeal open. Some muted talk, and I thought maybe it was crazy, drunk Finn Barber come back. But when I turned from the stove and glanced behind me, I saw Ruth Graves standing in the doorway of the kitchen, partially cloaked in the shadows of the hallway.

I just stared at her—at her tight, sober face and those tar-black, probing eyes. My throat suddenly felt tight and I could feel the hairs on the back of my neck stand up.

She's come for me! I thought, terrified. *She knows what we've done and she's come for me!*

My father appeared beside her. "We'll be in my office for a bit, Andrew."

As she moved down the hall after my father, her eyes widened the slightest bit, so that the lights of the chandelier over the kitchen table reflected in her pupils. I could see it clearly, and it was like watching her eyes light up from the inside.

My knees went weak at the sound of my father's office door closing. *She knows and she's going to tell him what we've done.* A moment later, and I could smell the smoke from that night, that sentient cloud drifting over the old Ribbon Road along Gracie Point, burning my sinuses and causing my eyes to water. My right eye suddenly burned, too, and it set my nerves further on edge. I hurried to the bathroom and examined my face in the mirror. Aside from the grief-stricken terror I saw staring back at me, I looked otherwise normal.

She knows and she's telling him everything she saw that night . . .

I returned to the kitchen to find the sandwiches burning in the pan.

Fifteen minutes later, Ruth Graves reappeared, my father leading her down the hallway toward the door with one hand against the small of her back. When she'd gone and my father had returned to the kitchen, he went to the refrigerator and took out a beer after all. He seemed heavier somehow when he settled back down in his seat. I tried to read the expression on his face, to determine what he now knew about me and what I'd done, but I couldn't. My father's face was impassive.

"Why was she here?" I asked, mustering enough courage to speak.

"She just needed someone to listen." He was wearing his reading glasses now, which he did whenever he worked. It made him look older than he was.

"About her son?"

"She doesn't trust the police. She doesn't think what happened to her son was an accident."

"But he just fell," I said, as if to drive this point home.

"Autopsy report came back. Official cause of death was asphyxiation due to drowning."

I felt a pair of invisible hands slowly tighten around my throat. Suddenly, in my head, I could hear Tig shouting, *He's still alive down there! He's still alive!*

"According to police, he went out there to light off some fireworks—cops found evidence of that at the scene—and happened to injure himself. Looks like one of those fireworks went off and struck him in the face. The jolt of it sent him over the cliff, where he hit those rocks below. According to the coroner, he broke his neck in the fall but was still alive and breathing until the tide came in and drowned him."

In my head, Tig was still screaming, and I was watching over and over again as Robert's mouth came open in a futile gasp for air . . .

"I'm telling you this so you can see how something that seems harmless and maybe a good time can turn into big trouble if you're not careful, Andrew." And then he said something that made my blood turn to ice: "Ruth Graves said she saw a white pickup truck that night outside their house, shooting off fireworks. She said her son went to confront whoever it was. She said she didn't want him to go, but that he went anyway. She told this to the police, but she said they didn't follow up on any of it."

"Oh," I uttered, my voice barely above a whisper. I felt my stomach tightening into a fist. Suddenly, the smell of that burned toasted bread was making me ill. "What are you gonna do?" I managed to ask. "About helping her, I mean."

"There's nothing I *can* do. I think she just needed an ear."

"People say she's a witch."

"Don't let that old drunk's story spook you, Andrew," he said, referring to the crazy drunken tale I'd heard Finn Barber relay earlier that afternoon.

"Not just him," I said. "People have always said it. They say she talks to birds and casts spells on the town. All the weird stuff that's been happening lately…" I trailed off, not wanting to sound like a frightened child. "I mean, why would she come to *you* for help? Do you know her that well?"

My father removed his reading glasses, set them on the table, then pinched the reddened bridge of his nose. "No, Andrew, I don't know her that well at all. The Graves family has lived in this town for generations, but they have always kept to themselves. In fact, Kingsport used to be called Graves, but that was before my time. I've come across it when doing some real estate research for a client years ago."

"What happened?"

My father hoisted one shoulder in a lazy suggestion of a shrug. "What usually happens, I guess," he said. "Industry came to the shore, developers started buying up the land, putting condos and beach houses and gas stations on them. Pretty soon, the Graves family were nothing more than a house out there in the middle of nowhere. The house was like a commune back then, the whole Graves clan living there. There was some legal wrangling over the property by some of the developers and the county, and even some . . . well, let's say nefarious attempts at driving the Graves family out of that house, and out of town for good."

"They wanted everything *and* the house, too?" I didn't truly know who the *they* were in my comment, but I imagined some faceless, greedy thing in a suit with hands like bear traps, snapping.

"Greed breeds greed," said my dad. "Anyway, after a time, most of the family died off, until it was only Ruth living out there on her own. I guess those developers and county folks figured it was only a waiting game at that point. But then she had those kids, someone to pass the house onto. A lineage, you know? And now the Graves family just *are*, and no one really bothers with them anymore."

"What about Ruth Graves's husband? I mean, the father of her kids?"

Again, my dad shrugged. "Never knew anything about a husband or father. Some ignorant fools like to spread rumors, say there never *was* a father, that Ruth Graves simply witched those two kids into existence all on her own. Not only because she'd grown lonely in that old house all by herself, but to keep it in the family once she was gone."

"I've heard people say that those kids aren't really kids at all, and she made two of her creepy dolls come to life."

My dad sighed. He looked instantly exhausted. "Listen, Andrew, I know what people say about Ruth Graves and her kids. Someone acts differently, they're shunned. They become outcasts. People make up stories about them, mostly because those people are dim-witted and mean, but sometimes it's because it makes it easier to hate someone if you believe they're a monster. That's just the way it is. Small-town life can be like that sometimes. And I hear what people are saying about Ruth Graves now, after what's happened to her son, and what people like our friend Finn Barber claims to have seen out in the bay. A witch's curse."

"Yeah," I heard myself say.

"But that woman's no witch. Her daughter is just a little girl. Her son is—*was*—just a regular teenage boy, just like you."

I felt something like a white-hot sewing needle press against the muscle of my heart.

"She homeschooled those kids, kept them cooped up in that house, because Ruth Graves has become distrustful of folks, and maybe she's even grown a little crazy because of it over the years. Maybe that's just what happens to someone when strangers come in and take what belongs to them. Sometimes it's not a single dramatic incident that ostracizes someone, but a lifetime of small differences." He pointed to the charred sandwiches in the trash.

"Sorry. I can make some more."

He waved a hand at me. "Not hungry."

I leaned against the counter, that needling sensation still piercing my heart. I was terrified by the thought that if my father looked at me—looked directly into my eyes—he would know the truth without me having to speak a word.

"I hear what people are saying now," my father continued. "That Ruth Graves, in her grief, cast a curse over this town. Punishing this town for letting her boy die, and for saying it was just an accident."

"Why doesn't she believe it was an accident?"

"Because grief is a funny thing, Andrew."

"What do *you* think?"

He seemed to consider this, his eyes searching for truth on some distant horizon. After a time, he said, "I don't really know, Andrew. But if it *wasn't* an accident, then I feel for Ruth, because I know this town, and she's right—the truth will stay buried." He smiled wearily at me. "Sometimes, unfortunately, that's the cost of living in a small town."

Something struck the window over the sink. The suddenness of it caused me to jump, and I twisted around to face the window. A second thump followed, reverberating against the glass, and this time I caught a glimpse of a pair of fluttery wings out there in the dark.

I took a step back, my eyes glued to the greasy smear of small white feathers imprinted on the windowpane.

"What was that?" my father said, looking past me at the window.

"A bird," I said. "A bird hit the window. Two of them, I think. I saw—"

There came another muted thump from deeper in the house . . . and then another. And another. It sounded like a barrage of fists pounding against the windows all throughout the house. When another bird struck the window over the sink, I happened to see it—the frenzied beating of wings, there one second, gone the next, leaving behind a streak of blood on the windowpane.

My father rose from his chair and hurried out into the hall. I quickly followed; it felt like we were under gunfire and I did not want to be left in that kitchen alone in the event one of those birds came bursting through the glass.

From the hall, we could both see the slurry of birds on the other side of the living room windows, a tornado of them, suicidal in their shared madness, hurling themselves over and over at the glass. The sound was like someone pummeling a punching bag, only my dad and I were *inside* the punching bag, and I brought my fists up to my ears in an effort to blot out the sound.

It could have lasted five seconds, it could have lasted five minutes: I would never be sure. But once it was done, the silence that simmered throughout the house sounded like the silence after an earthquake—an eerie, cottony thickness that seemed to fill your head with gas.

My dad went down into the living room and right up to the windows that looked out onto the backyard. The birds had struck the glass with such force, they had imprinted themselves on it, a design that looked almost deliberate. Feathers were stuck to the windows, along with smoke-dark beads of blood. A few hairline cracks ran the length of some of the windows, too, and my father went to one of these cracks and ran a thumb down the length of it.

"Oh. Some are still alive." My voice sounded hoarse and insubstantial to my ears. When my father turned and looked at me, I pointed beyond the sliding glass door, to where some of the birds twitched and flopped on the concrete patio.

When my dad went back out into the hall and tromped down to the front door, I called after him, asked where he was going.

"Outside to have a look," he said.

"Don't."

"Andrew, it's okay. It's over."

"What *was* it?"

My father didn't have an answer for that. Instead, he opened the front door and stepped outside into the night. I hurried after him, followed him down the porch steps . . . then paused when I saw how the dark ground fluttered and flapped. I didn't want to go down there. I couldn't walk through that morass of dead and nearly dead birds.

My father must have sensed my apprehension. He told me to stay on the porch as he went down the steps and crossed in front of the house. He was staring at the ground, and at the random scatter of small birds whose wings whipped at his ankles.

The E. LARIMER, ATTORNEY-AT-LAW shingle swung on its chains in the breeze, making a bird's squawk sound which sent me down those steps, hopping over those dead and dying birds, and rushing up to my father's side. I felt childish, having been spooked in such a fashion, but my father said nothing about it. He was too busy examining the cracked windowpanes, the feathers stuck to the glass, the tiny smudges of blood here and there, like some sort of coded message left behind for us to figure out.

My father crouched down and examined one of the dead birds at his feet. It was small, with mottled black-and-white feathers and a yellow apron along its breast.

"These are meadowlarks," said my father. "I don't think I've ever seen one around here, let alone a whole flock."

"Why did they do that? Why did they hit the house like that?"

My father didn't respond for a long time. Finally, when he stood, he mumbled something about radar signals from the Naval Academy in Annapolis messing with the birds' migratory patterns, or maybe something about high-voltage power lines or wind farms. Whatever it was, I knew he had no idea; that he was trying to rationalize this for himself, not provide any answers for me. What answers could there be?

I looked around at all those dead meadowlarks lying in the grass, or snared in the branches of bushes, and how my dad had just stood there with his hands on his hips, attempting to digest it all, to understand it all, the pragmatic man he'd been all his life. It was in that moment that I nearly told him what had happened and what we had done . . . and why he might actually be wrong about Ruth Graves and her ability to curse this town and all the people in it. But instead, I cried. And much like the barrage of birds striking our house, my sudden tears confounded him.

"Hey," he said, very softly. "Hey."

He slung an arm around me, drew me close to him. Maybe he thought something about the birds had frightened me to tears, because he never asked what had upset me so badly. And then the moment passed, and I never again considered telling him anything about what had really caused me to cry.

iv

In the fall of 2010, a woman named Trudy Loman went on a blind date with a man who had recently graduated from the police academy. He was young and handsome, with the type of athletic body Trudy appreciated. He was also surprisingly modest and self-aware for someone so good-looking—a rare combo, in Trudy's limited experience.

They had a nice dinner at an Italian restaurant in Stevensville (she smiled to herself when she saw the sign that read Love Point Road, wondering if that might be a good omen), and then they talked for hours while sharing a bottle of Chianti.

At one point during the conversation, Trudy, who was still in her early twenties and had never known anyone who'd been a police officer, asked this man if he really believed he could draw his gun and kill another human being.

"Absolutely," said the man, without hesitation. Then he added: "It's not the killing that's the trouble, I would think, but the mess that follows."

PART THREE

THE LITTLE GIRL
FOUND ...
... AND THE SICK ROSE

SIXTEEN

E ric picked me up that evening at the train station in Baltimore. I was already exhausted, not just from the stress of going back to Kingsport and all that would inevitably entail, but in having to lie again about where I was going and what I was doing to Rebecca. Before stepping off the train, I unscrewed my wedding band from my finger and looped it onto my keychain for safe keeping this time.

Eric's car was idling against the curb across the street from the train station when I stepped outside. It was the jade-green Toyota Corolla with a dent in the rear passenger-side bumper. As I approached, Eric leaned over the passenger seat and shoved open the door for me.

It was a ninety-minute drive from the train station in Baltimore to Kingsport, give or take. Eric did nearly all of the talking.

The night before, Eric had been jarred from sleep by a pounding on his front door. Actually, Eric's *wife* had heard the pounding, and she had shaken him awake. He pulled on a pair of cargo shorts, tugged a T-shirt over his head, then crept downstairs without turning on any lights. There was a vertical strip of window glass beside the front door, covered with a sheer curtain; Eric turned on the outdoor porch light, peeled back the curtain. His late-night visitor was Meach.

Eric opened the door, but he didn't invite Meach inside. Instead, he stepped out onto the porch, and gave him the once over. Meach was dripping wet and streaked with mud. His feet were bare and fresh rivulets of blood trickled down his shins, as if he'd run through a field of thorn bushes.

"What happened to you?" he asked Meach. "What are you doing here?"

It wasn't the first time Meach had shown up on Eric's front porch in the middle of the night, unannounced. Usually he was high or drunk (or both), but tonight, regardless of whatever poison he may have had buzzing through his veins, he looked as sober as a judge. Frightened, even.

Meach said, "I found her."

Eric didn't need to ask for clarification.

They drove all the way out to the sharp bend at the height of the old Ribbon Road, where the Gracie Point Lighthouse was visible in the clear, cloudless night. Meach was a live wire in the passenger seat, sitting bolt upright, hands on his knees, his eyes wide and scanning the darkness that lay ahead of them. He smelled of the bay, that brackish, salt-rich aroma, vaguely fishy, and Eric cracked a window while he drove.

"How did you find her?" he asked Meach.

Meach turned his head away, gazing intently at the darkness beyond the passenger window. He gnawed ravenously on his lower lip.

"Goddamn it, Meach. Tell me how you found her."

"Robert led me. It's what he's been wanting me to find all along."

"Look at me."

Reluctantly, Meach turned and stared at him.

"What are you on right now? Don't lie to me."

"Just some weed. A few beers earlier." Meach kept staring at him with those wide, almost childlike eyes, and Eric could sense desperation—hopelessness—coming off him in waves. Fear, too. Finally, Meach turned away again, and stared back out at the darkness. "I know you think I'm fucked up, Eric. That I'm losing my mind. I'm sorry you think that. I'm sorry you can't see this for what it is."

He felt a pang of pity for Meach, the idiot, in that moment. He said, "I think we're all just under a lot of stress."

"You've seen him, too," Meach said. It was a statement, not a question. "We all have. I know it's true, even if you don't want to talk about it. Even if you won't admit it to yourself. Robert's come back. He's coming for us, and he's getting stronger. He *knows* things."

"Cut it out, Meach."

"There's some endgame here, and it's all about the curse. It's all about revenge. We can't fix what we did, but maybe we can—"

"I said shut the fuck up, Meach."

He went silent, his whole body stiff in the passenger seat of Eric's car.

When they got to the place where Meach said he had scaled down the side of the cliff earlier that night, Eric parked along the shoulder. He unlatched the glove compartment, took out a heavy-duty Maglite, and then they both got out of the car. It was slightly cooler out here, high on the bluff above Kingsport and the bay. Out in the distance—in what could have been outer space, for all its black, bleak openness—stood the Gracie Point Lighthouse, its beacon rotating indefinitely within its lantern room. As they crossed the road, the low, mournful moan of a foghorn sounded somewhere out along the water.

They arrived together at the edge of the cliff. Eric peered over the side, and felt a fleeting vertiginous sway overtake him. It was a good thirty feet to the bottom, maybe more, although it looked like there was nothing but sand and surf directly below. Slightly farther up, along the bend, was where Robert Graves had gone over. Eric looked in that direction now, and despite the darkness, could make out the biting, angular shapes of the rocks where Robert, all those years ago, had fallen to his death. Something about the symmetry of all this made Eric think this was all a bad trip on Meach's part— that he had something more sinister than booze and marijuana shuttling through his system, and he was getting the past and the present confused.

"The lifeline is only in my dreams or visions or whatever they are," Meach explained, though to Eric, it only confounded him further. "In real life, though, you gotta use rocks and roots and stuff to get down."

Meach proceeded to climb over the edge of the cliff, but Eric gripped him about the forearm, yanking him back onto solid ground. "You'll break your fucking neck going down like that."

"I've been doing it for weeks," Meach protested, and then he did what Eric considered to be a curious thing: he looked down at the palms of his hands. They were filthy, streaked with muck and grime, the fingernails practically black. But there were also lacerations crisscrossing his palms, and they looked fresh.

Eric clicked on the Maglite, directing its beam down the road in the direction they had driven. The old Ribbon Road rose gradually until it reached the zenith of Gracie Point. But in the opposite direction, the height was less dramatic, and Eric knew there was a path worn through the side of the cliff that made traversing down to the bottom less treacherous than trying to scale the wall this far up.

"Come on," he said, and began marching in that direction.

Meach came up behind him, his bare feet slapping along the ground. "She's back that way."

Eric ignored him. When they reached the section of the bluff where the path wound down to the beach below, Eric went first. It was still a steep descent, but he'd done it before when chasing teenagers away from the beach at night, and he was careful to keep the flashlight trained on the ground ahead of him so that he wouldn't trip over anything.

When they reached the bottom, Eric's sneakers sank into the soft, wet sand at the shoreline. The tide was up, and foam clung to the rocks up ahead. Eric shined the flashlight in that direction and could see a set of footprints—likely Meach's from earlier, he surmised—running along the beach until they vanished into the surf.

"Come on, I'll show you," Meach said, sprinting ahead of Eric, his bare feet kicking up fans of wet sand.

Eric followed at a more cautious pace, pausing only when he realized Meach was moving deeper into the surf to avoid the outcrop of jagged black rocks where Robert had fallen to his death. Beyond, Eric could make out what appeared to be a narrow opening in the face of the cliff: the slender, nearly imperceptible entrance to a cave. It was in that direction Meach was headed.

He followed Meach through the surf, which was cold enough at this time of night to cause an ache in his ears, the tide rising up to mid-shin. He did his best to maneuver around that outcrop of rocks, much as Meach had, but smaller, sharper ones were submerged beneath the surf, and Eric felt them slicing and poking the exposed flesh of his shins.

"Meach! Goddamn it, wait for me!"

Up ahead, Meach slipped into the narrow opening of the cave.

"I thought he was high on something, that I'd follow him into that cave and find a wadded-up bed sheet or a jumble of litter, something that he'd twisted around in his head to think was a body," Eric said. We were still driving through the darkness toward Kingsport. He glanced at me, his face illuminated in the glow of the dashboard lights, and that look on his face said all there was to say about what Matthew Meacham had found in that cave. But then his expression changed, and he said, "What was that thing you said over the phone about the cellar in your dad's house?"

I shifted sweatily in the passenger seat. "It's nothing. There's been a smell, that's all. Like something had died down there. I let my mind get carried away."

His eyes hung on me a moment too long, perhaps assessing the truthfulness of what I'd just said. Then he redirected his gaze toward the road and continued his story.

About twenty feet inside the cave, there was a body wrapped in a sheet of heavy-duty industrial plastic. Eric could tell it was a body by the shape of the thing inside that partially transparent plastic sheet. But also: a pale, slender leg poked out, the skin mottled and bluish gray. There were chunks taken out of the flesh along the calf, and a few of the toes had been chewed down to the bone by sea creatures.

"This . . . is what Robert . . . wanted me to find," Meach said, breathlessly. He leaned forward with his hands on his knees, sucking down great gasps of air, and staring at the thing wrapped in plastic.

The inside of the cave teemed with flies; Eric swatted them away, then shined the flashlight around the cramped interior of the cave. Tiny crabs raised their claws menacingly from just beneath the surface of the water as the light washed over them, but as Eric waded through the water in their direction, they sank down into the murk and then bolted in various directions.

"I know it's her, I don't even need to see her face," Meach was saying. "But should we open her up? Like, unwrap her? Have a look to be sure?"

"Don't touch anything, Meach."

Eric repositioned the light. Minnows were nibbling on flecks of greasy flesh floating in the water. The crabs were already returning, their pincers pulling and tearing, stuffing tufted particles into their segmented mandibles.

Jesus Christ, Dale, Eric thought.

"I mean, it's *her,* right?"

"How did you know she was in here?"

"I told you, goddamn it," Meach said. "Robert led me here. With the lifeline."

Eric redirected the flashlight to shine it on the shape beneath the plastic sheet, half submerged in the water.

"I know you think I'm nuts, Eric. I know you think I'm a fucking mess—"

"I just need you to shut up for right now, Meach."

"—but here she is. I'm *not* nuts. And now you gotta believe all the stuff I've been saying."

Eric turned the flashlight on Meach, causing him to turn his head and hide his eyes behind one arm. "That's really your statement to me? That some ghost led you here?"

"Whatever he is," Meach said, hands still shielding his eyes, "I'm not sure he's just some ghost."

Eric lowered the flashlight and stepped deeper into the cave. He was shining the flashlight around the dark crevices between the rocks along the ground now, searching for anything important that might have washed up back there. Anything the murderer—Dale—might have left behind.

"Hey, Meach," he said, and when Meach didn't immediately look at him or respond, Eric snapped his fingers to collect his attention.

The sound echoed throughout the cave. "Why don't you head back to the beach, wait for me there?"

Meach frowned. "I want to stay here. I want to see her."

"I know, but your feet are all cut up and they're bleeding over a crime scene, buddy. Go stand out there."

Meach glanced down at the soles of his feet, then trudged back out into the night without further protest.

Eric took a step closer to the body, his wet sneakers balanced precariously on a ridge of uneven rocks. Something black and slimy got spooked by him, and slithered off into the water, soundless as smoke. Eric considered the situation for a moment, running over all the potential hazards of what had been laid out before him against what he might do. In the end, he decided to unwrap the body and get rid of the plastic sheet.

"Wait," I said, interjecting on his story for the first time since he'd started telling it. "I mean, giving me that file was bad enough, but now you're telling me you've implicated yourself in this whole—"

"I needed to do it, Andrew." His voice was unnervingly calm. We were driving over the Bay Bridge now, a vast expanse of black nothingness far below us. "Wrapped in a sheet, it's homicide. Dale would be standing before a judge in no time, especially if that fucking sheet came from his house or one of his construction sites. Damn thing probably had his fingerprints all over it. But a body down there on its own . . . I mean, she could have wandered drunk over the cliff, fell into the bay, and just washed up, right? Plenty of witnesses saw her drinking down at The Rat that night, acting weird."

"That was risky," I said. "What if you unwrapped that sheet and found that she's got a bullet hole in the center of her forehead?"

"That's not what I found," Eric said.

—◇—

Eric propped the flashlight between two large stones, then inched his way through the water toward the body. Minnows flashed like lightning bolts around his ankles. He looked around for a clear section of the sheet that he could peel away, and when he found one, he tugged at it gently. That single exposed foot rocked rigidly in the surf. Unhurried, he unrolled what was inside, careful not to jostle the remains too much, for fear they might come apart and drift all over the place. He knew damn well what happens to a body that's been submerged in water for over a week, and he didn't want to start chasing body parts through the surf.

When he was done and the plastic sheet lay in a heap on the rocks nearby, Eric found himself standing above the remains of a murdered woman. She wore a flimsy floral dress, cut at the knee, with thin shoulder straps. It might have been a bright, festive yellow at one time, but the brackish, unforgiving waters of the Chesapeake Bay had bleached it to a colorless tallow hue. Her flesh was gray and peeling, and when one of Eric's Nikes accidently brushed along one arm, the skin sloughed off in a semitransparent sheet, drawing the crabs out of their hiding places to gobble it up in bits.

"My God, Dale," he said, shaking his head.

It was Cynthia Walls, all right. Eric could tell it was her, even though her face had begun to decompose, the blade of a cheekbone thrusting up through torn flesh along the right side of her face. Her eyes were gone, feasted upon by the things that lurked in the darkest depths of the bay. Her hair swayed like fronds in the surf, still a stunning gold, still somehow alive, despite the rest of her.

Eric took another step toward the body, and crouched down near the head. He trained the flashlight on a section of scalp, and in that harsh, unforgiving circle of light, he could see a grotesque dent in the upper portion of her skull, where her forehead met her hairline. The bone had broken and there was a ragged cut along one edge of the crater. Blunt force trauma.

After some deliberation, Eric collected the sheet of plastic off the rocks, folded it over and over until it was no bigger than a hardback book, and then he tucked it under his arm. He headed back out of the cave, grateful to be away from the smell and the buzzing curtain of flies.

Meach was sitting in the wet sand, the foamy surf lapping at his bare feet, as Eric approached him. A gentle rain had begun to fall, cool against their grimy, sweat-sticky flesh. Meach looked up at Eric with bleary eyes, then glanced down at the sheet beneath Eric's arm.

Without saying a word, Eric extended a hand to Meach, and Meach took it. He hoisted Meach out of the sand, and then they proceeded to climb back up the side of the cliff toward the road together in mutual silence.

At the car, Eric dumped the plastic sheet in the trunk. Then he went around to the passenger side, yanked open the door, and told Meach to get in. The drizzle had turned to rain by the time Eric went around to the driver's side and climbed in behind the wheel.

They just sat there in the quiet darkness for the length of several heartbeats.

"We need to get your story straight," Eric eventually told him. "No more talk about Robert. No more talk about curses or ghosts or witches, Meach. You were down here tonight because you *often* come down here. You look for junk on the beach. You come down here to smoke dope where no one will bother you."

Meach just stared at him from the passenger seat. His eyes were rimmed in red and the muddy streaks on his face looked as prominent as war paint.

"You went into that cave because you know random junk sometimes washes up in there. But when you went inside, you saw a woman's body."

"Just her foot," Meach said. "I only saw her foot at first. But I knew what it was. I knew *who* she was."

"Not a foot, Meach," Eric said. "You saw her whole body, lying there in the water, on the rocks."

Meach shook his head. "I didn't. She was wrapped up in a plastic sheet."

Eric gave Meach a sad little smile. "There was no plastic sheet, Meach."

"Jesus Christ, Eric, I *saw*—"

"Listen to me," Eric said, leaning closer to Meach. He even put a set of fingers on Meach's shoulder. "There. Was. No. Sheet. Do you understand me, Meach? Do you understand?"

Whether Matthew Meacham understood or not, the point was clear. Numbly, he nodded his head, and Eric Kelly retracted his fingers from his childhood friend's shoulder.

"Let's consider this your official statement," Eric said, and then he cranked over the ignition.

"What about her?" Meach asked, peering with those wet, sloppy eyes past Eric and beyond the cliff. Straight out to the lighthouse, perhaps. "We can't just leave her down there."

"I'm gonna call it in as soon as we go over your statement a few more times."

Eric watched Meach swallow a lump of spit that made his Adam's apple jump, and then he heard something click dryly in his throat. "You know I always listen to you, Eric. At least, I try to. But this is different, man. He's already very angry at us. He wanted me to find her, and I did, so now we gotta do what's right—"

"We're doing it, Meach," Eric said, his voice impeccably calm.

"We're doing all the things. Don't you worry about it, Meach-Man. You just keep listening to me."

Meach's eyes shifted from the darkness beyond the cliff back over to Eric. "Okay," he said finally, and then turned his head away, as if ashamed.

"Anyway," Eric continued, "Meach and I went over his story a few times, I took an official statement, and then I radioed it in. I went that night to inform Dale, too. And to try to talk to him about what the hell really happened."

"How did he react?"

"That's why I got you back here, Andrew. He wouldn't say anything to me. He's terrified. He's losing his mind and he's about to crack."

"Can an autopsy tell if that blunt force trauma happened from a fall over those cliffs or, say, a hammer?"

"A good examiner can, probably. The body went to the OCME in Baltimore, so we should know more in the next day or so." He reached down between the driver's seat and the center console and produced a manila folder. He tossed it in my lap and said, "You okay looking at stuff like that?"

"Stuff like what?" I said, opening the folder, and seeing a color photo of Cynthia Walls's decomposing corpse partially submerged in water, surrounded by black, glossy rocks. The police lights made her look garish, the floral yellow dress nearly translucent. The angle of her head reminded me of birds with their necks broken, and I was suddenly thinking of the summer of 2003, and the immediate aftermath of Robert's death—the night all those meadowlarks threw themselves at our house and died with their necks broken in our yard.

"How the hell do you think Meach really found her?" Eric asked. "You think he was involved somehow?"

"Meach? No, Eric, I don't think he's involved in this. Come on."

"Then what was he doing wandering around in some cave in the middle of the night? How'd he know she was there?"

"He thinks he's on some quest."

"Yeah," Eric muttered, "from beyond the grave. But that doesn't explain how he knew where to go."

I turned to the second photo, a close-up of Cynthia's face. The dent in the upper portion of her skull was just as Eric had described it—a severe indentation with a dark red laceration around one half of it. The skin was mottled and nearly blue. There was a cut on her cheek, too—bloodless, but I could glimpse a hint of bone protruding.

"Maybe he didn't," I said. "Maybe he just stumbled upon her by accident."

"That's not the crazy bullshit story he told me."

I closed the folder and looked at him. "Do you believe him? That he had some . . . I don't know . . . precognition that her body was in that cave? I mean, the location where she was found, and Meach of all people being the one to find her."

His eyes flicked briefly in my direction then returned to the road. "I don't believe in that stuff," he said.

"It just feels weird to me," I said, and turned to look out the window.

"Just let me handle this," Eric said. "I'm taking you straight to Dale's tonight. You need to pump him on the details of what exactly happened that night. And for the record, I didn't tell him about the plastic sheet. Far as he knows, Meach found her body in the cave. I never mentioned anything about a plastic sheet and neither did Dale when I told him about her."

"Why lie to him? He obviously knows he wrapped her up in it."

"Andrew, you think I want that guy having any more dirt on me? There was no sheet." The muscles in Eric's jaw tightened as he shook his head. "That stupid fucking imbecile. What a mess he's made."

I sat there for a while in silence, considering all that Eric had told me. "That thing Meach said to you—he said you'd seen Robert, too. That even if you didn't want to believe it, you've already seen him. What'd he mean by that?"

"I told you," Eric said, eyes on the road, "Meach is out of his mind."

"But have you?" I asked him. "I don't mean seeing ghosts. I mean, I guess . . . have you been seeing anything strange lately?"

"Like what? Bigfoot? Aliens?"

"It just feels weird being back here," I said, although I knew I had been feeling strange even back in New York, before I'd ever gotten the phone call from Dale. I'd told Rebecca it was nothing more than nerves, that I was stressed out about becoming a father. I'd even managed to make myself believe that, despite the increasing sense of guilt and deceit that kept swelling up inside me. Did I believe in ghosts and witches' curses? No, I did not. Yet had I been experiencing small, intimate confusions that I couldn't rationally explain? I couldn't deny that. And I couldn't deny that they had only gotten stronger the closer we came to the twenty-year anniversary of Robert's death.

Without looking at me, Eric said, "You need to keep your head screwed on, Andrew. Don't let Meach or anyone else spook you. You're smarter than that."

"I'm just saying, what are the odds that Cynthia's body is found right around where Robert died, and that *Meach* of all people happened to find—"

"Stop. Do you hear me? Stop." He glanced at me, then back at the road. "Don't let Meach poison your mind with his bullshit. It's bad enough he's been freaking out Dale and Tig. Keep your head clear. You and I are the only ones who stand a chance of making this go away."

I knew he was right, but it made me feel cold and empty, nonetheless. Frightened, even, if I was being honest.

"Keep your shit together, Andrew," he warned me. "Remember: this isn't a ghost story."

SEVENTEEN

It was close to midnight by the time we pulled into that eerie ghost town of a development that Dale had abandoned mid-construction. His was the only lighted house in the entire cul-de-sac, looking like a moon-base all the way out here in the middle of nowhere. I was exhausted, I wanted a cigarette and to crawl into bed—my own bed, back home—but I knew I wouldn't be able to sleep without confronting Dale. Moreover, I wasn't too enthused about returning to my father's house, with its fetid stink and its buzzing circus of flies. I was already planning on finding a motel out by the highway.

Eric said, "Shit."

He rolled the steering wheel and parked us alongside the curb.

"What's wrong?"

"Tig's here." He nodded toward a banged-up Jeep Wrangler with a COEXIST bumper sticker parked beside Dale's Navigator in the driveway.

"She doesn't know, does she?"

"She knows the body's been found. The whole town knows by now. If she knows anything beyond that, I can't say."

We got out and went to the front door. Eric rapped his knuckles on it.

Tig answered. She didn't look surprised to see either one of us standing there on the other side of the doorway.

"Hey," she said, stepping aside. "Come in."

Dale was in the living room, reclining on the red sofa. He had his head back, his fingers tangled in his hair like he was giving himself a scalp massage. There was a bottle of Laphroaig single malt on the glass table in front of him, along with a couple of half empty lowball glasses, and what looked like the last remaining slice of a microwave pizza.

"Hello, Dale," Eric said, coming up behind me.

Dale dropped his hands in his lap and leaned forward on the sofa. He hung his head for a moment, then stood and faced us.

"Jesus, Dale," I heard myself say. "What happened?"

He had a twist of bloody Kleenex curling out from his left nostril and some dried blood smeared along his left cheek. There was a constellation of dark red spots on the front of his powder blue polo shirt, too. When he plucked the Kleenex from his nose, I got a better look at the pasty, haggard expression on his face. The wet, messy eyes, the signs that he'd been crying, the uncombed hair standing up in corkscrews.

"I ran into a wall," he said. "Yeah, that old excuse. But it's true."

"Where's your son?"

"He's staying with my sister in Odenton until this whole thing blows over."

Until this whole thing blows over? Did Dale Walls actually grasp the severity of his situation?

Tig came out of the kitchen carrying two more glasses. She brought them over to the glass table, uncorked the bottle of scotch, and began to pour—

"I'm not drinking," Eric said.

"None for me, either, thanks," I told her.

"Oh." She stopped pouring and looked up at us. Surprised, almost. She re-corked the bottle and set it back down on the coffee table. Then she picked up the glass with the half-pour and downed it.

"What about Bonnie?" Eric asked her. "Where's she tonight?"

"At home. With a sitter." Tig frowned. "What's with the third degree, you guys?"

"It's late, Antigone," he said. "I'm going to drive you home. We'll take your Jeep." He tossed me his own car keys. "Andrew, you take my car, get it back to me tomorrow."

Tig came up behind Dale, put a hand on his back. Dale had been staring gloomily down at the bloody tissue he was pinching between his thumb and index finger, but jerked his head up at her touch, as if suddenly spooked by her presence. I could see red, threadlike blood vessels networked across the sallow pits of his cheeks, circumnavigating the slightly swollen tip of his nose.

"I don't want to leave him alone tonight," she said. "Not tonight."

Dale exhaled a shuddery breath. I saw his eyes begin to fill up with tears again.

"He won't be alone," Eric said. "Andrew will be with him. They need to talk. In private."

I tried to read her face, tried to see how much she already knew, how much Dale had told her. But her expression was characteristically stoic. I thought about how our friendship and our budding teenage romance had been cut short because of what happened that night, and how it was something we had never been able to get back. How she had remained cold and distant to me ever since.

Tig folded her arms across her chest. Hugged herself, as if she'd grown instantly cold. "All right," she said quite simply, her voice barely above a whisper. Then she leaned over and kissed Dale on the cheek. "I'll check in with you tomorrow."

Dale smiled wanly, rubbed her arm. His voice sounding far away, he said, "Thanks for always looking out for me, Tig."

Without another word, Tig marched right between Eric and me, snatched her car keys off the dining room table, and stalked outside. I waited for her Jeep to start before speaking, so that I knew she was out of earshot.

"Does she know?" I asked Dale.

"Everybody knows," Dale said. He folded his arms and leaned back against the sofa. That red streak of dried blood smeared along his cheek looked like the fiery contrail of a comet.

"I don't mean that she's dead. I mean about how she died."

Dale's eyes sprung up at me. For the first time since I'd walked through his front door tonight, he looked alert. "Christ. Christ, Andrew. No. Jesus Christ. You think I want Tig to think . . . think that of *me* . . . ?"

A single sob found its way out of his throat; he pressed a hand to his mouth to contain it, and hung his head, but not before I saw his eyes filling with tears again.

"We'll talk tomorrow," Eric said, and then he was gone, too.

I went to the front windows and waited for Tig's Wrangler to pull out of the driveway and turn out of the development before I turned back to readdress Dale.

He was sitting on the sofa again, leaning forward over the coffee table. He had one of the lowball glasses of scotch in front of him, and with both hands, he kept turning it around and around and around on the table.

I came around and sat opposite him in an armchair.

"I thought you said no one would ever find her," I reminded him.

He made a noise that could have been a laugh, could have been a sob, or maybe a combination of the two. He knocked the rest of his drink down his throat, set the glass back down loudly on the table, then leaned back against the sofa. He rubbed his face with his big hands, the skin pale, the knuckles filigreed with wiry black sprouts of hair.

"Drop the act," I told him.

He balled his fists, drove them down on his knees. "You think this is a fucking act? That I'm a goddamn suspect in my wife's murder? That I'm gonna go to fucking *jail*?"

"You need to calm down and listen to what I'm about to tell you. Can you do that?"

"Don't talk to me like I'm one of your degenerate clients."

I blinked at him.

"I'm here to help you, Dale."

This sentiment seemed to breach his armor. He sniffled, then nodded profusely.

"I looked at the police report while I was back in New York, and Eric spent the entire drive back from Baltimore bringing me up to speed on things here. So hear me out, Dale, before you start freaking out—*there is no evidence that ties you to what happened to your wife.* You, me, and Eric are the only people who know the truth. We'll wait for the coroner's report, and you'll see that it'll say the cause of death was blunt force trauma."

"Jesus Christ," he said, hanging his head again.

"But they won't be able to determine if that happened from a drunken fall down the side of the cliff, or some other way." I didn't know this to be fact, but I wanted Dale to calm down, and it sounded reasonable. If the autopsy report came back with anything other than that, we would deal with it then. For now, I just wanted this guy to keep his wits about him and not go over the deep end.

"There was . . . I mean, I wrapped her up . . ."

"Spit it out."

"I wrapped her in a plastic tarp. They're gonna know someone killed her. It was so fucking stupid of me, I know, I freaked, but now *they're* gonna know that someone . . . that *I*. . ."

It suddenly made perfect sense to me why Eric had lied about this bit of information to Dale.

"There was no plastic tarp," I said. "She must have come free of it in the water. It was just her body that washed up in that cave, Dale. Just her body. See what I'm saying? It could have just as easily been an accident, that she wandered out there drunk that night and fell over the side."

"It's miles from The Wharf Rat. You really think the police will believe she walked that far, drunk, with no shoes on? Jesus Christ, I'm a fucking idiot!"

His comment about her shoes—or lack thereof—reminded me of the story Eric had told me about finding Cynthia standing barefoot in a snowstorm last winter in front of the Graves house. And on the heels of that, I recalled something Meach had said to me the night I'd discovered him living in my house: a dream or a hallucination—a *reflection,* he'd called it—where he'd glimpsed a vision of Cynthia Walls standing outside Ruth Graves's house while things like bits of ash floated around her. *Did he mean snow?* I wondered, then immediately chased that ridiculous thought away.

"If she'd been found wrapped in plastic, we'd be having a different conversation," I told him. "But she wasn't. And I keep reiterating, Dale, that there is no evidence against you other than your own conscience. So let's work on striking that."

He nodded again. Ran a finger under his nose. I could tell he was eyeing the liquor bottle, but I didn't want him drinking any more tonight. I still had a million questions, and Dale Walls owed me a story.

"Tell me what happened," I said.

Dale looked away from me. I watched his left leg bounce, watched his fingers dig themselves into the knees of his slacks. He kept glancing over his shoulder at the picture window at the front of the house, as if expecting someone to come up the walk.

"Dale," I said. "I need you to focus."

"I'm not some child," he groused, shooting me a look.

"I just want you to tell me what happened."

He took a breath, then exhaled. I could smell the booze on him from across the room. He looked back up at me and said, "The night it happened, I was home, Andrew. Asleep. My cell phone rang and it was Tig. It was one in the morning, and she was calling from the bar to find out if Cynthia made it home safe. I was so fucking embarrassed, I said she was home and she was safe, but that she was drunk and sleeping it off in the guest room. That was it. And I hung up."

He paused here, and I couldn't sense whether or not he was willing to continue, so I asked him what he did next.

"I got up and got dressed. I checked to make sure Barrett was asleep in his room—he was—then I got into the Navigator and drove down to The Rat. I figured maybe I'd find her car run off the road or wrapped around a tree or something. She'd done it before. Or maybe I'd find her making out with some guy in his truck in the parking lot. At that point, Andrew, nothing would have surprised me.

"But I didn't find her car run off the road or wrapped around a tree. And when I pulled into the parking lot of The Wharf Rat, I could see no other cars in the lot. Even Tig had gone home by then. So I drove around the side, where the piers and the dumpsters are, and I saw Cynthia's car. I thought maybe she'd fallen asleep in the backseat or something. That's happened before, too. But she wasn't in it. I saw her purse inside, though, and so I opened the door—I mean, the fucking car was unlocked—and looked around in it. Her wallet was in there, her cell phone, her car keys. Like I said, she'd disappeared from time to time before. But something about all that just bothered me. It felt *different*. I don't even know why."

"What'd you do next?"

"I got in my car and headed back home. I didn't want my son waking up and finding the house empty. But then, just as I was coming off the main road and heading up the construction road that led back up here to the development, I saw her walking in the middle of the street."

"Your wife?"

"Goddamn right, my wife. She was weaving down the center of the road, drunk as a skunk, her shoes in her hand. I pulled over, rolled down the window, told her to get the hell inside."

"What'd she do?"

Dale laughed, but there was no humor in it. "She cursed me out. Laughed at me. I guess she cried a bit, too. She was a mess, really. With as much as she drank, she never could learn to hold her liquor. But in the end, yes, she acquiesced, and climbed into the car, and I drove her home.

"By the time we pulled into the driveway, she was passed out in the passenger seat, and I figured I'd leave her there to sleep it off. So I left her, and went back into the house. I checked on Barrett—he was still asleep, thank God—and then I got into bed. But then like five minutes later I could hear her stumbling through the front door. I didn't want her to wake up our son, didn't want him seeing her in that condition, so I got up and went out there. I figured I'd put her to bed.

"She was standing in the kitchen. Just standing there in her bare feet. And I saw her and I said . . . I mean, I don't really know *what* I said, or what *she* said. I don't really remember now, you know? All I know is that she was shouting and then she started hitting me with her fists and I didn't want my son to hear, and I kept telling her to be quiet, to calm down and be quiet, but she just kept striking me and striking me, and, I don't know, something snapped inside me, and I grabbed her—I grabbed her around the mouth, or tried to, trying to shut her up, but I couldn't, so then I was pushing her . . . or trying to grab her . . . I can't be sure, I can't remember . . . and then she, well . . . she fell. She fell down. She struck her head on the corner of the kitchen table and then she fell to the floor. And I thought, okay, that's bad, but at least she's *stopped,* at least she's *calm,* and maybe I could get her into bed . . . but then I saw she wasn't moving. And I saw her head, and there was like, I guess, um . . ."

He paused here as his voice hitched. He looked away from me, his eyes filling with tears again. That leg kept bouncing, and his fingers were digging into the knees of his pants once more.

"It's all right, Dale. Take your time."

He sucked in a breath, then said, "I knew she was dead the second I looked at her lying there. I just knew it. I mean, her eyes were open . . . just staring up at the ceiling. And that wound on her head."

"Was there any blood?"

He seemed to consider this, as if his recollection of such a vivid detail was somehow eluding him. Finally, he said, "Only a little. It was more like that part of her head had just been pushed in."

"What'd you do next?"

He didn't say anything for a long time. I sat there for a while, waiting for him to continue. A trick of the trade is to never interject, never break the silence when someone is confessing—you just let them go, and if there's an awkward silence, you let them fill it with words. Let them be the one made uncomfortable by the absence of talk.

"I panicked," he said eventually. "I didn't know what to do. I kept thinking of Barrett waking up and coming out of his room, seeing what had happened. Fuck, Andrew. Fuck!"

He reached for the bottle of scotch and I didn't stop him.

"I had some plastic tarp in the back of the Navigator," he said, filling a glass with scotch. He filled a second—one of the clean glasses Tig had brought over—but I didn't touch it, and he didn't seem to notice. "I wrapped her up in it, carried her out to the car, and drove around for a while trying to think of what I should do. I didn't know what I should do, Andrew. I was freaking out. I just kept thinking about my son."

His hand shook as he brought the drink to his lips.

"What did you ultimately do?" I asked him.

"I was thinking of Robert, I guess. He'd been on my mind lately, mostly because Meach had started talking all this nonsense and riling up old ghosts, you know? Fucking Meach-Man. Anyway, I thought of the night up at Gracie Point, out on the old Ribbon Road. How he'd gotten hit by that firework and fell over the side. How he'd died down there on the rocks."

The way he'd phrased this wasn't lost on me—*how he'd gotten hit by that firework and fell over the side.* It had been Dale who'd fired it at him, trying to scare him. Yes, it had been an accident, but Dale was the responsible party.

"And I thought how lucky we all were to have gotten away with it that night," he went on. "It could have had repercussions that carried through our entire lives, but it didn't. It didn't."

I shifted uncomfortably in my chair but said nothing.

He took another sip then set his glass on the coffee table. "So I brought her to the cliffs and threw her in the water. Hoping for another bout of luck, I guess. I knew it was a mistake to wrap her in that plastic the second she went over the side, but the way she sank . . . I mean, bodies are supposed to float, right?"

"I guess," I said.

"She sank like a stone, Andrew. Like a fucking stone. And so maybe that was luck, too."

And then he hung his head and wept.

I got up, went to the kitchen, and poured myself a glass of water from the tap. My own hand was shaking. I was tired from the trip down, and my mind was weary from all that I'd had to digest over the past few weeks. I didn't want to be here and I didn't want to hear any more of Dale's terrible story . . . except I was beginning to think Eric was right. I had little faith that Dale would keep his mouth shut about Robert if someone from the D.A.'s office really put the screws to him. And I couldn't let that happen.

I got a second glass, filled that with water, then went back into the living room to find Dale slouching forward on the sofa, his head in his hands. He was making wet sniffling sounds that, to me, sounded strangely childlike.

I set the glass of water down on the coffee table in front of him then told him to finish the story.

He raised his face to meet my gaze. Tears leaked from the corners of his eyes and his face was patchy and red. "I came home and took a shower. I felt disgusting and wanted to wash myself. I must have showered for over an hour. I don't know. Then I crawled back into bed, but I couldn't sleep. I just laid there until the sun came up and I heard Barrett's feet padding down the hallway. And that broke my heart, Andrew."

"And then what?"

"Christ," he said, swiping a jittery hand across his eyes. "You're a heartless bastard, you know that?"

"I'm not here for a good time, Dale. What happened next?"

"I made my son breakfast, all right? Motherfucking pancakes."

"What happened the next day?"

"Christ, I don't know . . ."

"Dale," I said. "You need to know. You *have* to know. Tell me what you did the next day."

"I went back and got her fucking car, all right? I drove it home, and it was here until the cops came around and impounded it. Okay?"

"Which was days later," I said, "because you waited a while before reporting her missing."

"I just didn't know what the fuck to do."

"Why didn't you tell me all of this when I first came out here?"

He looked me dead in the eyes and said, "Because I'm a *shit*, Andrew. You think I wanted to tell you *that*? I hadn't seen you in years, and you think I wanted to drag you back here and confess to being some kind of monster? I needed your *help*."

"And I'm here," I said.

"Yeah, yeah," he said, nodding his head and looking miserable. "That's right. You're here."

"What did you do with the blood?"

"What do you mean?"

"I asked if there was any blood. It happened in the kitchen, right? How did you clean it up?"

"There was just a little on her head. It didn't get on the floor or anything."

"What about in the Navigator?"

"She was already wrapped in plastic in the Navigator."

"All right," I said. I knew even the most microscopic particle of blood could be detected under ultraviolet light.

"Eric said it was Meach who found her," Dale said.

"That's right. How do you think that happened?"

"What do you mean?"

"I don't really like coincidences, Dale. Is Meach wrapped up in any of this? Be straight with me."

"Meach?" He laughed. "You think I'd confide in that guy?"

"You said you tossed her over the cliff, which means the current probably dragged her into that cave. Yes, it's right near where Robert died, but that's no coincidence, since you went deliberately to that location that night. But I just can't reconcile Meach stumbling around some cave in the middle of the night and coming across your wife's body. Help me understand that."

"I'm telling you, Andrew, I never said shit to Meach. Do you think I'm stupid? Look at him. He can barely stand up straight some days. I'm gonna tell him my deepest, darkest secrets?"

I believed him. It didn't explain how Meach had found the body, but I was confident Dale hadn't said anything to him. I stood and cleared the glasses from the table.

"Leave the bottle," Dale said.

I left the bottle, took the dirty glasses to the kitchen, set them in the sink. And I couldn't help myself: I scanned the floor, the corners of the kitchen table, for any signs of distress. Clearly there wouldn't be visible splotches of blood, but I couldn't help—

Something *whumped* against the window over the sink. Startled, I looked up and saw nothing there. I stepped closer, peering out into the night. There was a little shelf outside the window with some plants in it. A small gray bird with a yellow bib lay dead in one of the ceramic flowerpots. Its neck was clearly broken.

I stood there for the length of several heartbeats, unsure what to think, what to do. I felt like the brunt of some joke—like I was being set up, and this whole thing was a ruse to prank me. I suddenly wondered if Cynthia Walls might not walk through the front door at any moment and yell *surprise!*

Unnerved, I stepped back out into the living room. Dale had gotten up from the couch, and stood now before the front windows, that bottle of scotch clutched in one beefy paw. He wavered drunkenly as he gazed out at that moonscape cul-de-sac. His reflection in the glass swayed along with him.

Without looking at me, he said, "There's more, you know. I almost don't want to say it."

"You need to tell me everything, Dale."

"Even this? This . . . nonsense that's been scaring the shit out of me?"

"Everything."

Silence simmered between us. For a long while, I thought he wouldn't say anything more.

"I'm being haunted," he said. "You remember when I said I'd been cursed? Well, I didn't mean it in some metaphorical, guilt-ridden way." A sound lurched out of his throat that might have been a humorless laugh, or maybe just an expulsion of tension. "Someone's been coming into my house."

"What do you mean? Who?"

"I don't know *who*," he said. "And I don't know how to explain it. You live in a house, it's your home, you know if something's wrong, right? Someone's been in this place when I haven't been home. Walking around in here, going through my stuff, my office. Going through my wife's stuff, too. I thought maybe it was the cops with a search warrant, sneaking in here looking for clues, but Eric said it doesn't work that way."

"Maybe it was your son going through your things?"

"It's not my son."

"Or maybe . . . I mean, you've been under a lot of stress, Dale..."

"You think it's all in my head, huh? Look at this place, Andrew. It's immaculate. I've got a woman comes twice a week to clean up, doesn't leave a speck of dirt behind. But then a couple nights ago I notice a footprint on the carpet in my office. Not *my* footprint. I don't fucking know. I thought about calling the police, but then I thought I was in enough trouble with them already and didn't want to look like some paranoid lunatic on top of everything else."

"Has anything gone missing?"

"I don't know."

I thought of what Eric had said about Dale earlier that night, as he drove me out here from the train station: *He's terrified. He's losing his mind and he's about to crack.* I was suddenly concerned that maybe Eric Kelly was all too right on that score.

"There's something else, too," he said, his voice shaking.

"What?"

"That night I called you? Something . . . well, something happened. I wasn't lying when I said Eric suggested I get in touch with you, but Eric wasn't the reason I called. It was what happened. What I *saw*."

"What did you see?"

"Don't think I'm crazy, Andrew. Don't think I'm like Meach. Please, okay? Please."

"Goddamn it, Dale, just tell me."

He lifted one hand and pointed out the window. There was nothing but darkness out there, except for that wreath of streetlamps, so I couldn't tell what he was trying to show me. A part of me wondered if he was going to tell me he'd seen birds striking the window for the past few days.

"That house right there," he said, still pointing into the darkness. "The night I called you, Suzanne had taken Barrett, and so I'd gotten drunk. Eric had told me to reach out to you, that it was time, and I had been thinking about you all night, thinking about calling, but I just couldn't bring myself to do it. So I was just sitting on the sofa getting even more drunk when I heard fireworks go off."

"Nothing unusual about that," I told him, even though I was beginning to feel a cold unease rise up in me. "It's almost the Fourth."

"They were coming from inside that house," Dale said. "I could see them flashing there behind the windows. Greens, reds, purples— *boom, boom, boom*. I thought I was losing my mind at first, but then I thought maybe some neighborhood kids had come out here, thinking the whole street was deserted, and that they were vandalizing the place.

"I keep a gun in my office, so I went and got it, then went across the street to the house. Those lights kept flashing in the windows . . . only each flash was a blinding white, and it's stupid, and I was drunk, but for a second as I was standing there, I thought I was staring into the Gracie Point Lighthouse. The closer I got, the more uncomfortable I became. I could smell the smoke from the fireworks inside the house from the street. And as I got even closer, I could see a figure standing in one of the front windows. I couldn't make out any detail, but I could see their silhouette backlit from those flashing lights. Only . . . only they weren't so much flashing anymore. Kind of like . . . I don't know . . . *revolving* . . .

"I almost didn't go in. I thought about calling the cops again, calling Eric. But in the end, probably because I was drunk, I went up to the door, typed in the code on the cipher lock—it took me three tries to get it right—and then I went inside."

I stood there, waiting for him to continue, while also not truly wanting him to continue. I didn't want to hear about what he found over there in that house. I was thinking of my *own* house, the one here in town, with its flooded, foul-smelling cellar and its rooms and corridors choked with black flies. A house like a drowned corpse. But also my apartment back home, and the creeping anxiety I'd been feeling there throughout the duration of Rebecca's pregnancy. All this time I had been fighting my way to the end of this third trimester under the belief that once the baby was here, my anxiety—that pale, ghastly wraith—would vanish. But what if this was only the beginning? What if things only got worse once the baby arrived?

"What did you find in the house, Dale?"

I watched him glance absently down at the palm of his right hand. His entire arm trembled.

"Dale."

I didn't want to know.

I had to know.

"You," he said. "I found you. At least, I thought it was you. At first, anyway. The house was filled with smoke from the fireworks and it was hard to see through it. Everything was dark inside. The figure

I'd glimpsed in the window stood at the far side of the room. Like a drunken idiot, I reached for the light switch on the wall, but there's no power going to any of those houses yet. So nothing came on."

"Why did you think it was me?"

"Because you were wearing a necklace made out of metal pull-tabs."

He turned and looked at me, and I felt myself recoil internally from the cadaverous look of him in that moment—the dead, runny eyes, the slack jaw, the listless pallor of his skin. That red contrail of dried blood on his cheek stood out as garish as a clown's greasepaint.

"Remember?" he said. "You were wearing it that night, out at Gracie Point. I remember making a comment about it earlier that night, thinking it was weird, until I realized later Tig had probably given it to you." Some muscle twitched in his face as he said that last part. "Anyway, that necklace was all I could see in that room, because it was dark, and because of the smoke, except that the moonlight was coming in through the windows and reflecting off all those little metal tabs around your neck. I think I even spoke your name."

"But it wasn't me." I felt foolish stating this—it was obvious, of course; I'd been in New York on that night, still blissfully unaware of all that had transpired here in Kingsport—but I felt the need to get this point across nonetheless. For Dale, but maybe also for myself, too.

"No," he said. "It wasn't. It was Robert."

I just stood there and said nothing.

"He was looking at me through that cloud of smoke, and if he hadn't spoken, I would've just convinced myself that he was part of that smoke, too. A black smudge in the room. A black stain on my psyche, maybe."

"He spoke? What'd he say?"

"He counted. Very quietly. *One, two, three, four, five.* Just like that."

"Then what happened?" I was speaking very quietly now, too.

"I was drunk," he said, "so I raised the gun and fired three rounds at him."

"Did you really? What happened?"

"What do you think?" he said. "Nothing. You can't shoot a ghost, Andy." Again, he turned his bleary eyes on me. The liquor in the bottle sloshed. "But I nearly blew my eardrums out and I fucked up one of the walls. Robert just sort of vanished, like ghosts do, I guess, and then I heard what sounded like pocket change falling to the floor. And then when the smoke cleared—the fireworks smoke, the gun smoke, the smoke in my head: all of it—I saw that he wasn't there anymore. Or maybe he hadn't been there at all. But when I went over to where he'd been standing, I could see all those little aluminum tabs scattered all over the floor.

"It scared the shit out of me, so I got the hell out of there, came back home, and called you. It was like the last thing I needed to see, the thing that scared me enough to call you. So that's what I did."

"I think maybe you've been letting Meach's ghost stories get to you."

"Yeah, that's what I thought the next day, too. But there have been other things lately that . . . I don't know . . . I can't explain."

"Like Meach finding your wife's body in that cave," I said.

Dale offered up a pallid smile. "Like Meach finding my wife's body in that cave. Yeah. Have you talked to Tig?"

"About your situation?"

"No. About Robert. About what's been happening to her, too."

"She's told me some stuff."

"What do you think?"

"I think we're all spooking ourselves."

"She's terrified. She's worried about her kid."

"Maybe all of us together is just heightening our anxiety. Our guilt."

Dale seemed to consider this. He set the bottle of booze on the dining room table then went over to a low table with a lamp on it. He kept massaging the heel of his right hand.

"What's wrong with your hand, Dale?"

"Burns. On and off. I burned it that night when that last fireball shot off. Lately, it's come back like a phantom pain." He opened the drawer. "Anyway, maybe you're right. Or maybe the old Meach-Man is right, and we've got a hex on our heads. Time to pay up. I mean, July Fourth is breathing down our necks, twenty years later, almost to the day. It can't be a coincidence this is all happening right now, can it?"

He took a handful of something out of the drawer, carried them over to the dining room table, and let them all spill out: countless aluminum pull-tabs clattered to the tabletop.

"I kept thinking of that sound just before he vanished," Dale said. "Kept thinking about all those little metal bits lying on the floor over there. That sound like loose pocket change falling to the floor. I spent all this time convincing myself that I had been drunk and I had hallucinated what happened in that house, but then I thought, what if it had been *real*? So I went back in there tonight, stumbled around in the dark, and found these. Walked into a wall, too, which is how I bloodied my nose. I wasn't lying about that part."

Those pull-tabs could have come from anywhere. They could have been left behind by kids partying in that house. Or maybe Dale was making this all up to ensure I'd stick around and help him out of his jam—that I could be convinced to stay by some otherworldly magic, if not the desperation of an old friend.

"I don't believe in any of this nonsense," I said, though my voice to my own ears did not sound quite so convinced. "That poor old woman is not a witch and there is no curse on our heads. It's just guilt. That's all."

The grin that he gave me was thin and humorless. "Well," he said, "in for a penny, in for a pound, I guess."

EIGHTEEN

I t was summer on the shore, and with the Fourth of July drawing
closer, this meant that all the motels out along the highway were
sold out. Without another option, I drove Eric's car back to Kingsport
and to my father's house, bracing myself for the deluge of flies and
stink that would rush toward me the moment I stepped through the
front door.

I was not disappointed.

I had spent a full week back home in New York with Rebecca,
but walking through the front door of my old home again, it was
like I hadn't left this place—not since last week, and not since I was
a teenager, too. Something about it had metastasized in my bones.
I need to sell this house and be done with it. Be done with Kingsport.
Be done with all of it. I kept hearing Dale's story in my head about
how he'd fought with his wife and how she'd struck her head on
the kitchen table. How he'd wandered, drunk, into a vacant house
and took potshots at a ghost. I kept seeing him open his hand to
let all of those pull-tabs spill out and scatter. I kept thinking about
meadowlarks breaking their necks on windowpanes.

I stood in the hall and called out for Meach. Waited to see if he'd
answer, if he was even still here. I had a six-pack of Budweiser under
one arm and a box of chicken strips in my hands, which I figured

might rouse him, if in fact he was still in the house. I wanted to talk to him, to dissect the details of how he'd found Cynthia Walls's body in that cave. I couldn't wrap my head around it; I didn't like where the avenues of thought took me. But it seemed like the house was empty, and I was alone.

I sat at the kitchen table, cracked open a beer, and dug a chicken tender out of the box. There were a few unread text messages on my phone, and I clicked on the ones from Rebecca. The first one, sent about two hours ago:

Baby's kicking. Will be a long night.

The next one was from an hour later:

Got some sleep but woke up. Nightmares again.
Dreamt someone was in our closet.

That text got to me. I read it three times. Digested it. Wondered if paranoia was contagious.

I scrolled to the third and final text from my wife, which read, simply:

spotting

It took me a moment to realize what that meant. And once I did, I dialed Rebecca's number, listened to it ring, and held my breath until I heard her voice on the other end of the line.

"It's late," she said.

"I just saw your texts. What's going on?"

"There was a little blood earlier. I called the doctor. It's no big deal. We're at the finish line."

"It scared me."

"I'm sorry. Are you back at your hotel?"

"I am."

"Tell Morrison I hate him taking you away from me so close to your birthday. Will you be home for it?"

I didn't know.

"I don't know," I said.

I heard the sound of blankets rustling over the phone, and then Rebecca said, "Do you want to know what my bad dream was about?"

"If you want to tell me."

"I dreamt a giant bird was coming after you. Did you ever watch those silly Godzilla movies as a kid? Sometimes they had these big, prehistoric birds in them. Well, something like that was chasing you, only it wasn't all rubbery and silly, it was scary, and you were running really, really fast to get away."

"Did I get away?"

"Do you want me to answer truthfully?"

"I guess that depends on the outcome…"

There was a pause. Then: "I don't want to talk about the dream, Andrew. I'm worried about you. Who are these clients? Are you in danger?"

"Danger from what? Getting a paper cut?"

"You've never had to just pick up and leave like this before. Something doesn't feel right about it. I'm worried about you."

"Bec, I'm fine. You're just missing me. And I'm missing you. Okay?"

Another pause. Longer, this time. Then: "Yes. You got away. In the dream, I mean. You're like Superman that way. You get away from all the bad business."

"Now you sound drunk," I told her. "You're nearly nine months pregnant, you shouldn't be drinking."

Rebecca laughed. "I'm drunk on missing you, my Superman." Her laughter subsided and she said, "You promise everything is okay?"

"I promise," I said, and then I saw a shadow shift along the hallway beyond the kitchen. "Listen, Bec, it's late. Get back to sleep. I just wanted to hear your voice, make sure everything was okay."

"Wait," she said. "Do you want to hear something weird? Do you know what I've been thinking about lately, for no apparent reason?"

"What's that?"

"The phone downstairs."

In the lobby of our apartment building, there was an old rotary telephone on the wall that no one ever used. It was a relic from bygone days, a thing Rebecca and I used to joke about sometimes. Saying, hey, if it ever rang, it's someone from 1965 calling to say hello. And we'd laugh. A silly, shared joke.

"Why have you been thinking about the phone downstairs?" I asked.

"I don't know. It's been on my mind. Whenever I walk past it, which is like several times a day, I stop and look at it. Once, I even picked up the receiver and put it to my ear."

"What did you hear?"

"Nothing. Not even a dial tone. What was I supposed to hear? The ocean?"

"I don't know, baby. Why are you so worried about a telephone?"

Those bed sheets rustled around again, and she said, "Did I say I was worried?"

"It's late," I said. "Why don't you get some sleep and I'll call you in the morning?"

"On the downstairs phone?"

I gave up a quiet laugh at that, but that comment bothered me in some way I couldn't quite comprehend. "Sure," I said, eventually.

"Okay. Goodnight."

"Goodnight."

And then she was gone.

I set the phone down, washed my hands at the sink, then stepped out into the hallway. Whatever shape or shadow I thought I'd glimpsed sliding down the hall, I could see no evidence of it now. Flies crawled along the walls, and the smell of that place was no less terrible than it was when I'd first arrived. This whole scene felt like a nightmare.

I walked down the hall to the master bedroom, where I'd let Meach crash last time I was here. The room was empty. I looked up at the windows at the far side of the room and saw cracks running down the windowpanes. Had they been like that before? I couldn't remember. I stood for a moment in this room, listening for the creak of a floorboard, of the exhalation of breath. But there was only silence.

I went back down the hall toward my old bedroom. Flies divebombed my face, and I swatted them away. Ducking beneath a garland of flypaper, I stepped inside my old childhood bedroom, turned on the light, and saw Meach lying dead on the floor.

Something in my chest clenched up. I leaned against the doorframe and stared at my old childhood friend, splayed out on the floor of my bedroom, his skin a mottled gray, his head leaning against the wall, his mouth partially unhinged. His eyes were foggy and unfocused, and there were flies crawling around his face. The old Ocean Pacific tank top and jeans shorts he wore were tattered and frayed. His feet were bare, and I could see that the soles were lacerated with abrasions, and there was dried blood on his shins, presumably from all his nighttime excursions. Strangely, the William Blake book that I kept in the nightstand lay beside him on the floor, upside down and opened up so that its spine was creased. Also beside him on the floor was a Ziploc bag of white powder and a plastic lighter.

A hypodermic needle stuck out of his arm.

"Fuck, Meach," I said, and went to him: dropping to the floor and feeling for a pulse at his neck, at his wrist. Nothing. Nothing. "Come on, Meach-Man." I gently slapped the side of his face, hoping this might bring some clarity into his milky stare, but it didn't. His head turned turgidly on his neck, and his skin felt like modeling clay against the palm of my sweaty hand. "Come on, man," and then shouted, "Come on, man!" And then—

And then I got up and walked back down the hall, through the kitchen, out onto the front porch.

My flesh felt feverish. My body trembled. For whatever bizarre fucking reason, I thought of Rebecca saying, *Whenever I walk past it, which is like several times a day, I stop and look at it. Once, I even picked up the receiver and put it to my ear.*

I sat down on the porch steps, and hung my head.

NINETEEN

Aftermath, July 2003

I didn't leave the house for those first few days after Robert's death. In that time, and aside from Eric Kelly's brief visit, I saw no one except my father. I felt marked somehow, like if I stepped out into the street, people would point and stare and recognize me as someone responsible for what had happened. But I couldn't remain like that forever, and so I began creeping out into the daylight and widening my sphere of travel like an old-world explorer making tentative inroads through uncharted lands.

One afternoon, I rode my bike all the way out to Rockfish Road, where the sign, MEACHAM MOTEL, stood above a scrim of trees. Meach's grandmother was sitting in a beach chair outside the motel's front office, her sizable bulk straining against the nylon straps of the chair. She was smoking a greasy brown cigarillo and spraying bug spray on her pasty white shins that lay exposed and as thick as lodge poles from beneath the hem of her housedress. Her feet were wedged into a pair of ratty blue slippers. She said nothing to me as I hurried past her, my head down, although I could feel her distrustful eyes follow me down the entire length of the motel parking lot.

Meach was in Room 1, running a vacuum along the fire-retardant carpet. The bed had been stripped, the sheets bundled in a ball on the floor. When he looked up and saw me standing in the doorway, he shut down the vacuum, then dug a pack of cigarettes from his pocket. He nodded, as if he'd expected my arrival. I didn't say anything; I just nodded back. He said, "Come on," and I followed him around the side of the motel, where a small dirt path led to a narrow channel of soupy brown water.

"Only one left," he said, shaking out his last remaining Marlboro from the pack.

"It's okay," I said.

We sat on the embankment and passed the smoke back and forth for a while without saying much. I noticed there were cuts on the palms of his hands, and dried rivulets of blood in the creases, but I didn't say anything about them. After too much silence had passed, Meach said, "You know, I can still smell the gunpowder from those fireworks. I thought maybe it was in my clothes, in my hair, or maybe even from those gross things my grandmother smokes, but now I think it's just haunting me, like a ghost." He turned his head and looked at me, his eyes glassy and red and unfocused. "Past few nights, I've woken up in the middle of the night and it's like my lungs are filled with water and I can't breathe. And the worst thing is that my eye—my right eye—keeps burning." He brought his face close to mine, and I could smell the cigarette on his breath. "Does it look messed up or anything?"

"It looks fine."

"Yeah, well, it keeps stinging me."

"Have you spoken to any of the others since that night?"

He looked instantly miserable. "No," he said. "Only you. I didn't really want to see anybody, you know?"

I nodded. I understood.

"Can I show you something?" he said.

"Sure."

We got up from the embankment, dusting the dirt and dead leaves from the seats of our pants, and I followed him back along the path toward the motel. Frogs leapt out of our way and plonked into puddles behind tall fronds. Meach's grandmother was still in her chair out front when we returned, still smoking and staring dismally at the road. We avoided her, cutting around the side of the motel instead, to where a jumble of overgrown ivy and thorny bushes rose up out of the woods and crowded this side of the motel. Meach swept aside thick vines so we could pass through, but then stopped so short I nearly ran into the back of him.

"I found some roadkill down the block, dragged it up here."

"Why would you do that?"

When he stepped aside, I saw the roadkill he was talking about: a raccoon, its belly unzipped, entrails glistening wetly and crawling with pearly white maggots. It was lying on a piece of cardboard, which was probably how he'd dragged it here. There was something else dead on the ground beside the raccoon—something that took me a moment to register.

"Jesus, Meach..."

It was a turkey vulture, bigger than the one that had struck the windshield of Dale's truck. It was lying on its side, its fleshy pink face crawling with flies, its bone-colored beak hinged open in a silent cry. Whitish foam had curdled around its open mouth.

"I dumped some rat poison on the raccoon, and that's how I killed that ugly fucker," he said, pointing at the bird. "Because they eat anything that's dead."

"Why?"

Meach shrugged. "It's just what they eat."

"No, I mean why would you do this?"

"Oh. Well, because I had a dream," Meach said. "That she was watching us through their eyes. Keeping tabs on us."

"Who was watching us?"

Meach lowered his voice and said, "The witch. Ruth Graves. She knows what we did to her son. She's still watching us, Andy. Even now. So I had to . . . to kill this thing . . ."

I took a step back from him, my eyes still locked on the gruesome scene on the ground beside the motel.

"I don't think you should be doing stuff like this, Meach."

"I've also been catching the frogs that fell from the sky. I keep them in jars in my bedroom."

"The storm blew those frogs into town," I told him. My father had told me of similar things happening in the past—waterspouts and cyclones scooping sea life from the ocean, carrying them miles in the air, then dumping them on some unsuspecting village.

"I sold one to the creepy guy who hangs around the Stop and Go for five bucks. It's crazy, because they're all over the place, and you can catch them for free. But they give me warts. I had to scrape them off with a pocketknife." Meach shook his head, then glanced down at the ruined, bloodstained palms of his hands. "Anyway, I got a lot of stuff to do around here, and I don't feel like hearing the old bag complain about how lazy I am."

I nodded, but said nothing. When he looked up at me and smiled, I wrestled a smile onto my lips in return, despite how disgusted and uncomfortable I suddenly felt.

"Just be careful out there, Andy. Okay?"

"Sure, Meach."

And then I got out of there as quickly as I could.

A few times I went to Tig's house, at a time when I knew her parents would be at the restaurant and she'd be home. On these occasions, I went around to the back door, knocked, and waited for her to open it. Once, I even heard her moving around in there, right on the other side of the door. I opened my mouth to speak her name, but changed my mind at the last second. She knew it was me standing out here; if she'd wanted to see me, she would have opened the door. So each time, I left with my head down, hurrying across the road so no one would see me, and taking the wooded trail back toward my section of town.

I made no effort to seek out Dale. I didn't go to his house like I did Tig and Meach, and I knew the reason was because the thought of seeing him made me uncomfortable. He had been the one to light that Roman candle, and he had been the one to fire it at Robert Graves. Yes, it had been an accident, but had he not done those things, everything would have been different. And while we were all responsible for fleeing the scene, I hated Dale the most for what he'd forced us to do.

But Kingsport is a small town, and it was only a matter of time before we ran into each other. Finally, one afternoon as I was at the Stop and Go, filling up a gas can so I could mow the lawn, I saw him smoking a cigarette and walking along the shoulder of the highway, on the opposite side of the guardrail. He had his head down, his longish hair swept in a bowl cut across the front of his face. I screwed the cap on the gas can, set it in the basket of my bike, then ran over to him.

He seemed startled by my sudden appearance, and physically recoiled from me as my shadow joined his on the pavement. I lit a cigarette of my own, then said, "Hey, man. You been okay?"

"What do you mean?"

I shrugged. "Haven't seen you in a few days. I thought about stopping by," which was a lie, "but then, well . . . I don't know . . ." I let myself trail off. That part had been a lie—I hadn't thought about stopping by at all. In fact, it made me uncomfortable to look at him and recall everything that had happened that night even now. I could still picture him launching those fireballs into the air, and the one that struck the road, bounced up, and blew a hole in Robert Graves's face, sending him backward over the side of the cliff. "I guess I didn't know what to say," I finished, which was at least the truth this time.

"What to say about what?" he said. He wasn't looking at me; instead he kept walking with his head down, perhaps studying our shadows on the ground in front of us. The ghosts of acne haunted his cheeks, miniscule divots that turned red in the summer, and each one now glistened with pockets of sweat. As I stared at his profile, he took a long drag from his cigarette.

"I mean," I said, my throat tightening. "I mean, about the whole thing..."

"Whole thing?" he said, still not looking at me. "I don't know what you're talking about."

Was he playing with me? Or had that night been so traumatic for him that he'd blocked it out? That seemed impossible to me, but I wasn't an expert. I was a sixteen-year-old kid, scared shitless about going to jail. What the hell did I know?

"Robert," I said, the word—the name—heavy on my tongue. "They're saying the fall didn't kill him. That there was an autopsy done and that the cause of death was drowning. Which means Tig was right. He was still alive down there. When we left him, he was still al—"

Dale whirled around and grabbed two fistfuls of my shirt. His cigarette dropped from his lips and he brought his face so close to mine, our noses nearly touched.

"It was an *accident.*" His teeth were clenched, and spittle showered onto my face. He kept pulling at my shirt, knuckles digging into my chest. "Do you understand? It was a fucking *accident.* Even the goddamn *police* said it was an accident."

And then he released me, shoving me backward with enough force that I nearly fell into the steaming, swampy culvert that ran along the shoulder of the highway.

"Don't try to turn this into something it's not," he said, and then he just stood there fuming, looking like maybe he wanted to say more, maybe wanted to even hit me or something, but lacked the conviction to do anything. In the end, he just stepped around me and continued in the direction toward town, his head down again, sweaty angel wings imprinted along the back of his T-shirt.

And I thought, *Why is he walking? What happened to his truck?*

I kept waking up in the middle of the night from a nightmare where I was drowning, only to bolt up in bed and feel the heaviness in my lungs and the salty, fishy taste at the back of my throat. And in my terror, all I could hear was Meach saying, *Past two nights, I've woken up in the middle of the night and it's like my lungs are filled with water and I can't breathe.*

And I kept seeing Robert Graves standing on the edge of the old Ribbon Road, pointing at each one of us, marking us. Saying: *one . . . two . . . three . . . four . . . five . . .*

There was one afternoon when I waited in the trees for Tig's parents to leave for The Wharf Rat. I hurried around to the back door, knocked furtively, then waited with increasing impatience for Tig to come to the door. Would this be another day of ignoring me or would she answer? I didn't know; I only knew that too much time had passed and I had to see her.

"Antigone! Come on, open the door."

She eventually came to the door, but she took her time, and when she opened it, she did so only a crack, so that just one half of her face was visible.

"What?" she said.

"I just wanted to see you."

"Well, now you've seen me."

"Hardly," I said.

She opened the door some more, revealing her full face. The sclera of her right eye was covered in a smudge of dark red blood. Just seeing it startled me, and I felt myself take a step back from her.

"What happened to your eye?"

"I don't know. I woke up and it was like this."

"Does it hurt?"

"Stings a little."

I shifted from one foot to the other. "I just haven't seen you around. I wanted to make sure you were . . . okay, I guess."

"Are you?" she said. "Are you okay?"

I didn't know how to answer that. The guilt over Robert had been eating me up. Moreover, the stories about Ruth Graves being a witch circulating about town continued to unnerve me, and in the wake of those birds hammering down on our house, I was finding it harder and harder to convince myself that we weren't, in fact, cursed.

"I just thought maybe after you'd heard about, uh, how he, uh," I stammered. Cleared my throat. Felt instantly impotent, and devoid of any coherent thought. *How he died,* was what I'd wanted to say, but I couldn't bring myself to say it. "I was just checking up on you, I guess."

"I saw Eric yesterday. He came by the restaurant."

"Oh," I said, because I didn't know what else to say.

"It never happened," she said.

"What never happened? Talking to Eric?" I didn't understand what she was telling me.

She eased the door closed a bit more, hiding that bloodshot eye from me. "Talk to Eric. And maybe don't come by here for a while, okay?"

That last part struck me like a punch to the chest. I had to catch my breath before I mustered out, "Okay, Tig."

She shut the door, and I just stood there for a bit, staring at my heartbroken, grief-stricken reflection in the semicircle of glass on the patio door. Then I headed back around toward the front of the house and the road, pausing only when I spied the maggot-riddled carcass of a small bird lying in the flowerbed on the side of the house. There was the body of a second bird a few yards away, snared in a patch of brittle, yellowed sea grass. I looked up at the house and saw bloody splotches on some of the windows, and a crack bisecting one of the windowpanes straight down the middle.

Seeing all that made me feel cold, and I fled that place as if some virulent, incurable disease lingered somewhere in the atmosphere, probing at my flesh with its invisible fingers to gain entry.

The police never spoke to Dale. They never spoke to any of us. If there was any suspicion in Sheriff Dean Kelly's mind that the death of Robert Graves was anything more than an accident, that was a suspicion that was never made public. In that sense, my father had been right: sometimes, this was the cost of living in a small town.

This reality only made me feel worse. It was as though a part of me wanted—no, *needed*—to be held accountable. The guilt was killing me. I felt part of some deeper conspiracy, which I was, only with each passing day, the noose around my neck only grew tighter. It was guilt, coupled with the paralyzing fear of being caught for what we'd done. When I learned that Dale had sold his truck soon after that night, I felt that noose grow even tighter. Someone must have told him that Ruth had seen his truck that night. Had it been Eric, who may have learned this from his father? Had it been Eric's father himself, whom Ruth had gone to see repeatedly in the aftermath of her son's death? How many whispers were being bandied about while I lay awake at night, petrified at the thought of getting caught yet desperate to unburden myself from this guilt? With the passage of each day, our silence was burying the evidence of what we'd done, whitewashing our role in the events of that night the same way Eric and I had whitewashed the back alley of the Stop and Go that time we were caught shoplifting. And that masking of the truth only made me feel worse.

On an unseasonably cool afternoon, I was home alone and alerted to the sound of an unfamiliar car pulling up the driveway to our home. I went out onto the porch and felt my bowels freeze as I saw a police car idling there, sheriff's emblem on the door. I knew without question in that moment that we had been found out and I was about to be taken to jail for murder.

The passenger door opened and Eric stepped out. He nodded at me, smiling, and I waved to him with some measure of uncertainty; since the incident on July Fourth, the five of us had, for the most part, kept clear of each other. This wasn't by design—not on my part, anyway—but more because whenever we got together, our guilt seemed compounded. To avoid each other was to try to convince ourselves that it never actually happened, that it had all been some horrible dream. Moreover, I found I wasn't comfortable around the others anymore—Meach with his newfound suspicion of birds and his collection of dead frogs in mason jars, and Tig with her bloodied eye giving me the cold shoulder every time I saw her around town. Dale, I just avoided completely. I didn't want to do it anymore.

"Hey, man," Eric said, and he was grinning like someone who'd just come off a roller coaster. He had a fresh shiner under his right eye, and I wondered what sort of hell he'd recently gone through at home with his dad.

At the thought of Eric's father, the driver's door of the cruiser opened and Sheriff Dean Kelly appeared. His buzz cut was silver at the temples and he looked much older than the last time I had seen him. He folded his arms and watched his son walk across the yard and halfway up the porch steps of my house.

"Just came by to say hey," Eric said.

"Hey," I said.

He glanced at his father, and then he lowered his voice. "Listen. We're all in agreement. It never happened. The five of us, I mean."

I just stood there, sweating like a hostage on my porch. I kept glancing at his father, the town sheriff, who was out of earshot. Eric was deliberately keeping his voice low.

"After this moment," he said, "we never bring it up. We never talk about it again. *It never happened.*"

I realized he wasn't asking for my input on this decision, but that the decision had already been made. And I wasn't about to be the outlier in my group of friends. Or former friends—whatever they were. Anyway, I wanted exactly that: to convince myself it hadn't happened and that it had all just been a bad dream.

"Okay," I said. Yet I kept glancing at his father and that police car. "Why's he here?"

"Hot today," Eric said. "Long walk."

I nodded. "Do you want to hang out or anything?"

Eric considered this for less than a second. "No," he said. "I'll just see you 'round."

He smiled, that shiner looking like the skin of an eggplant, and I watched as he headed back across the lawn and slipped back into the passenger seat of that police car. His father was still standing there, eyeing me with zero expression on his face. I thought he would never get back in that car and leave. But in the end, he did, and I stood on the porch as the town sheriff and his son backed out of our driveway, pulled out onto the road, and drove slowly on their way.

I ran into the house and was sick.

The five of us were never the same again. We avoided each other for the remainder of the summer, and when school started in the fall, we ignored each other in the hallways and classrooms. When Eric's father committed suicide, my dad and I attended the funeral. None of the others were there. Eric hardly acknowledged my presence, and I was grateful for it.

Dale shunned me, and I guess maybe I shunned him. Sometimes, I would catch him and Eric talking in the student parking lot after school, and when they'd sense my eyes on them, they'd look at me funny. Eric would occasionally nod his head, and I'd reciprocate. But that was about it.

Meach fell deeper into drugs. I lost track of him after a while, although I would occasionally have nightmares that he was walking along U.S. Route 50 in the middle of the night, collecting the carcasses of dead buzzards from the shoulders of the road.

Tig was the only one with whom I had made a half-hearted attempt at maintaining some sort of relationship. But my presence seemed to unnerve her, and I didn't want to be that guy. After a while, I kept my distance, and watched her ingratiate herself into a new group of friends. It broke my heart, but it was necessary. And maybe it was even what I deserved. There came a point when I had to stop hearing her scream at me in my dreams that Robert Graves was still alive and move on with my own life—for sanity's sake.

When I had an opportunity to leave Kingsport for college and not come back, I took it. If I couldn't unburden my guilt, then I could at least attempt to leave it behind, like something dark and terrible packed away in a box in the cellar of my childhood home.

Yet no matter how far away I ran, I would sometimes think, *Did the lighthouse see it all that night? Did its light wash intermittently over the scene, revealing what spontaneously happened in all its tragic glory one minute, slipping us all back into darkness the next? Close your eyes, make a wish, pretend for a moment it didn't happen until it comes back around again. Is there some knowledge—some truth—harnessed in that structure, way out there on Gracie Point, a secret hidden and held, just as we've held ours all these years, and if so, does it judge? Or does it simply observe, stately and benevolent, and wholly disinterested in the tribulations of the human creatures for whom its light brings into sharp relief when the nights are long and bleak and terribly, terribly dark?*

My father was right about small towns: the cost is sometimes higher than the return, and secrets, much like the things that lurk far below the surface of the bay, can stay buried for a very, very long time.

But in the end, everyone pays.

TWENTY

Two police cars came rolling up the street in the night. They had their sirens off, but their rack lights splashed the surrounding trees in alternating red and blue. I stood up from the porch, my cell phone feeling like a brick in my hand, and crushed out the cigarette I had been smoking beneath the heel of my shoe.

Both cars parked in the street. An ambulance followed, roving up the block with all the lethargy of some large, lumbering animal. I heard a radio squawk, a door slam. A trio of featureless figures glided up the driveway toward me.

I came down the porch steps and met Eric halfway down the drive. He was in plain clothes—the T-shirt and jeans he'd been wearing earlier when he'd picked me up at the train station—but he had on his gun belt and a large gold shield clipped to his hip.

"He's in my bedroom," I said, the first words out of my mouth. "Looks like he OD'd. He's got a hypodermic needle sticking out of his arm."

"Goddamn it, Meach," Eric muttered. He rubbed a hand along the unshaven portion of his face. "I thought the son of a bitch had quit that shit."

Two other officers came up the walk, both of them in their khaki uniforms. They both looked fresh-faced and straight out of high school.

I took them into the house and led them down the hall to my bedroom. The room hummed with flies. Meach was still where I'd found him, splayed out on the floor, his head propped up at an aggrieved angle against the wall between the bed and the nightstand. The lamp on the nightstand was still on from when I'd come in here earlier, the single bulb beneath the flimsy tan shade casting a part of Meach's face in shadow, dousing the rest in an almost spectral penumbra. From where I stood now, which was against the doorframe and no closer, I could only make out one gummy, staring eye.

The uniformed officers entered the room, and Eric gently placed a hand on my back. When he spoke, close to my face, I could smell coffee on his breath. "Why don't we go sit in the kitchen and let these guys do their thing?"

I nodded, and allowed him to lead me down the hall, just as a pair of paramedics came through the front door. Eric spoke with them briefly, then followed me into the kitchen once they'd departed for the bedroom.

In the kitchen, I searched the cupboards for coffee, but of course there was nothing. In the fridge was Meach's beer, some food in shrink-wrapped packaging with the red and white Stop and Go stickers on all of them. On the counter was a buckshot scatter of bottle caps and a half empty bottle of Wild Turkey. The six-pack and gas station chicken tenders I had brought home with me sat on the table beneath the glow of the dome light in the ceiling. I didn't know what I was looking for; I was neither hungry nor thirsty. Maybe I just wanted to keep my mind busy.

"Why don't you have a shot, calm yourself down?" Eric suggested, nodding toward the bottle of Wild Turkey.

I took a glass down from the cupboard, rinsed it at the sink, then poured a shaking finger of booze into it. I offered him one, but he declined.

Eric sat at the table. He gazed up at the ceiling, where the dangling, almost festive strips of flypaper curled down all around him. A fat, lazy fly landed on the back of his hand, and Eric shook it off.

I knocked the shot down my throat. Grimaced.

"This is going to kill Tig," Eric said, rubbing a hand along his bristling jaw again. I could hear the sandpapery wisp of his beard stubble against his palm.

"How long do you think he's been in there like that?"

"Maybe a day or two, by the look of him. Smells more like weeks, though. Jesus."

"That's not him," I said. "It's coming from the cellar. It's the smell I told you about. It's flooded and the water stinks."

"Flooded from what?"

"Maybe a pipe broke. I don't know."

"You can't stay here tonight. It's like a house of horrors." As he said this, a second fly lit upon the side of his face, crawled around his temple to his forehead, then took off. Eric rubbed absently at his brow, hardly noticing.

"I tried to get a room out by the highway, but they're all booked up because of the Fourth."

"You'll stay with me tonight," Eric said.

We watched the duo of paramedics wheel Meach's body out on a gurney then hoist him into the back of the ambulance. Eric returned to the bedroom where Meach had died and proceeded to gather up all of Meach's belongings—the backpack stuffed with his junk, his sleeping bag, his filthy clothes and shoes. When he picked up the William Blake book, I said, "That's mine," and so he set it on the nightstand, still open and upside down.

We went back out into the night and Eric tossed Meach's stuff into the trunk of his car, which I'd driven back here earlier that night and parked beside the house. When he opened the trunk, I noticed a large square of plastic sheeting folded up in there, too, and the sight of it thickened my throat. My own bag was still in the back seat of the car, and for one woozy second, I couldn't remember why. But then I recalled Eric picking me up earlier that evening at the train station in Baltimore, then shuttling me directly to Dale's house. At this ungodly hour, that now seemed like days ago.

I climbed into the passenger seat of Eric's car and rested my head back against the headrest, then closed my eyes. I was struggling with the impossibility of it all—of Matthew Meacham, the five-year-old boy I'd met rescuing a small bird at Kingsport Beach, having just been loaded into the back of an ambulance headed for the morgue. The words he'd spoken to me that night at The Rat echoed now inside my head: *It's almost twenty years to the day. The anniversary of Robert's death looming just over the horizon. We're all gonna pay now.* I thought, too, of the nightmare I'd had back in New York, Meach a specter at the foot of my bed, one icy hand clamped around my ankle, murmuring: *one, two, three, four.* Because one of us was now gone . . .

I listened to Eric's sneakers crunch along the gravel driveway, circumnavigating the car, until he popped the door and slid behind the Toyota's steering wheel.

"You okay?" he asked, and clapped a hand to my thigh.

"I will be."

He pulled out of the driveway and headed down the road, headlights cleaving the darkness ahead of us. The exhaustion I suddenly felt was so heavy upon me in that moment, it felt like my lungs were being crushed.

"What did Dale have to say tonight?" Eric asked.

My mind felt threadbare, full of holes. Nevertheless, I recounted for him everything that I could remember at that late hour. The only thing I didn't tell him was the strange story Dale had concluded with, about going into that vacant house in the cul-de-sac and seeing a figure standing in a room full of smog. Despite my exhaustion, I could still clearly see Dale dumping those shiny pull-tabs onto the tabletop whenever I closed my eyes—the way they clanked tinnily, scattered, shone in the light.

Not for the first time, I thought, *What the hell is going on here?*

"How did he seem to you?" Eric asked. "His state of mind, I mean."

"I don't know, Eric. He's a mess, man."

"He's a goddamn liability, is what he is."

"How long until the medical examiner releases an autopsy report on his wife, do you think?"

"They'll put a rush on it. Twenty-four hours. Maybe less. Could be as early as tomorrow afternoon." He glanced at me, and I saw the ghastly look of his pale face in the lights of the car's dashboard. "District attorney's gonna want Dale interviewed again, once the results of that report come back."

"Even if it's inconclusive what actually caused the trauma?"

"Yes," he said, flatly. "And this time, I won't be the one to do it. They'll bring in someone from the state police. Maybe even an investigator from the D.A.'s office."

"He's already given a statement. There's nothing more to ask him about."

"It'll be more interrogative this time. The D.A.'s not buying that she wandered drunk all the way out to Gracie Point, just to fall over a cliff. It's too far from The Wharf Rat."

"You said she wandered all the way out to Graves Road in the snow," I reminded him. Then added: "Barefoot."

"Yeah, well, let's keep that ace in our pocket for now."

"Dale's already given a statement," I reiterated, and eased my head back against the headrest. My eyelids fluttered closed.

"Speaking as his lawyer, huh?" Eric said.

"Speaking as his lawyer," I said. Then I thought of something and opened my eyes. "Do you think you can get me another police report? An older one?"

He glanced at me. "What report?"

"Robert," I said.

The car was quiet awhile.

"Why do you want to read that ancient history?"

"I'm preparing for every eventuality," I said, which was not wholly the truth. I'd been thinking lately of my father, and of the night soon after Robert's death when Ruth Graves showed up at our house. But I wasn't going to tell Eric this.

"Yeah, fine," he said, but he didn't sound happy about it.

Eric's was a small three-bedroom bungalow, with all the rooms spoken for. The sofa was a pullout, though, and once we'd crept silently into the house, Eric retrieved some sheets from a hall closet, which he and I stretched across the pullout sofa's flimsy mattress.

"You'll probably wake up with a cricked neck," Eric said, "but it's better than trying to sleep in that house."

"Someone should tell Tig," I suggested.

Eric raised a hand and seemed to pat the air between us. "Yeah, yeah," he said. "One thing at a time, huh? You need anything else before I turn in?"

"Not a thing," I said. "Thanks for letting me crash."

He smiled wearily at me. "You remember how many times I stayed the night at your place when we were kids?"

"Sure," I said, and I thought about the time I'd laid there in my own bed while Eric wept quietly to himself on the floor, swaddled in my old sleeping bag. He'd often spent the night at my house to escape whatever warpath his father had been marching down on any given night.

"Get some sleep," he said, clapping me on the shoulder, then he sauntered down the hall with his head hanging low, like some death-row inmate.

I crawled onto the mattress, heard the springs creak in protest, then felt a network of bars push against the small of my back the moment I laid down. But the sheets smelled clean, and there were no flies currently dive-bombing my head—not to mention that Meach's corpse had not just been recently excavated from this place—so all in all, I considered this an upgrade in accommodations.

Except that—

—a vivid dream accosted me at one point, so real that I woke moments later with the bed sheets in a sweaty tangle about my ankles and my entire body shaking: a dream, of course, because it could not have been reality to which I had opened my eyes. Eric Kelly's twin boys hovered above me in the darkness as I slept—or was I sleeping?—their heads pressed close together, an inquisitive and somewhat menacing air about them. Their eyes gleamed in the moonlight coming through the living room windows. I opened my mouth to speak to them, but only a hot rush of soundless air escaped. I tried to move, too, but found that my arms and legs refused to cooperate. There was a terrible taste in my mouth, like cordite or gunpowder, and with each breath I took I could hear an increasing rattle in my lungs.

One of the twins produced a lighter—one of those long-stemmed ones that people use to light barbecue grilles—and it went *clickity clickity clickity* until a narrow finger of flame sprung from the elongated tip. The boys' faces swam into focus behind that single dancing flame, their faces glistening with sweat, the pupils of their eyes alight with the reflection of that flame.

I was powerless to move as the flame drew closer and closer to my face. I could feel the heat from it; could see the way the shadows shifted across the boys' faces as that flame put distance between them on its way to me. It was coming for my eye, my right eye, and I could smell the lighter fluid burning off the tip of that flame. The taste of gunpowder still lingered in my mouth, too, and seawater filled up my lungs. Suddenly, I couldn't breathe.

That flame scorched the eyelashes of my right eye. I tried to recoil from it but couldn't. I tried to blink the burn away, to shut my eyes, but I couldn't do that either.

A figure stood behind the boys, untouched by the meager light—the narrow, scarecrow-thin suggestion of a person, head slumped to one side on the rigid stalk of its neck, a smell like death coming off it in waves.

And my mind screamed, *Robert?*

Suddenly, I could move again. Blinking my eyes, I found that I was lying on my back, sheets twisted about my ankles, my heart slamming against the wall of my chest. The room was dark, except for a shaft of moonlight coming through the living room windows. I rolled my head to the side, holding my breath in anticipation of seeing Eric's twin boys kneeling beside my bed with that elongated lighter at the ready, but there was no one there.

I was alone.

I rolled my head back and lay staring at the ceiling. I was gasping for breath, I realized; my lungs ached. It took several minutes for my heart to settle and my respiration to attain some semblance of normalcy again. I laced my shaking hands over my sternum and kept staring at the ceiling. For one fleeting moment, I thought I could hear that mechanical *beep beep beep* again, like someone's car alarm blaring far off in the distance. But I couldn't be sure if that wasn't all in my head, too.

Eventually, I closed my eyes. My mouth still tasted funny—like I'd been sucking on bricks of charcoal—and my lungs still ached, but I forced myself into some simulacrum of sleep, a pantomime of slumber, until the genuine article finally came and dragged me down, down.

TWENTY-ONE

I woke up disoriented, gazing up at a pair of matching pink faces staring down at me. Remnants from last night's nightmare came flooding back, and I jerked myself up on my elbows. Eric's twin boys stood above me, their round moonfaces gazing down at me. With perfect clarity, I saw a booger in one boy's nostril tick back and forth as he breathed. When they saw that they had sufficiently startled me, they scampered off.

An older girl motored by next, so preoccupied with her cell phone that she didn't notice me propped up on the pullout sofa. Eric's wife brought up the rear, marshaling them all down the hall toward the open front door. She paused to introduce herself to me—Trudy or Tracy; I forgot her name the instant she mentioned it to me—and then she said, "I hope that thing didn't wreck your back too bad. There's fresh coffee in the kitchen. Make yourself at home."

"Thanks so much. What time is it?"

"Noon."

And then the Kelly brood was out the door, piling into the family minivan, and shuttling off down the road.

Shying away from the daylight, I rolled off the mattress. My back protested, and as I stood upright, I could feel a dull throb directly above my left buttock. I rubbed at it, the muscle feeling like a peach pit beneath my skin. I'd slept in my clothes, and they felt damp with night sweat.

Eric came down the hall in uniform. He looked grim, and about as well-rested as I felt. I fumbled through some thank-you for letting me crash here, but he went straight into the kitchen without giving me much more than a curt nod. I followed him in there, where he stood at the counter filling a travel cup of coffee.

"I'm headed to Tig's before she leaves for work," he said. "I want to tell her about Meach before she hears it from someone else."

"I'm coming with you," I said.

We took Eric's squad car to Sea Grass Lane. I had a headache and was thankful that Eric didn't try to engage me in any conversation on the drive; he seemed preoccupied and lost in his own thoughts, and that was just fine by me. Tig's Jeep was still in the driveway when we arrived, but when we got out of the cruiser, walked up the porch, and knocked on the door, no one answered. Eric made a sound way back in his throat that suggested this was unusual. He banged harder on the door and called out Tig's name while I stood behind him on the porch. Directly above us, a pair of turkey vultures crisscrossed in the sky.

"Maybe she walked to work to avoid the road closures," I suggested.

Eric stepped to one of the windows. He cupped his hands and peered inside the house. From far off I thought I heard someone shouting. A woman's voice.

I went back down into the yard and walked around to the side of the house. Tig was striding urgently toward me from the backyard. I raised a hand over my head and waved, but something didn't feel right.

"Eric, she's back here!"

As Tig drew closer, I could see the state she was in—frantic, frazzled, her hair undone. She was wearing a Wharf Rat T-shirt and denim shorts, both of which were soaking wet. Her feet were bare, and brown streaks of mud ran along her shins and the tops of her feet.

"Tig, what's wrong?"

"She's gone." There was a slight rasp to her voice, as if she'd been screaming herself hoarse the night before. "She's gone, Andrew."

I could see that she had been crying, but more than that: there was a dark stain of blood in the white of her right eye, as if her tear duct had just excreted some poison into her.

Eric came around the side of the house and intercepted her before she could close the distance between us. "What's going on?" he said. "What's wrong?"

"Bonnie's gone! She's missing!"

"Calm down." He took her gently about the arms, as if to steady her. "Antigone, I need you to take a breath and calm—"

She swatted his arms off her. "Don't treat me like that, Eric! You knew this was coming, I *told* you this was coming, but you wouldn't fucking listen! You're so goddamned pigheaded!"

"Calm d—"

"Don't say it again." She jabbed a finger at him. Then she turned and looked at me, as if just now seeing me standing here for the first time. "What are you both doing here?"

"Just tell me what happened," Eric said.

"Well, I know you're not going to want to hear last night's bullshit, as you call it—"

"Antigone—"

"—so I'll just cut to the chase." She ran a hand through her tousled hair. "I got up this morning and she was gone, okay? The front door was open. I went down to the water, calling for her, but she didn't answer. She wasn't there."

"She's still sleepwalking? I told you to put a bolt on the door."

"I *did* put a bolt on the door. But the door was open. Goddamn it, Eric. . ."

"What about Reggie? He back in town? He's got a key to the house?"

"No, he doesn't have a key. And Reggie wouldn't come into the house and take her out of my bed in the middle of the night."

"And what happened here?" Eric said, lifting one hand and delicately caressing the soft pocket of flesh beneath her right eye with his thumb—the eye with the bloodstain.

"Forget about me." She pushed his hand away. "I'm fine. It's *Bonnie—*"

"I'm just saying, if Reggie's giving you any more prob—"

"It's not fucking *Reggie,* Eric, you're not listening to me."

He relented. Took a step back. Said, "Okay, okay. Don't worry. We'll find her." He glanced at me for some reason, and said, "Let's go to the front. I'll radio it in from the car." He looked back at Tig. "Everything is going to be all right. I promise."

"Jesus Christ," she said, and rubbed her hands down her face.

Eric nodded at me, then he headed back toward the driveway.

"Come on, Tig." I put a hand on her shoulder and led her back around to the front of the house. She moved with all the zeal of a zombie. By the time we got to the edge of the driveway, Eric was already leaning into the open door of his squad car. I heard him prattle off some instructions to dispatch over the radio.

"This is us," she muttered, her fingers over her lips. "This is our fault."

I didn't know what she meant, and I didn't care to push her on it; clearly she was a mess. "Eric's right," I told her. "Everything will be fine."

She fixed her eyes on me again. That bright red bloodstain was as prominent as a gunshot wound. "What are you *doing* here?" she asked me again.

Before I could respond, Eric approached and stepped between us. "I put the word out, the guys are gonna do some neighborhood drive-bys. I'm gonna drive the block a few times, head down to the inlet and then back up through Kingsport Park. She couldn't have gotten far."

"You don't *know*, Eric."

"Just wait here at the house with Andrew, in case she comes back."

"I don't want to wait at the house! You *know* what I've been saying, and I don't want you to shut me down anymore. This is my *daughter*—"

"I'm not shutting you down, Tig. Just let me go find your daughter." He looked at me. "Andrew, make sure she stays at the house. The both of you."

He got back inside the squad car and ran over some lavender as he backed out into the street, then drove off.

Tig stood for a moment, staring after Eric's cruiser while I stared at her. Then she turned to me, studied me with that one bloodied eye. She looked unsteady on her feet.

"Let's get you inside," I said, placing a hand on her shoulder.

The house looked like it had been ransacked: chairs were knocked over, items had been pulled from closets and lay in heaps on the floor. Tig wandered down the hall and disappeared into the bathroom.

I picked up an end table off the floor and righted it. There was a broken lamp beside it, triangular chunks of ceramic scattered about the carpet, the lampshade dented. Behind the couch was a plastic Playskool desk and chair, a bunch of art supplies on it. I went over and peered down at the crayon drawings and watercolor paintings that lay spread across its top. More birds, more lighthouses. The one at the center of the desk depicted some sort of sea creature leaping from spiky blue water—a thing that could have been a mermaid except that its face looked like a skull, its hair a wiry mop of green algae.

When Tig came back into the room, she was wearing fresh clothes and the streaks of mud had been washed clean from her legs and feet.

"What happened in here? It looks like you were burglarized."

She sat on the couch and laced up a pair of cross trainers.

"Where are you going? Eric said to wait here."

"Fuck that," she said. "And fuck Eric. He hasn't listened to a damn thing I've been saying since this whole thing started."

I shook my head. "What are you talking about?"

She got up from the couch and snatched a set of keys from a hook on the way.

"Where are you going?"

She ignored me, and instead made a beeline for the front door. I hurried after her and caught up with her halfway to her Jeep. I reached for her but she swung her arm with such force that she clocked me in the jaw.

"Goddamn it, Tig!"

She jumped behind the wheel of the Jeep, and I rushed over and climbed up into the passenger seat just as the engine growled to life. The Runaways blasted out of the high-end speakers, belting out "Cherry Bomb." I switched the radio off just as Tig stomped on the gas and we rocketed across her front yard in reverse, kicking up plumes of dust.

"Jesus, Tig, you're gonna get us killed . . ."

"I didn't ask you to come."

"Please," I begged. "Slow down."

She looked at me from the side of her eye—her ruined eye—and then slowed down a bit once we were on the main road. I stole a glance at her, could see the muscles flexing in her jaw. She was angry, I could tell, but she was afraid, too. I recalled the story she'd told me about her daughter sleepwalking, and how she'd found her in the middle of the night down by the water behind her house.

"I'm sure she's fine, you know. Maybe she's curled up asleep in a field somewhere."

"Don't be so naive, Andrew."

The Jeep jounced over a series of potholes and my back teeth gnashed together.

"You said something to Eric about him knowing this was coming? That you knew he wouldn't want to hear about last night's bullshit?"

She glanced at me, those jaw muscles still flexing, that hemorrhage in her right eye looking like a splotch of bright red ink on a blotter.

"He doesn't want to hear it." She spoke low, her voice barely audible over the rumble of the Jeep's engine.

"What do you mean?"

"He thinks we're all crazy, that we're all losing our minds. Drinking Meach's Kool-Aid." She shook her head as a tear raced down her cheek.

At the mention of his name, I suddenly remembered that Meach was dead. A wave of nausea washed through me, and I actually leaned forward in my seat and gripped the dashboard, suddenly worried that I might be sick. Tig's driving didn't help matters.

"Do you want to know what happened last night?" she said. "Or will you think I'm crazy, too?"

We hit another bump in the road and I felt my stomach lurch. She wasn't headed into town, but instead she was taking us to the outskirts of Kingsport, where the cornfields grew, and great metal grain silos stood in ranks against a horizon fecund with trees.

"Yes," I heard myself say. "Tell me what happened last night."

Her grip tightened on the steering wheel, knuckles turning white.

"Tig," I said.

And then she told me.

Last night, after they'd left Dale's house and she dropped Eric off at his home, she arrived at her own home in a jumble of nerves. Eric hadn't spoken to her the entire drive; she felt like he disapproved of her being there for Dale in his moment of need, and if that was the case, Eric could go fuck himself. She wasn't an idiot; she could see the walls were closing in around her old friend.

She parked, shut down the Jeep's engine, and just sat there crying for a while before going inside to relieve the babysitter. Millie thanked her for the extra cash, said Bonnie had been a sweetheart all night, then left. Still shaken from the cold shoulder Eric had given her on the drive back, she went to the kitchen, poured herself a shot of whiskey, and tipped it down her throat. Then she went to the bathroom and washed her face and hands, trying to get herself under control.

There was a small red circle of blood on the sclera of her right eye, near the tear duct. She brought her face closer to the mirror, pulled her eyelid wide with her thumb and index finger. A spot of blood, no bigger than a ball bearing. But there nonetheless.

The bathroom lights fluttered.

She went down the hall and into the kitchen, saw that the microwave was blinking 88:88, and knew that the power had monetarily gone out in the entire house. There was a transformer out on Rock Beach Road that was fairly unreliable, but it only went dead during a bad storm. Tonight, the air was still, and there hadn't been a cloud in the sky.

She crept back down the hall and peered into Bonnie's bedroom.

Bonnie's bed was empty.

279

A finger of panic rose in her throat. Images flashed before her eyes of the night she'd found the kitchen door open and her daughter standing along the cusp of the bay, staring out into the darkness at . . .

What?

A dead boy?

She was about to turn and run down the hall, out the door, down through the yard toward the water, until she realized that the window beside her daughter's bed stood open. And not just *open,* but the screen was gone, too. As she stared at the open window, a large black fly entered, zigzagged around the bedroom, then disappeared down the hall.

Tig hurried to the window, poked her head out. The screen was on the roof, as if someone had pushed it away from the window from the inside. She looked farther down the slope of the roof and saw nothing at first, fearing the worst . . . but then she could see Bonnie standing along the edge of the roof, her white undershirt and panties nearly aglow in the moonlight.

"Bonnie! Bonnie!"

The girl did not respond.

Tig climbed out onto the roof and crawled on her hands and knees toward her daughter. Heat lightning bisected the sky directly in front of her, startling her, and in that flash she could see the way Bonnie's head was sleepily cocked to one side, her arms limp, her knees about to buckle. If she fell, she'd go right over the side of the roof—

Tig reached out, snatched one of her daughter's wrists, and dragged her into a tight embrace. The girl went effortlessly, her body as lifeless as a ragdoll's. Tig tipped her daughter's head back, shocked by the clammy coolness of her daughter's flesh, the horrible rolling whites of her eyes, the long black fans of lashes fluttering, fluttering . . .

"Baby? Baby?"

A second bolt of lightning directly over the house illuminated a

figure in the yard below. In that pulse of light, Tig saw him, Robert
Graves, gazing up at her with his one remaining eye. Where his
other eye should have been was a smoldering crater that emitted a
pearlescent blue light.

All the lights in the house blew out.

Tig screamed, and dragged her daughter back through the open
bedroom window, down onto Bonnie's bed, the girl's head limp
against Tig's arm, the wind picking up and whipping leaves into a fury
against Tig's face through the open window and into the bedroom, Tig
muttering, "Come on, baby," gently slapping Bonnie's cheek, those
fluttery white orbs unchanged, "come on, baby, come on," slapping her
with a bit more force, "please, now," and the girl's mouth yawned open
and her eyes suddenly looked up at her mother, her body stiffening, her
arms coming up in a tight embrace around her mother's neck, a scream
that made no sound, and Tig, casting one final glance out the window
and down into the yard to see if that dead boy was still standing there,
still staring up at her, still waiting for her daughter to come back out
onto the roof and to step off the ledge and into the night—

She could see no one down there. Still holding her daughter
against her, she closed the window with one hand, then backed out
of the bedroom and out into the hall. She didn't want to take her eyes
off the window, expecting at any moment that shape from the yard to
appear on the other side of the glass, the dead boy's empty eye socket
ablaze, hands pressing against the windowpane, sliding down the
glass and gripping the sill, wresting the window back open . . .

No.

In the hall, she toggled the light switch but nothing happened.
The storm had knocked out the power. Lightning pulsed in all the
windows, followed by a peal of thunder that shook the world.

Something shifted at the far end of the hallway. Tig turned and
stared down the throat of that black chasm, not quite seeing anything,

yet at the same time overcome by the unshakeable certainty that there was something *big* and *encroaching* clawing its way toward her in the darkness. A sentient blood clot slowly filling up the corridor to block her passage; a storm cloud with many minds.

Against her neck, Bonnie said, "Mommy, I'm scared..."

Tig backed into the master bedroom, closed and locked the door. She carried Bonnie over to the bed, set her down on the mattress—

"Mommy!"

—then dropped to her hands and knees on the floor.

She kept an aluminum baseball bat under the bed for protection, in the event someone broke into the house in the middle of the night, or if Reggie ever came back around again, drunk and handsy and looking for trouble.

"Mommy..."

"Shhh, baby. Shhh."

She stood there in the dark, baseball bat at the ready. Something else stood in one darkened corner of the bedroom: she took a swing at it, but the bat passed through the darkness unimpeded. A floorboard creaked behind her and she took another swing. But there was no one there.

"Mommy! Make the lightning stop!"

"It's just a storm, baby!"

But the house was rattling: the windowpanes shook in their frames and the closed bedroom door bucked on its hinges. There was a popping sound, and then the bedroom door swung open. Tig felt a gust of wind pass right through her. She swung the bat again, twirling around like a ballerina in the dark. Something—someone—was in the house and they were toying with her.

"Leave us alone!"

Swing.

Swing.

Swing.

A shape flitted down the hallway.

"Stay in the bed, Bonnie."

"Mommmm . . ."

"Stay in the bed!"

Tig pursued the figure down the hall, swinging the bat erratically. It collided with a wall, showering the floor with plaster. Robert was there, just out of reach of the bat, gliding backward down the hallway—a shape that was barely visible in the shafts of moonlight sliding through the windows, but there nonetheless. Another bout of lightning, and Tig saw his gangly form slip away into the living room.

"You bastard." It came out in a breathy expulsion of air. "You lousy son of a bitch, *leave me and my daughter alone!*"

She staggered down the stairs, swinging blindly. A lamp crashed to the floor. An end table toppled over. She backed into a closet and items came avalanching out onto the floor, pelting her about the shoulders. Still swinging, swinging—

"You son of a bitch!"

Swinging—

"Momm-EEEEE!"

She paused, sweat coursing down her body in rivulets, and stood in the center of the darkened house, catching her breath. When Bonnie shrieked again, Tig rushed back up the stairs and down the hall to the master bedroom.

"I'm here, baby. Mommy's here."

She crawled onto the bed beside her daughter, hands still gripping the bat. The house creaked like a ship on the sea. Lightning stuttered in all the windows. Thunder bowled across the rooftop.

She grabbed her daughter's sweat-damp head and drew it against her chest. The girl wrapped an arm around her, squeezed her tight.

"It's just a storm," Tig whispered into the child's ear. Wide-eyed, she searched the darkness for a figure who could not be there, could not exist. "Close your eyes, baby. It's just a storm. It'll pass. It'll pass."

"I'm scared!"

"It'll pass, baby. It'll pass."

And it did.

Soon, Bonnie was asleep against her, the girl's soft, warm breath coursing over Tig's sweat-spangled flesh. She set the bat down beside her on the mattress, her own eyelids growing heavy, lulled by the sound of the wind outside, bullying the house. When she thought she heard the ringing of a bicycle bell from far off, she opened her eyes and gazed into a swirling black cloud that hovered in front of her face—a cloud that was really a thick ball of flies, was really a multitude of fluttering bird wings, was really the dark crater of an eye socket with a dim blue light emanating from its distant core. But then she heard the bell again, opened her eyes again, and realized she'd only been dreaming.

"In the morning, Bonnie was gone. The front door was open. I *did* have a deadbolt put in, but that had been unlocked, too, and it's too high for Bonnie to reach. There weren't even any footprints in the mud outside, because there *was* no mud. There hadn't been a storm last night."

Tig was right. I'd spent most of the night awake, and what sleep I'd gotten had been sporadic and restless on Eric's pull-out sofa. But I knew one thing for certain: it hadn't stormed at all last night.

I didn't know what to say. Too many things had come at me in such a short span of time that I felt like the butt of some terrible joke, because there was no way all of this was *real*, no way all of this was connected and actually *happening*.

Tig slowed the Jeep down further, and I was grateful. I could hear my heart slamming in my ears over the surge of the engine.

"You're a lawyer. Let me ask you something."

"Go ahead."

"Realistically, what would happen to us? If we all came clean, I mean. It was so long ago and it was an accident. Would we go to jail for murder? For manslaughter? Is it worse that we've kept it a secret all these years?"

"Why are you bringing this up now?" A minute earlier, I noticed she had driven us onto Graves Road, and we were coasting along it now at a steady clip, winding through a matrix of cornfields. The humidity that boiled into that Jeep made me feel feverish and sickly. "Where are we going, Tig?"

"Enough is enough," Tig said, and she pushed down further on the accelerator.

As we rocketed around the wooded bend, the Graves house came into view. I was suddenly overcome by the certainty that we were being beckoned, like animals lured into a trap.

"What are we doing here, Tig?"

"She took her," Tig said. "The old witch came in the night and took my daughter. Just like witches do."

"Tig, please—"

She jerked the Jeep to a stop in the middle of the road, right in front of Ruth Graves's house. It had been years since I'd seen the place, and I wasn't surprised to find it every bit as hopeless and inhospitable as I remembered it: the cement house covered in veins of ivy, the front yard filled with a profusion of those hideous child-sized dolls adorned in animal bones and bird feathers. A tree stump in the middle of the yard that held my attention for longer than it should have.

Before I could say another word, Tig jumped out of the Jeep and was marching across the road. I jumped out, too, and chased after her.

"Hey," I said, gripping her high on the forearm.

She jerked her arm free. "One more son of a bitch grabs my fucking arm today and I'll break their jaw."

"This is crazy. Please, Tig, get back in the car."

"I can't, Andrew. I don't have a choice anymore."

"You don't know what you're doing. We shouldn't be here."

"I don't have a *choice*, Andrew. Don't you get it?"

She shoved open the gate—the hinges shrilled—and headed up the weedy, overgrown path toward the front of the house. The phalanx of dolls that lined the walkway looked like sentries, observing her every step.

"Antigone!"

She ignored me.

"You want to know what could happen?" I called after her. I was careful to keep my voice down, but to also put some authority behind it. I was suddenly panicked and shaking. My whole world felt like it was tilting to one side. "We could go to jail. Not just for what happened, but for what we did afterward—us fleeing the scene and not getting help. Then for conspiracy to cover it up all these years. We could all go to jail and you'd lose your daughter. Eric would lose his family. Dale's son will have no parents left. Is that what you want?"

She turned and looked at me.

"What I want," she said, her voice calm, though I could see tears beginning to well in her eyes, "is for my daughter to be safe. That's all."

Just then, the front door of Ruth Graves's house opened. Both Tig and I turned to look, just as the old woman herself ambled out onto the porch. She wore a long-sleeved cotton frock and had her hair—now completely silver—twisted into a braid running down the front of one shoulder.

The sight of her caused Tig to pause at the foot of the porch steps. Ruth Graves turned her head to examine Tig without a hint of emotion on her face. Then she redirected her black-eyed gaze toward me, to where I was still standing farther down the walkway near the fence, flanked on both sides by a procession of her hideous dolls, sweating in my damp, unwashed clothes.

"Where is my daughter?" Tig demanded.

The old woman's lips thinned. She took a step closer to the edge of the porch, and I could hear the floorboards creak. "Your daughter?" she said.

"Don't bullshit me! You did something to her. You've been doing it for weeks! It has to *stop*. I want my daughter back. Goddamn you, I want her *back*..."

"You think your little girl is somewhere in my house?" Ruth said. "Is that why you're here?" Those black eyes sparkled as she turned to examine me standing in the yard again. Then she extended a hand and addressed her open front door. "You're welcome to go inside and look around. But I assure you, your daughter is not here. There are no little girls in my home."

Tig proceeded to climb the porch steps, but I rushed up behind her and took her by the wrist. This time, when she tried to shake me off, I refused to let her go. "Stop it, Tig. Bonnie isn't here."

Tig looked at me. That red hematoma had spread; there was only a small section of sclera in the corner of her eye that was still white. "This has to *stop*," she said to me. Her voice was reed-thin and shaking. "Please, Andrew. Please help me make things right."

"This isn't making things right. This is making things worse."

"Worse?" Something akin to a laugh ratcheted up her throat. "My daughter is missing! Wake the fuck up!"

I groped for her again, but she moved quickly up the porch steps and out of my reach. She dropped to her knees before Ruth Graves.

"Please," Tig said. "Please give me back my daughter. I'm sorry. We're all sorry."

Ruth's head leaned to one side. "What exactly are you sorry for, dear?"

"Antigone," I called to her, attracting the old woman's attention.

"For what happened," Tig said. "For what we did. *Please*—let me have my daughter back."

"I do not have your daughter," Ruth said, eyebrows knitting together slightly. She was looking at me now, not at Tig. I remembered the way the kitchen lights had shined in her eyes all those years ago when she'd followed my father down the hall of our house, like they had been lit up from the inside.

"Tig," I said, and crept up the porch steps toward her. "Bonnie isn't here. We need to leave."

"Please," Tig begged at the feet of Ruth Graves.

"Tig, honey," I said, and placed a hand on her shoulder. I helped her to her feet, then slid my hand into hers. Her fingers slipped between mine, and squeezed. The sweat in her palm made a squelching sound.

I looked up at Ruth, and those oil-black eyes swiveled once again in my direction.

"She's just upset," I said. "Her daughter's missing and she's—"

"Oh, I know who she is," said Ruth.

I felt Tig's grip on my hand go limp.

"Go back to the car, Tig," I said.

Tig's hand dropped from mine. She stood there a moment, tears streaming down her face, staring first at me, then at Ruth, and lastly at the door that stood open at the front of the house. For a second, I thought she was going to bolt for it, and I held my breath. But then she turned and retreated down the porch steps. Her shadow followed, bobbing down the steps until it withdrew into the tall, sun-bleached grass. Above her, two turkey vultures wheeled lazily in the sky.

"I know who *you* are, too," Ruth said, staring at me.

"That's right," I said. "My name's Andrew Larimer. My father was Ernest Larimer. He was an attorney here in town. I grew up here. I used to . . ."

Something like a smile tugged at one corner of Ruth Graves's mouth. Above her head, hanging from the porch awning was a wind chime made of small, slender bones and wire, adorned in iridescent black feathers. It made a sound like distant horse hooves in the breeze.

"I hope your friend finds her little girl, safe and sound," Ruth said, still staring at me.

"I'm sure she will. I'm sorry for the trouble."

I backed away from the house, just as Ruth Graves stepped to the edge of the porch. Her face remained in shadow, but one pale, talon-like hand reached out and wrapped a set of bone-white fingers around the railing. I imagined I could hear the rigid tendons creaking along her knobby finger bones. Loose strands of silver hair whipped about her face, although the air was hot and still and motionless in that moment.

I retreated down the walk and hurried out into the street. Tig stood there, staring up at the house and at the woman on the porch, sweat rolling down her face. Her eyes—even the bloodied one—were moist. I ushered her around to the passenger side of the Jeep, then was about to climb into the driver's seat when I paused and glanced once more over my shoulder.

I could see the old woman still on the porch. She appeared to be muttering something to herself. And although I couldn't hear what she was saying—and yes, I will admit that perhaps my overtaxed mind could have been reading into things, imagining things to be one way when, in fact, they weren't—I thought I could make out what it was by the repetition of those words on her thin, dry lips.

She was counting.

One, two, three, four, five.

Over and over again, the old witch was counting.

"Don't take me home," she said.

"Where do you want to go?"

"Just drive, goddamn it. Look for my kid."

I took the first turn I could, heading down through a section of A-frame houses toward the beach roads, where we coasted by the dunes and the wharfs and the crumbling wooden fishing shacks that lay in abandoned disrepair along the cusp of the bay. We made this loop three times, circling in that Jeep like some predatory bird, and by the end of that third circuit, we passed police cars heading in the opposite direction.

"Do you want me to follow them, see where they're going?"

She considered this for a second. Then said, "No. Take the old Ribbon Road out to Gracie Point."

"She wouldn't have gone that far, Tig."

"Just fucking do it."

I turned around and headed back along one of the old beach roads that would connect us with the old Ribbon Road along the coast and take us straight out to Gracie Point. In this moment, I would be lying if I said the encounter at Ruth Graves's house hadn't left me rattled. It wasn't just about how close Tig had come to saying something damning and irreparable; it was the way the old woman had probed me with her dark eyes, as if some unspoken knowledge was swirling around inside her brain, some unspoken language transmitted between us. As if she knew more about me and my life than I cared to think about. I knew that fretting over such a thing was nearly as ludicrous as Tig's assertion that the old woman had crept into her house, witchlike, in the night to abduct her daughter from her bed . . . yet I couldn't help but think of all those old fairytales about gingerbread houses and naive young children kept in cages until they were plump enough to eat.

I know who you *are, too,* Ruth Graves had said to me.

Ridiculous.

"Stop here."

"Come on, Tig."

"Now, Andrew."

I didn't argue with her.

I eased the Jeep to a halt in the middle of the road. Tig got out, and I watched her take a series of small steps to the edge of the cliff. She peered over the side, and to the rocky shore below. Out in the distance, the Gracie Point Lighthouse looked like a scratch on the surface of a bit of film.

I reached for the door handle, but in that moment, my cell phone chirped. It was Laurie O'Dell from New York, and I debated about answering it, but then decided that I had to.

"Larimer, where the hell have you been? Morrison is fuming."

"I had an emergency come up out of town."

"You know you missed a scheduled meeting with Remmy Stein this afternoon."

"Shit."

I'd forgotten all about it.

"Yeah, shit is right. Whatever the emergency is, clean it up ASAP and get your ass back here."

She hung up before I could say anything more.

I slipped the phone back in the breast pocket of my shirt, then got out of the Jeep and went over to where Tig was standing at the edge of the cliff. The day was hot and the air was still, but I felt a chill as I came up beside her and peered down at the unfathomable drop to the stony beach below.

"What are we doing here, Antigone?"

Her stare was locked on the rocks below, where the surf crashed and foamed and lapped at the shore.

"It's funny," she said, her voice low. She could have been talking to herself for all the authority in it. "How every significant outcome in life hinges on a confluence of a million different things coming together at just the right moment to form the perfect storm. How some split-second decision or some thoughtless action could change the trajectories of all our lives. How it could *end* a life. Is that how fragile we are? As people, I mean." She looked at me. "You ever just drive your car over a bridge and think, one jerk of the wheel and that's all it would take to turn out the lights?"

I didn't know what to say to that.

"Life is so delicate, Andrew. It's a wonder any of us survive." She turned and looked back out over the water. "Why did you and Eric come to my house today?"

Out of nowhere, I felt a heaviness in my lungs, an ache in my chest.

"Maybe now's not the time, Tig," I said, which all but cemented the fact that she would pull it out of me. I even winced inwardly as I said it.

"Goddamn you, Andrew. Tell me. Is it about Dale? What's happened?"

I took a breath and said, "It's Meach. I came home last night and found him there in the house. He'd overdosed on something, and I couldn't—"

She clamped her hands to her ears and said, "No, no, no, no, *no*..."

"I'm sorry, Tig."

She dropped her hands and shouted out over the abyss: *"Fuck!"*

And then she turned and just stared at me.

I felt an overwhelming sense of failure for some reason as I stared back at her. As if I'd done something to let her down. To let Meach down, too. Something to cause all of this. As if there had been one more misstep in the story of our lives that had brought us to this point, just as Tig had suggested, and it was all my fault . . .

A jerk of the wheel.

"Antigone—"

"No. Stop. Stop talking."

She turned away from me and looked out across the bay again. The lighthouse stared back at us, its lantern room dark at this hour of the day. Tig hugged herself as if suddenly cold, and then she turned and headed back to the Jeep.

We drove the rest of the way back to her house in silence. When we pulled into the driveway, I barely had the Jeep in park before she was out the door and striding toward Eric's police car that was idling in front of the house. Eric was standing on the porch, but he had turned at our approach and was coming down the steps to greet Tig as she hurried toward him. I shut down the engine, hopped out, and jogged after her.

"We still haven't found her," Eric was saying. "We've got DNR searching the waterways and I've radioed in to the state police. Meantime, we've assembled a group of folks to help search throughout the community. We're combing the woods and the beaches, and all the way out to the highway. I've also put out a BOLO on your ex, just to cover all the bases here. Bottom line: there's not a person in town who doesn't know we're looking for her, Tig."

"Go talk to the witch," Tig said.

Calmly, Eric said, "I'm not going to do that." He leaned closer to her and said, "Your eye is getting worse."

"She's slowly killing me. That woman. That witch. She burned the bar, she killed the power in our house, and now she's killing me. She's killing me, she's killed Meach, and she's taken my daughter!"

Eric glanced disapprovingly in my direction.

"I know you don't believe in this bullshit, Eric," Tig went on, "but Meach dies the same night my daughter disappears? Am I supposed to believe that's just one more goddamn coincidence?"

"Meach needed help," Eric said. "He had a drug problem. His clock was going to run out sooner or later."

"Listen to you! That's *Meach* you're talking about. Our *friend*. He's not some goddamn statistic. This wasn't just an accident!"

"I didn't mean it like—"

"You know what I think? I think Meach was right all along. Instead of calling him crazy and ignoring everything he had to say, we should have *listened*. You said they were just ghost stories, Eric. Well, stories didn't kill him!"

"That's right, Tig. Stories didn't kill him. Heroin did. Nothing supernatural about that."

"Fuck, Eric, we should have gone for help that night! He was still alive. We could have saved him."

"Please, Tig. Stop this." Eric's voice was calm.

"Ruth Graves knows what we've done," Tig said, not stopping this. "Maybe she has from the very beginning. Maybe she's just been sitting here biding her fucking time. And now we're all paying for it."

"Listen to yourself, okay? Think logically. Even if you believe this witchcraft nonsense, why would that woman wait twenty years to take revenge on us if she knew what had happened all along? It doesn't make sense."

"I don't know, Eric. I don't know. Maybe she's got her reasons."

Eric reached out, placed a hand on Tig's shoulder. "What happened to Meach has nothing to do with your daughter's disappearance. Bonnie is going to be fine. We'll find her. I promise."

"I'm going to be sick," she said, and then she hurried into the house.

"I thought I told you guys to stay here," Eric said. "You've been driving around town all day."

"She didn't want to stay. She's upset." I swallowed what felt like a fistful of gravel, then added, "She drove us out to Ruth Graves's house earlier today, begged the woman to give her daughter back."

Eric's face had been beet-red from the heat since his arrival, but now I watched as all the color drained from it. His expression—stoic, calm—did not falter, however. "What happened?"

"Nothing, really. I mean, she just—"

"What the hell happened, Andrew? What'd the old woman say?"

I know who you are, too, Ruth had said, and I literally shook my head to jostle the cobwebs of her voice from my memory.

"Nothing," I said. "Tig was upset. She wasn't making sense. Nothing was said. Nothing happened. I just wanted you to know."

Eric put his hands on his hips and paced around the front yard. I was still feeling that ache in my chest from earlier, only now, it seemed like the physical reverberation of that night all those years ago on the old Ribbon Road—the pain from Eric striking me across the face and making my nose bleed having trickled down into my chest, my lungs, metastasizing throughout my body. What had Dale called it while furiously rubbing the heel of his hand?

Phantom pain.

"You know," he said, "this is your fault."

"*My* fault?"

"You humor her crazy stories, you pretend like Meach wasn't the fucking lost cause train wreck junkie that he was—what's she gonna think? Huh? People like that, you've got to *contain,* Andrew. You've got to *control.* You can't let their fears and their weaknesses overrule common fucking sense."

"Jesus Christ," I said. "I don't even want to be here."

"It's self-preservation time, buddy. This isn't a game."

"Eric—"

"I'm serious, Andrew. This isn't a fucking game."

Tig came back into the yard, looking a bit more collected. To Eric, she said, "I want to go with you and look for her. If she's gone down to the water . . . to the beaches . . ."

"I really think it's best you stay—"

"I'm not sitting in this house while my daughter is out there somewhere."

Eric sucked on his lower lip. "All right," he said after a moment. "Come ride with me."

"I'll come, too," I offered.

Tig pushed past Eric and hurried toward his police cruiser.

"No. Take Tig's Jeep," Eric said. "If this goes on too long, I want you to drive her home."

I watched them get into Eric's car and pull out of the driveway. On my way back to Tig's Jeep, I paused to glance up at the sky, where a large black bird was pulling slow rotations through the air directly above my head.

TWENTY-TWO

We searched until dark, several dozen people along the beaches of Kingsport, the cuffs of our pants rolled up to just below the knees, wading through the surf. No Bonnie. Once the sun had set, large fluorescent lamps were set up along the beach, making the whole scene look like the set of a movie. An hour after that, Eric approached me as I was creeping through a wedge of itchy sea grass.

"I tried to convince her to have you take her home," Eric said. "She refused, and I'm not going to fight her on it. Come with me."

I followed him back across the beach and up to the road, where his police car sat on the shoulder with the rack lights twirling. The pavement was still warm against the bare soles of my feet.

"What exactly happened at Ruth's house today?" he asked me.

I told him what had happened. The only details I left out were how I saw—or thought I saw—Ruth Graves mumbling those numbers as we left, and the sinking, desperate fear I'd felt when I'd looked into that woman's raven-black eyes.

"Do I need to go out there, have a chat with the old recluse?"

"No," I said. "I don't think so. I think we're okay."

Eric seemed to mull this over. I watched as a large black fly landed on the side of his face; Eric casually brushed it away. Then he opened the rear door of his police car and took out another pastry box, similar to the one he'd given me that night at The Wharf Rat containing the open investigation into Cynthia Walls's disappearance. This one said GO NUTS FOR DONUTS on the side.

"Autopsy report came back," he said.

"And?"

"Not good. The body sustained lacerations and some broken bones consistent with a fall over the side of the cliff, but they were all postmortem. The head wound was not. Obviously. Medical examiner estimates anywhere between forty minutes to two hours between the time of the head wound and the other injuries."

"Jesus Christ, Eric."

"Yeah, I know. D.A.'s gonna release a statement tomorrow, they're actively pursuing this as a murder investigation now. She's gonna ask Dale to come in for another statement. We knew this was coming. You can't say no at this point, Andrew."

Something was drilling deeper and deeper into my sternum.

I wanted to call Rebecca.

I wanted to hear Rebecca.

"Listen," he said, and he surprised me by grabbing me high up on the forearm. Squeezed to exert some authority. It was a strangely intimate gesture. "Go home and read the report. I'm gonna come by and get you later tonight."

"What's happening later tonight?"

"We're going to look for blood," he said.

As I drove back to my father's house, what I thought were premature fireworks was actually thunder rumbling out over the bay: I took the coastal road and could see a bulkhead of dark storm clouds brewing way out on the horizon, black as soot. The slender beacon of the

Gracie Point Lighthouse stood resolutely before those clouds like that famous photo of the man standing before a column of tanks in Tiananmen Square. I watched lightning flash within those clouds as I curled around the ribbon of roadway back toward town, and I swore I could feel static in the air stiffening the hair on my forearms.

The house had been waiting for me in my absence. Flies congregated on the walls, and that fetid smell was back, emanating up from the cellar, more potent than it had been last night. I felt Meach's death resonating through the rooms and hallways. I sensed, too, a stirring in the darkness around me, something with a consciousness that was making its presence known. *It's me,* I told myself. *The wraith.* But the incident at Ruth Graves's house earlier that day continued to strum through my bones and mess with my head, and I couldn't trust myself to parse reality from imagination: there, at the end of the hallway, something watched me from the dark.

I flipped the light switch, but only a single bulb came alive in the ceiling midway down the hall. *She burned the bar, she killed the power in our house, and now she's killing me,* Tig had said. Here, alone, sensing something in this house with me, those words took on a gravity that tightened my throat, causing my heart to jackhammer in my chest.

I set the donut box on the kitchen counter, then crept down the throat of that black hallway, eyes locked dead ahead on some indistinguishable space. I thought I caught a whiff of sulfur buried somewhere within the stink coming up out of the cellar. The deeper I went down that throat, the more sweat was wrung from my pores. Flies swarmed my face.

When I stopped before the cellar door, a terrible thought occurred to me—so terrible, in fact, that I nearly fled that house and drove back down to the beach to find Eric and have him and his police buddies do this dirty work. But I didn't. Instead, I turned the crystal-cut glass knob, pulled the door open, *skreeeet*, and gazed down at the water, so high now that it was halfway up the staircase.

Please be wrong, I told myself. *Please be wrong. Please be wrong.*

I stripped off my shoes and socks, activated the flashlight app on my phone, then descended the stairs.

The water was cool, the surface covered in brownish foam. I forgot about the broken step, which nearly sent me splashing to the water below, except I grabbed onto the handrail at the last moment. More cautiously, I lowered myself into that cesspool, casting ripples across its surface as I sank deeper—past my ankles, my shins, my thighs, right up to my waist. Thinking the entire time: *Please be wrong, please be wrong, please be wrong* . . .

Because the cellar stank like death.

I cringed when my bare feet touched the cold dirt floor of the cellar. A body would float down here, wouldn't it? A child's small body would float . . .

I roved back and forth, wall to wall. The cobblestones were veined with algae now, and pale blades of sea grass poked up from the surface of that murky pool in places. Every time my bare feet thumped against something, the breath caught in my throat, and I waited to see if a child's pale, drowned face might come bobbing to the surface. Every time an impossible tendril of seaweed would curl itself around my ankle, I bit back a cry of horror, picturing the narrow fingers of a child's hand pawing at me from below. In my mind, I was already attempting to piece together how this might have happened—how Meach might have somehow done something terrible to Bonnie here in this house and then deliberately overdosed on heroin because he couldn't live with the guilt, and if the timeline of those things actually lined up, because Meach was found dead in this house last night, which was also when Bonnie had gone missing from her house—

(Meach dies the same night my daughter disappears? Am I supposed to believe that's just one more goddamn coincidence?)

—and Bonnie would have known Meach, would have trusted him, and what terrible, heinous thing was my mind cobbling together in these bleak and desperate moments?

Please be wrong, please be wrong, please be—

I turned and redirected the beam from my phone onto a particular area of that panel of dark, stagnant water—a place in the far corner of the cellar. I didn't see it at first . . . but then I did: something luminescent and bulbous suddenly materializing from the murky depths only to drift momentarily along the surface. Terrifyingly skull-like in appearance . . .

Jesus, no . . .

I followed it with the light and realized that I was observing not a human skull but the mesoglea of a very large, whitish jellyfish, drifting there just beneath the waterline. I watched it pulsate, its myriad tentacles expanding just below the shelf of that black water, as a dull bluish light emanated from deep within its formless, membranous body.

There was nothing else down there.

Back upstairs, I left a trail of muddy water on the floor as I went to the bathroom, showered, then got dressed in some fresh clothes. There was still something in this house—some flash or flicker, determined to collect my attention—but I couldn't settle on it. And I refused to continue to act like a frightened child.

I took the donut box into my bedroom, sat on my bed, and opened it.

The coroner's report was on top. I read through it, looked at the photos, and made notes on a legal pad. Already I was working through an argument for these findings, but I also knew it was going to be difficult.

There was another report at the bottom of the donut box—a smudgy photocopied stack of papers, thin enough to be stapled together. I took it out of the box and opened it to the first page.

It was the police report detailing Robert Graves's death, the one I'd asked Eric for and he begrudgingly agreed to get for me. The investigative file included the autopsy report, a fairly antiseptic document that made no suppositions, of course. I had expected as much in that regard. I flipped through the police report, hunting for any statements provided by Ruth Graves—particularly statements about a white pickup truck coming by their house that night, and fireworks being set off on their property, causing a fire. It was what Ruth Graves had told my father that night twenty years ago when she'd come to our house, and what she had supposedly told the police . . . yet no such statements were here in the report of investigation. In fact, there were no statements attributed to Ruth Graves at all throughout the entire report. I'd seen enough police reports in my line of work—had torn them apart on the stand, in fact—to know when one had been whitewashed, and this one certainly had. It was cursory at best, and conclusions were drawn about how Robert Graves died—an accident involving fireworks and a fall from a cliff—with minimal evidence.

It was Sheriff Dean Kelly's signature on the report.

I leaned back against the headboard of my bed and picked absently at the staple in the upper left-hand corner of the report. Had Eric, in a moment of weakness, confessed what had happened to his father? I remembered the black eye Eric had been sporting days later, when he came around my house, his father's police car idling in our driveway like some unspoken threat: had he told his father all we had done, suffered a beating, but ultimately had the whole thing covered up?

Moreover, was that why Dale had sold his truck? Had there been some secret discussion about what Ruth Graves had seen that night between Eric, Dale, and Eric's father—the one thing Sheriff Dean Kelly had made sure stayed out of the report?

And then, just a few short months later, Sheriff Kelly drives out to the Narrows Bridge to put a bullet in his head, I thought. Suicide rates among law enforcement officers, I knew, were among the highest of nearly any profession in the country. I supposed that if I were someone like Meach—or maybe even Tig, given her current state—I might draw some conclusion there: that Sheriff Dean Kelly's whitewashing of the Robert Graves investigation ended with a curse upon his head, too, and had resulted in the grimmest of outcomes.

But I wasn't Meach.

I wasn't Tig.

I refused to make myself believe in such—

Something shifted in the dark rectangle of my bedroom doorway. I froze, waited for it to reappear and assert itself, but it never did. Still, I stared at that dark—

(rectangle)

—space for several heartbeats more, my mind now struggling to piece something together, something I had already overlooked, something that was right here in this house with me. My eyes shifted to the wall across the room, where an old mirror hung. I caught the reflection of half my face in it now, one weary eye gazing out, the post of my bed beside my face, and the drawing that Bonnie had given to me that day at The Wharf Rat taped to the wall beside the headboard. The number 13 was reflected backward in the mirror . . .

(it's not a firteen)

. . . and I sat bolt upright in bed.

Because I suddenly knew what I was looking at in that drawing.

v

In the vestibule of a nondescript Manhattan apartment building, a seemingly out-of-service and mostly forgotten payphone suddenly begins to *ring . . .*

TWENTY-THREE

B y the time I'd moved away from Kingsport, the Meacham Motel had already been forgotten by most of the local residents. Unlike the bigger motels and hotels out along the highway, which catered to summer travelers and vacationers alike, the Meacham Motel had earned a reputation over the years as a place of ill repute, where married men stayed for a few days once their wives got fed up and kicked them to the curb, where drunks went on benders, or where so-and-so might slip away with his mistress for an hour or two during lunch. As kids, Meach used to regale us with all sorts of sordid stories about who came and went, and the things he'd seen—condoms lying limp on the floor like deflated bladders; splotches of blood on the bed sheets from rigorous bouts of lovemaking; a forgotten bag of cocaine left behind on the toilet tank. Some of those stories we believed, and some we didn't.

I was thinking of those stories now, as I drove out to the place, and saw what remained of the motel sign rising above the trees. The word MOTEL was missing its first three letters, and as I came up the dark road from the rear of the property, I glimpsed what remained of that sign in reverse. The EL backward resembled the number 13. To a six-year-old child, anyway.

It was clear, upon my arrival, that the place *had* been condemned—there were signs everywhere, and the foliage had become so overgrown that large, leafy branches scraped along the sides of Tig's Jeep as I took the turn off Rockfish Road. Yet I could only drive so far: someone had strung a chain across the entranceway of the motel, with a NO TRESPASSING sign dangling from it. I glanced up and could see the motel sign more clearly above the trees. It looked weatherworn and was entwined in thick reddish-green cables of poison ivy.

I drove farther up the road, until I found a place where the trees thinned out, then steered Tig's four-wheel-drive Wrangler off the road and parked it beyond the shoulder, so it wouldn't get rear-ended if anyone else happened to come along this desolate stretch of roadway. I got out of the Jeep and hoofed it back in the direction of the motel, where I climbed over the chain, and walked the rest of the way up the gradual incline toward the old Meacham Motel.

When the motel came into view, the sight of it caused something to hitch in my chest. Condemned, yes, certainly—but this place looked like it had been dropped from some great height only to crash to the earth. It had never been a good-looking place, this cinderblock train-car of a building, with its peeling, chipping paint, patchy roof, and bombed-out parking lot. But now it looked downright *treacherous,* and with the way the trees and shrubbery had encroached upon it, the building looked in the throes of being reclaimed by the land itself. The juxtaposition between this place and Dale Walls's antiseptic, unlived-in development couldn't be further apart. It seemed the Meacham Motel was now paying the price for its role in a lifetime of sin and degradation.

I went to the front office, stepping over brambles and discarded bits of lumber, and found that someone had stacked two-by-fours in front of the door. This struck me as a deliberate attempt to dissuade anyone who might be looking to break in (although why someone would desire to break into this dump was anyone's guess). I wiped a smudge of grime away from the window, cupped my hands around my eyes, and peered inside.

There was the front desk, what looked like a pair of office chairs, and an old wire magazine rack slouching emptily in one corner. An old pinup calendar from 2017 hung on one wall, the pages yellowed and its corners curling. Otherwise, the office had been gutted—there was nothing else on the walls, nothing left behind on the desk, and nothing (from what I could see) lying about the floor in there. There had once been a corkboard lined with keys behind the desk, but that was gone, too.

An ear-piercing whistle ruptured the otherwise quiet night, followed by a *sssst*-BOOM! that shook the trees. Birds took flight, startling me further. I looked toward the horizon and saw the remnants of fireworks dissipating in the sky beyond the trees. I realized that tomorrow was the Fourth of July—my thirty-sixth birthday—and the Kingsport rebels were already declaring their independence a day early.

I crept away from the front office and negotiated around some other debris—a turned-over shopping cart, some old crab pots, a few cans of paint, what looked like the torso of a dressmaker's dummy—and peered down the length of doors that lined the outside of the motel. The motel was a small one, with only five rooms that faced a weedy, gravel parking lot. The paint had peeled away from each door, exposing a termite-ridden, marrow-colored wood beneath. Each room had its own window, the panes a murky cataract, the cheap plastic shades the color of skin drawn tight as eyelids. A distinct pattern on the glass of the nearest window drew my attention due to its unmistakable birdlike shape; I approached the window, feeling a chill ripple through my body, and scanned the ground below it. No dead bird, though that shape imprinted on the glass was undeniable. And larger than a meadowlark.

The door to Room 1 stood open about two inches: I could see that vertical sliver of darkness against the peeling paint of the doorframe in the light of a second explosion of fireworks at my back. I went to the door, placed a hand against it, and gently pushed it open on hinges that moaned dismally.

The room was dark, but there was moonlight at my back so I could make out the bed against the wall, the credenza with its ancient, tubed television set, an armchair, and what looked like a coat rack in one corner. I ran my hand along the wall for the light switch, but of course this place hadn't been getting power for years, most likely. I stepped inside, and immediately knocked over a large trash bag that had been leaning against the wall. Its contents spilled out across the floor, and I didn't need to see those items to tell what they were, since the sound was so specific: empty aluminum cans. As my eyes acclimated to the dark, I could see several more bags lined up against the wall on the far side of the bed. There was a dim, electrical sound coming from someplace. Like the basement in my house, there was also a sour, damp smell in here, and when I drew closer to the bed, I could tell it was coming off the sheets. The outer spread was pulled up to the headboard, and not only could I see something lumpy beneath it, but I could make out dark stains seeping through the fabric.

Stop, said Rebecca. *Come home.*

I couldn't stop.

I couldn't come home.

Not now.

I took my cell phone from my pocket and switched on the flashlight app. Motes spiraled in the narrow beam of light, and bugs zigzagged before it. I pinched one corner of the bedspread between two fingers and slowly drew it down the length of the bed. It came away wetly, and I suddenly recognized what that distant electrical humming sound was when a slurry of large black flies came with it. A smell, too—not the damp odor I'd originally smelled upon walking in here, but one very similar to the fetid swamp of water that had flooded the basement of my father's house.

It took me a moment to realize what was lying on the bed. And even when I realized what it was, I found my brain too slow to actually process it—as if some part of my mind was trying desperately to detach itself from this situation and deny all.

It was the carcass of a large, black bird—a turkey vulture, or what remained of one. Its xylophonic ribcage was exposed, and one wingtip where the feathers had fallen away poked into the air, accusatory as a finger. Things squirmed and writhed along the flank and face of the bird, which made me think of the flies—a rolling mass of pale white maggots, blindly probing while they fed, so many of them that when I held my breath and took a step back, I could audibly hear the moist, tacky movements of their bodies as they wriggled overtop one another.

Each of the five rooms were accessible from the parking lot, but they also maintained doors inside each room that, if unlatched, would lead into the adjacent one. The adjoining door inside this room, I saw, was not only unlatched, but was already partway open. As if someone had passed through it recently.

I went over to it, pushed it open further.

The buzzing was suddenly all around me. I brought my hands up just as a whirlwind of flies whipped across my face. I turned away, spitting them out of my mouth and swatting at the air around my head.

It was too dark to see anything from where I stood, even after shining that slender beam of light in there, so I entered the room, holding my breath. The smell in here was comparable to the stink coming up from the cellar back in my father's house, and I held my breath as I made my way across the room to the window. I grabbed the brittle plastic shade and let it retract.

The window was so filthy that only a trivial amount of moonlight was able to penetrate the room, but it was enough by which for me to see more clearly, and to recognize that what'd I'd seen in the previous room was only a preview of the madness that lay out on gruesome display in here.

The bed had been stripped, and on the mattress lay a charcuterie of dead birds in various states of decomposition. They weren't all turkey vultures, although they appeared to make up the majority of the flock, and the smaller ones were tucked between the rotting carcasses of the larger ones. The mattress itself looked black with some foul fluid, and the storm cloud of flies that hovered over their bodies was as thick as steel wool.

At the head of the mattress, a series of birds' bones were laid out. Some were as fine as toothpicks, some as thick as drumsticks. They were arranged in intricate patterns, as if to form sigils. It made me think of Eric's story about Cynthia arranging chicken bones on her dinner plate at a restaurant. I shined the flashlight beam toward the ceiling and saw mobiles of bones dangling from the light fixture from catgut.

Covering my mouth and nose with one hand, I repositioned the light on my phone and saw several boxes of rat poison atop the credenza at the foot of the bed, as well as a number of mason jars filled with soupy brown water, inside of which the unmistakable shapes of frogs could be discerned.

Christ, Meach, you went and lost your fucking mind in here . . .

I cast the beam of light toward the floor and could see that the same black ichor that had soaked through the mattress had extended wandering fingers across the moldy, threadbare carpet.

A pair of reflective eyes stared out at me from beneath the bed.

I jumped back, slamming my shoulders against the wall, just as a possum glared at me, hissed, then retreated beneath the bed. There had been blood along its pointy snout.

The door to the next room also stood open.

Don't, Rebecca said.

But I had to.

I passed through into the next room, my hands shaking, a film of sweat running down the sides of my face. There was another smell in here, comingling with the stench of rot—that of gasoline—and my eyes immediately began to water. I reached out and let the window shade roll up. Murky moonlight fell upon a bed whose sheets were stained to a yellow-brown tobacco color in the shape of a person. It was as if some mummy had lain in this bed for years, decaying upon it, until someone had carried it off.

That gasoline smell was making me dizzy. I looked over and saw that where the TV should have been on the credenza stood a line of ancient metal gas cans. I lifted one and found it was empty. I lifted another; it was nearly full. There were burns on the carpet in here, and scorch marks on the wall behind the credenza. Looking more closely around the room, I could see that sections of the wallpaper had been burned away, leaving charred, black tendrils unspooling from the walls. There were newspaper articles pinned to one wall, perhaps a dozen of them. I went over to one, which depicted a photo of an institutional-style building. I shined the flashlight on it so I could read the headline: RESIDENT SETS FIRE TO REHAB FACILITY. I could see Meach's name mentioned prominently in the article. I remembered what he'd told me about setting a fire while in rehab in an effort to escape, and burning his arms in the process.

"Jesus Christ, Meach," I said, my voice sounding eerie and unsettling in this terrible place.

I moved down the wall and read the headline of another article: ARSON SUSPECTED IN BALTIMORE CITY DUMP FIRE. And the one beside that: BOATYARD FIRE CLAIMS FIVE VESSELS, INVESTIGATION INITIATED. There was an accompanying photo that showed the charred husks of several yachts partway submerged in a river.

What the hell is all this?

The headline of yet another: LANDMARK RESTAURANT SUSTAINS FIRE, ARSON SUSPECTED. Beneath this headline was a photo of The Wharf Rat. I looked at the date and saw it was only from a handful of weeks ago. I recalled the somewhat cryptic statement Meach had made to me on the night I found him living in my father's house: *Tried to help Tig, get her out of this town for good, but . . . well, I don't know. Sometimes I don't think things through, and I just wind up making shit worse.*

The rest of the articles were similar in nature—suspected arsons, inexplicable fires—except for one. This one was pinned in the center of all the others, the Kingsport *Bugle*'s masthead prominent at the top. It hung at eye-level, the centerpiece of this morbid collection. The headline was simple enough:

LOCAL WOMAN MISSING

In the photograph that accompanied that article, Cynthia Walls stared out at me. The newsprint pixels of her face were smudged, as if someone had repeatedly rubbed their fingers across it, but there was no denying who it was.

Get out of here, Rebecca's voice spoke up in my head. *Leave this place.*

But I couldn't.

Instead, I pushed through into the next room, feeling like I was descending through Dante's circles of hell. This room seemed darker than the others. I went to the window to retract the shade, found that it was stuck, and so I just ripped it off its brackets. It clattered against the window, then the ancient radiator, and then tumbled to the floor, where it unrolled and disappeared under the bed.

In the moonlight that struggled through that cracked and dirty window, I saw what Meach had done in this room, and felt my throat tighten at the awfulness of what it all meant. In some distant part of my head, I could hear Dale saying, *Someone's been coming into my house. Walking around in here, going through my stuff, my office. Going through my wife's stuff, too.*

There was a tapestry of floral dresses nailed to the walls. They hung there like exorcized ghosts, damp and drooping from the humidity in this place, nail heads snared through the shoulder straps. One dress I recognized in particular: it was the one Cynthia Walls had been wearing in the photo in Dale's home office, the one where Dale was leaning on a golden shovel surrounded by his family.

Also pinned to the walls were small photographs, the kind you'd find in a photo album. The ones with Cynthia by herself were unmarred; the ones where she appeared with others, those extraneous faces had been scratched out so that only Cynthia's timid smile and sparkling eyes were visible.

There were items spread out along the bed, too—a hairbrush, a pair of nylon stockings, a tube of lipstick, a fan of credit cards. I went over to the cards and lowered my face close enough so that I could read Cynthia's name on all of them.

It was now Eric's voice rattling around in my head: *How the hell do you think Meach really found her? You think he was involved in this somehow?*

It had seemed a ridiculous question at the time . . .

Get out of here, Rebecca spoke up once more, her voice drowning out all the others. *Leave this place, baby, and come home to me.*

But I couldn't.

Not just yet.

There was only one room left—the fifth—and in my head, I could hear Robert Graves saying, *One . . . two . . . three . . . four . . .*

"Five," I said, and pushed open the door to the fifth and final room.

TWENTY-FOUR

B onnie stood in the center of the room, facing a large, hollowed-out hole in the wall that appeared disconcertingly in the shape of a person. I could make out the suggestion of a head, the arms spread at each side, the dual posts of its legs. It looked as if a man on fire had come barreling straight through from the other side. The wallpaper all around it had been burned to black carbon, and great sheets of it had become unglued and peeled away from the wall or lay in large black flakes on the carpet. The whole room smelled of an old fire.

"Bonnie..."

I rushed to her, knelt beside her, gently touched her on the shoulder. Her skin radiated heat through the fabric of her thin T-shirt, and beads of perspiration glistened across her forehead and the side of her face. In one hand, she held what looked like a shiny chrome bicycle bell; in the other hand, she was gripping what appeared to be a thick, pinkish vine that looked strangely moist and covered in a sheath of fine hairs. The vine was suspended in the air, trailing from Bonnie's hand and disappearing into the hollowed-out chasm in the wall, as if connected to something on the other side that I could not see.

Not a vine, I thought. *Umbilicus. Lifeline.*

315

Bonnie stared as if hypnotized into that man-shaped opening in the wall.

I turned and stared at it, too. I recalled Meach's story, and how he'd said Robert had started coming to him in his dreams at first, but then at some point, the dead boy had physically come through the wall of the motel—had been *birthed* from it, was how Meach explained it.

A rasp of air escaped Bonnie's lips. I looked at her just as she began to speak, and her words chilled me to the bottom of my soul: "And his dark secret love . . . Does thy life destroy . . ."

I stood and felt a soft breeze rush up and cool the damp, sweaty patches at the front of my shirt. I watched as the hanging, curling flaps of charred wallpaper billowed out from that opening. My pulse thickened in my throat, and as I moved closer to the opening in the wall, sweat trickled into my right eye, stinging it. The walls in the motel were thin, with cinderblocks beyond, but in that moment, that man-shaped chasm seemed unfathomably deep—as if I could step right through it and disappear into another world.

A dull, pulsing white light began to emanate from within that hollowed-out, man-shaped hole in the wall. I watched as it brightened then grew dim, brightened then grew dim. No, not pulsing—*revolving*.

I stood and approached the opening. I could smell the ancient smoke and the charred wood behind the plaster, but I could also suddenly smell the briny aroma of the Chesapeake Bay, which was impossible all the way out here. Nevertheless, I looked down and saw a tendril of water oozing out from one of the burned-out leg shapes. It snaked along the threadbare carpet in my direction like something capable of conscious thought. The smell of the bay grew stronger, all around me now, as if I was drowning in it. My lungs began to feel heavier, and I felt myself gasping for breath. Yet each inhalation only made it more difficult to breathe, as if I was sucking down water instead of air. Absently, I reached down and wound my fingers around that fleshy umbilicus, feeling it grow taut within my grip. Feeling it respire like something alive and breathing.

I ducked my head and slipped through the opening, my hand trailing along the shaft of the umbilicus as a guide. The flashlight on my phone abruptly died, dousing me in complete darkness, except for each time that cold, white light came back around. It was impossibly faraway, and as I pursued it, I felt as if I was moving slowly through a cave buried deep beneath the earth. My rational mind knew this was impossible, yet it also felt like I was—

(sleepwalking)

—moving through a dream, and so I thought, *Of course this can happen in a dream. Anything can happen in a dream.*

The light came back around, blinding me . . . then as it faded, I thought I could see the coastline of Kingsport beyond—more specifically, the cliffs of Gracie Point. Suddenly, I was in the lantern room of the Gracie Point Lighthouse, overlooking the town.

She sees from here.

I didn't know what it meant or why such a thought had popped into my head, but I found myself thinking it over and over again: *She sees from here. She sees* everything *from here.*

The soles of my shoes fell upon something metallic. I groped blindly in the dark and felt something like a metal railing to which the umbilicus was tied. I took a step down, then another, then another, and realized I was descending some impossible spiral staircase sinking deep into the earth.

No, not the earth, I reminded myself, my mind a wall of fog. *Not the earth, but high above it. The lighthouse.*

I heard a noise far below me: someone moving about down there. Footsteps grating across the stone floor. A metal chain clanging. Laughter?

I thought about Dale Walls, and the story he'd told that night at The Wharf Rat—the story of a memory, of an actual event, when we'd dared Meach to enter the Gracie Point Lighthouse and go all the way to the top. Only he had gotten frightened by someone calling out to him, a man's voice calling out his name—

"Meach!" I shouted down the length of that spiral staircase. "Meach, is that you down there?"

I was about to take another step down when I heard the shrill ringing of a bell.

I blinked my eyes and realized I was only about a foot inside the wall, still gripping that strange vine. I glanced back over my shoulder and saw Bonnie holding the bicycle bell in my direction. Her eyes were still foggy and unfocused, but as I stared at her, she rang the bell again—*rriiing!*

That snapped me out of my trance.

I extracted myself from the wall, then tugged the vine from Bonnie's hand so that it fell limply to the floor. I knelt before her again, speaking her name over and over until her eyelids fluttered and her eyes focused on me.

"Hey, Bonnie. It's Andrew. Remember me? Your mom's friend?"

She reached out and placed a hand against the side of my face. The gesture was so completely *adult* that it stunned me into momentary silence.

"Let's get out of here," I said, and gathered Bonnie up in my arms. She came willingly enough, wrapping her hot, sweaty arms around my neck. She nestled her damp forehead against the side of my face, and I could smell the mixture of bay water and firework smoke briefly in her hair.

There was something on the edge of the bed that caught my attention—something I hadn't noticed upon first entering this room. I had seen it before, but here in this place, it took me a second to realize what it was, and to reconcile what it meant to find it here—

A sheet of plastic tarp, neatly folded.

It was the same one I had glimpsed in the trunk of Eric's car last night when he'd confiscated Meach's belongings from my father's house after the paramedics wheeled away the body. The tarp that Cynthia Walls had been wrapped in when Dale had tossed her over the side of the cliff.

Bonnie squirmed in my arms, suddenly agitated.

And I realized she and I were not alone in this room.

Go, said Rebecca. *Leave. Now.*

It was the wraith. The wraith was me, but it was also the—

(dark secret love)

—dark secret that had hung over my head all these years: a furious, fuming thing that swirled around my wife and unborn child like a gas fire, swirling, swirling, a thing that was *me,* but was also the thing that was *anchored* to me, a thing that would engulf us all if I wasn't careful, a thing that was approaching through the opening in that wall, hungry and desperate for revenge—

An explosion rang out somewhere high above the motel, and through the window I could see a spray of fireworks in the deepening light at the horizon.

Get the hell out of here, Rebecca said.

I got the hell out of there.

TWENTY-FIVE

I realized my phone was dead as I drove Bonnie back toward town, so I couldn't call Eric or Tig to tell them that I had found her. As I drove, the girl bounced along in the Jeep's passenger seat and seemed wholly unaffected by anything that had happened to her in the past twenty-four hours. I wanted to ask her a million questions, but did not want to disrupt the silence. Maybe a part of me wasn't prepared for whatever answers Bonnie might give. As it was, I was still trying to comprehend what had happened back in that motel room. Had I suffered one of Meach's hallucinations, thinking I'd followed some sentient umbilical cord through a wall that led me into the Gracie Point Lighthouse? Had I been the voice all those years ago that had called out Meach's name and frightened him so badly? I found I couldn't clear the smoke from my head; I felt drunk and aloof and wholly unanchored.

Yet I couldn't stay quiet for the entirety of the drive. Moments before we reached the beach road, where I could see the glow of the battery-powered fluorescent lights stationed along the bulkhead and the bobbing heads of the massive search party, I turned and looked at the girl in the passenger seat.

"What was that you said back there in the motel room? The thing about a dark secret?"

Bonnie looked at me. Her face was expressionless in the glow of the Jeep's dashboard lights, and she was cradling her bicycle bell in her lap. I could still smell the Chesapeake Bay on her, like a pheromone.

She said nothing.

"Where did you hear that before?" I asked her.

After a moment, she said, "I don't know what you're talking about." And then she turned and stared out the windshield and at the band of fluorescent light simmering along the horizon of the beach road.

At the sound of a rising commotion, Tig sprinted across the dunes and gathered her daughter up in her arms. People were applauding, some were looking heavenward and thanking God for Bonnie's safe return. With Bonnie still in her arms, Tig rushed toward me, kissed the side of my face, my lips, pressed her sweaty forehead briefly to my collarbone, then faded back into the crowd. She was too preoccupied with her daughter's safe return to question how I had found her.

Eric Kelly was not so preoccupied. He had some of the other deputies corral the crowd, and then we walked over to his police car, where he offered me a cigarette.

"I found her in one of the rooms at Meach's old motel," I told him. My hand shook as I tried to light the cigarette, so Eric took the lighter from me and held it steady. "Thanks."

Eric nodded slowly. His eyes were heavy on mine. "What the hell made you go all the way out there?"

"I don't know," I said, not wanting to explain the drawing Bonnie had given me, and how I'd felt some presence shifting about inside my father's house, vying for my attention. Too many inexplicable events had converged to arrive at this outcome, and I couldn't wrap my head around any of it. "I was just thinking about Meach, and everything that had happened, and I guess I just thought I'd drive out there and see."

"What did you see?" Eric said. His voice was flat.

"Uh," I said, and rubbed at my forehead. I felt weirdly lightheaded. Something, I feared, was wrong with me. "The place is . . . the place is a horror show. I think maybe you were right. I think Meach *was* involved with Cynthia's murder somehow. I saw Cynthia's clothes and some personal items in one of the motel rooms. A bunch of newspaper clippings on one wall—arsons, mostly, but one about Cynthia's disappearance. There were a bunch of dead birds in a bed."

I did not mention the fact that I'd suffered some sort of hallucination in that horrible place, and that I was still reeling and unbalanced from it. But there was also one *other* thing that I had witnessed that I deliberately did not mention: the plastic sheet that had been neatly folded on the edge of the bed.

"Meach lost his mind for good in that place," Eric said, and then that was all he said. He handed me his pack of smokes and told me to stay put. I was happy to oblige. I stood there chain-smoking while the crowds dispersed, the fluorescent lights went dark, and the deputies helped direct traffic along the beach road.

Her daughter still clinging to her, Tig came over to me. She looked at peace, though the hematoma in her right eye now looked as black as squid ink in the night. More gently this time, she kissed the side of my face again.

"How did you know to find her in that old motel?"

I shook my head. "I don't know, Tig. I don't know."

"How did she walk all the way out there on her own?"

I didn't need to repeat myself.

"It's not going to stop, you know," she said, her voice a hoarse whisper. "This will just keep happening. Maybe next time we won't find her. Or we will, but it will be too late."

I could say nothing to that, either.

Eric drove Tig and Bonnie home, and I followed them in Tig's Jeep. The house was dark, but the lights came on when Tig hit the switch in the foyer; she and I froze, looking around, and marveling at the sight.

Bonnie was asleep in Tig's arms, and she didn't want to wake the girl to clean her up, so she just carried her straight into her bedroom, then returned to the foyer, where Eric and I had remained standing, not speaking.

"You both better do something," she said. "This isn't the end. This was just a warning." And then she said: "Thank you."

Eric and I left, clomping down the porch steps as Tig shut the front door on our backs. I heard the bolt turn. As we made our way to the police car, Eric said, "I hope you're not tired."

I was about to ask him what he meant, but then I remembered.

We had a date with blood.

TWENTY-SIX

Eric drove us back to his house, where he exchanged his police car for his Toyota Corolla, and then together we drove out to the ghost town cul-de-sac on the ridge where Dale lived. As we drove, I leaned my head back against the headrest. My mind was a tornado of confusion and mounting panic. I kept seeing that folded plastic sheet in that motel room, and kept wondering if Eric *knew* I'd seen it.

As for the hallucination I'd suffered back at the motel, I saw it now for what it had been, exactly that: a hallucination brought on by stress and probably all those gas fumes. A bit of momentary delirium. Nothing more.

"I'll admit one thing," Eric said, after too much silence had permeated the car. "In just a few hours, it'll be twenty years to the day. I think if I was a superstitious fellow, the timing of all this might make the hairs stand up on the back of my neck for sure."

I looked at him, saw that he wore a sharp, toothy grin, and then turned away again.

"I want to talk to you about that motel," he said, and I wondered if he could perhaps sense my thoughts crackling like static in the air between us. "I couldn't sleep last night. I kept thinking about Meach, and how upset Dale was going to be when he found out. In fact, I drove out to see him last night, after you'd fallen asleep on my sofa. Had a long conversation about poor Meach."

I looked at him, feeling cold. "You went to see Dale last night?"

"And that got me thinking about Dale's whole situation," he said, ignoring me. "You know how sometimes when you lay in bed, just thinking, one thought will randomly collide with another, and you suddenly see something in a way that you hadn't before?"

"What are you talking about?"

"I'm talking about the newspaper articles on the walls in the motel," he said. "All of Cynthia's stuff in there, set up like a shrine." He glanced at me. "The plastic sheet I put on the bed."

I met his eyes, and felt an iciness flow from his stare over to me. "You put all that stuff there," I said. It was not a question.

"Last night," he said. "I drove out to Dale's to tell him about Meach, and that's when I told him my plan." Eric glanced at me. "I mean, I had to act fast, but it's a good plan. Dale agrees. He gave me some of his wife's clothes and some of her stuff. We've got an archive of old newspapers at the station, so I had access to all the articles. The last thing was the plastic sheet. I went out there and set the place up." He glanced at me again. Said, "Meach's death doesn't have to be a tragedy. It can also be an opportunity."

"So you plant all that stuff in Meach's motel and make it look like he killed Dale's wife. That he had some obsession with her, collected her things, and then murdered her. That he's already a lunatic, because he's got a bunch of dead birds rotting away on a bed and all those newspaper articles about the fires he's started, plus the one article about Cynthia's disappearance."

"Hey, the dead birds were all Meach," Eric said, and he actually chuckled to himself. "I wasn't kidding when I said the poor son of a bitch lost his mind out there."

I felt my throat grow increasingly tight, while a sickness began to creep about inside my gut.

"It's just a matter of having the right person find all that stuff," Eric said. "I was going to have someone dispatched to the motel tomorrow morning under the guise of looking for Bonnie, had we not found her by then. It would have worked. I mean, I didn't think the kid would actually *be* there, or that you—or anyone—would think to check that place."

"Yet Bonnie *was* there," I said. Which was when another thought occurred to me—one that seemed to teeter on the borderline of implausibility, yet I found I couldn't dismiss it. "Did you take Bonnie and put her in that motel, Eric?"

Once again, he glanced at me. His face was hard, his eyebrows knitted together. "Are you crazy? No, I did not kidnap our friend's daughter, Andrew."

"Because the timeline of you going there last night would be around the same time Bonnie would have gone missing."

"That kid has been sleepwalking for weeks."

"So it's all just coincidence that I found her in that motel the night after you planted all that stuff?"

"Hey," he said. "Maybe everything's a fucking coincidence. Meach finding Cynthia's body, the timing of all this with the Fourth of July tomorrow. You deciding to *coincidentally* go to that motel in the first place. What was it again that made you go there? I forgot what you said."

I held nothing back this time. "Bonnie drew a picture and gave it to me when I was here last week. Tonight, I realized it was a drawing of the motel. So I drove out there on a whim."

"And there she was," Eric said, quite matter-of-fact. "I mean, you think a six-year-old girl drew you a map to the place she was going to sleepwalk to a week later? Or can we just chalk that up to coincidence, too?"

I rubbed my hands across my eyelids. "I don't know, Eric. I don't know what to make of any of this anymore."

"Nothing," he said. "You don't have to make anything of it."

"So we're just going to frame Meach for Cynthia's murder. Jesus Christ, Eric."

"He's dead. What does it matter now?"

I considered all that he'd just told me, then said, "It won't work, you know."

"Yeah? How's that?"

"That plastic sheet will be analyzed. They'll find remnants of Cynthia's DNA on it, sure, but I bet they'll also find Dale's fingerprints."

"Of course they will," Eric said. "The sheet *belongs* to Dale. He's got a stack of them in his garage, and a bunch more in all his company vehicles. He's got a fucking *warehouse* full of them. But he's also got Meach doing some work for him under the table—hanging drywall, doing some painting. He gave Meach the keys to one of the company vehicles, which also happened to have Dale's house keys attached . . . which would explain how Meach was able to get inside their house, take all those items out, build that creepy shrine in that room. And let's face it—it's the least creepy thing in that whole fucking place. So, yes, Dale's fingerprints will be on that sheet, as they should be. Everything fits."

"But not Meach's," I said. "Meach's prints won't be on it."

"There are some latex gloves in a dresser drawer in that motel. Let's say Meach was cautious."

"The state of that motel doesn't suggest a cautious man."

"It'll work," Eric said.

Feeling ill, I turned and looked out the window.

I didn't want to talk about this anymore.

—◇—

We arrived at Dale's development, where all the houses save one were dark, and Eric parked in the empty street. Before we got out, I said, "Dale went along with this whole motel plan?"

"He doesn't want to go to jail, does he?" Eric said, and then he climbed out of the car.

I stepped out, too, and caught a whiff of gunpowder in the air. "You smell that?"

"Kids were lighting off fireworks earlier. Quit getting spooked, Andrew."

Eric went around to the back of the car and removed a rugged black Pelican case from the trunk. He carried it up the walk to Dale's front door, knocked once (strictly as a formality), then opened the door and let us both inside.

Twenty seconds later, Dale came staggering down the hall with a gun in his hand. His hair was sticking up and he had a sleepy, faraway look in his eyes.

Eric scowled at him. "Jesus Christ, Dale, what the hell are you doing?"

"I thought you were burglars," he said, somewhat detached. His sloppy little eyes kept volleying back and forth between Eric and me, confused to find us standing here in his house. "Someone's been coming into my house."

"He's fucking drunk again," Eric said to me. Then, to Dale, he demanded: "Put the fucking gun away before you accidentally kill one of us."

Dale blinked, and seemed to shake himself out of a stupor. "Yeah. Right. Okay. Sorry." He turned and padded back down the hall, that patch of hair sticking up at the back of his head. I heard a glass break somewhere on the other side of the house and then Dale muttered a series of drunken curses.

Eric opened the Pelican case and took out the long slender wand of a UV light and a can of Luminol. He dug a pair of latex gloves from a hollowed out section of foam inside the case and pulled them over his hands.

"Don't say anything to him about the autopsy report," Eric said. "I don't want him freaking out."

"I won't say a word."

Dale reappeared, this time carrying three lowball glasses and a bottle of bourbon under one arm. He was actually grinning, like this was some party.

"No one's drinking," Eric informed him. "Put that shit down."

Dale's grin faltered, then vanished altogether. He set the glasses on the coffee table, the bottle of bourbon next to them. The glasses clanked together violently enough that I was surprised none of them broke.

"Show me in the kitchen where it happened," Eric said.

Dale grimaced, as though he suddenly found this whole scene distasteful. He ran his tongue across his upper teeth, hitched up his pants, then wandered around the sofa and into the kitchen. Carrying the UV light and the Luminol, Eric followed him. I brought up the rear and remained standing in the doorway of the kitchen, not wanting to go in there. Not wanting to be a part of any of this, really. Not anymore.

"What is this?" Dale asked.

"It's an ultraviolet light," Eric explained. "I'm going to look for blood."

"There's no fucking *blood*, Eric—"

"You don't know that there's no fucking blood, Dale, so just show me where it happened."

I spent the next two minutes watching Dale move through a drunken pantomime of his struggle with his wife, how she had struck her head on the corner of the kitchen table, and where she'd ultimately come to rest on the floor. Eric had him go through the whole routine a second time, which was when I started to feel ill like I had back in Eric's car, so I retreated into the hallway.

Somewhere in the distance, I heard the familiar *BOOM-sizzle* of an exploding firework. I glanced out the front windows in time to see the reflection of the colored lights raining down across the darkened windows of the empty houses along the street.

That's what Dale saw that night, I realized. *Not fireworks inside the house, just reflections off the window.*

Yet I looked down at the dining room table and at those flecks of aluminum that still littered the tabletop.

For some reason, I felt like bait in a trap.

Eric found no evidence of blood on the kitchen floor, on the kitchen table, or anywhere in the vicinity where Dale said the incident had taken place. Afterward, Eric took the UV light and the Luminol out to Dale's Navigator, sprayed the entire interior of the car, but could find nothing there, either.

As Eric went back inside the house to pack up his gear, Dale and I smoked outside on the curb.

"Meach," he said. His voice sounded thick. "We should toast to fucking Meach. I can't believe he's gone." He looked at me through a veil of cigarette smoke. "Eric told you about the plan? The motel?"

I felt that speaking aloud might somehow incriminate me further, so I just nodded my head once, perfunctorily.

"Do you think it will work?"

"I think we're digging a deep hole even deeper," I said.

Something stiffened behind the doughy bulwark of Dale's face, and I could tell he did not like my answer.

"Let me ask you something," he said, "but I want you to be completely, one hundred percent honest with me. Okay?"

"Okay."

"Did you ever fuck Tig?"

"Jesus, Dale."

"I know you guys were, like, dating, or . . . I guess . . . messing around or whatever you want to call it back then. When we were teenagers, I mean. So I'm just asking."

"No, Dale. We never had sex."

"Really?"

"Really," I said. "What's it matter to you, anyway?"

The expression on his face did not so much soften as it sort of drooped. His eyes were bloodshot, and there was a glister of spittle in one corner of his mouth. "I just want to know what kind of friend you are. Or were. Back then, I mean. Because you knew I liked her, right?"

"I'm the kind of friend who shows up here to help you with this whole mess, Dale. That's the kind of friend I am."

"But you knew I liked her back then? Right? You knew."

"It was a long time ago."

"But you *knew*," he said, and this time it did not sound like a question.

"Hey," I said. "My turn to ask something."

He sucked on his smoke, exhaled, said, "Okay, shoot."

"Did you do this to your wife because you've got something going on the side with Tig? Is that what this is all about, Dale?"

Something behind Dale's eyes grew hard. His face, previously slack, tensed up again. The moment I saw his lips tighten, I knew the drunken fool was going to take a swing at me.

"Hey!" Eric yelled, coming out of the house, just as I sidestepped Dale's clumsy haymaker. "The hell's going on out here?"

"This guy," Dale said—no, he *whined*. "This guy *says* he's your friend, but then he says these terrible fucking things. Not just about me, but about Antigone." He glared at me, his eyes rimmed red, his nostrils flaring. "Real fucking classy, Larimer. Real fucking classy."

"Get in the house and go to sleep," Eric instructed him. "You're drunk."

"Ask him what he said!" Dale shouted. "Go on, Eric! Ask him!"

"You're lucky you've got no neighbors," Eric muttered. He popped the trunk of his car, dumped the Pelican case inside, then slammed it shut. I noticed that Meach's bags were still in there, which did not sit well with me. Yes, it had clearly been a suicide, but those items should have been taken as evidence until a report could be finalized. Not sitting in the trunk of Eric's personal vehicle. "Now go inside. We'll talk more tomorrow."

"This is bullshit," Dale muttered. He staggered up to the porch, but turned around when he reached the door. "None of this matters anyway, you know. We're all fucking doomed! We're all fucking cursed! Andrew thinks your motel plan is bullshit, Eric, and he's probably right. But even if it works, that only gets us off the hook with the cops, you dummies. Robert Graves has been in my house, has been wheedling into my head, and into all of yours, and now we're all fucked! So happy Fourth of July, America! And happy fucking birthday, Andrew Larimer!"

He went inside and slammed the door.

I glanced at my wristwatch and saw it was ten minutes after midnight, July Fourth. Happy fucking birthday, indeed.

"The hell did you say to him?"

"I asked him if he killed his wife because he was having an affair with Tig."

"Don't be so stupid," Eric said.

"Stupid? Sounds pretty logical to me."

"I'm not talking about the logic," he said. "What the hell does it matter what his motive was? You were stupid for antagonizing

332

that drunken imbecile." He took a step closer to me, so close I could smell the sweat on him. "I got him to buy into this motel thing, so don't try to fuck with that by planting doubt in that moron's head. The more he thinks we've got things under control, the calmer he'll be. Understand?"

I understood, but again, I couldn't bring myself to speak about it. Instead, I told him to take me home. And in that moment, he seemed relieved to be rid of me.

Back at the house—back in my room—I plugged my cell phone in to the charger and realized it was too late to call Rebecca. Oddly, I had no missed calls or texts from her. This unsettled me, but I forced myself to think rationally and not become worried. She'd probably just fallen asleep. I would call her first thing in the morning.

I stripped down to my underwear and then climbed onto my bed. Bonnie's drawing was still there in the reflection of the mirror across the room; it was still there taped to the wall beside my head.

My right eye itched.

I looked over and saw the William Blake book still on the nightstand, where Eric had left it after collecting all of Meach's belongings. I picked it up and a couple of pages fell loosely out of the book. On one page was the poem "The Little Girl Found," which opened with the line, "All the night in woe." On the other page was the poem "The Sick Rose," and while that title was less distressing than the first, I felt my skin grow cold as I read two specific lines:

> And his dark secret love
> Does thy life destroy.

It was Bonnie's voice I heard recite those lines in my head.

◇

Several hours later, I was awoken by the sound of someone knocking on the front door. I sat up stiffly, wincing at the daylight streaming through the window. I got out of bed, pulled on my clothes, and staggered down the hall.

Rebecca stood there on the porch.

A wave of disorientation washed over me. For a second, I thought maybe I was still asleep and dreaming. All I could muster to say in that moment was: "Oh..."

"What are you doing here?"

I cleared my throat and said, "Rebecca, what—"

"Why did you lie to me about coming here?"

"There was . . . I had to do . . . some..." I stammered. Then I cleared my throat again and said, "I had a friend who's in trouble. I came here to help him."

"And you thought you had to lie to me about that?" she said. Her green eyes looked like pale fire. Behind her, I could see a rental car in the driveway. I was still trying to wrap my head around what was happening when she said, "We never lie to each other, Andrew. Never."

"Right," I said, the word numb and useless on my tongue. "But . . . how did you know I was here?"

Those green cat's eyes narrowed just the slightest bit. She was wearing a plain white cotton dress, the mound of her belly cradled at her center; she ran a hand across her belly now, in a gesture that, for some inexplicable reason, abruptly made me feel like an outsider and a violator.

"My mother called me," she said.

"You haven't talked to your mother in five years."

"That's right. Not a single word in five years. She never even knew where I was all this time. She knew nothing about where I'd gone, or what you and I had created together. Because we both promised each other we'd never look back." Her voice trembled the slightest bit. "Yet the phone rang just the same, and now here I am."

"Rebecca—"

"She told me you were here in town, that she saw you. I didn't believe her, so she said to come see with my own eyes. And now I'm standing here. Seeing with my own eyes."

I kept shaking my head, desperate to wake from this nightmare. "Bec, please, come inside—"

"She told me something else, too," she went on. "Will you answer me truthfully? Or will you lie to me again?"

"Honey, please—"

"She said you and your friends killed my brother."

"Rebec—"

"Is that true?"

"Of course it's not true. Of course it's—"

"Are you lying again now or are you telling me the truth?"

I reached for her, but she took a step back. For some reason, I felt powerless to leave the doorway.

"You lied to me about coming here." She glanced down at my hand—at the finger that no longer wore a wedding band. "You've lied to your friends about being married to me, too, I see. Secrets from them, secrets from me. Is there no end to your secrets? Is there no end to your deceit?"

"Your mother is crazy," I said, and groped for her again; once more, she took a step back. "You've said that for years. She's making up stories to get you to leave me and come back home. I swear to God, Rebecca."

"No," she said, her voice calm. Eerily so. "Don't do that, Andrew. Don't."

"Listen, Bec, it's *me*. It's—"

"Stop." She held up one hand. And despite how calm she seemed, I could see her eyes welling up with tears. "Just stop."

"Please," I said. "Come inside."

She seemed to consider this for a moment. But then she shook her head. One tear loosed and slipped down the side of her face. "No," she said. "Not right now. I need to be away from you right now."

"Don't do this. Please."

"I need to be away from you right now," she repeated, and then I watched as she went down the porch steps and got into her rental car.

Some spell had broken, and I felt myself able to pass through the doorway and out onto the porch. Down the stairs, out into the driveway. I chased after the rental car as she backed out of the driveway and into the street.

"Rebecca! Rebecca!"

I ran down the middle of the road after her as she drove away, until my bare feet bled and my lungs burned.

And his dark secret love does thy life destroy . . .

PART FOUR

THE KINGSPORT CURSE
. . .

. . . AND THE WRAITH
REVEALED

TWENTY-SEVEN

2017

M aybe this is a love story . . .

Six years ago, in the fall of 2017, I received a phone call from a man named Luther Fisk, who proceeded to inform me of my father's passing. Even lawyers have lawyers, and Fisk had been my father's personal attorney for many years. At the time, I was working as a public defender in Manhattan, which meant I had to clean out my savings account to purchase a roundtrip train ticket from Penn Station to Baltimore, then rent a car to make that joyless ninety-minute drive to Kingsport.

It was late autumn, the leaves had already changed, and once I crossed over the Bay Bridge to the Eastern Shore, I could see that the cornfields and rows of wheat that flanked U.S. Route 50 had already turned brown and desiccated. Produce stands now sold apples, strawberries, and jugs of cider along the highway, their large, hand-painted boards advertising their goods. The palm readers and psychics had their neon signs on in the black, smoky windows of their homes, and the gas stations, spaced out like moon bases in vast, yellow, unencumbered fields, had gone quiet ever since the last days of summer.

I met Fisk at his office in Queenstown. He was a fastidious, surly fellow whom I had occasionally glimpsed maneuvering in and out of my father's home office when I was a kid, though I couldn't recall if I'd ever actually spoken a single word to the man, let alone had an entire conversation with him. True to form, he presented me with a stack of documents for me to sign without uttering a word, then exhibited too much consternation as he deliberated over which pen to select for me from a ceramic mug on his desk.

"The house is yours, of course," Fisk said. "It's paid off. I've taken the liberty of getting the name of a reputable real estate agent in your area, if you'd like to sell it. There was also a small savings account at First National. It's all in the paperwork."

"How did he die?" I'd neglected to ask this question of Fisk when he'd called; I'd been overwhelmed at the news of my father's death, and I had merely listened to what the man had to say, agreed to come out there to settle things, and then hung up the phone in a daze. I had then gone out onto the fire escape, had a cigarette, and let a few silent tears roll down the side of my face.

"Heart attack," Fisk said. He dropped his considerable bulk down behind his desk, into a maroon leather chair piped with brass tacks. The chair legs groaned.

"Was he at home?" I imagined him in that house, dead for days, before someone came around looking for him.

"He was out for a walk," said Fisk. "A motorist found him in the road. My condolences once again, Mr. Larimer."

I couldn't recall if he'd passed along his condolences previously, but I just nodded my head. The text on the document in my lap blurred. "He'd been going for walks every day for the past year," I said, more to myself than to Fisk. "He'd put on a little weight in his old age and wanted to keep healthy. I guess that's irony, huh?"

"I can have Linda assist you with the funeral arrangements," he said.

"Thank you."

He leaned forward, that chair creaking again, and plucked a Kleenex from a box on his desk with a magician's flourish. "Your nose is bleeding, Mr. Larimer," he said, and handed it to me.

There would be a small funeral service held in Kingsport, at St. Gregory's, in three days, and then my father would be laid to rest in the plot he'd had the foresight to purchase for himself several years earlier. (For some reason, the knowledge that he'd gone and done this without me knowing hit me with such a profound sense of grief that I had to excuse myself from Linda Montrose's office and disappear for a while in the restroom.)

When I arrived in Kingsport later that day, I went straight to the house. It had been years since I'd been back here—once I'd left for New York, I never wanted to look back; and while my father was happy to take an annual trip to Manhattan, usually around Christmas or Thanksgiving, to visit me, much of our relationship in those latter years was relegated to weekly phone calls.

I wended through the halls and rooms of that house like someone who'd just had a lobotomy. I was numb; I was, in every real sense of the term, orphaned. My mother had died at such a young age that I had no memory of her. I had no siblings. Both of my parents had been only children, so I had no aunts, uncles, or cousins. One heart attack on the side of a road later, and I was a solitary diode floating alone in the vastness of space.

What would I do with the house? What would I do with all his stuff? I had the real estate agent's card in my wallet, the one Luther Fisk had given me, and I suppose I could have Linda Montrose assist me in setting up an estate sale. But in that moment, I couldn't think about those things. It was three days until my father's funeral.

A normal person might spend those three days in this house, going through their deceased father's belongings, walking the town, maybe catching up with old friends. But I was not a normal person: there was a darkness waiting for me at the center of Kingsport from which I had fled years earlier—a darkness in the shape of a dead teenage boy—and I was in no frame of mind to consort with it. So I hopped the train back to New York to wait out the days until I'd have to return for the funeral.

St. Gregory's was a small stone church that stood on a hill overlooking downtown Kingsport. My father had never been an overly religious man, and his predilection for attending church every Sunday was more for the hour of serenity it offered him than anything remotely divine.

In his time, my father had been a respected member of the community. He did pro bono work for nearly everyone in town, and once, he was awarded a plaque that proclaimed him KINGSPORT'S CITIZEN OF THE YEAR from the local chamber of commerce. But many of those residents had either died themselves or retired to warmer climates, which meant the church was only sparsely populated on the day of Ernest Larimer's funeral service.

The only face I recognized that day was Dale's. As I stood greeting people at the door of the church, I looked up to see a man of about my age come noisily into the church from the rear doors. He was dressed in a tight-fitting suit (a dark blue, but passable for black) and there was a sheen of perspiration glistening on his forehead despite the mildness of the weather. When he saw me watching him from across the church, he came over, and that's when I realized who he was.

Most people are happy to see old friends. The emotion I felt upon seeing Dale Walls ambling over to me from the opposite side of the church was akin to tasting a candy you once loved as a child, only to find it overly bitter in your mouth as an adult.

He shook my hand, then pulled me against him for a one-armed embrace. He smelled like a concoction of cigarettes and pungent cologne. "I'm so sorry about your dad, man," he muttered into my ear. "So sorry." Then: "It's good to see you, Andrew."

Dressed in my only plain black suit, I spoke a few words to the congregants from the pulpit, then sat in the first pew while the priest did the rest. Dale sat behind me, and at one point, I felt him place a hand on my shoulder. It felt overly intimate and it made me uncomfortable, though I guess I appreciated the gesture. He'd been the only one of my childhood friends to show up, and while I hadn't expected to see any of them, I realized now that their absence was both welcome while also disappointing at the same time. I shifted a bit in my seat until his hand fell away, and that's when I noticed a young woman sitting near the back of the church. She was dressed in a plain black dress, no makeup on her face, hair swept back behind her ears.

When the service was over, I resumed my place at the door, and thanked everyone for coming. Dale asked if I wanted to go out for beers, but I lied and said I had to catch the train home, and he seemed relieved by this, to be honest. It was a lie—I planned to spend the next few days at my father's house, going through his junk, packing up what stuff of mine remained, and deciding on what I should ultimately do with the place. But I needed to be alone to do it. Reliving old memories with Dale Walls over a couple of beers sounded exhausting to me at that moment.

When I stepped out into the brisk, gray afternoon, the woman in the simple black dress was standing on the curb, looking up at me.

"I know you, don't I?" I said, going over to her. "You're Ruth Graves's daughter."

"You don't remember my name, Andrew?"

"Rebecca," I said, the name coming to me on a flash of light.

"I'm sorry about your father."

"Thank you for coming. I mean, you didn't have to . . ."

"I wanted to pay my respects."

"Did you know him?"

"No," she said. "I came to pay my respects to you."

In the aftermath of Robert's death, and with my friends having grown cold and remote, I felt myself overwhelmed by the guilt of all that had transpired. Not just what had happened to Robert, but the gnawing, termite feeling of keeping that secret bottled up inside me.

Like some sort of self-imposed penance, I found myself walking along Graves Road at least once a day, my shoulders burning beneath the summer sun, my entire body leaking sweat. I wasn't sure how I'd feel when the Graves house came into view; and as I kept on walking past it, there was really only a sense of numbness that washed over me.

One afternoon, I noticed Robert's little sister sitting on a tree stump in the front yard, surrounded by those unsettling wicker dolls. She was maybe eleven years old or so, and wore an oversized white frock and sandals on her feet. She had a book open in her lap, and her head bent low over it, almost as if she was deliberately hiding her face from me as I walked by. She wasn't actually reading, but crying soundlessly; I only knew this because of the way the sun shone on her face and reflected in her tears. I wanted to say something, but I didn't: what could I say? So I just kept walking. My chest hurt, my heart hurt, but I just kept walking.

And then one day, for reasons I couldn't fathom at the time, I decided to stop on the other side of that white picket fence along

Graves Road, steeling my nerve, my guilt rattling around inside me like a penny in a tin can, so loud in my head that I could actually hear it, and I cleared my throat just as Robert's sister looked up at me from her book-reading perch on the tree stump, and summoning all my courage, whatever there was left of it, I said, "Hi."

After the funeral, we drove together in my rental car to the next town over, where we had lunch at a roadside diner, although we hardly ate. Rebecca asked me about my life in New York, and I tried to make it sound a bit more glamorous than it was, which was difficult. I was still toiling away among the dregs of society in a dingy courtroom in Manhattan's lower east side, and most of my suits, no matter how many times I'd had them dry cleaned, still stank vaguely of that desolate, dismal place. Still, Rebecca listened intently, her green cat's eyes growing wide as she digested all I had to say.

"What about you?" I asked her.

She was twenty-five years old and single. She had never gone to college, but had taken courses online at the local library, where she also worked as a librarian's assistant. Her passion was books, specifically books of poetry, and she said her dream was to someday work for a publishing company as an editor.

"I remember you reading that one book over and over again that summer," I said. "What was it?"

"*Songs of Innocence and of Experience*," she said. "William Blake. You really remember that?"

"Of course."

"You came by the house just about every day that summer to talk to me. It was very sweet. To take pity on a little kid, I mean."

"I didn't take pity on you. Not at all."

345

"You didn't feel bad for me?"

"I just thought you looked lonely."

"That's pity."

"It's not," I said, smiling. "I swear."

"You never walked by my house before."

"It's a small town," I said. "It was bound to happen eventually."

Rebecca reached across the table and squeezed my hand. "I had a hole ripped into me the night my brother was killed. I had never felt more alone in my life. I didn't know what I'd do, how I'd survive without him, all alone in that house with my crazy mother. And then, like magic, you show up one day on the other side of that fence and said 'hello.'"

"I said 'hi,' not 'hello.'"

She smiled, then withdrew her hand. "But then at the end of summer, you just stopped coming by. Why?"

I knew why, but I didn't want to say. I also caught the way she'd referred to her brother's death—not *the night my brother died,* but *the night my brother was killed.*

"I don't know," I said.

"Well, I know my mother didn't approve. I know she used to watch us talking in the yard from the porch, and that she was a scary old witch. She never said anything to me about you coming around, but I knew she was distrustful of the whole thing. I was eleven years old, you were some teenage boy from town, and my mother spent her life distrusting everyone from town. So when you stopped coming around, I think she was pleased."

That was one of the reasons I had stopped coming around—that the guilt had been slowly metastasizing inside me and I could no longer bottle up the grief and fear and culpability I felt each time Ruth Graves crept out onto her porch and stared me down with those soulless black eyes of hers. It was as if she'd *known.*

She smiled at me, and I smiled back at her. But then something behind Rebecca's startling green eyes appeared to grow dim.

"What is it?" I said.

She shook her head the slightest bit. Looked away from me. Folded her arms over her chest and just gazed out the plate-glass window of the diner. She had her bright copper hair tucked behind one ear, and the constellation of earrings along the outer part of her ear sparkled in the daylight coming through the windows.

"I'm sorry. Did I say something to upset you?"

"No," she said, but those eyes—

(those eyes)

—spoke a different truth.

She came back to the house with me. It was her idea, not mine, but I found I was happy to stay in her company. We stepped into my father's house together, looked around at the place.

"Were you close with him?"

"I don't know. I guess so. All we had was each other when I was growing up. I wish I'd seen him more over the past few years."

"How often did you come back to visit?"

I almost said the truth—*never*—but then decided that sounded too horrible. So I said, "Very seldom. He mostly came to the city to see me."

"What will you do with the house?"

"Sell it, I guess."

"And all this stuff?"

"Estate sale, maybe? I don't know. I need to go through it all and see what I want to keep, what I want to get rid of."

"Then let's do that together," she said.

—◇—

She poked her head into my father's office, where I was going through his file cabinets for any papers that might be important, and held up a piece of paper, my chicken-scratch handwriting all over it. Said, "What's this?"

"Oh. The local newspaper asked me to give them a write-up about my dad. You know, a summary of his life, I guess." I shook my head. "It's terrible, isn't it?"

"I wouldn't say that. I mean, you seem to have an aversion toward hyphens. 'Small-town lawyer' should be hyphenated, stuff like that. If I were to analyze you, I'd wonder if that means you have an aversion for joining two unrelated and wholly separate things together into one."

"That's pretty deep."

"I'm deep," she said, smiling at me from the doorway. And in that moment, I felt something lurch inside my chest. I suddenly felt weak, powerless, a confusion of emotions roiling around inside my body.

"I guess I don't know what to write," I said. "How do you sum up a guy's life in a couple of paragraphs?"

"Well," she said, "I think you start by talking about what he meant to *you*. Everything you've written here is about his career, his status in the town, the work he did for the people here. That's all fine, but what about what he meant to you as a father?"

"I didn't think about that," I said, but then quickly amended: "I guess what I mean is, that stuff is even harder to write than what I've already written."

"I'll help you."

She found a cheap bottle of red wine in the kitchen, filled two glasses, and then we sat in the living room together. She had a notepad balanced on one knee, a ballpoint pen at the ready.

"How do we even begin?" I asked, hopeful.

She considered. Then said, "Tell me one of your stories?"

—◇—

There were stories. As I told them, and as she wrote them down, something happened to me: a gentle yet undeniable tug on a lifeline of my own, you might say. I began to study the delicate profile of her face, the tiny seashell whorls of her ears, the almost preternatural quality to her luminescent eyes. Hair that shined like new pennies. When she found something funny or amusing, her eyes would go large and she would tip her head down so as to study me from beneath a slightly downturned brow. When she grew pensive, her lips would part and she would study some upper corner of the world with her eyes. I felt a thing awaken inside my chest, yawning and stretching wide its arms, its roots casting throughout the core of my body and through all my nervous, trembling extremities.

Tell me one of your stories?

We fell asleep that first night right there—Rebecca lying on the couch, me on the carpeted floor below her. We talked in the dark for hours, mostly about simple, quiet things, nothing serious, nothing that would break either one of us. I told her about my dream of someday working for a law firm, and how I wanted to live in a nice house, and have a family—that I wasn't simply satisfied as my father had been to eke out an existence without experiencing my full potential. In the dark, somehow, I could tell she smiled when I said that.

"Sometimes I feel so overwhelmed in that city," I confessed. "I'm not where I want to be and I'm struggling to keep my head above water. I feel like a flame that's slowly growing smaller and smaller until I'm going to eventually gutter out."

"But you're doing it," she said. "You've left this place and you're in New York City. You're making it happen for yourself. And I know you'll get to where you want to be."

"Yeah? How do you know?"

"Because you speak with passion. And you're not a dreamer—you're a doer."

I asked her about the tattoo I had seen on the small of her back earlier that day as she bent over a box of my childhood toys, and she said she'd gotten it in remembrance of her brother. Then she spoke of her mother, and how she needed to find a way to leave that terrible woman and that awful house—that someday she would do it, just walk out the door and never look back.

"My mother is ill," Rebecca said. "In her head. To this day, she believes Robert was murdered, and that this town covered it up to protect their own. Sometimes I even catch myself saying stuff like that, because her influence on me has been so strong for my entire life. Robert used to be a buffer between us, but after he died, it was just her and me."

"Do you still live there with her in that house?"

"I have no place else to go," she said, and I could hear the misery in her voice. "Do you want to hear something silly? I'm afraid that if I spend too much more time with her in that house, that I'll go crazy, too. As if neuroses is something you can catch, like a cold."

I listened but said nothing. When her hand came down off the couch and rested atop my chest, I was startled at first. But then I reached up and took it, gave her hand a squeeze, and kept it right there where, all night, she could no doubt feel the frantic beating of my heart.

We lived like that together for three days—sorting through my father's stuff (and my own junk that I'd left behind when I moved to New York) in the daytime, falling asleep with Rebecca on the couch and me on the floor in the dark of the living room in the evenings, just

talking straight on into the night. With the passage of each day—
the passage of each hour, to be honest—that tumultuous whirlwind
of emotions inside me only increased. At the end of day three, we had
an early meal of Chinese food and a bottle of wine in the kitchen,
and then she gave me a present wrapped in a small, flat box.

I opened it and saw that it was her copy of William Blake's *Songs of
Innocence and of Experience*. The very same one she had been reading
on that tree stump in front of her house whenever I walked by on those
first few days, struggling to find the courage to say something to her.

"You're not some flame that's going to gutter out," she said. "Open
it to the first page."

I did, and saw the simple, two-word inscription in Rebecca's
handwriting:

burn bright

I offered to drive her home that evening before I left for the train
station, but she insisted that it was a nice evening, and she wanted to
walk, and to be alone with her thoughts—and her emotions—for a
while. We stood for a time on the porch, holding hands, and I could
tell she was feeling that same tumultuous whirlwind inside of her
that I was.

"There are a lot of publishing houses in New York looking for
good editors," I told her.

She smiled at me. "That's what I've heard."

"If you ever find a way out of here, come look me up, okay?"

"If you ever see me in New York City," she countered, "then you'll
know I've finally run away from that terrible woman and this dead-
end town. Just promise me you'll never let her find me. Promise me
we'll hide from her for as long as we can."

"I promise," I said.

And then she leaned in and kissed me softly on the lips. That was it—just one soft kiss. And then I watched her go down the stairs, down the driveway, her body—her essence—seeming to pull some thread of mine along with her, unraveling me, and it was all I could do not to call to her and tell her to come back, come back.

But what was the use of that? Because there was also a darkness there, too, at the center of that bright, revolving light—a secret that would forever stand like a wedge between Rebecca and me. There was no future there, because my cowardice would not allow it. My dark secret would destroy us.

Before leaving for the train station, I cleaned up the rest of the house, and realized I wasn't so sure that I wanted to sell this old place after all. I went into the kitchen, threw the leftover food away, and saw the William Blake book still sitting on the kitchen table.

Burn bright.

I nearly put it in my luggage, but in the end I thought it best to let the past be the past. I was haunted enough as it was, and despite my feelings for Rebecca Graves, I knew any future with her would be impossible. So I slipped the book in the drawer of my nightstand, and hoped to forget about it.

Hell is a three-hour train ride in the opposite direction of the thing that makes you whole.

A week later, I received a letter in the mail, a simple handwritten sentence from Rebecca wishing me well, and hoping that I was achieving all I wanted to achieve in the Big Apple. She included in the letter a clipping from the Kingsport *Bugle*, the article she'd help me write commemorating my dad. I sat on my bed that evening and read it several times, noting all the perfectly placed hyphens, and all the dressing up Rebecca had done to make me sound literate and wise. But more than that—it was the stories of my father she had drawn from me that made the obituary what it was. *Tell me one of your stories?* It had been as simple as that with her.

I reclined on my bed and stayed that way as the evening darkened to night outside my apartment window, and the sounds of the city below tried desperately to mask the thoughts in my head and the feelings in my heart.

Something like three months later, as a light snowfall dusted the streets of Manhattan and the Christmas lights sparkled in every storefront window, I came out of my apartment to find a pair of bright green eyes and a shock of shining copper hair standing on the curb in front of my building, a suitcase on wheels at her side.

She smiled hopefully at me, snow swirling all around her, the lights of Third Avenue reflecting in her shining emerald eyes.

We were married six weeks later at the court house. She had run from her mother in the night, abandoning both her heritage and the town in which she'd been born. "Promise me we'll never look back," she said on our wedding night. I promised, even though a part of me would be forever looking back. A part of me was looking back every time I looked at her. *Will this work?* I wondered on those first few nights together as husband and wife, lying beside Rebecca in our small Manhattan apartment. *Can I pretend there's no dark shadow clinging to me? Can I pretend there isn't some wraith that sleeps between us each night? Could I fool myself into forgetting?*

Try, said a voice.

So I tried. And for a while—for years—it worked: we were strangers, and we could fill in the parts of our lives that we'd missed with any story we wished, and leave out all the bad things. We could leave behind all our ghosts, all our secrets.

Tell me one of your stories?

They could be whatever we wanted them to be.

TWENTY-EIGHT

I thought maybe it was Rebecca coming back when I saw a car appear on the horizon. I stood there in the middle of the road, catching my breath, while the vehicle approached. My head was swarming with flies, my thoughts muddled and confused. I glanced down at my hands and saw they were shaking uncontrollably.

It wasn't Rebecca, but Eric in his police car. He glided to a stop in front of me, and rolled down the passenger window. He frowned when he took in my appearance. "What are you doing in the middle of the road?"

"I . . . uh . . . needed cigarettes, but forgot I didn't have a car."

"I've got a pack. Get in."

"Where are we going now?"

"Come on," he said, instead of telling me.

"Give me a sec," I said, and jogged back to the house where I put my shoes on and grabbed my cell phone. I washed my face in the bathroom, desperate to rinse away the mask of horror I wore, the guilt and sin radiating like radium through my flesh. That smooth band of flesh at the base of my ring finger nearly burned. I kept seeing Rebecca standing on the porch every time I closed my eyes.

Back outside, I got into the passenger seat of Eric's police car. He pulled a U-turn in the middle of the road and drove at an easy clip.

"The D.A. is going to issue an arrest warrant for Dale tomorrow," Eric said. "We need to reiterate to him that we've got things under control. We can't have him lose his shit right now."

"What's the probable cause for the arrest?"

"All of it—his lie about Cynthia being home when Tig called, him waiting days to report her missing. Now that the autopsy report is in and shows foul play, the D.A. thinks she's got enough to bring him in and break him."

"Jesus . . ."

He looked me over. "You okay? You look like shit."

"This whole thing is spiraling, Eric." I heard my own voice tremble.

"No," he said, firmly. "It's not. We've got this. And we've got the motel as our get-out-of-jail-free card. Literally."

"I don't like it," I said. "I don't like any of it."

"Just stick with me on this," he said, and drove a little bit faster.

Dale came to the door looking like he'd been beaten the night before with a baseball bat: there were dark pouches under his bloodshot eyes, bright red gin blossoms crisscrossing the ridge of his nose, and what looked like a bruise darkening the left side of his face. He stank like a brewery.

"Oh," he said, like some child, when he opened the door. He let us in, and the first thing I noticed was that the bottle of bourbon he'd brought out and set on the coffee table the night before was now empty. "What're you guys doing here?"

"We need to talk," Eric said.

"Right, right." Dale was nodding his head like a windup toy. Those bleary, bloodshot eyes shifted wetly in my direction. "Hey, listen, Andrew—I want to apologize for, uh, you know . . . what happened last night . . ."

"Forget it," I said.

"The district attorney is going to issue an arrest warrant tomorrow, Dale," Eric said. "Andrew's going to walk you through everything you need—"

"What?" Dale said. His lips were pulled back, and he was suddenly all teeth. "What? What's this?"

Eric raised a hand. "Relax."

"What?" Dale said. He was looking between Eric and me, trying to comprehend. "I don't understand. How . . . how can they do that?"

"Andrew will explain it to you."

"Everything is going to be okay, Dale," I told him, although I found I couldn't convince myself of that. "Let's go sit in the kitchen and talk."

"Get him some water and aspirin," Eric said.

"I don't understand," Dale said. "Am I going to jail? I can't do that. Eric, what about the motel thing? Why can't we do that? Christ!" He kicked the leg of a dining room chair, sending it clattering to the floor.

Eric and I exchanged a look.

"Where's your aspirin?" I asked.

"Fuck," Dale said. He had his hands planted on the arm of the sofa, his head down. "Goddamn it."

"One more thing," Eric said. "You've got a registered handgun in the house. I need to confiscate it."

"This is bullshit."

"It's procedure. Where's the gun?"

"Un-fucking-believable."

"Dale, where's the gun?"

"In the back. In my office." Dale pushed himself off the sofa, rubbed his face with his thick-knuckled hands, then led Eric down the hall to his home office.

I went into the kitchen where I searched the cupboards until I found a bottle of aspirin. I shook two tablets into my hand, dry swallowed them, then hung my head beneath the faucet to wash them down the rest of the way. I was about to take a glass down from a shelf for Dale when I heard Eric shout something unintelligible from the far end of the house. I leaned out into the hallway—

—and heard the sound of three gunshots echo throughout the house.

Fireworks, I thought.

Because of course they were.

But I *knew.*

I hurried down the hall, and froze in the doorway of Dale's office. Eric stood there with his service weapon drawn, the barrel still smoking. On the floor in front of him lay Dale, on his back, three perfect asterisks of blood widening across the front of his pale yellow polo shirt. Dale's eyes were open, but they stared blindly up at the ceiling. There was a safe in the wall above Dale's head, the door hanging open, and there was a handgun on the floor less than a foot away from Dale's right hand.

The room seemed to tilt. I clutched the doorframe, desperate not to pass out.

"Fuck," Eric said, and he quickly holstered his weapon. He dropped to his knees beside Dale, tipped his ear to Dale's lips, then felt for a pulse at Dale's neck.

Somehow, from very far away, I managed to ask what happened.

Eric began to administer CPR. The bloodstains along the front of Dale's shirt spread wider with each compression, and in a matter of seconds, Eric's knuckles were slick with Dale's blood. He kept going like that for an untold amount of time, while I slouched against the doorframe, feeling hot and slimy in my clothes.

Finally, Eric sat up. There was blood on the floor now and in the creases of Eric's palms, which he examined with an almost passing disinterest. I took that to be the result of shock. When he looked up at me, he was suddenly sixteen again, peering out at me while standing before his father's grave.

"What did you hear?" he said.

"What?"

"What did you *hear*."

"I heard you yell something. I heard a gunshot." I glanced at Dale's body, at the bloody rents in his polo shirt, and recalibrated: "Heard three gunshots."

"I yelled at him to put the gun down."

"Okay," I said.

"He took it out of the safe and pointed it at me. Said he wasn't going to jail. I had no choice. It was self defense."

"Okay," I said again.

"I picked you up today because I was going to confiscate the gun," Eric said. He kept staring down at the blood on his hands. "I knew you were his lawyer and I wanted to do things by the book. So I came and got you and brought you here. Do you understand?"

I nodded and said, for the third time, "Okay."

"Poor bastard lost his fucking mind," Eric said. He was gazing down at Dale's body splayed out before him on the floor. Then he dropped his hands and looked up at me. "Call 911," he said.

It took paramedics less than five minutes to arrive, but by then, Dale Walls was already dead. The sheriff showed up with some deputies, as well, and they took Eric out to the back patio to talk for a while. Eric appeared shaken, but he went with them without hesitation; his hands were still covered in Dale's blood. One of the other deputies confiscated Eric's service weapon, which they sealed in a plastic evidence bag.

Someone told me to sit in a kitchen chair and not move. So that was what I did. People in various uniforms came in and out of the house, but I was only half seeing them. A deputy—one of the young fellows who had showed up at my father's house when I'd discovered Meach's body—stood in the kitchen with me, arms folded as he leaned against the refrigerator. He kept looking over at me, no doubt trying to puzzle out how I happened to find myself in the vicinity of two dead bodies in the span of forty-eight hours.

I was attempting to puzzle that out, myself.

"Hey," said the deputy. "You've got a nosebleed."

I pawed at my face, then stared at my bloodied palm like someone who'd never seen blood before.

"Use the sink," he said, nodding toward the counter.

After what felt like an eternity, I was summoned to the back patio as well to give a statement to the sheriff. He was a thin, silver-haired man of middle age, fit beneath his uniform, and with eyes the color of cobalt. By the time I stepped out onto the back patio, Eric was near the side of the house, talking with two other deputies, and the sheriff was seated by himself in a wicker chair. He asked me to sit in the chair facing him, and I did so quickly, before my legs gave out.

"My name's Hal Harmony, and I'm the sheriff," he said, which struck me, in my frazzled state, as nearly preposterous. Like he was quoting the opening line to an old Springsteen song or something. He asked me my name, asked who I was, and asked what I was doing here today. He seemed amenable enough, but I wasn't so out of it that I was fooled into trusting him.

"My name is Andrew Larimer," I said, "and I'm a little too shaken up at the moment to give a proper statement, if that's all right with you."

Sheriff Harmony licked his lips, like some jungle cat daydreaming about a gazelle, but there was nothing predatory that I could read in his eyes. Quite simply, he said, "All right. I'll be in touch." Then he rose from the wicker chair and sauntered back inside the house.

The distant sound of thunder snapped me from a daze a few minutes later. *Rebecca, Rebecca.* I looked out beyond the yard and out toward the bay, where a battalion of dark black storm clouds was gradually advancing along the horizon.

I hung my head.

Later that afternoon, I was driven to the police station to give an official statement by the young-faced deputy who'd been staring at me while slouched against Dale's refrigerator. I rode upfront in the deputy's car, like I was partners with the guy, and he even offered me a much-needed cigarette.

"Some shit luck for you these past few days, huh?" he said, by way of conversation.

"Something like that," I muttered. I cracked the window and blew smoke.

"Weren't you also the guy who found that kid last night?"

"No comment," I said.

The deputy chuckled, like I'd just told him a joke.

The last time I'd been in the police station was when I'd been hauled there for shoplifting from the Stop and Go at age thirteen. Because fate likes symmetry, it was once again Eric and me in the hot seats, or so it felt. Unlike last time, however, I wasn't left sitting in a plastic chair in the lobby waiting for my father; this time, I was ushered to a small conference room where Sheriff Harmony sat behind a desk, shuffling some papers around.

"Andrew Larimer," the sheriff said, smiling from behind his silver mustache. He waved a hand at the empty chair before his desk. "Have a seat, sir."

I sat.

"Let's cut to it, shall we? Tell me what happened in the house."

I told him I was Dale's attorney, and that Eric had picked me up because he was going to confiscate Dale's handgun and he knew Dale would want me present. As for what happened in the house, I relayed it exactly as it happened—that Eric and Dale went to retrieve the gun; that I had been in the kitchen when I heard Eric shout something from the other end of the house; that I heard three gunshots follow. I had hurried down the hall to find Eric with his service weapon drawn. Eric then began to administer CPR before telling me to call 911.

"What did you hear Deputy Kelly shout?" Sheriff Harmony asked me.

It had been unintelligible, but Eric had also told me what he'd said. I weighed the response to this question, and ultimately said, "I heard something. It was muffled."

"You didn't hear anything specific?"

I felt myself on a precipice. I could end this, could follow Eric's lead and close the book on this whole nightmare. "I heard him tell Dale to put the gun down," I said.

"Yeah? How exactly did he say it?"

"Just like that—'put the gun down.'"

"And that wasn't muffled?"

"It's what I heard."

"Did you hear Mr. Walls say anything?"

It was Eric whispering in my head now, saying, *He took it out of the safe and pointed it at me. Said he wasn't going to jail. I had no choice. It was self defense.*

"I don't think so," I said.

One of Sheriff Harmony's silver eyebrows arched. "You don't *think so*, Mr. Larimer?"

"I didn't hear anything."

"Did your client confess to the murder of his wife, Mr. Larimer?"

"That's privileged."

"Not when your client's dead, it's not." He looked down at the mess of papers spread across the top of his desk. "You found that missing girl last night up in that old motel, didn't you?"

"I already gave a statement about that."

"Yes, that's right, you did," he said. "You gave it to Deputy Kelly, as I recall. How long you two been friends?"

"I think I'm done here," I said, rising up from the chair.

I expected him to coerce me to stay, to sit back down and continue our little chat, but he didn't. He just smiled at me and told me to have a nice day.

I stepped out of the police station with every intention of walking home, but saw Tig's Jeep parked against the curb beneath an increasingly overcast sky. She was leaning against the door, smoking, and when she saw me coming toward her, she pitched the cigarette to the sidewalk and hurried into my arms.

She sobbed against my neck.

"Hey," I said, hugging her tight, wondering how she'd heard. "I'm sorry, Tig. I'm sorry."

"What the fuck *happened*?" she said, still hugging me.

What *had* happened? Even now, it was all jumbled in my head. *Poor bastard lost his fucking mind,* Eric had said, but I wasn't going to say this to Tig.

"I think the stress of it all got to him," I said.

Tig pulled away from me, and I was shocked to see her right eye leaking bloody tears.

"Antigone, your eye . . ."

"Shhh," she said, hugging me again, and crying bloody tears into the crook of my neck.

I drove Tig home and sat with her for a while. Whenever she felt herself becoming upset again, she'd sneak off to the bathroom, leaving me alone on the couch. I kept replaying the whole thing over and over in my head—Eric's muffled shout, the three gunshots. I knew from experience in trials that it wasn't unusual for a police officer to empty an entire magazine into a suspect in the heat of the moment, so Eric's three shots didn't strike me as excessive. In my mind's eye, I kept seeing him doing those chest compressions, kept seeing the blood on his hands.

My cell phone kept buzzing; each time, I dug it out hoping it was Rebecca, but it was Bryce Morrison's private number. He kept leaving voicemails, which suggested I was on the precipice of losing my job if I didn't get my ass back to New York right away.

Everything is falling apart, I thought, and then noticed a single bulb of blood on the back of my right hand. I touched my nose and found more blood. There was a mirror on the wall, and I went to it, finding a slick crimson thread oozing from my left nostril. I blotted it hastily with a Kleenex I found in my pocket as I heard Tig's footfalls coming back down the hall.

"What will happen to Eric?" Tig asked as she stood in the doorway to the living room.

"There will be an internal investigation to determine whether or not it was a good shoot," I said.

"What an awful fucking phrase. Tell me what happened, Andrew. Please. I need to know."

"Eric said Dale pulled a gun on him. Said he wasn't going to jail."

"No."

"I'm sorry, Tig."

"He thought shooting Eric would keep him from going to jail? That doesn't make sense."

"It was suicide by cop, Tig. Dale just cracked under the pressure. I saw him last night, after Eric and I took you and Bonnie home. He was drunk, he was raving, and he even took a swing at me. He came to the door carrying a gun. He'd become unhinged over this whole thing."

"So what happens now?"

I stood up from the couch but did not go over to her. "I really don't know, Tig. But I can't stay here anymore. There's something I need to do right now, and then I'm hoping to get on a train tonight and go back to New York."

"And what about the rest of us? What happens to me and my daughter?"

"There's no curse. The thing with Dale is over. We can all get back to our lives."

"Isn't it pretty to think so?"

I went to the door, then turned back.

"Is it okay if I use your Jeep a bit longer? There's someplace I need to go."

"Use it," she said. "Will you bring it by the restaurant tonight? Before you get on your train and go home?"

"Yes."

She nodded, and I headed down the hall with the Jeep's keys in my hand.

"Just be careful, Andrew," she called after me. "I have a feeling something really bad is about to happen."

TWENTY-NINE

Rebecca's rental car was parked in the driveway of her mother's house. With the encroaching storm creeping up from the bay and darkening the skies, the Graves house looked more ominous than before, and I felt my stomach knot as I parked Tig's Jeep on the shoulder of the road and shut down the engine. Before getting out, I dug my own set of keys from my pocket. My wedding band was still on the key ring; I twisted it off then pushed it back onto my still bleeding finger.

As I came up the walk, a large turkey vulture coasted down from a drooping willow tree and landed on the tree stump in the front yard. I paused and stared at it, just as it stared back at me. It cranked open its wings, as if to hug me, its fleshy head slung low on its neck, its hooked talons digging into the stump. I caught a glint in one of its tarry, oil-spot eyes.

I went up the porch steps just as a soft and not unpleasant breeze shuttled through the yard. Those wicker dolls standing watch in the overgrown grass made the hairs stand up on the back of my neck, and each time I looked away from them, I thought I could see them moving in the periphery of my vision. When a series of fireworks boomed in the distance, I paused to catch my breath. I turned and saw a spangle of shimmery lights in the distance. My hands were shaking.

Before I could knock, the door opened.

Ruth Graves stood there, her pale face pinched, her cheeks sunken, her mouth a straight, lipless slash—but no, that was just how I'd remembered her from before. She just looked like a regular woman now, with that thick silver braid draped over her left shoulder. She had one hand on the door, and I saw that her fingers were not hooked into talons like the turkey vulture on the stump, but were simply bent out of shape from arthritis.

"Is she—" I began, but Ruth Graves did not need me to finish: she opened the door wider and allowed me to enter.

The place was gloomy and under-lit, the air stale. The old furniture and ancient sepia-toned photos on the walls suggested this house and its occupants had existed one hundred years earlier, and had, in the passage of all that time, remained unchanged. Bell-shaped birdcages stood on both sides of the foyer, meadowlarks agitating about within. I walked down the hall, through a beaded curtain, and into a sitting room where more of those strange, voodoo-like wicker dolls stood around like faceless servants. A large one—nearly the size of a full-grown adult—stood in one corner, behind an ornate wingback chair. It wore a headdress of black feathers and a necklace of delicate white bones. A knitted vest covered its wicker torso. One of its hands was extended, and I could see black twists of wire protruding from the stump where its fingers should have been. The longer I stared at it, the more I could discern an expression in the weave of its featureless wicker face.

"Where is she?"

Ruth Graves pointed in the direction of a narrow hallway beyond a second beaded curtain.

I stepped forward, brushed the curtain aside. Birds flitted in the air, arcing back and forth in that corridor. The walls were lined with handmade birdhouses—countless, innumerable birdhouses—and

I had to duck my head to avoid the frenzy of small, chirping birds darting back and forth from perch to perch. I continued down the hall, where most of the doors were shut, except one: through this doorway, I glimpsed a room with pale walls decorated in large black feathers—feathered mosaics on the walls, and what looked like dreamcatchers hanging by strings from the ceiling. Sigils made of bone stood along the far wall, intricately assembled, suggestive of some ancient, forgotten language.

There was a wooden cradle in the center of the room, unpainted, and built by what in my estimation appeared to be unskilled hands. A headdress of black feathers lined the headboard of the cradle, which made the whole thing look sinister and nearly alive.

The sight of that cradle unnerved me.

There was a set of glass patio doors at the back of the house, and I could see someone out there in the yard. I went to the doors, eased them open, and stepped outside.

Rebecca turned and faced me. She was wearing what looked like a hemp gown the color of silt and there was a crown of daisies in her hair.

"I'm sorry," I said. "I should have been honest with you. I came out here the first time because a friend of mine's wife went missing and he needed a lawyer. I came back out here this time because she was found dead."

Rebecca just stared at me, her face impassive.

"I didn't want to tell you the truth because I know how this town made you feel. I know you never wanted to think about it because of what happened to your brother, and I didn't want to stir those emotions up in you so late in the pregnancy. I've been worried about this baby for months now—you know I have—and I didn't want to do anything to jeopardize you or the baby."

"I see your ring is back on," she said. "Why would you lie about being married to me?"

"I didn't want anyone to know our personal business. It was easier to say I wasn't married than to come up with some lie about who I was married to. And you know I don't like coming back here, either. I never have. I wanted to keep our life in New York separate from this place. We've both always said that—let's forget about Kingsport. Let's never look back."

"But you looked back," she said. "Like Lot's wife, you looked back. You *came* back."

"And you said you never wanted to see your mother again. That she was crazy and that she was holding you down and making you crazy right along with her. That her neuroses were contagious. When you came to New York all those years ago, you said you'd vanished, that she'd never find you. That she'd never find out about *us*."

Rebecca shook her head. The expression on her face was one I was unfamiliar with—a look that suggested she pitied how foolish I was. It made something ache inside my stomach.

"I would have understood why you had to come back here, if you'd only told me the truth," she said. Her eyes were swelling with tears, and I could see the anger, the frustration, the *cheat*, that she felt of me, right there beneath the surface. That pity, too—still there. She took a step toward me through the grass, and I glanced down and saw that her feet were bare.

"I just didn't want to upset you," I said.

"That's not true." A tear rolled down her cheek. I went to embrace her, but she took a step back, held her hands up. Her face was red but her expression held firm. Her voice shaking, she said, "Tell me one of your stories?"

"Rebecca, come home with me."

"I can't, Andrew. I can't. I need to know the truth. I need you to tell me."

I felt a presence behind me. I turned around and saw Rebecca's mother standing in the open doorway. Ruth Graves's eyes nearly shone, as if they were outlined in steel pins.

"Please," Rebecca said. Her voice held tough, but she was crying openly now. She—

(cradle)

—cradled the bulge of her belly in both hands. Delicately. "Please, Andrew. Just tell me the truth. *Just tell me the truth of what happened.*"

"Nothing," I said. "Nothing happened."

"About my brother . . ."

"Nothing *happened.*" I glanced at Ruth once more, still spying on me from the open doorway, then back at Rebecca. "I swear, Rebecca. Nothing happened. Nothing happened. Your mother is . . . is confused."

Rebecca smiled sadly, and began nodding her head. The tears continued to spill, and her hands continued to swim all over the swell of her belly—a psychic's hands skimming over the shell of a crystal ball. What portents could she see in her mind's eye in that moment?

"I'm going to purchase two train tickets for Penn Station," I told her. "We can leave here tonight from Baltimore and never look back. We can go back to New York and be a family again—"

Rebecca turned away from me. Slowly, she walked across the field, in the direction of the tombstones that tilted this way and that in the tall grass of the side yard.

"Baby, please," I called after her. "Rebecca!"

A small sparrow bolted from a tree and slammed into the side of the Graves house, a mere few inches from my head. I jumped back, then looked down at the flagstones where the bird lay, its body twitching, its feet jerking spasmodically in the air.

From behind me, Ruth Graves said, "Baby. Yes."

I turned to the old woman. "She's going to go into labor any day now. She needs to come home with me."

"It's none of your concern any longer."

"She doesn't even *like* you," I said. "She's terrified of you. She came to me to get *away* from you. How did you even find her? How did you even know about us?"

A second bird darted from a nearby bush and thwacked against the window closest to me. The collision was not fatal; the bird struck the patio, flapped about until it regained some composure, then flew to a nearby holly bush.

"She's my wife," I said. "It's my baby."

Something behind Ruth Graves's eyes flashed—a fireworks display in those pitch-black pupils, limned in gold. "Do you really think so?" she said, and then she smiled at me.

I turned back and saw Rebecca wending through the tombstones, the overgrown grass whisking against the hemp fabric of her dress.

"I think, my boy, it is time for you to leave," Ruth said.

THIRTY

With the exception of the William Blake book, there was nothing more I needed from my father's house, so there was no packing. I decided to sell the place for good, and be done with it, and with all of Kingsport, too. But I knew I couldn't do that just yet—not with Rebecca still in town. On my phone, I pulled up the Amtrak app, and purchased one train ticket for later that night. My plan was to return to New York, apologize to Morrison for my recent absence and hope he wouldn't fire me, then beg to go on early paternity leave. If Morrison gave me any pushback, I'd tell him there were complications, which, in truth, was not a lie. And then I would come back here and hunker down in this miserable shell of a house to wait for Rebecca to come around. It was all I could think of to do. Maybe she just needed some time.

Before leaving, I opened the cellar door and stood before it, gazing down. The water had risen even further, its surface black as ichor, flat as a pane of glass. The smell was still there, of course. I stood there for a while, just staring down into that midnight pool, remembering how Meach had said Robert had shown him visions—*reflections*—in the surface of the water.

And then I heard it again—that mechanical *beep beep beep* that caused me to look around in a panic. In an ordinary house, it could have been anything making that sound—the batteries dying in a smoke alarm, the dishwasher alerting the homeowner that the cycle is done, the timer on a microwave—but this wasn't an ordinary house. This was the *shell* of a house and there was nothing that functioned within these walls any longer. Myself included.

I closed the cellar door, tucked the William Blake book in the rear waistband of my pants, and fled that place.

It was dusk by the time I arrived at The Wharf Rat. The parking lot was empty and the place looked closed; had Tig not specifically instructed me to meet her here tonight to drop off her Jeep, I would have thought the place deserted.

As I climbed out of the Jeep, I saw Eric's Toyota pull into the lot. He parked beside me and got out of the car. He was in plainclothes—a T-shirt and jeans again—and his face looked recently shaved.

"What are you doing here?" I asked him.

"Tig called, said to come by."

"She's broken up about Dale. Someone told her."

"Yeah," he said. "I told her. I didn't want her to hear it from someone else, and I didn't want a repeat of the Meach fiasco."

"What about Dale's son?"

"Sheriff Harmony paid Dale's sister a personal visit to tell her the news. What did you say at the police station today?"

"I told them what we discussed. That you picked me up because you were going to confiscate the gun. That I was in the kitchen when you and Dale went to retrieve it. That I heard you tell him to drop the gun, and then I heard the gunshots. That it sounded like a suicide-by-cop scenario."

"What else did you say?"

"That's all."

"Yeah? That's all?"

"I was in there for less than five minutes."

"You didn't say anything about finding Bonnie in that motel?"

"Sheriff asked about it, but I wouldn't answer. I got up and left."

"State police went to check out that motel today. I was stuck at the station all day, answering questions, so I didn't get a chance to clear all that stuff out. The plastic, the newspapers. I hear they bagged up a lot of evidence."

I just shook my head.

"There was a gas leak in that place, you know. Meach must have gone nuts and hit a gas line when he was setting fires and breaking through walls. Could explain why you felt like shit after you got out of there."

I hadn't told him that I'd felt like shit. I hadn't told him that I'd hallucinated while passing through that man-shaped hole in the wall. I hadn't told him any of it.

"Maybe they'll think Meach and Dale were in on it together somehow. Or maybe it'll just become one of those unsolved mysteries you see on Netflix. Either way, it's not going to come back to us."

"There is no *us*, Eric. I had nothing to do with that motel setup."

"Yeah, I'm getting that impression, that there is no *us*," he said, and I could see him eyeing me up and down. Sizing me up, almost. "I think maybe it's time for you to go back home to New York."

"I've got a train ticket waiting for me in Baltimore tonight, in fact."

"Perfect," he said. "I'll drive you."

There were some candles lit around the bar and on a few tables, but otherwise the interior of The Wharf Rat was dark. It was also humid as hell, with the air feeling thick and swampy. Tig stood behind the bar, rummaging around some bottles that chimed softly together. She looked up and smiled sadly at Eric and me as we came into the place.

Both her eyes were blood-red.

"Jesus, hon," I said. "Your eyes."

"It's the price I pay, I guess." She set down a bottle of Macallan just as I placed her keys on the bar. "I hear this is what all the big-time attorneys drink in New York City," she said.

"I don't want a drink, Tig."

"We have to drink. All three of us. That's why I told you both to come here. One last hurrah, right?" She began to set a series of lowball glasses on the bar, counting each one aloud as she set it down: "One, two, three, four, five."

I shot Eric a look, but he wasn't looking at me; he was staring at Tig, and although she wasn't staring back, I could see that his gaze was uncomfortably intense.

Tig uncorked the bottle and poured about an inch into each of the five glasses.

"There we are," she said, pleased, and set the bottle back down. "One for each of us."

In that instant, I almost expected Dale and Meach to come walking out of the shadows—Dale with his yellow polo shirt covered in blood, Meach with that hypodermic needle jutting from his arm.

Tig picked up one of the glasses, then looked at Eric. And then she looked at me. "Well?" she said.

"What are you doing, Antigone?" Eric asked.

"I'm saying goodbye to my oldest and dearest friends." She met his stare, gave him a dose of that intensity right back, bloodied eyes and all, and then she looked back at me. Her face softened somewhat. "There have been a lot of secrets. And secrets are poison." She set the lowball glass further down the bar, in front of an empty barstool. "Tell me how Meach died."

"You already know this," Eric said. "He overdosed on heroin."

She looked at me. "You saw him?"

"I found him that way in my house," I said. "I told you this."

"What's this about, Tig?" Eric said.

"Meach said something was after him," Tig said. "After *us*. Not a *someone*, but a *something*. Robert's ghost. Robert's mother. A curse."

"This isn't a ghost story," Eric said. "He had a needle sticking out of his arm. We've been over—"

"No, no, I know. I know what we've been over, Eric." She looked to me, and offered an unsettling smile.

"Cut out the bullshit, Tig," Eric said.

"All right." She picked up Meach's glass, downed it. Then she picked up another glass and set that one farther down the bar, in front of another empty barstool. "Now tell me about Dale."

"Tig, please," I said. "What are you doing?"

"No, Andrew, I want to hear it from Eric."

"I already told you this, too," Eric said quietly.

"I want to hear you tell it again."

"Christ." Eric ran a hand through his hair. A vein throbbed at his temple. "The D.A. was going to indict him. Dale got spooked. I had to confiscate his firearm, but when he took it out of the wall safe, he pointed it at me. Said he wasn't going to jail for killing his wife. I told him to put the gun down but he just pointed it at my face. So I fucking reacted."

Tig shook her head. A single tear spilled from her bloodstained eye and rolled down the side of her face; in the candlelight, the tear itself looked like blood. "Why would he do that, Eric?"

"Because he felt backed into a corner. He wasn't thinking straight. He thought this was some kind of way out."

"See, though, that's bullshit." Tig slid one of the lowball glasses in front of Eric now. "Dale's only concern throughout this whole thing was his son. His *son*. So why would he do something like that and leave his only kid an orphan? It just doesn't make any sense."

"It's like I said, Tig. He wasn't thinking straight." Eric picked up the glass that Tig had placed in front of him and knocked the shot back.

She looked at me. "Did you see what happened?"

"I was in the kitchen. I heard Eric yell for him to drop the gun, then I heard the gunshots."

"Gunshots?" she said. "How many?"

"Jesus Christ, Antigone," Eric said, and he walked away from the bar.

"Three," I said, when she turned back in my direction.

"You shot him three times," Tig said to Eric. She leaned over the bar and watched him pace the floor. "You shot one of your oldest friends three times."

"Cops aren't trained to pull their gun and fire one shot," he barked at her. "You shoot until the threat goes down. And I don't need to explain any of this to you, because I don't like where you're going with this. You've known me practically your entire life. You're going to pass judgment on me now?"

She placed one of the two remaining glasses in front of me. "Did you hear what Dale said to Eric from the kitchen?"

"I did not," I said.

"Do you believe him?" she asked me, and pointed to Eric. "Do you believe it happened the way he said it did?"

"Of course," I said, though I heard my voice falter.

She studied my face for the length of several heartbeats. Another crimson tear rolled down her face. Her bloodstained eyes were so dark, they looked like empty eye sockets in the dimness of the restaurant.

Then she smiled. "Okay, drink up," she told me.

I hesitated with the glass halfway to my lips, but then kicked the whole thing down. In my head, I heard Laurie O'Dell saying, *Be careful, counselor. Your blue collar is showing.*

"I guess it's my turn," Tig said. She picked up the last remaining glass. "You see, Eric, I know you're full of shit. Dale didn't say that to you, and he wouldn't have pulled that gun on you. I know what Dale *said* he did, but he didn't do it."

Eric took a step closer to the bar. "What are you talking about now?"

Tig's hand began to shake. When she spoke, her voice held steady, but those bloody tears wouldn't stop coming. "Dale didn't kill Cynthia," she said. "It was me. I did it."

I watched as Eric's hand froze midway toward Tig, then slowly lower to his side. I was watching Tig's face, and the bloodied orbs of her eyes. Something inside my belly clenched fist-like.

"Yeah," Tig said, her voice soft. "She left here drunk that night alone, everyone saw her go. But as I was closing up, she came back. She accused me of having an affair with her husband. Then she said she knew about what happened to Robert, that Dale had told her, and she wanted to hear me say it, too. She *scared* me," and here Tig's voice *did* tremble, "and I told her to leave. But she wouldn't leave. And then something changed behind her eyes—like some light going dim, I don't know how else to describe it—and before I knew what was happening, she was coming at me. She was trying to wrap her goddamn hands around my throat."

With her free hand, Tig dragged one of the giant glass ashtrays down the length of the bar until it sat like a talisman before us. In fact, each of us gazed down at it, as if to divine some knowledge from it.

"I grabbed one of these," Tig said, tapping the rim of the ashtray with her lowball glass, *clink*, "and I hit her in the head with it. Hard."

"Jesus," I said.

"It happened right there." She pointed toward the end of the bar, where it cut a ninety-degree angle to form an L. "She went down, and I thought I'd only knocked her unconscious at first. But then I saw the funny indentation in her head, and then it started to bleed. I tried to wake her, but she wouldn't wake up. Her eyes were still open, but they looked all funny, and I guess I just *knew* . . ."

She tapped her glass against the ashtray again, *clink*, and the ringing sound it made reverberated in my molars.

"I panicked. I called Dale, told him what happened. He came out here, got down, looked her over. I was a mess, I didn't know what to do. And then he said she was dead, and I think maybe I passed out or something. I don't remember.

"Dale left, then came back with a big plastic tarp. He wrapped her up in it, and I asked him what the hell he was doing. He just told me not to worry, that he'd take care of it—that he loved me and he wasn't going to let anything bad happen to me. He told me to go straight home and that we would talk about what happened in the morning. And then he carried her out to his car and drove off."

She wiped the bloody tears away from her face with one hand, then held up the glass of scotch. The amber liquid rocked back and forth at the bottom, and her fingers left crimson prints on the glass.

"When I left here that night, I didn't go straight home. I drove out to Gracie Point where I threw the ashtray into the bay."

She brought the glass of scotch to her lips and drank it down, more slowly than she had the other two shots. When the glass was empty, she set it squarely on that enormous glass ashtray—*clink*.

"So that's how I know you're full of shit, Eric," she concluded. "That's how I know you killed our friend in cold blood, and just to cover your ass. Dale would have never confessed to the police about Robert because that would implicate *me*, and he wouldn't have done that to me."

Eric took another step closer to the bar. He extended a hand toward her, said, "Antigone," but she just shook her head and moved away from him.

"So here's the end of my little story," she said, still swiping tears from her eyes. "I love you both, I really do, but I can never look at either one of you ever again. We should have gone for help that night. We should have tried to save him. We should have said something to someone—the truth. But we didn't, and now *this*. This *is* the curse. And you're both a part of it. Please—don't ever set foot in here again. Don't ever come around to try and talk to me. Don't—"

"Antigone, come on," Eric said.

"—don't ever come to my house or talk to my daughter or try to make me think differently on this. I will not think differently on this. I love you both, and I always will, but I never want to see either one of you again. Now get the hell out of here."

THIRTY-ONE

I stood beside Eric's Toyota, clutching the copy of *Songs of Innocence and of Experience* Rebecca had given to me all those years ago, while Eric remained inside trying to talk sense into Tig. But when he joined me outside less than a minute later, I knew he'd been unsuccessful.

"She's upset," he said. "She'll come around."

I stared at him over the top of the car as he fumbled his keys and got in behind the wheel. Then I glanced down at the book in my hand, opened now to "The Sick Rose," and then flipped back to the inside front cover, where all those years ago Rebecca had written: *burn bright.*

I felt like I had a lead weight on my chest.

A light rain began to fall as we drove. In the distance, I thought I saw lightning flash within the clouds, but then realized it was fireworks.

Happy fucking birthday, Andrew Larimer, I thought.

Main Street was closed for the Fourth, so Eric took the detour that sent us along the outskirts of town. Soon, the Chesapeake Bay was shuttling by along the left side of the road in all its grandeur.

"Is she right?" I asked him after a time.

"Is she right about what?"

"About why you shot Dale."

He said nothing.

"You once called him a liability. Remember?"

"What are you asking me, Andrew? If I'm a murderer? If I killed Dale to shut him up?"

"Yes," I said. "That's what I'm asking."

"You know what? I'm not going to say it as eloquently as Tig did back at the bar, so here goes—I don't like you, Andrew. I don't trust you. I think you're a weak man who's got secrets of your own. You think I didn't notice you're wearing a wedding ring now? I'm a fucking cop, you idiot."

I glanced down at my hand and saw that I was, in fact, wearing my wedding band again. I'd put it on when I'd gone to see Rebecca but had forgotten to take it off again.

"You're *also* a liability," Eric said. "And I never want to see you again, either."

My heart was beginning to beat faster.

"What about Meach?" I said. "You know, I went through his backpack when I lost my wedding ring, and I didn't find any heroin in there."

Eric just smirked and shook his head.

"And yeah, it's entirely possible you would have put that plastic sheet in the motel room that night, because I saw it earlier that evening still in the trunk of your car. But those newspaper articles? Cynthia's dresses and all her things laid out on the bed? You wouldn't have done all that in the same night. Dale said he thought someone was coming into his house, going through his wife's things—was that you? Had you been taking stuff from the beginning, planning to set Meach up before things got too out of control? After all, Meach was a liability, too, wasn't he?"

Eric laughed, but I could see moisture collecting in the corner of his eyes. I remembered him once more as a boy, weeping silently on my bedroom floor when he thought I'd been asleep. The way—

He shoved the heel of his hand against the side of my face. The right side of my head cracked against the passenger window, and stars exploded before my eyes.

My vision cleared just in time to see his fist come around. I brought my hands up, caught his fist between the X of my wrists, but it was still enough to drive his knuckles into the bridge of my nose. I expected him to continue striking me, but he didn't. I pinched my nose between my thumb and forefinger, then peered over at him through watery eyes.

"You were always a weak son of a bitch," he said. Yet his voice trembled and he kept readjusting his hands on the steering wheel, like he wasn't sure what to do with them. I watched and watched and kept waiting for that tear to spill from his right eye, but it never did. All the windows in the car were beginning to fog up.

We should have gone for help that night, Tig had said. *We should have tried to save him. We should have said something to someone—the truth.*

The truth.

"Stop," I said. I was still pinching the bridge of my nose, which gave my voice a nasal quality. "Stop driving. Take me back."

"Back where? She doesn't want to talk to us."

I wasn't thinking of Tig.

I was thinking of Rebecca.

"Just stop the car and let me out."

We had just turned onto the old Ribbon Road and were advancing up the incline toward Gracie Point. I watched the trees shuttle by on the right, the wide expanse of the bay to the left. There was no moon—the storm clouds had seen fit to erase it from existence—but I could see fireworks reflecting along the black surface of the bay.

"Stop!" I shouted, and grabbed the steering wheel.

The Toyota swerved to the right, but Eric swatted my hands away and readjusted.

"Just stop the fucking car and let me out!"

"You're—"

Something large and black rushed up in the periphery of my vision. I turned my head just in time to see a pair of outstretched black wings come swooping toward the windshield. I had time to think *turkey vulture* in the moments before it crashed into the windshield, webbing the glass and spraying it with blood, feeling it thump and roll over the hood of the car, *whump whump whump*, feeling Eric overcorrect as the Toyota fishtailed, hearing the fireworks *pop!* of a blown tire, followed by the *thump-thump-thump* as Eric lost control of the vehicle and the chassis rolled over unpaved ground.

Within the frame of the windshield, I watched the world spin out of control. First it was the road ahead of us, and then it was the rotating beacon of the Gracie Point Lighthouse out there on the bay. I watched the edge of the cliff rush up and fill the windshield, and then there was nothing but darkness—pure black nothingness—veined with the occasional flicker of distant fireworks.

I felt the sensation of falling, falling, falling. The darkness filling the windshield became water, black water, and in the moments before we plummeted down into it, I swore I saw Robert Graves standing in the surf, his flesh a sickly green, his one empty eye socket aglow with a pale blue, magisterial light.

And then—

Darkness.

THIRTY-TWO

Eric Kelly was killed in the crash. In the days that followed, an autopsy would determine that he'd died from a head injury sustained when the Toyota plummeted off the cliff and plowed through the surf, where its front end struck the ground below. The car then tipped over, coming to rest in the dark, murky, unforgiving waters of the Chesapeake on its roof. The vehicle quickly filled with water. So, in that regard, Eric Kelly's suffering was nonexistent.

His wife and children laid him to rest at St. Gregory's, just a few plots over from where my father was buried, and right beside Eric's own father, the former Kingsport sheriff (and infamous suicide), Dean Kelly. On the day of the funeral service, a fierce storm touched down, and Kingsport was pelted for three days straight with rain. Some locals claimed they saw frogs falling from the sky like back in 2003, and indeed there were many countless frogs seen hopping along the stretch of the old Ribbon Road, down by the wharfs, and clamoring all over the boats moored down at Kingsport Marina in the days that followed. A few people reported small black-and-white birds with yellow bibs—meadowlarks—flying into the windows of their homes, too, and there was certainly a number of them found strewn about people's yards, their necks broken, their bodies contorted to impossible positions.

On the night Eric and I drove along the bend of the old Ribbon Road, moments before I grabbed the steering wheel and tried to get him to pull over, Rebecca collapsed to the floor of her mother's house. She screamed and clutched at her belly as her contractions began. They came like thunder. Rebecca's mother, Ruth Graves, stood above her. She watched as Rebecca's water broke, and a snakelike tendril of fluid carved a serpentine passage along the floor between my wife's legs. It looked nearly alive. Rebecca screamed, said she needed to go to a hospital, but Ruth would have none of that talk: she knelt beside her on a pillow, brushed the sweaty hair from my wife's forehead, and whispered certain cryptic things into her daughter's ear.

As Eric and I fought in the car, my wife pushed down, screaming, crying out, while Ruth Graves clutched at her daughter's hand with one bony talon, still muttering those magic incantations, still speaking in tongues. Birds darted frantically above their heads, restless and agitated by the sounds Rebecca made in the throes of childbirth. Other sounds, too—the faint rustling whisper of wicker dolls slowly contorting themselves to observe—could be heard throughout that house.

And the smell in that house was of the bay.

As Eric and I plummeted over the edge of the old Ribbon Road, the car's headlights suddenly reflected up at us from the surface of the water below, my wife gave birth to a tiny baby boy, purple of flesh, squealing, fists thrusting at the air. The birds were frantic, frenzied, screeching and fluttering up and down the hallways. Ruth collected the child, snipped the—

(umbilicus)

—umbilical cord with a pair of sterilized sewing shears, then clutched the tiny being to her breast. On the floor before her, Rebecca lay panting and spent, crying out, groping blindly at the air for the mother who had been there one moment, gone the next. Calling out for the baby who had been taken from her.

Ruth carried the child to the bathroom, where she cleaned him up in the sink. She muttered some words over him, then dipped her thumb in a basin of warm oil. She traced the oil around the circumference of the child's head, then kissed him on the soft spot at the top of his skull. The child, after a time, quieted down.

Rebecca, too, quieted down. Eventually. And when she next opened her eyes, she was lying on a soft bed covered with a down comforter, her baby already feeding at her breast. She was dressed in a white linen gown whose sleeves were preposterously rimmed with stiff black feathers.

Her mother stood beside her in the semidarkness, and to Rebecca, it seemed that her mother's eyes radiated a dull yet piercing light. Ruth came closer to the side of the bed and rested her old crone's hand against the base of the child's skull as he fed. Cradling it.

"I have a terrible, terrible feeling, Mother," said Rebecca.

Ruth Graves smiled warmly down at her. "Quite the opposite, my love," she said. "All is now right with the world."

And the child's eyes gleamed.

After the accident, I awoke floating on my back in a dark, foul-smelling chamber. I thought I might have flown free of the car during the crash and that I was bobbing somewhere out along the bay, but when I righted myself, my feet touched solid ground, and I realized I was in a small, black, cobblestone room. There was nothing distinguishable about the place except for the runner of wooden stairs that climbed one wall, all the way to a door that was mostly closed. There was a strip of light coming from the other side of the door, and I could hear a steady mechanical beeping sound coming from up there, too.

I waded through the water toward the stairs, but movement in the corner of my eye caused me to stop. I peered through the darkness, and as my eyes acclimated, I could discern the vague suggestion of someone standing just beyond the narrow shaft of light that spilled out of the open door at the top of those stairs. A dim light radiated from the place where an eye should have been.

I climbed the stairs and tried to push the door open, but it wouldn't move. I peered through the inch of space between the door and the frame, but the light out there was too blinding, and I couldn't see anything. That beeping was too loud, as well, and I covered my ears with my hands.

It was down there in that black water that I was shown the reflections of things: Eric's death and funeral; Rebecca giving birth to our son in her ancestral home while a cacophony of birds frenzied above her head; Meach following a lifeline halfway across town and conversing with a dead woman on a barstool in the middle of the bay. Meach again, kneeling before a small but growing fire in the darkened kitchen of The Wharf Rat, a cigarette lighter trembling in one hand, his eyes—like the fire itself—ablaze, his lips repeating a single, prayer-like instruction to a woman and a friend who could not hear him: *Leave this town, leave this town, leave this town ...*

I saw Tig chasing a ghost through her house in the dark, swinging a baseball bat in frantic desperation. Six-year-old Bonnie wandering along the shoulder of a dark highway toward the ruinous remains of the Meacham Motel, her eyes unfocused, a bicycle bell clutched in one sweaty palm. Poor, doomed Cynthia Walls meandering barefoot along Graves Road during a midnight snowstorm, the expression on her face no different than Bonnie's the night she trekked to the motel, only Cynthia stopped in the middle of the road directly in front of the Graves house. She stood there for an impossible amount of time, the flimsy nightclothes she wore no protection against the icy winds and the snow that spiraled down like ash all around her. I watched as a dark cloud formed in the air, swirled about, then moved in a sentient current toward Cynthia Walls. When it reached her—

(i'm smoke)

—she breathed it in.

I saw my father walking along this same road in a white button-down shirt and pale trousers, the sun shining at his back. When he passed in front of the Graves house, movement in the periphery of his vision caught his attention. He looked out across the front yard and at the assemblage of wicker children that stood there, outfitted in inky black feathers and necklaces of bleached animal bones. A head tilted. A pair of arms repositioned themselves. My father paused in midstride, staring. The subtlety of their movements could not be denied, yet it wasn't possible. They were advancing toward him through the tall grass, in the dark spaces when my father blinked his eyes, and the impossibility of it all—

My father's heart gave out, and he collapsed to the road.

I watched as Rebecca came back to our apartment building after a late-night dinner with a client in downtown Manhattan; how she stopped to check our mailbox in the lobby of our building when, out of nowhere, that forgotten relic of a telephone began to ring. Startled, she whirled around and stared at it. The receiver practically jumped off the handset with each shrill ring. It frightened her—I could tell that in the reflection of her rippling along the surface of that stagnant cellar water—but in the end, she went to it, lifted the receiver, placed it to her ear, and whispered, *Hello?*

Upon that surface of water, I saw Ruth Graves carrying the child to a room filled with black feathers, placing him in a cradle with a feathered headdress, a name painted regimentally across the headboard:

ROBERT

The child's eyes gleamed green.

And I thought (in whatever passed for thought in the place I was currently in) that if Ruth Graves *had* known all these years, that she had seen it all from the lantern room of the lighthouse and had waited, had bided her time, until this very moment, it was in order to get back the one thing—or, perhaps, the *two* things—that had been taken from her.

I smoothed my hand across the surface of the water and saw my wife nursing the child. The image flickered and was replaced by another—of Rebecca moving all of her stuff from New York into her mother's house. This image was replaced by yet another—of Antigone, eyes bloodied and body weakened, creeping up the porch steps of Ruth Graves's house on her hands and knees, clawing at the door. Blood dribbled from her eyes onto the porch, and the pores of her skin wept brown, brackish water. Her hair had begun to look like seaweed, her fingernails like tiny scalloped shells. When the door opened, Tig begged forgiveness of the old witch, who glared down at her with eyes like fire. The old witch placed a hand on Antigone's head, mumbled something inaudible, then cast my friend back out into the street. Days later, Antigone's body returned to normal, and six-year-old Bonnie stopped sleepwalking. Days after that, she picked up her daughter and fled Kingsport for good.

I ran my hand along the surface of the water and saw yet another image: Rebecca, sitting up at night in bed, the child asleep in her arms, my wife's eyes full of tears as she gazed absently at the darkness ahead of her at the far end of the room. Once, she even spoke my name.

I smashed my fists through the water, and the image dispersed. I called out to her, begging to tell her one last story—

(tell me one of your stories?)

—and to own all the guilt, all the heartache, all the pain that I had buried all these years, but that I so rightfully deserved. All of it. All of it.

In my fury, I looked back at the figure with the glowing eye socket who had retreated back to the shadows of the cellar. Instead of speaking to me, the figure just pointed up the stairwell and at the partially opened door. That sliver of light looked like salvation.

I waded through the water and ascended the wooden stairs as the dark figure looked on from the shadows. At the top of the stairs, I pushed against the door, but it wouldn't budge. I thought of Meach pushing against the lighthouse door, thinking we were all leaning against it from the outside, trying to scare him.

I was scared.

That strip of light was blinding, the mechanical beeping coming from the other side of that door incessant, but I listened, and heard speak of a coma, of minimal brain activity, of a thing lying in stasis that would never return to consciousness again. I pressed my face against the door and peered through the opening, only to find—

—the wraith on the other side. Not the sinister ghoul that had tormented me for the duration of Rebecca's pregnancy, but a version of me in a hospital bed, unconscious, hooked up to a wall of noisy machinery.

Beep . . .

Beep . . .

Beep . . .

And I cried out—

I'm here.

I'm here.

But you don't hear me, Rebecca.

And after a time, those wooden stairs break apart, until they are only planks of wood drifting along the surface of this watery grave in the darkness. I can no longer reach the door because of this. And anyway, that light has grown dim, dimmer, until it fades completely to black, and that mechanical beeping abruptly stops. The door eases closed, and here I am, trapped in this sightless black void as the water rises, rises, rises, and my body—what exists of it—goes numb.

ACKNOWLEDGMENTS

These are the people who, in some form or fashion, helped get this story to you:

Cameron McClure, Katie Shea Boutillier, Matt Snow, Sophie Robinson, Daniel Carpenter, Paul Simpson, Rebecca Rowland, Tyre Lewis, Kevin Kangas, Rhodi Hawk, Robert Jackson Bennett, David Liss, Hank Schwaeble, Katharine Carroll, Bahar Kutluk, everyone at Titan Books, my family, myself.

Here are some of the random places I visited while writing this book that, in some form or fashion, helped get this story to you, too:

Maryland's Eastern Shore, New York City, Dallas, Austin, Hartford, Springfield, Orlando, Pittsburgh, Annapolis, Haverhill, Severna Park, Williamsburg, Marlborough.

Here is some of the music I listened to while writing this book that, in some form or fashion, helped get this story to you, as well:

Billy Squier, Rick Springfield, Def Leppard, The Runaways, Joan Jett,

John Mellencamp, The Cars, Scandal, Pat Benatar, Night Ranger, Mike Oldfield.

And they say writing is a lonely endeavor...

RONALD MALFI
November 27, 2023
Annapolis, Maryland

ABOUT THE AUTHOR

Ronald Malfi is the award-winning author of several horror novels and thrillers, including the bestseller *Come with Me*, published by Titan Books in 2021. He is the recipient of two Independent Publisher Book Awards, the Beverly Hills Book Award, the Vincent Preis Horror Award, the Benjamin Franklin Award, and his novel *Floating Staircase* was a finalist for the Bram Stoker Award®. He lives with his family along the Chesapeake Bay, and when he's not writing, he's performing in the rock band VEER.

ronaldmalfi.com
@RonaldMalfi

For more fantastic fiction, author events,
exclusive excerpts, competitions, limited editions and more

VISIT OUR WEBSITE
titanbooks.com

LIKE US ON FACEBOOK
facebook.com/titanbooks

FOLLOW US ON TWITTER AND INSTAGRAM
@TitanBooks

EMAIL US
readerfeedback@titanemail.com